MISSING
IN PLAIN VIEW
an Alex & Hazel mystery

Nick Planas

© Nick Planas 2019

ISBN 1799117669

This book is a work of fiction. The names, characters and incidents portrayed are the work of the author's imagination. Any resemblance to actual persons, living or dead, events or localities is entirely coincidental.

Studio65

www.nickplanas.com

DISTANT VENGEANCE
the first Alex & Hazel mystery

In 1874 Joseph Palmer, a signalman on the London and Western Railway, is wrongfully sent to prison for manslaughter after a railway inferno claims twenty-one lives.

In 1946 an old lady confesses a terrible crime of vengeance to her great nephew.

In 2018, young Alex Phipps, one of Joseph's descendants, finds an old file his father had made about the accident. Father and son investigate further and discover a tale of conspiracy and murder which still echoes around the old village of Salmsham. They find enough evidence for the police to open an historical murder enquiry, but by clearing the name of one ancestor, they may have tarnished others...

COMING SOON...

ONE by ONE by ONE
the third Alex & Hazel mystery

A school trip ends in tragedy when 14-year-old Patrick Skeete slips and fall to his death. The trauma of the experience draws the small group of youngsters closer together, then a few years later the group suffers another loss as Lorna Vernon dies on holiday during a mountaineering trip.

Over the next twenty years, more tragedies affect the group until Derek Ashley and Annelise Dillon are the only two left. Annelise mentions this in passing to her niece Hazel Burns. Fresh from solving another historical mystery, Hazel and her boyfriend Alex Phipps investigate further and discover a chilling pattern of supposedly accidental deaths.

To fit the pattern, another death must be imminent. The trouble is, who is the victim and who is the killer?

Things are seldom what they seem,
Skim milk masquerades as cream;
High-lows pass as patent leathers;
Jackdaws strut in peacock's feathers.

Black sheep dwell in ev'ry fold,
All that glitters is not gold;
Storks turn out to be but logs,
Bulls are but inflated frogs.

Drops the wind and stops the mill;
Turbot is ambitious brill;
Gild the farthing if you will,
Yet it is a farthing still.

W.S.Gilbert - H.M.S.Pinafore

1

9th October 1937 - Crystal Palace, London, England

The policeman stood attentively at the paddock gate, carefully watching every individual who approached, noting every truck, car and trailer which came in. He didn't directly engage with anyone, but stood back and listened as the young official on duty checked people's passes. He had been given strict instructions to look out for one particular car, but as no-one seemed to know whether it was being driven on the road to the circuit, or carried on a trailer or the back of a truck, he was having to keep a keen eye on every single vehicle in the line. Meantime, his Inspector was busy harassing the race officials in the control office.

"We'll let you know, Inspector, as soon as we hear word from him or his team, but as I say, he's not signed on yet. It's not unusual for one or two cars to turn up halfway through the day either, it depends on the traffic, or whether they've had any last-minute problems" the Clerk of the Course said patiently.

"It seems pretty inefficient if you ask me." replied Inspector James Walsh. "If I was running this meeting, there'd be a cut-off time, and if they weren't here by then I'd exclude them."

"Well, you're not running this meeting; I am, and I will decide whether to let people race or not." The Clerk of the Course and the Inspector glared at each other for a few seconds.

"And another thing, Inspector; perhaps you might ask your colleagues to do something about the

1

atrocious traffic jams around the circuit. It's not as if it's been a secret that we're holding an international race meeting here, is it?" The Clerk of the Course slammed his clipboard down on the desk with irritation. "Oh, and by the way, this is a sport for teams and drivers; without them there'd be no race. We're not in the army or the police force and they are not our underlings. If they want to turn up late, they can, they just get less time to practice."

"I see. Well, what's your cut-off time then? What's the latest you'll accept them turning up?" The Inspector was not used to being treated like another member of the public.

"Frankly, Inspector, if they've entered, as long as they're on the grid tomorrow they'll get to race."

"What, even if they don't do any practice beforehand?" the Inspector asked incredulously.

"Yes... as long as we get to scrutinise the car before the race to check it conforms to the regulations, and is safe, they can race. Now, if you don't mind, I've got a lot of work to get on with..."

"Hmph!" The Inspector turned and left the room, hurrying down the steps and crossing the paddock to connect up with his two constables. He could see one of them at the paddock entrance; the other had been posted outside of the grounds, on the approach road to the circuit.

"P.C. Rowles! P.C. Rowles!" the Inspector called out as he marched swiftly towards the constable on the gate, narrowly avoiding a car and trailer which was being reversed awkwardly into position. "Any sightings yet?"

"No Sir," replied the constable, "and I tell you, there's been a lot of cars coming in, but no sign of either the Bugatti or the driver."

"Have you spoken to any of them?"

"One or two, Sir, but none of them have seen anything."

"Well, they have to be here soon, surely. Well, don't let up. Keep a good look out, and remember, any signs of anything or anyone suspicious, let me know straight away. No need to stop them yet, just let me know and we'll move in together."

"Right-ho, Sir." Rowles looked a little fed up, which he was. He'd already been on duty for three and a half hours, with just a short comfort break, and the thrill of seeing the latest top-level racing cars had worn off some time ago.

He wasn't even sure of exactly why they were searching for this one particular car. Apparently, this was part of an international effort to capture a wanted fraudster, on the run from the French police. When he'd asked for more details, he was told he didn't need to know; normally this would have irritated him, but he realised that his Inspector actually didn't know either. They were simply following orders to stop and arrest this unknown Frenchman "on suspicion of committing various fraudulent acts on the European continent" and then, once apprehended, he would be handed over to a higher authority.

Suddenly, he became aware of a slight fracas between the young official on the gate and a motorist who did not appear to have a pass.

"I 'ave a pass, but it is in ze boot of my car along wiz the rest of my singz." said the driver in a heavy French accent. "You want me to get it out now? Surely you know who I am?"

"No I don't, actually, but even if I did I can't let you in without a pass, as you must know."

Ready to make a name for himself, P.C. Rowles stepped in. Within minutes, the Clerk of the Course once again found himself arguing with the Inspector from Scotland Yard, before French motor racing ace René Dreyfus was finally released to enable him to practice in his Delehaye…

2

The same day – Abbots Park Racing Circuit, Bristol.

The mechanic was hunched over the open bonnet of the car, his left hand guiding a long-armed socket spanner into the depths of the engine bay, while his right hand started to undo the sparking plug. His driver looked on impatiently, his carefully waxed moustache seeming to quiver as he began to shake with rage. Suddenly he grabbed the socket spanner and began to bawl at the mechanic. "Not like zat, you *ambyseel*!" he shouted in heavily accented English, as he barged the mechanic out of his way and began to quickly undo the plug.

Alongside them, in the next grid slot, two members of the private Italian Scuderia Verde grinned at each other and shrugged. Their driver, Paolo Fontana, sat impassively in the three-year-old Maserati as they put the finishing touches to the car. There was no panic surrounding the Maserati; one mechanic was quietly checking the bonnet catches, the other was checking the over the right rear suspension, which he'd been working on overnight.

By comparison, the scene beside the privately-entered Bugatti could have been straight out of a French farce. The mechanic wiped an oily cuff across his sweating upper lip, leaving a grey smudge under his nose. The driver finished changing the sparking plug, almost threw the socket spanner at his bemused mechanic, and slammed the bonnet down. The mechanic leaned forward to make sure it was secure front and rear.

"I hired you because you come wiz good – how you say – credentials! *Sacre bleu*, Sah-monze, I should have checked wiz more people before asking you to work wiz me." He walked around the old Bugatti, checking each corner of the car, while the chastened Simmons wiped the edge of the bonnet with a rag, removing the greasy fingermarks which he'd unavoidably added when he'd rushed to see what the problem was after the car had arrived on the starting grid from the paddock.

Several rows ahead, the mighty Auto Union and Mercedes works teams were lined up, each car surrounded by what seemed to be crowds of mechanics, but what was in reality two mechanics to each car, and several other team personnel, and quite a large number of hangers-on. Both teams were heavily state-sponsored, to show off the might of German automotive engineering; by splitting the funding between the two teams Germany had ensured that competition was fierce at the front of the grid. The cars were in another league, and were expecting to dominate the race, as they had at the Donington Grand Prix just one week earlier. Those with their smaller *voiturettes* at the back would be racing for class honours only.

A large crowd of spectators watched the starting preparations in various states of excitement and amusement. Word had spread since the Donington race, and many people were fascinated and awed by the mighty display of automotive dominance from the two competing German teams, not to mention the almost military efficiency of their teamwork on the grid. Of course, some of the smaller cars were racing at Crystal Palace, in the Imperial Trophy race, but even so, the Abbots Park organisers were pleased to have a field of 21 cars for the 30-lap race, more than enough for what was a relatively narrow circuit.

Those spectators towards the back end of the grid, however, were more entertained by the almost comical show of technical amateurism from the teams at the tail end. More than a few were wondering how the old Bugatti was even allowed to compete, and why anyone would want to enter an 8-year-old car for a race featuring up-to-date machinery, with no hope of success even in the smaller *voiturette* class for 1,500cc cars. The Mercedes W125 5.6 litre supercharged machine was more than six times as powerful as the humble Bugatti Type 39, although the Bugatti was a much lighter and nimbler machine; bigger-engined versions had once dominated grand prix racing for several years, but that was way back in the 1920s. The practice lap times were a stark reminder; the fastest Mercedes lapped the winding hilly circuit in just over 3 minutes; the Bugatti another 32 seconds slower.

Moments later, an official walked across the front of the grid with a one minute board, and the first few engines were fired up, while the hangers-on left the grid swiftly. The driver got into the car, flicked a switch and gestured to the mechanic, who quickly cranked the engine. Almost immediately it spluttered into life, and the driver revved it a few times until it ran cleanly, nodded at his mechanic and gave a thumbs-up. The mechanic leaned over and took a quick look at one of the gauges on the small fascia, nodded, and patted his driver on the arm.

"Good luck" he shouted above the roar of the

engine, but his driver did not respond. He was already thinking about the mad dash to the first corner; his face was now set; the moustache was still; his piercingly blue eyes were focussed into the distance with a steely determination.

At the '30 seconds-to-go' signal, the driver put his goggles over his eyes, and waved briefly to the mechanic, who turned and left the grid. The last few mechanics from other teams also left the grid, leaving their charges in the hands of their skilled drivers; men who regularly put their lives on the line for the sheer pleasure of dicing at breakneck speeds around narrow circuits with little or no protection if they should leave the circuit at any speed.

As soon as the man with the '30' board had left the grid, and somewhat less than thirty seconds later, a fellow official raised the union flag in full view of the field of cars. Engines revved higher until the flag dropped, clutches were released, and the pack of 21 cars moved off almost in complete unison, the sound of individual engines briefly lost as one deafening roar signified the start of the 1937 Abbots Park Vendolet Tyres Gold Trophy race.

A cloud of dust, mixed with oil and tyre smoke, drifted across the startline as the mechanic returned to his pit; a narrow affair just wide enough for four people to sit on the pitwall side by side. The pits were open on both sides, and were little more than a low brick wall, behind which was stored various spare parts, a new set of wheels complete with tyres, a couple of fuel churns, and a large tool box. The driver had also slung his overjacket and a travel bag in one corner of the pit. Sitting on a bench on the pitwall was a youngish looking dark-haired woman, wrapped in a short coat, and wearing a headscarf. She held a stopwatch in her left hand, and on her lap was a clipboard holding a lap chart. The mechanic looked at her, smiled and shrugged. Her piercing brown eyes stared straight back at his almost comical visage – not only did he appear to be totally incompetent as a mechanic, but there seemed to be more grease on his face than on his overalls; a smudged half-moustache which seemed to start just under his nose and finish halfway across one cheek. She curled the sides of her mouth briefly into a half-hearted smile, not matched by her eyes.

Neither of them were expecting much from this race, but they had at least made it to the track, got the car through scrutineering and practice without serious mishap, and started the race, thus ensuring that they would be able to collect the starting money, such as it was. They both knew it was a paltry sum compared to the four-figure sum alleged to have been offered to the German teams

They could hear snippets of excited commentary from the distant loud speakers, facing away from them on the opposite side of the track. It sounded as if one of the Mercedes cars had got into the lead; the commentator thought it was Rudolf Caracciola's Mercedes, from the Auto Union of Bernd Rosemeyer and the similar car of Rudolf Hasse, then two more Mercedes cars. The first of the British cars, the privately-owned ERA driven by Raymond Mays, was lying 10th after passing the spinning Maserati of Santorello at the third corner. Mays had withdrawn from the Crystal Palace event due to engine failure on his works car, so he was more than happy when he was offered the last-minute chance to take part in this race in a colleague's own car.

As the cars disappeared from the view of the far observation tower, the spectators at the startline waited excitedly to see who was leading. The distant engine notes rose and grew steadily louder until suddenly the leaders burst into view through the trees, two, sometimes three abreast as they left the final sweeping bend and barrelled past the pits, the first five cars separated by less than a second.

While the crowd were awed by the sheer spectacle of the gaggle of German cars which thundered past them, the mechanic simply counted off the numbers until the first fifteen cars had past. Then he looked back down the track towards another group of cars, this time the leading voiturette racers. He was surprised, and not displeased, to see that the Bugatti was holding its own in 18th position. He smiled to himself as he remembered the trouble they'd had with officialdom, trying to get the last-minute entry accepted even after having been offered suitable starting money by the organisers. Perhaps now they could see that this little car was still able to properly compete; there was no way it was simply a 'starting money special' as one official had so bluntly put it.

It was not long before the field began to spread out, and the mechanic was able to hang out a pit board giving the car's position in the race. Having not had much hope going into the race, his competitive juices were starting to stir as he noted with continued surprise and pleasure that the 'old' car was able to pull away from its pursuers until it was a good half a minute ahead of them. Not only that, but it was catching the ERA ahead of him, although that car had a misfire which was becoming more obvious as the race wore on. After ten laps of the gruelling circuit the two team members in the pits heard the commentator's excited voice shouting "Cantin… that's Pierre-Henri Cantin…he's passed Westwood's ERA!" and they were up to 15th place thanks to an audacious outbraking and overtaking manoeuvre pulled on the ailing ERA, and a retirement higher up the order.

At the 15-lap mark, one of the Mercedes had retired through accident damage following a spin, and the Maserati of Santorello had also stopped with gearbox problems. The Bugatti was now running in 13th place, but as if to appease those of a superstitious bent, the car began to smoke slightly. The commentator at the far side of the track spotted a few wisps as the Bugatti passed him, and as he excitedly passing this information on to his colleague in the starting area, he speculated as to whether there would be another retirement.

At first the commentators and observers thought that the smoke was coming from the exhaust pipe, but it wasn't long before it was realised that there was something seriously wrong under the bonnet. Smoke, or was it steam from the radiator, was billowing over the front of the car and threatening to obscure the driver's view. Trackside observers noted the smoke but at this stage, as there was no evidence of any liquid being dropped on the track, no warning flags were being displayed.

As the Bugatti went past the pits at unabated speed, the driver was seen to be leaning out to the right of the rudimentary windscreen, and waving his hands to one side. Whether the hand waving was a signal to the pits, or simply the driver trying to clear his vision was not obvious, but the mechanic began to wonder whether he would see the car pass him again. Meantime, officialdom had taken note, and the mechanic was visited by a large man with a jacket and armband, carrying a black flag.

"If your chap doesn't come in this lap, we're black flagging him, alright?" the official said. "I'm not sure if he'll make it anyway, but he's leaving a trail of smoke and probably oil all round the circuit."

"Yes, alright" the mechanic agreed. "I'll call him in as well". With that, he attached a large arrow to the pitboard and stuck the word "IN" on it as well.

"Cantin has just gone passed us leaning right out of his car so he can see over the smoke!" bellowed the commentator. "Let's hope he can make it round to the pits, he's driven a storming race so far and it would be a great shame if he has to stop."

No-one watching could be in any doubt that the Bugatti would be asked to pit the following lap. The mechanic stood and watched as Manfred von Brauchitsch, now leading the race, screamed past in his W125 Mercedes, followed closely by the sister car of Hermann Lang, two Auto Unions and the original leader, Caracciola. They had already lapped the voiturettes for the second time, so his man would not be far behind. He glanced at his watch, and waited. Then he checked his watch again, as the ailing ERA of Philip Westwood tore past, its driver maintaining a consistent pace despite the fairly obvious misfire. He waited another minute or so, and then heard the commentator saying something about the Bugatti missing from the order. He turned, shrugged, and put the pitboard down against the pit counter, wondering exactly what had happened around the back of the circuit.

He lit a cigarette and sat down. The young woman with the stopwatch, who had been passing him information throughout the race, shrugged too, and folded her lap chart away. He offered her a cigarette too, and the pair of them sat silently waiting for news of their man. Neither of them was too concerned; all the evidence pointed to an engine failure which would most likely have resulted in the car simply stopping; the driver would find a safe place to pull over and that would be that.

Another official appeared, and gestured to the mechanic. He idly stood up and wandered over.

"I'm afraid your man's had a bit of a big one, old chap" said the official.

The mechanic frowned. "What do you mean, a big one?"

"It seems he got blinded by all that smoke, and went straight over the edge of the er... hillside... round the back, down into the trees."

"The trees? What's happened to him?" The mechanic could see the look of fear in the eyes of the other man, and knew something bad had happened.

"We think he's gone off the edge, down the gorge into the river."

"Bloody 'ell! How is he? I mean, is anyone with him?"

"That's just it. We don't know. The car's gone off the track, and ended up halfway down the slope, upside down... sort of, in a tree."

"In a tree?"

"That's what they're saying. And there's no sign of your man... we think... we think he's in the river."

"What! You mean, you don't know where he is?

Didn't anyone see him?"

"He was thrown out. There's no spectators there – they can't get to that part of the track. And the only marshal there said the driver was thrown out."

"Bloody 'ell! What shall I do? Shall I come with you? I don't really want to leave his young lady here on her own."

The official looked past him. The young woman was sitting casually on the pit counter, cigarette in hand, looking back down the track as the leaders roared into view once again.

"I tell you what, old chap…" the official offered. "You stay here with her while we find out more information. We won't be able to retrieve the car till the race is over anyway, and we've got some people heading down there now. I'll come back in a few minutes and let you know what's going on."

3

The corner marshal stood on a small grassy ledge about a foot below the level of the roadway, protected by the official car which had parked carefully on the outside of the track. An ambulance pulled up behind the car, and the occupants began to gather their gear. The chief marshal, who had emerged from the official car, peered down through the trees. He could just pick out what looked like the underside of a car, about sixty feet below.

"Bloody hell, son, what happened?" he asked the corner marshal.

"Well, I didn't quite see everything, but by the time he went past me the whole car was like a ball of smoke. He wasn't going that fast but he didn't seem to be braking and I think he may have been blinded by the smoke. I turned and saw my colleague grab the oil flag and when I turned back I saw the car tumbling off the edge of the track. Like I say, he wasn't going very fast but he just went straight on, between those straw bales, and straight through the trees. We left a spectator waving a flag at our post, and ran down here but I couldn't see him anywhere. There's a couple of people looking down there now, my flag marshal and a spectator."

The chief marshal told him to go back to his post, and beckoned to a couple of colleagues from his car. They were joined by the two ambulancemen. "I need a couple of you to go down and see if you can see him. I need to phone race control and let them know what's going on. We'll put a permanent yellow flag on for this corner, and I'll get a couple more people down here to help man the marshals' post."

As he headed back around the corner to use the field telephone at the marshals' post, the two officials and one of the ambulancemen stumbled their way down the steep slope towards the wrecked Bugatti.

"We need some rope here – several I think" said one of the officials. "I'll go back and ask them to send some, and a breakdown crane. It's going to take a lot of manpower to get that car out of these trees."

"Alright, Frank. Be careful!"

"You too Johnny. There's a bloody river down there, you know. I hope our chap didn't land in it." replied Frank as he clambered back towards the track, the roar of engines reminding them all that the Grand Prix was very much on still.

Johnny and the two ambulancemen stumbled on, occasionally slipping on the steep earth, using saplings and small tree branches as hand holds. As they approached the wrecked Bugatti they saw it was suspended about six feet in the air, upside down, and with the nose nearer to the ground than the back. There were two men already there.

"Don't go near the edge, chaps" said a tall, gangly looking young man wearing a marshal's armband. "It's almost vertical there, and we're about a hundred and fifty feet up from the river."

"Where's the driver?" asked the ambulanceman, who introduced himself as Malcolm.

"Arthur" the marshal said in response. "And the driver could be anywhere. This chappie here saw the whole thing. He says he saw him come right out of the car, didn't you?"

The other man was fairly short and slender,

looked about 28-years-old, and somewhat worse for wear. He tried to wipe the dirt and tree-bark from his face, and puffed "I was spectating up there, at the next bend. I know I wasn't meant to be there but… well it's a most spectacular piece of track this. Anyway, I saw the car go straight on into the trees, and then as it started down the slope it hit some small trees and went end over end. The driver came up and went straight over the bonnet. I couldn't see much beyond the car as there was so much smoke, but I'm pretty sure he's gone over there."

He pointed to the edge of the tree-lined slope. Beyond that the drop was almost vertical. All four men were struck simultaneously by the utter madness of racing cars around a track with such a dangerously steep slope beside it. But that summed up the sport, of course. Utter madness, which is why it attracted so many passionate people, from the spectators who liked to watch men risking their lives on the track, to the men themselves who craved the thrill of driving on the limit, knowing that they could easily pay the ultimate price for a mistake.

"Have you searched anywhere else for him?" asked Malcolm. "We've only been here a few minutes, but he's definitely not around here. But you should have a good look too."

Arthur went back to the edge of the gorge and looked over it. "Can't see anything in the river. We'll need a search party down there."

Malcolm and the spectator started to widen their search around the area.

"The marshal up there said he wasn't going that fast when he went off the track. Is that what you noticed?" Malcolm asked.

"No, that's right. Now you come to mention it, he wasn't going fast at all." The spectator wiped his brow on the short sleeve of his shirt, leaving another smudge of dirt across his visage. "I suppose that's what made me think he was blinded by the smoke. Maybe he was just pulling off the track and couldn't quite see where he was going. Even so, when the car turned over, it was as if a spring had gone off under him; he really shot out. That's what made me think he must be in the river, but I hope I'm wrong."

The two men carried on searching, heading off in opposite directions, while the marshal went back to the car and started to look for any clues. All four wheels seemed to be intact, although one of the front wheels was pointing straight out, and the front of the frame was clearly twisted. The radiator was still hot, and water dripped down silently to the forest floor.

Suddenly, there was a shout from the spectator. "Over here! I think we'll need the ambulance!"

Malcolm and the marshal rushed over to a small bushy area, about thirty or so yards from the wrecked Bugatti, and slightly higher up the slope. The spectator was bent over a small figure – at first sight it looked like a piece of blanket, but then they saw the twisted figure of a young boy, half sitting, half lying. He was propped up against a thick branch of the tree, his leg folded awkwardly under his body. He stared straight ahead, clearly very dazed. The spectator was holding his hand reassuringly. He had several small lacerations to his head and arms, but Malcolm was able very quickly to establish that he was very much alive, if only half conscious.

"Right, sonny, let's see what's happened to you. Can you hear me alright?"

The boy nodded, and opened his mouth to speak, but no words came out.

The spectator leaned over him. "Can you tell us your name? What's your name?"

"Tow… tow..ee…" the boy muttered.

"Tony? Is that it?"

Malcolm carried on with a question of his own. "Alright, Tony, what happened? Can you tell me?"

The boy summoned some more energy. "Toby… my name's Toby. I was… we were up by the track… the car… it came straight towards us."

The spectator stood up to make room for the marshal, who knelt down beside Malcolm. The ambulanceman had opened his bag and got a sponge out to wipe Toby's forehead with. "You were up by the track? What, on the outside up there?"

Toby nodded, and winced slightly as the sponge was dabbed over a large cut on his forehead.

"My friend and I… we crept round there. You get the best view… OW!"

"There's a reason we stop people going there, young man. You could have been killed…" The marshal was interrupted by Malcolm.

"Toby. Did you say you were with a friend?"

Toby nodded again. "Harry… He was… I think the car hit him as well. I don't… I can't remember anything really. I thought I was being strangled…"

"Strangled? No son, you must be confused. You've had a nasty bang on the head and I think your leg might be hurt, but I don't think the car could have strangled you."

Within a few more minutes, several more officials and marshals had joined the search for the missing driver, and the other boy, Harry. Meanwhile,

Toby was carried carefully up the steeply winding path to the trackside, and the waiting ambulance. The chief marshal reappeared, and the spectator who'd seen the accident was introduced to him.

"We'll need to take a statement from you, of course, sir. Perhaps you could come back to race control with me in a while? If you could leave us to it now, that would be good."

"That's fine. I'd like to go and retrieve my camera and bag, if you don't mind. Should I head back to the startline area then?"

"Yes, but we probably won't be back until the race has finished. If you'd like to wait up at the top, we'll give you a lift."

"That's most kind. Thank you very much. I might well do that, but if not, I'll meet you back at race control."

"Alright then. Oh, what's your name, sir?"

"Watson. David Watson."

"Alright, Mr Watson, I'll see you soon."

The spectator climbed back up through the wooded area, using the tree branches to help. It was a very steep slope indeed; of all the places to come off the track, the Bugatti driver couldn't have chosen a worse place. Reaching the path near the edge of the track, he made his way further round the circuit in the direction of travel. He noticed that the race was still very much on; as he looked across he saw Mays's ERA chasing down one of the Maseratis ahead of him. After nearly two hours' running of the Gold Trophy the drivers were still putting heart and soul, and not a small amount of sheer brute strength, into their racing.

"Oi! This is a restricted area!" said a voice. He

looked up to see another marshal gesticulating urgently at him. "Get out of the way, you idiot!"

"Sorry! I've just come from helping out with the accident actually" said the spectator as he ran to join the marshal at his rudimentary post. "David Watson. They've asked me to go back to race control. I saw it all happen from just behind you, and I've left my camera and bag up there so I need to go and fetch it."

"Round there? No-one's allowed there, that's a restricted area. How come I never saw you then?" asked the marshal, indignantly.

"Look, I know I shouldn't have been there, which is why you couldn't see me. I was up there, just behind that tree." He pointed. "There's a small ledge on the hillside. I can see the track, but you can't see me. I can get some splendid photographs from up there, you know. It took me ages to find it last year, so I wasn't going to miss it this time round. When I saw the accident, your friend from the other post went running and I followed him but further down in the woods. There's a young lad called Tony down there who was hit by the car, but he's in the ambulance now. We've been searching for the driver, but I think he's ended up in the river, poor chap."

"Bloody hell, what a way to go." said the marshal. "Mind you, this has to be the most dangerous bit of race track in the world."

"Oh no," replied the spectator, "you should go to the Nurburgring. It's much more mountainous than this, and over four times as long. You really wouldn't want to crash there. I mean, the cars go airborne several times a lap, especially these things..." He pointed as von Brauchitsch thundered past, his bright red leather helmet making him easily identifiable. For a few seconds the two men could not speak, as the rest of the German cars roared by.

"I say" he continued "they're damn close to each other after all this time, aren't they?"

"I reckon they're doing this for show, old chap" replied the marshal. "It's one thing turning up to show how good you are, but really this is taking it a bit far, isn't it?" He suddenly turned and grabbed the yellow flag, as a passing backmarker lost control and looped into a gentle spin. "Well caught, sonny boy." he muttered under his breath, as he waved the flag vigorously at two oncoming racers. After the two cars had passed, the spinner dropped his clutch and started off down the track. For a moment, he looked set to rejoin the race, but suddenly his engine cut and he coasted to a halt. The driver hopped out, and after a cursory glance at his car, waved at the marshal and ran across the track to join them.

"Right, I'll go and get my camera and bag then, and head off." said the spectator. "By the time I reach race control, the race will have finished. They've asked me for a statement, so I must be getting back there. Cheerio!" and with that, he clambered back down to the pathway, just as the stricken racer walked around the back of the marshals' post.

It was over an hour after the race had finished before the crumpled wreckage of the Bugatti could be finally dragged up from its shaky perch in the trees, and craned onto a flatbed truck for the journey back to the paddock. The mechanic had helped with the operation, having sent the young woman home in the driver's own road car. As the car was lifted onto the back of the breakdown truck, he had a quick look at the remains.

"It's difficult to see what could have caused all that smoke. The exhaust is broken, and one of the oil pipes has become detached, but I'll have to strip the car down first before I can say what the cause was."

The Clerk of the Course, who had also arrived at the accident scene, nodded.

"Well, of course, we'll have to investigate this thoroughly. Our resident engineer here will give it the once over with you. He'll let us have a report as soon as he has a chance, although to be honest, I'm much more worried about your driver, and apparently there's a young boy missing too, who was hit by the car. There's no sign of either of them, and the police are going to have to search the river."

"Yes, of course." The mechanic nodded grimly. "I don't even want to think about what has happened to him. This is a terrible place to go off."

"Quite right. We'll have to talk to the track owner about putting more straw bales up to stop cars crashing down there. Maybe we need them all the way along, and three bales high."

The sporting headlines the next day told of the sensational 1-2-3 victory by the Mercedes team, lead by von Brauchitsch, followed by Lang and Caracciola, after the Auto Unions had all succumbed to mechanical issues. A brief mention was made of the accident to the Bugatti, the injured young boy, and the missing French driver, Pierre-Henri Cantin, who was thought to have been thrown into the river following a spectacular plunge through the trees. In the more sensationalist papers, another kind of headline highlighted the tragic death of 13-year-old

Harry Levenson, whose body had been found at the bottom of the steep drop beside the river, having been mown down by the Bugatti as it plunged through the trees.

Following the discovery of Harry's broken body, the police searched the surrounding area for two days but found no trace of the missing driver. After a third day of searches, including the use of a diver to search the river in the immediate vicinity, the Chief Inspector of Police issued a statement in which he stated that the missing driver was most likely drowned in the river, and that because of the proximity of the coast, his body may have been carried out towards the sea.

Later in the month, the Motor Sport magazine carried a race report by 'RGP', in which the mystery of the missing driver was barely mentioned, other than the seemingly callous comment that the police expect a body to be washed up in the next couple of months further down near the mouth of the river.

An unsympathetic article in the Daily Express referred to Cantin as an 'obscure French businessman' and harped on about the inherent dangers of the sport of motor racing. It questioned the sanity of the participants who thrived on those dangers, and the wisdom of accepting an entry for such a high-profile race, from a little known foreign driver driving an eight-year old car.

Nowhere in any of the British press articles was any mention made of an investigation by French police into the financial activities of the business owners of a large industrial manufacturer of automobile tyres.

4

Saturday 5th January 2019 – Milnefield

Hazel Burns sat straight-legged on the large beanbag under the window of Alex Phipps' bedroom, staring intently at her phone, while Alex lay propped against the pillows on his bed, tapping away on his laptop. To an outside observer, especially an older one of parental age, the pair might have been ignoring one another, or maybe had a tiff, but the truth was much simpler – both 14-year-olds were just trying to work out where to go that evening. It would be their last 'night out' before the start of the spring term, and more serious GCSE coursework. Hazel was keen to see a film – any film – while Alex, not much of a cinema goer himself, just wanted to go wherever his girlfriend wanted to go. He would have happily settled for a long walk, as long as he could have Hazel alongside him.

"Here you go!" said Hazel enthusiastically. "Ghostblade! It's meant to be really spooky, with lots of blood and dead bodies and so on…"

Alex smiled and raised his eyebrows. "Nice. What time is it on?"

"There's one at 3.30, then 6, then 8.30. Then we could have a pizza maybe? Lauren and Sam want to come along as well, and your sister, of course."

"Do I know Sam?" asked Alex.

"He's in Year 11, but you'll like him. He's mad about trains. He'll love all that Salmsham stuff." Hazel's thumbs typed rapidly on her phone's screen.

25

Alex snorted. He'd had more than enough of that for the last year – solving the mystery of the true cause of the Salmsham Railway Disaster had taken up six months of his spare time since last February, and he'd been trying to put it out of his mind since. It had been a very intense period, saving the reputation of one of his ancestors only to implicate others in murderous revenge, and leaving him slightly uncomfortable whenever he remembered the more gruesome details.

"So, what time shall I tell them then?" asked Hazel, flicking her long blonde hair back over her shoulders.

"Why don't we go for the 3.30 showing and then we can all have a pizza afterwards." Alex suggested. "Then we've still got time to hang out or whatever. What time have you got to be home?"

"Well, Mum said 10, Dad said 10.30, so 11 it is" Hazel grinned.

"Right, I'll make sure I see you home by 10 then. I don't want to be in trouble with your 'rents."

"You won't be in trouble with them, I will. Anyway, you don't need to see me home…"

"Yes I do. It's only right!"

"Oh, stop being the gallant man, Alex! This is 2019, not 1919. My parents aren't expecting you to see me home. Anyway, then you've got to walk home yourself from my village."

"I know… but I want to. It just feels right, and anyway, I'll get my mum to pick me up." said Alex.

"Whatever… anyway I've messaged Lauren and she's up for it. How long before the bus leaves for town?"

Alex glanced at his watch. "We've got another

twenty minutes, so we might as well see what this film is all about."

"Well, duh, it's a ghost story, hence the name Ghostblade!" teased Hazel.

"Sounds okay, I suppose." said Alex, half-heartedly. "If you like that sort of thing!"

"Yeah, I do. Anyway, the special effects are meant to be the best ever. The ghosts really look as if they're passing through walls and everything. But they get trapped in an old dungeon or something, and then they're defeated after a lot of blood has been spilt…"

"So these ghosts can go through walls but manage to get locked up in a dungeon, so presumably they just forgot about the wall stunt…"

"Yeah, well, it's a story. If you don't like it…"

"It's not that. I'm just not into ghosts. They don't scare me or anything. They're just figments of people's imagination."

Hazel raised her voice. "You don't have to believe in them; it's just… entertainment. Anyway, there's lots of records of real ghosts doing things like walking through walls, and all that."

"Haha really? Lots of records? Wow, I'll go and look them up to find how many times ghosts have done this over the centuries…"

"Stop it, Alex! Why do you always spoil things by taking the mickey!" Hazel put on her best hurt expression and threw her phone onto the floor.

"I'm not taking the mickey, I just think these stories aren't that scary, especially as I don't believe in ghosts."

"Yeah, I gathered that. But you still got freaked out by that skeleton last summer, didn't you?"

"That was a real person, and a murder victim too." Alex shivered slightly as he recalled going to see all that remained of the man who accused his ancestor of manslaughter many years ago. "There's no such thing as ghosts. They're all in the mind."

"So you keep saying. But I happen to think you're wrong. I believe they really exist." Hazel looked away dismissively.

"I'll agree to disagree, Haze. Anyway, we'll definitely have a pizza afterwards, eh?" Alex was already feeling hungry just thinking about the evening meal.

"I don't care really."

"Oh, okay. Well, we can decide when we've seen the film then." Alex flipped his laptop closed and looked across at his girlfriend. She was staring at the far wall of his room, looking thoughtful.

"'Sup?" he asked.

"Our family's got a ghost in it. Or a ghost story anyway. But I don't suppose you care about that."

"Oh, really?" Alex tried to sound interested.

"Yep. Really. My Uncle Toby, I think. He saw a real ghost once." Hazel sounded very sure of herself, and looked at Alex as if challenging him to try and deny the possibility.

"Did he? Was he the only one who saw it?"

"I think my grandma saw it too. But anyway, he's convinced several people in our family it was true, and he's built up quite a story around it too." Hazel frowned as she tried to recall some details. "Something about a car crash, in a race or something. Anyway, this racing driver was killed but years later my uncle saw his ghost in broad daylight, but as soon as the ghost saw him, he vanished into thin air.

28

Just… disappeared, literally right there and then."

"Sounds too fantastic for words." said Alex dismissively. "Anyone can say they saw anything, and insist it was true."

"Yep, I suppose. But one time, he was with my grandma and she says she saw it too."

Alex shrugged. "Oh well, sounds like a nice bit of storytelling to me."

"Well yeah, but there was definitely this car crash, in a race. It really happened apparently. They've got a newspaper cutting somewhere."

Alex's ears pricked up. "Ah, now this sounds more interesting. Another historical mystery to get our teeth into."

"Oh yeah, we could go and do our detective work on this one, couldn't we!" Hazel started to try to get up out of the beanbag. "I'm stuck down here!" she giggled. "Help me… I'm actually stuck!"

Grinning, Alex slid off the bed and reached his hand out to pull Hazel up. As she stood she lost her balance and fell forward into his arms, and they toppled back onto the bed, just as the door opened and Olivia Phipps, Alex's older sister, came in.

"Oh children, please! Come on, if you want to catch the bus into town, we need to go now."

Hazel stood up quickly, giggling while she brushed herself down. Alex went a deep shade of red and stammered "She fell on me, Livvy!"

Olivia grinned and rolled her eyes. "Yeah right, and I'm the Queen of England! Anyway, you've got about three minutes to get ready, you two, otherwise you'll miss the bus." She shut the door behind her, chuckling to herself as she did so.

Alex and Hazel both snorted with laughter for

a moment, then gathered their phones and jackets and made their way downstairs. Later on, as the bus slowly meandered its way around the new estate, Hazel told Olivia about the ghost story. "Alex reckons we could do a bit more research and solve another mystery."

"Really? You must be mad, little bro'. Wasn't one crazy mystery enough for you last year?"

"Well, no… I mean, I like the idea that something's happened and there's clearly some loose ends which haven't been tied up. It'll make a change to be someone else's family as well."

"That's true!" chuckled Olivia. "I hope you're not both expecting me to use up my precious spare time on more newspaper reports though. Uni work is a lot harder than A levels, you know."

"Yeah, we know." Alex grinned. "Anyway, I reckon I know what to do now, and if we get stuck…" he winked at Hazel "we'll ask Jake to help us instead."

"Don't you dare!" said Olivia, turning serious for a moment at the thought of her boyfriend getting involved with another mystery. "It's bad enough us being at different unis this year, but I had enough of him spending more time last year with my ancestors than with me!"

Alex liked the idea of a new mystery to solve, especially if it meant spending more time with Hazel. He hated to admit to anyone – and especially to Hazel herself – that he was infatuated with her, and he found it impossible to gauge whether she felt the same way about him. He resolved to take a lot of interest in her ghost story, and see whether it would bring them even closer.

5

"Here you are, here's the newspaper cutting." Meredith Burns slipped a clear plastic sheaf across the kitchen table toward Alex and Hazel. Inside was a neatly cut out portion of newspaper, with a couple of paragraphs under the heading: 'Missing racing motorist feared drowned'.

"Thank you, Mrs Burns." said Alex, enthusiastically. "Do you mind if I take a copy?"

"Not at all, Alex. And please, call me Meri; all Hazel's other friends do – it's what I've always been known as, since I was a little girl."

Alex was too shy to say anything, so he just frowned and lined up his iPhone to take a picture. After taking two or three copies, he started to read the cutting to himself. Hazel leaned over and prodded his arm. "Come on then, read it out!" she cajoled. "See what you make of it."

"Okay" said Alex, "here goes: *'Missing Racing Motorist Feared Drowned. The search goes on at the Avon Gorge for the missing French racing motorist, Pierre-Henri Cantin, who was flung from his Bugatti racer as it plunged off the circuit during the Abbots Park Ven...* Ven-do-let Tyres...'

"It's pronounced *von-du-lay...*" interrupted Meredith. "The company. *Von-du-lay* not *Vend-O-Lett*. It's French. And the driver's name is *Can-tahn*."

Ah, okay" Alex was glad of the help. "*'The Abbots Park Vendolet Tyres Gold Cup Trophy Race last*

*Saturday, killing a young spectator. Police are currently searching the river for a considerable distance from the place where the driver is thought to have fallen. The accident was witnessed by a lone spectator, Mr David Watson of London, who had been watching from a restricted area. He saw the car leave the track 'quite slowly, with smoke billowing from under the bonnet.' Mr Watson said the car tumbled end over end down through the trees on the steep slope, and he saw the driver ejected from his seat 'as if on a spring' and flung over the edge of the steep slope. The car came to rest in some trees. Rescuers searching for the driver found the body...*Oh gosh!" Alex stopped, took in a quick breath and read on silently for a moment.

"Go on." Hazel leaned forward to try and see what he was reading.

"Sorry... I was just... it says *'Rescuers ... found the body of a young boy, Harry... Levenson, 13, who had been struck by the car as it left the track. Another boy, Toby Allen, 12, who was spectating with Master Levenson in a prohibited area by the trackside, was slightly injured. Police say it is likely that if the driver was unconscious, he may have been washed out towards the sea. The search continues.'* So... which one of these is the ghost?"

Hazel frowned. "Mum?"

"Well, that little boy, Toby Allen, is my Great Uncle. He's still alive; he's in his 90s now, of course. He reckons he saw the dead driver several years after the accident. In fact, he swears blind that he's seen him several times." Meredith smiled. "He used to tell me the story when I was a young girl; frightened me something rotten, he did. He was always deadly serious about it too. I mean, I believe he really thinks he saw the ghost of the dead racing driver."

Alex raised his eyebrows. "But I presume you think it's a load of rubbish, don't you? I mean, we all know ghosts can't exist. It's obvious that either he was mistaken, or the driver survived the accident."

"You can try telling him that, and he won't have it. He's sure the driver was killed. There was an eyewitness; the man who he reckons saved his life."

"Who was that?" asked Alex. "It doesn't say anything about it in the paper."

"Not directly, no." replied Meredith "But it was the spectator, Watson who found Uncle Toby. He was lying on the ground underneath the car, and he said that this Watson chap pulled him out, and got the ambulancemen to him just in time, as he was choking to death. Anyway, Uncle's friend Harry was killed and Watson was a key witness at the inquest, so it was all thoroughly looked into at the time. They never found the driver, and reckon he was killed when he hit the water, and his body floated down the river and then got washed out to sea."

Alex frowned. "Well that's easily solved then. The driver was thrown free, and not drowned at all. So your Uncle's ghost must have been the living driver, because he hadn't actually been killed."

"That's what we all thought, but then as Uncle Toby says, they had a lot of people searching high and low for the driver. He would have had to pull off a really clever stunt to survive a crash like that, and not be noticed. And why would he do that?"

Alex shrugged. "Dunno. Still, it's a neat story. I think Hazel and I should do a bit of detective work."

"You are kidding me?" said Hazel in disbelief.

"Well it's your family, Haze!" Alex shrugged, while glancing knowingly at Meredith Burns at the same time. "I could get my Nana to do a quick search of your family tree. And don't forget Livvy can look up those newspapers and things online."

Hazel ignored him and turned to her mother. "Mum, where does Uncle Toby live now?"

"Oh… somewhere up near Bristol, Yatton I think it's called. He's still living in his own home; I think one of his friends' daughters looks after him."

"Could we go and see him? I mean, soon? Maybe to do an interview or something."

"Hazel, he's... what, 93 now and he'll probably be too infirm to see anyone, and certainly to do an interview with a stranger, or even a relative."

"Can't we at least try him?"

Meredith Burns sighed and looked at her eager daughter's bright eyes under her raised eyebrows, as she looked on pleadingly. "Darling, how on earth are you going to get over there? I'm not letting you travel by train on your own…"

"Well, I thought you could take us, Mum."

"Us?" Meredith raised an eyebrow.

"Yes. You and me and… Alex?"

Alex squirmed a little, embarrassed to be seen to be too enthusiastic in case he fell out with Hazel's mother before he'd really got to know her.

"Please Mum? You won't regret it. We're going to solve the mystery of the ghost driver for all of the family, not just for us." Hazel did her best 'hard-done-by' look and stared pleadingly at her mother.

Meredith sighed again. "I'll ring him up tomorrow, Darling, but not at this time. Look, it's nearly 10 o'clock; far too late to ring anyone, let alone a 93-year-old man. I have no idea what time he goes to bed or anything."

6

Half term could not come quickly enough for Hazel and Alex. The start of Year Ten had been something of a wake-up call to both teenagers, after a year of handing in bits of homework here and there, fitting it in around researching and helping to solve the Salmsham disaster. Now, after the first round of mock exams just before Christmas, they found themselves with serious amounts of studying and homework. Alex was already feeling pressured by his teachers' high expectations of him. Hazel seemed slightly less stressed but nonetheless, they had nearly fallen out twice in the past weeks over petty things.

Now, however, a trip to Bristol was on the cards; the Burns family had arranged to stay with Meredith's cousin Martina in Henleaze, one of Bristol's northern suburbs, for a few days. Geoff and Meredith had formally invited Alex along as company for Hazel. Hazel's younger brother Maxwell was away on a school residential; his school being on a different half-term week, it meant he would be away all of this week but home the next, much to Meredith's annoyance. The two teenagers were suffering under the weight of what seemed to be a ridiculous amount of coursework for the half-term week, but with a little bit of parental assistance, and the incentive of another mystery to work on, they had spent the first Saturday of half-term working solidly so as to free up the rest of the week.

The following day was Alex's birthday, although he was more excited about the upcoming trip with Hazel's family than he was about celebrating being fifteen. After opening his presents, which consisted mainly of clothes and useful items for teenage students, the family had an early Sunday roast dinner. Olivia had come home from university, and his mother's parents had come over for the day too, so Alex felt genuinely spoilt and happy, although he wished he could to have Hazel there too. After lunch his parents surprised him by slipping him an extra present – the latest model iPhone.

"Thanks Mum, thanks Dad! I'll take it with me and set it all up on holiday" he enthused.

The Burns family arrived later in the afternoon to collect Alex. Hazel had already told him that his present from her was the holiday, so he was even more surprised when she gave him a small wrapped package and told him not to open it until he was on his own that evening.

They reached Henleaze a little later than planned on the Sunday evening, having seen Hazel's brother Maxwell off on his residential on the way. The trip had been somewhat torrid, not helped by appalling weather conditions and a serious accident which closed the main road through Bath. Their hosts house was one of the older Edwardian properties on the southern fringe of the suburb, with ample room on the drive for Geoff's Range Rover.

Martina Heath greeted them at the door with huge hugs for Meredith and Geoff, a hug and kiss for Hazel, and a handshake for Alex. "Lovely to see you all; I'm so sorry you've had a rubbish journey. This weather's just ghastly, and it's not possible to go anywhere in this country without hitting some sort of delay, is it?"

"Oh, one delay would have been fine, Martina, but there every diversion we took ended up being worse, with roadworks and floods and blasted caravans crawling along..." Geoff was still feeling tense from the drive.

"Well, come in and sit down everyone. I expect you could all do with a drink?"

Everyone agreed, and a few minutes later they were all ensconced in Martina's living room with various hot drinks, pleased to be out of the car at last.

"So Alex. Happy Birthday, Dear. I've heard all about you and your railway adventures. I gather your family has solved a murder mystery, or something?" Martina gushed.

"Well... yes... I mean, I had a lot of help from Hazel and my parents, but we did manage to get this train crash investigated again after 144 years."

"So I've heard. Gosh, you sound like a regular Sherlock Holmes from what I've been told!"

Alex felt he couldn't blush any more if he tried.

"...and I gather" Martina continued "that you and Hazel are going to look into our family's little ghost story."

"Well..." Alex began.

"You'll love Uncle Toby. He's wildly eccentric; completely batty, but don't be fooled - he has a pin-sharp mind. You'd be hard pressed to outwit him, I must say."

"Well..." Alex tried again.

"But I expect he'll like the attention all the same. He loves to relate the ghost story, or rather the ghost stor*ies*." Martina continued

"Oh gosh, yes!" said Meredith. "The only thing is they change every time he tells them."

"Well, yes but only in a few little details. The essence is always the same though. He saw this racing driver chappie killed before his very eyes, and then he saw him in the street bold as brass, two or was it three times? And each time he vanished into thin air, before his very eyes."

Hazel glared at Alex. "I told you, but you wouldn't believe me."

Alex blushed even more. "Look, I never said…"

"He doesn't believe in ghosts, Auntie Tina," Hazel said "which is why we're here, of course."

Martina Heath could sense Alex's acute embarrassment and came to his defence. "Well why would he, Hazel? Frankly, I don't believe in ghosts either. But I know for a fact that Uncle Toby does believe in them, and won't be moved about it."

"Well…" Alex stammered again "I'm quite sure that there must be something to erm… Uncle Toby's story, otherwise he wouldn't keep on telling it, but I'm also quite sure he's not being seeing a real ghost. But after what Hazel and I have found out in the last few months, there's always an element of truth in all these stories."

There was a silence, during which Alex realised his statement of the obvious had probably come across as extreme arrogance in the eyes of a family who had lived with Uncle Toby's ghostly tales as a staple since they were all young children.

Finally, Meredith Burns spoke. "Yes, well, as Alex says, there must be some truth in these tales, so the reason Alex is with us is to try to make sense of it all. I'm sure we're all too close to the story to challenge any of it."

"You're not just challenging the story, you're challenging Uncle Toby!" said Martina. "Good luck with that, everyone…"

"Sometimes, Mrs Heath, it needs an outsider to come in and ask awkward questions. That's exactly what Hazel did when we got to the bottom of the Salmsham Railway Disaster." Alex was so far out of his comfort zone that he was starting to babble now. "She was pretty amazing actually; she came up with a different slant on the whole affair…"

"Which turned out to be wrong, Alex…" Hazel interrupted. "But thanks for the compliment anyway."

Both teenagers laughed with embarrassment. Martina looked at Alex and smiled kindly. "Well, you're most welcome anyway, Alex, and it's nice to meet you. We've heard so much about you from Hazel, and it was all good."

Now it was Hazel's turn to blush. Alex smiled and winked at her. "Oh, that's nice. You must tell me these good things about me as well, Haze."

"Maybe, one day, if I can remember them. Anyway, Auntie Tina, when are we going to meet Uncle Toby?"

"Tomorrow, dear, and please… you're old enough to just call me Tina, especially as I'm not actually your auntie; we're cousins. Same for you Alex – it's Tina, okay?"

"Okay." Alex smiled at her, but couldn't quite bring himself to say her name this time.

"After tomorrow you've pretty much got the

rest of the week free to sightsee, but don't forget I'm taking Meredith here to see a museum on Thursday, and on Friday evening we're going to see Annelise in the opera."

"Of course, I hadn't forgotten" said Meredith. She hadn't seen her younger sister on the opera stage for several years, and was delighted when she mentioned that she was performing nearby. "Where is it again?"

"On the S.S. Great Britain, just down in Bristol Harbour. It's a lovely venue."

Hazel sighed. "I suppose we've got to go and watch, have we?"

"Yes you have! This is your aunt, you know. She's a very fine singer."

"Yes, but… opera? I mean, it's not exactly our sort of music, is it." She looked across at Alex, who looked at the floor, wondering what it was he was being dragged along to see.

"Oh, I think you'll love it!" said Martina. "It's H.M.S. Pinafore, a Gilbert and Sullivan comedy. I took Lucy along last year to see another one they did and she loved it. It's nothing like you think."

Hazel shrugged. "So it's not fat ladies wearing helmets with horns and singing in foreign languages then? Okay, I'll go… just for Auntie Annelise."

Martina smiled. "Right, now that's settled. Meri, let's show you all to your rooms. Hazel, I hope you don't mind having Lucy's room. It means you'll have to share with her when she comes back from guide camp on Thursday." Martina led them upstairs and pointed to a room at the end of a small corridor off the landing.

"That's cool, thank you." Hazel trotted along

and gingerly opened the door. "Oh, wow! Cool wallpaper! Did Lucy choose it herself?"

"Yes – and she helped to decorate it." Martina turned the other way and pointed to a larger double room on the left. "That's you and Geoff, and Alex has got the attic room. – this way." She led Alex to the far end of the corridor, and opened a smallish door which could have passed for a cupboard.

"Just up there, Alex. It's a bit steep, but you've got a nice big room, and it has its own bathroom as well. My son Lucas is away on his gap year, so you have the room to yourself."

"Thank you very much, Tina." Alex managed her name, and thought how grown up he sounded, and felt, as he made his way up to the room. Tina and Hazel followed him. "Oh, Alex, mind that low beam...!" Tina called out, but Alex ducked too late to avoid the wooden beam at the top of the stairs, and gave himself a fair knock on the temple.

"Oh... it's fine, it didn't hurt!" he said, grimacing in a vain attempt to hide the pain and his embarrassment. Hazel stood in front of him and looked at his forehead.

"That looked *very* painful, Alex. You sure you're okay?" She winked at him knowingly. "Shall I get you some ice?"

"No, it's fine thanks. But I may have a bit of a lie down for a minute or two." He sank down onto the bed, feeling decidedly dizzy.

"You're not the first person to do that, and you won't be the last. I'll leave you here for a few minutes; Hazel – you need to go and unpack, dear."

Hazel ignored her aunt's hint, and looked at the small bump which was starting to show on

41

Alex's forehead. "That's going to be quite spectacular if we don't get some ice for it, you great numpty."

"I'll be fine, honestly. I think I just need to shut my eyes for a few minutes."

"Oh crikey! He's got concussion now" she grinned, "that'll be a great help when we try to solve the Mystery of Uncle Toby's Ghost. I'm off to get you an ice pack, no arguing."

"Whatever…" Alex replied, falling back onto the pillow, as Hazel moved off downstairs.

When she returned with the icepack a few minutes later, Alex was sitting on the bed with the little present she'd given him on his lap. She sat beside him as he unwrapped it, and opened the small white box.

"I know you don't wear stuff like this but… well… I bought it myself. My folks don't know." Hazel blushed as Alex held up a necklace with a small gold bar on it. He read the inscription out loud.

"Alex and Hazel forever" he smiled.

"There's more on the back."

He turned it over and read "'*You take my breath away*'! Oh wow, Haze… Thank you!"

He slipped his arms around her, and kissed her boldly, more boldly than he had ever done before.

"Right, you two. Your birthday's nearly over, Alex" Meredith grinned as she appeared in front of them, making them both sit back in surprise. Alex quickly dropped the necklace out of sight by his feet. "I can tell that bump on the head hasn't done you any damage. Come on, Hazel, it's bedtime."

7

During a brief chat over breakfast, Martina Heath mentioned that Uncle Toby would probably struggle to cope with all five of them, and so it was decided that Meredith would take the two teenagers over to visit him, while she and Geoff would spend the morning exploring Clifton, which he had not visited for many years.

"Well I must say, young Meredith, your children have turned out well, haven't they?" Toby Allen sat in an old armchair in the corner of the living room of his house, looking at Hazel and Alex who sat awkwardly together on the sofa opposite him. His friend's daughter Julia, who visited him daily, had brought in a glass of squash for each of them, and pulled out another chair for Meredith from a small bureau which was tucked against the far wall.

Meredith couldn't help smiling at his mistake. "Thank you, Uncle Toby. Of course, only Hazel is mine. My son Max is on a school trip. Alex here is Hazel's boyfriend."

"Oh." said the old man matter-of-factly, staring straight at Alex, who fiddled nervously with the necklace which he had put on proudly before he got into the shower that morning. He was already feeling very self-conscious about the small bruise on his forehead from the low beam, and couldn't decide whether there was a hint of distaste or not in Toby's brief comment. After a short pause, he realised it

43

may have been a cue for him to speak.

"That's right, Mr Allen. Hazel and I recently worked on solving the mystery of the Salmsham Railway disaster, and we thought we'd, erm…" He let the sentence die away, rather than appear to challenge the old man's ghost story before he'd heard it first-hand.

Meredith finished off for him. "We'd like to hear the story of the ghost, Uncle. These two sleuths think they may be able to solve the mystery for you."

"Mystery? What mystery? My dear girl, as you well know, there is no mystery at all. You've heard my story many times. I saw the ghost of Pierre-Henri Cantin several years after he died in a racing accident which I saw with my own eyes."

"I know that…"

"And again," Toby interrupted, "in 1968. He saw me staring at him, and vanished into thin air straight away. And then I realised I'd seen him other times too, but had often thought I was mistaken."

Alex was about to make a comment, when Hazel dived in instead. "Uncle Toby, we've only heard the story second hand, and some of the details are a bit unclear. Could you start at the beginning?"

Toby shifted uneasily in his chair. "Really? Well… it's quite a long story…"

Julia poked her head around the door. "I'm just off, Toby. I'll see you tomorrow, luv. Bye everyone!"

"Yes, thank you Julia… lovely girl that. A great help to me around the house."

"Please, Uncle Toby." Hazel stared at him with an exaggerated pleading look on her face. "Will you tell us all of it? It would make it easier for us to solve the… problem. Well, try and find an explanation."

"Very well, young Hazel, I'll tell you everything I can remember. But I warn you, this might take a couple of hours."

Hazel and Alex sat expectantly on the edge of the sofa; Alex turned his iPhone to record and placed it in the middle of the coffee table.

"It was in November 1937. My friend Harry Levenson and I were eager to go to the Donington Grand Prix, but Harry's father did not have a car, and my father had to work that Saturday, so we couldn't get to Donington. We were both very disappointed. You see, we were both mad about motor racing then. We would see the newsreels at the cinema and hear about all the grands prix around Europe, and we read all the magazines we could. So anyway, about three weeks before the Donington Grand Prix we heard about another race which was due to be held the following weekend, nearer to home, at Abbots Park, in Bristol. It's very near here, actually… you should go there and have a look around. Some of it is still open to the public. At least, it was about 25 years ago…" He paused, looking down at his feet, as he tried to remember the nitty-gritty of the day's events so as not to cause even more confusion with the two eager youngsters.

"So my father took Harry and me to Abbots Park. My mother came as well… or did she? I'm not sure… No, she must have been there, because… well anyway, we got into the track and my father told us the best place to see the real action was around the back of the track, just as the cars come over the hill which they called The Leap. Those German cars… my God, they would be airborne for a good few

45

yards, and then when they landed they had to turn into a right hander which was faster than it looked. So, we settled down there, and there were a couple of demonstrations, and then a race for little Austins first, before the main race. Harry and I loved it all. It was such a thrill to see these cars being driven flat out. I remember the first race was won by… oh, what was his name again? Leslie Stokes? Stock?"

There was a long silence as nobody knew the answer, and neither Alex nor Hazel wanted to interrupt the flow of memories from the old man.

"Anyway… Harry and I were thrilled at the sound of the engines approaching The Leap, through the woods. It was… well it was almost magical. They were really driving flat out through the wooded area, and you didn't know who was leading until they burst over The Leap. Well, we wanted to see more of this, so Harry and I asked my father if we could go a bit further along; the other side of The Leap. Father said we could after the main race had started, as long as we came back before the end.

"I think he and Mum had set out all our stuff on the ground. In those days, you drove your car right in and you could park on the grass by the track, and Dad had his camera equipment there. I remember we had a picnic lunch before the main race started. Egg and cucumber sandwiches, that was it. Wrapped in foil. Lots of them. And sausage rolls, and a special treat, fizzy pop. It was a really nice moment; it's etched in my memory, I suppose because of what happened later that day, but I remember that picnic because Harry said something to us about wishing every day could be like that.

"Anyway… then came the main race. I tell you,

we were so excited. We'd heard about the big German cars; the Mercedes and Auto Unions, and we'd read the report from the Donington Grand Prix. We could hear the commentators talking about the power of these great German machines, and when the cars were lining up on the starting grid we could hear them from the other side of the park. In those days, the cars didn't do any warm up laps, they were just pushed onto the grid and that was it, so we didn't actually see them until the race started. Imagine that – it was so exciting!

"And then the commentator said 'The flag is up… and down, and they're off!' and we were shaking with excitement. Remember, in those days, like most people, we didn't have a television, and we had only seen pictures of these cars. I'd been to a few minor races with my father, but never a Grand Prix. This race was run with mostly the same cars that had raced at Donington, so it was like a Grand Prix to us.

"Well, we could hear these cars going round the park in the distance, and then the commentator said 'the cars have disappeared from view' and the next commentator was further round the track from us, so he couldn't see them. I remember him saying 'I can hear them coming round The Ledge… and I can just see them now…' and then they appeared over The Leap. Well, the sound, and the sight, was indescribable. It was so exciting, and so incredibly noisy. Every one of the German cars was airborne, one after the other, and then almost immediately the little voiturettes as well…"

"Excuse me…the little what?" asked Alex.

"Eh? Oh, the voiturettes. They were… it's a French word for little cars. They were using much smaller engines. Fifteen-hundred CCs... that's one and a half litres in modern terms. They used them to fill out the grand prix field, otherwise you'd only have twelve or so cars. You can imagine, with all these other cars there was quite a race going on towards the back as well, and these chaps were racing for the voiturette trophy as well, so the racing was just as serious at the back as it was at the front.

"Well, after a few laps, Harry and I asked if we could go the other side of The Leap and watch the cars coming out of the corner. Dad said fine, just come back by the end of the race, which was wonderful. You probably don't know it, but in those days, these races went on for three hours or so, so we were very excited. I think my mother was sitting in our car by now; she didn't much like the noise. Well, Harry and I walked down to the corner, out of sight of my father, of course, because we'd gone over The Leap. We kept walking round the corner, but then there was a fence and it said 'No Spectators Beyond This Point'. Well, that was like red rag to a bull to us, so we walked back a little way, and went away from the trackside, into a bit of woodland, and then climbed over the fence where no-one could see us.

"We could still hear the cars as if they were right next to us, so then we went on a path that was below the level of the racetrack for a bit. You need to know that we had the track on our left, about six feet above the path, and a very steep drop on the right through the woodland. You see, we were near the edge of the gorge. That's why they didn't allow spectators there, of course, or they might have fallen down into the gorge. Well, we kept well away from the edge; we were just following the sounds of the engines as they got louder.

"After a short while the path got closer to the level of the track, and eventually we found we could see the cars. We hadn't realised quite how close they were until we found a little flat patch of land by a bush. If we stood just behind the bush, we could see over it and the track was about six feet away at just below our eye level, so these cars were thundering past us and we could look almost into the drivers' eyes as they went past. Sometimes you could see a car, if it was on the inside of another one, but… well I tell you, they used to say on your ticket 'Motor Racing is Dangerous' and it really was. But we were so thrilled. We must have been there a good ten minutes or so. We couldn't hear what was going on though, because of course they hadn't put the tannoy around that part of the track because we weren't meant to be there. We didn't see any officials or anything, so we thought we'd got away with it.

"Anyway, I remember one lap this chappy came past in a Bugatti with smoke coming out from under the bonnet, and we looked at each other and said we wouldn't be seeing him again, but next lap, there he was, chugging slowly towards us, even more smoke. I can remember it clear as day… the driver was peering round the outside of the bonnet because the smoke was so thick. And then Harry said 'watch out! He's coming straight at us!' I think Harry waved or something, because I remember seeing the driver's eyes getting wider and wider, then the car just came straight off the edge of the track, right over us. I jumped to my left and remember hitting the ground hard, then everything was a complete daze. I do remember the noise of the car going over us, and I heard Harry shout 'Damn!' and remember thinking that Mum wouldn't be happy about him saying that, then the next thing…"

Toby Allen paused for a moment, then took a deep breath.

"The next thing I remember is waking up with this chap leaning over me, shaking me and saying 'You stupid little fool, you stupid little fool' and then he called out 'over here!' and someone came running. I had a terrible pain around my neck, and I felt like I was choking, so they gave me something to drink. My shin was badly bruised too, but oddly enough it didn't really hurt. The man who had found me looked into my eyes and said 'do you know your name' so I told him and he thought I said 'Tony' but then I corrected him and he said I was lucky to be alive. It turns out he was a spectator and we found out later he was also hiding from view, because he said The Ledge is the best place to take… spectacular pictures from. Well anyway, I got taken off to the field hospital, but I managed to tell them where my parents were and I think they found my mother… yes, of course they must have done, because she was in the ambulance when they got me to the field hospital. They checked me over and then my father turned up and he was white as a sheet because they'd found Harry. He had fallen backwards and gone off the edge of the slope with the car. They found him at the foot of the drop, next to the river, quite dead."

More silence. The three listeners shuffled uneasily, wondering what to say to the old man as he stared at the far wall.

"Yes… poor Harry. He… he'd been hit square

on by the car I think. I don't know, but anyway, where I'd jumped to one side and caught myself on a branch round my neck, he'd gone straight back... I don't know really, how he ended up going off the slope, but he did." A pause, then "Hmmmm."

The old man seemed to be away with his thoughts. Meredith Burns stirred first. "So what happened to the driver, Uncle?"

Toby Allen jerked his head up and looked at her. "Well, this is where my story really starts to be... unusual. You see, this spectator chappy had seen everything, and he saw the car tumbling down the slope, end over end he said. And he said the driver sort of came out of the car as if he had a spring beneath him, and went flying over the treetops and down into the river, but they never found his body. I've often wondered if he actually saw Harry's body flying through the air and not the driver's, but then... well it's a mystery. But then he also said at the inquest that he didn't see us at all. Now, if he didn't see me, then he surely can't have seen Harry either. I reckon Harry went under the car, and then tumbled down through the trees sort of dragged by the car. But the car got stuck in the trees, so Harry must have just carried on and gone over the edge. They found him... anyway I can't remember all of that. I know there was an inquest because I had to go along and explain what we were doing. I remembered being really scared that I was in a lot of trouble, but no-one told me off, and the man in charge... the coroner... told me I wasn't in trouble, and it's true. No-one ever told me off; not my parents, not Harry's parents; no-one. Isn't that strange?"

51

8

"So it wasn't Harry's ghost you saw then?" asked Hazel.

Toby looked down at his feet in deep thought. "No. No, I've never seen Harry's ghost. In fact, do you know, I can't even remember his face, which I find strange. He was my best friend and we did everything together. But now, I can't remember his face, or his voice, or anything."

"So where was the ghost again?" Hazel shuffled with slight impatience.

"I'm coming to that, young Hazel. You know, this is quite a complicated story so you'll need to bear with me." He took a sip from his glass of squash, and then stared towards Hazel's feet. She resisted the temptation to move but was wondering whether she'd accidentally put different shoes on each foot, such was the intensity of his gaze.

"You know, soon after this all happened we went to war. I was 14 when the war started, and I was lucky that my father was too old to be called up to fight. He was 47 years old, and was working for an engineering firm. Well, we had to move as he was transferred to Coventry to work on engines for the warplanes. I had to go to a new school and I suppose it helped that no-one knew me there so I wasn't constantly reminded about Harry and the accident. I was a sensitive lad, though, and my way of dealing with it all was to go into my little shell. I decided to study engineering and I found I was quite good at it. I loved the technical drawing side of it all, so I used to help out in the drawing office – it was all official and part of my education. Because of this, I was given special dispensation to avoid call-up. I didn't actually realise this at the time, but my father's company had arranged it all apparently. My older brother – your grandfather, Meredith, had gone into the RAF as a navigator, so I rather liked the idea that he might be flying with one of our engines – all very fanciful, of course, but at the time it was a great comfort. I ended up helping out with aircraft testing; we would design a new part, test it and then arrange for it to be manufactured. By the time I found out my call-up had been postponed it was too late really, the war was almost over and my father persuaded me that I was making a far bigger contribution doing what I was doing, than I would as a single soldier slogging my way across Europe. That was fine, I wanted to help but I didn't much fancy being in the front line. I'm not a coward, you understand, but I wanted to make a real contribution and I think I did.

"Well, after the war finished I carried on working for this firm, making engine parts for various companies. One day my father asked me if I wanted to go to see another motor race. Of course, I said 'Yes' straight away, so we went to this little old airfield in Northamptonshire called Silverstone, and we went in and had a wonderful day. Dad was worried that I would have flashbacks but I don't think it even occurred to me to think about it. Some of the cars racing that day were the same ones racing in 1937, so the sounds and everything were familiar. We watched the races from outside of the track, but then at lunchtime Dad asked if I'd like to go to the paddock and see the cars close up. He had several friends working there, and as he was a popular man he had been invited to see them, so anyway, I don't know how we did it, but we ended up in the paddock where they prepare all the cars.

"We went to see this friend of Dad's, called… erm… Mike. Mike Ferris, that was it. Ferris. Well, we were chatting away, standing next to this car. It was an ERA, and there were a couple of mechanics working on it. I was watching them, and I think I got talking to one of them about the engine, and he was bending over and doing something around the bottom of the block… I can't remember. Mike was talking to Dad, and I happened to look up, and there was someone standing looking straight at us… just standing there, staring. I looked at his face and realised it was the face of Cantin, the racing driver who had died in the Abbots Park accident. I mean, it was him. He had the same bushy moustache, the same mouth shape, eyebrows… high cheekbones. And he looked straight at me as if he knew me. I opened my mouth to speak… and nothing came out at first. Then I managed to say "I say! My God! Look! It's Cantin!" and he… he just disappeared. Just like that. Before my very eyes. Totally disappeared. One moment he was there; the next he was gone."

Alex Phipps sat up, excitedly. "Did he say anything back to you?"

"Not a word. There was no time. He literally vanished. My Dad and Ferris looked at me and said 'What was that?' and I told them I thought I saw the racing driver Cantin standing right there. I remember Ferris looking at me oddly and saying 'I think you must be seeing things, young man. There was no-one there', and then the mechanic looked up and said he hadn't seen anyone. They all knew who I was talking about though, and my father just said, very matter-of-factly 'I think you must have seen a ghost, son'. Well, that was it. I think I fainted, and then I don't remember much about the rest of the day. I vaguely remember walking back to Dad's car, and then I can remember arriving home. I was still living with my parents back then. I remember my mother saying I must be feeling ill. Hallucinating, they both did. After all that, I realised they didn't really believe me. I didn't want to get into a row over it, so I decided not to mention it again to them, and I didn't."

"Couldn't Cantin have survived the accident though?" Alex said. "I mean, they never found his body, did they?"

"Young man… I've thought about it often, and I've questioned it many many times. But please let me tell you the rest of the story and you can ask me questions afterwards. My memory is not what it used to be but I can assure you I remember these moments as if they had just happened."

"I'm sorry, I'll wait." Alex said apologetically.

"You saw the ghost again, didn't you Uncle?" asked Meredith, trying to prompt Toby to carry on. She was worried that, at this age, he might suddenly have to stop and rest.

"I did, yes… I'm trying to think when I next saw it. I think… we didn't go to many races after the Silverstone incident, but Dad went quite often, and one day I asked if he would take me and another friend to the British Grand Prix. Now this was in… 1954, I think. I was nearly 29 years old, and I had a friend I'd met at work, another Mike. Mike Henshaw. You might have heard of him, he invented the Henshaw ignition system which they used for a while before… I think he was bought out by Lucas in the end. Anyway, Mike Henshaw and I went with my Dad. By now I'd stopped thinking about the ghost; I think I bought my parents' idea that I'd been ill and hallucinating. It didn't even occur to me.

"Well, we went to the Grand Prix. It was a fabulous race, won by Juan Manuel Fangio. You've probably never heard of him. He was the Michael Schumacher of his day."

"Michael who?" interrupted Hazel. "Is he a racing driver?"

"Uncle, I think Schumacher is a bit old hat now. These two are only 14. If you mean the Lewis Hamilton of his day…"

"Yes, of course, sorry Meredith… the years just fly by at my age. Anyway, we went into the paddock again and met up with an old friend of my father's, and lo! and behold, there was Cantin again, standing there staring straight at me. This time I kept my eyes on him. I didn't speak, but I did raise my eyebrows, and nudged Mike and pointed. Mike looked up, followed the line of my finger and said 'what are you pointing at?' I said 'that man, right there.' But as I said it I looked across briefly at Mike. 'What man?' he asked, and when I looked back there was nobody. Nobody at all. Gone. Vanished into thin air.

"I told him, 'Mike, I just saw Pierre-Henri Cantin, the driver who died in the Abbots Park race in 1937. I've seen his ghost before; it doesn't scare me but I wish I knew what it meant.' Well, Mike just laughed and said 'it must have been someone else' but then, as I pointed out, he hadn't seen anyone at all. Dad thought I was making it up, so I just shrugged and carried on looking around the paddock I didn't feel scared or anything, unlike before when I was feeling faint. So anyway, then we watched the race and, ah… it wasn't Fangio, it was that big chap… you know… Gonzales."

The others nodded as if they knew what the old man was talking about. There was a short silence, broken by Meredith's gentle questioning.

"Who was Gonzales? The winner?"

"That's right, yes. In a Ferrari. Yes, definitely Gonzales, because I remember we crowded round him afterwards. He was a big chap… his nickname was the Pampas Bull. Anyway, after the main event, we joined the traffic and went home.

"This time my Mum asked if we'd had a good day and my Dad didn't even mention the ghost, so neither did I. I did remember to write it down in my diary, though, because I thought I ought to make a note of the date. I also remember I met a young lady there as well…" The old man paused, and took a sip of squash from his glass. "She's the reason I wrote the date in my diary. We went out for a while."

Hazel and Alex exchanged glances; neither of them could imagine anyone dating Uncle Toby.

"Well, anyway, I must have gone for years without giving the ghost another thought. Life went on, I worked my way up in the firm until I became the southern area sales manager. As well as supplying components into the automotive industry, we also had a minor sponsorship deal with some racing teams, mainly the semi-privateer teams, to help them stay competitive. I visited one or two race meetings every year, mainly checking to see whether our customers were happy with the product."

9

"In 1968 we had a small sponsorship arrangement with a couple of the privateer Formula One teams racing at the Race of Champions, at Brands Hatch in Kent. I didn't really want to go for the race; too much traffic; so I went down on the Saturday for the practice sessions. I actually took your mother, Meredith. I think she was about 19 at the time, and she wanted to go along and see these racing cars. I remember… she came along wearing an old Lotus jacket she'd got from somewhere, and she spent most of the day getting autographs.

"Well, anyway, we were in the paddock. One of my teams was in real trouble. They had a Swiss driver, Jo Siffert. Now, Siffert had crashed their Lotus in testing earlier in the week, and then they'd had a terrible fire at their garage which destroyed the car completely, as well as a lot of their equipment and things. I went into the paddock after the first practice, and I remember bumping into Siffert near the Lotus team; he was walking around looking a bit lost, and he had a sticker on his jacket which read 'Merde alors!' I was commiserating with him when I saw, over his shoulder, Pierre-Henri Cantin looking straight at me. He was wearing a modern looking set of mechanic's overalls, but he didn't look any older than when I'd last seen him, and he just stood there, staring. He didn't smile, he didn't blink, or make any facial expression. Just then Siffert patted me gently on the shoulder and moved off. I turned to wish him all the best, then when I turned back the ghost was gone. But this time, we were in the middle of the paddock.. I said to your mother 'Lindy, did you see that mechanic' and she said 'Yes, the one staring at you. He looked a bit odd. Where's he gone?' and then I told her who I thought he was.

"Well, we looked around. There was nowhere for anyone to hide. There were no buildings nearby. I suppose, if he'd been a real person, he could have nipped into another team's van or something. I walked along the row of vans, and looked at all of the mechanics working on the cars. Most of them were wearing team gear, so you could tell the Lotus mechanics from the Ferrari mechanics. The BRM crew were wearing similar coloured overalls to Cantin's ghost, so I had a good look at each of them. Of course, they knew me, so we were able to have a few minutes' chat. I checked that I had seen every one of them, and none of them matched Cantin's appearance even slightly.

"By now I was sure that I had made a mistake; either Cantin had survived the crash and was working as a mechanic in a privateer team, or I had just seen someone who looked a bit like him. After all, I had not seen him alive since that brief moment in 1937 when I had looked into his face as he drove straight towards me. I had seen photographs, of course, so I remembered his face from those. Anyway, Lindy and I spent the rest of the lunch break between practice sessions going from team to team, chatting to their mechanics and team managers. I was welcomed everywhere, and in those days paddocks really were just grass and gravel. The teams used to rope off a small working area and carry on working in full view of everyone else, so you could meet everyone in the team. Even the drivers used to just sit in the back of the trucks, and eat their sandwiches. Quite often you'd see them looking over the cars; one or two even helped their mechanics. People like Graham Hill... he'd been a mechanic before he was a racing driver, so he used to muck in and help the mechanics. I'm not sure they always liked it, but anyway, he was there too.

"Well, we checked everywhere. There was not a single person who looked anything like Cantin, so I realised I'd seen his ghost again, and your Mum saw him too, Meredith. But the thing I don't understand... and I'm not sure any of you will be able to help me with this, but... what did the ghost want with me? And why haven't I seen it since... ever! I don't know. I have no idea, but anyway... that's my story. I've spent some time over the years trying to make sense of it, but I can't. So, if you young folk think you can do any better, I'd be very surprised. I don't have the energy or even the desire now, to be honest. It's been a mystery to me all my adult life, and I can't see it changing now."

There was a short silence while his audience processed the transition from being transfixed with the narration to sorting out their numerous questions into some semblance of coherence.

Alex was the first to speak. "Wow, that was some story. Thank you, Mr Allen. Do you mind if I ask whether you've got any papers about the accident that we could look at?"

"Of course I have. I'm not sure where they are, but they're still in the house. I've kept all the press cuttings from those days in a box; you're very welcome to have a look at them, if I can find it."

"That would be great, thank you."

Hazel stretched her legs and said "Uncle Toby, can I just ask you whether you were ever married?"

"Hazel! Don't be so cheeky!" her mother said quickly. "Sorry, Uncle Toby."

The old man smiled. "Don't worry, young Meredith, it's fine. No, my dear, I never married. Not because I didn't want to, but… let's just say I've held a few hands in my time, and leave it at that."

"What, you mean you've had a few girlfriends, or… I'm confused." Hazel had missed the subtlety of her great great uncle's last sentence.

"I've been in love, I've been out of love. I've also been hurt by love, and I've probably hurt others. I've been a little unlucky, that's all. Or perhaps I've been lucky, who's to say. But all of that's in the past now. I'm very contented with how I've lived my life, and I'm happy to have my lovely extended family; of which you are, of course, a precious member. I have no regrets."

"Ah, okay. I just wondered if you had any children." Hazel blushed a little as she asked the question, and her mother took a sharp intake of breath and rolled her eyes.

"If I had, I'd like to think they'd be sitting here now with us, don't you?" he smiled. "No, I have my nephew and nieces, and grand nephews and nieces, and their children too. You are all like children to me. I don't have any of my own; or if I do, I am unaware of it."

Hazel raised her eyes in slight shock at the thought of Uncle Toby having children he wasn't aware of. How old would they be now? Gosh, he's 93 so they could be in their 70s. Shocking.

61

Meredith looked at her great uncle. He looked quite tired, but his eyes were sparkling still. "Well, Uncle Toby, you've been a great help, but I think maybe we should leave you in peace now."

"Definitely not, my dear. I could do with a cup of tea, but then perhaps I'll try and find these cuttings for this young man, and see if he can make sense of them."

Meredith stood up and went towards the kitchen. "That's a great idea, but you must let me sort it all out, Uncle."

Quick as a flash, the old man was up and out of his chair. "No you won't, Meredith. You don't know where anything is." He strode towards the kitchen and followed her in. The two youngsters could hear them arguing gently as they prepared elevenses.

"What do you think, Haze?" said Alex.

"It's an interesting story, but I reckon it's what you said. This Cantin guy wasn't killed and was still out there. It's that simple, surely."

"If it was that simple, they would have found out when Uncle Toby reported it."

"He didn't report it though, did he? He just told his parents."

"Good point." Alex paused. "Actually, that's a really good point. The only people who know about these ghost sightings are immediate family."

"Yeah, so… I wonder if Cantin did live, and he just wanted to warn Toby away. But if so, why would he want her not to know."

"I really don't get it. I tell you what, though, Haze. This is quite a mystery, isn't it? Much more exciting than the usual history coursework."

"Agreed. And don't keep calling me Haze,

otherwise I'll call you Lexi."

"Ooooh get you. Okay, Hazel it is, unless you'd prefer Miss Burns?"

"Don't be stupid, just stop calling me Haze. None of my other friends call me that; I'm just Hazel to them."

Just then the door from the kitchen opened and Meredith appeared with a tray of drinks. "I assume you all wanted tea. I know you will, Hazel!"

"Thanks Mum." Hazel took a mug from the tray and put it down in front of Alex. "For you, Alex dearest."

"Thank you very much, Miss Burns." Alex grinned.

"My pleasure, Master Phipps." said Hazel, smiling at him and taking another mug for herself.

"Master? Don't you mean Mister?" said Alex. "I'm not a little boy anymore. I'm fifteen now. I'm getting 'all growed up!'"

Toby Allen followed Meredith in from the kitchen with a plate of assorted biscuits, and put them on the table in front of the two teenagers.

"Oh alright, if you say so, *Mister* Phipps!"

As she spoke, the old man started slightly.

"Who... what did you say, my dear?"

Hazel looked up at him. "Oh, nothing, Uncle Toby. We were mucking about; Alex was teasing me about my name so I'm just getting him back. And thanks for the biscuits."

"Yes, but what did you call him just then?"

"Mister Phipps. He's Alex Phipps."

"Alexander actually." Alex added.

The old man sat down frowning. "My God. Phipps. You're a Phipps." He stared oddly at Alex.

"Where is your family from then, erm… Alex?"

"Oh, we live in Milnefield, but I think my grandparents were from Belcote, near Salmsham."

"Are they English?"

"Oh yes. Buried in the churchyard in Belcote. I've seen my great grandparents' grave there too."

"Were they English as well?"

"Yes… You mean the Phipps's? I'm sure they were, but I can get my Nana to check if you like."

"Yes, if you wouldn't mind." Toby Allen seemed slightly troubled, and Alex didn't want to query what was to him an odd request. Meredith, who had sat down herself and was sipping her tea and eyeing up the most chocolatey biscuit, sensed the slight tension.

"Why did you need to know about Alex's family, Uncle? They're nothing to do with us. They're Somerset born and bred."

"Maybe so, but I knew someone with a similar name, and… well… maybe it's nothing but… How did you get interested in all this again, young man?"

"Well, Hazel and I worked on the Salmsham train crash mystery, and anyway we were going to the cinema to see a ghost film, and Hazel just happened to mention your ghost story. We seem to like mysteries, and we just thought it was a mystery worth looking into. That was all." Alex felt even more uncomfortable, as the old man continued to stare at him, as if trying to verify his honesty.

"So no-one in your family put you up to this?"

"No. Not at all. I mean, they didn't object to me coming on holiday with Hazel, but… well they didn't even know about this until I told them."

Alex felt as if Toby Allen didn't believe him,

but he couldn't work out why. It would be a while before the truth revealed itself to him and Hazel.

Meredith and Toby spent the next few minutes catching up on family matters, while Hazel and Alex sipped their teas in silence, listening to the family gossip. Eventually, Alex leaned over and whispered in Hazel's ear "do you think he's remembered the box of cuttings?"

She whispered back "I'll ask him in a minute." at which moment Meredith chuckled and said "Look at those two lovebirds whispering sweet nothings to each other."

"Mum! Stop it! We were not whispering sweet nothings, and we're not lovebirds. That's so sick. We were just wondering about the cuttings Uncle Toby was going to show us after we've had tea."

"I haven't forgotten, my dear." Toby said, "In fact, I'm just off to find them now. I won't be too long. Just give me a few minutes."

He disappeared from the room, and a few moments later they heard his footsteps slowly ascending the stairs.

"What was all that about your name, Alex?" said Hazel. "I thought he thought you were another ghost or something!"

"Yeah, that was freaky." Alex said. "I wonder whether he knew another Phipps or something."

"Yeah, maybe, but he went all defensive, didn't he? Did you see that, Mum?"

Meredith nodded. "Yes, it was a bit odd. I shouldn't let it worry you, Alex. Let's see what these old papers and cuttings show us. I can hear him coming back now…"

10

Alex's eyes widened as he saw the pile of papers in the box that Toby Allen placed on the table in front of them. On the top was a small booklet with a colour painted front cover, proclaiming the Abbots Park Vendolet Tyres Gold Trophy for Grand Prix cars, above a picture of what looked to him like two very old cars speeding towards the reader.

"This is the programme for the race." said Toby "I found it in my father's papers after he died. It's been written in, as my father made notes about the race. Interestingly, Pierre-Henri Cantin was not on the original entry list, but he was added on at the end. There…" he found the page, and pointed to the entry list, "you can see it in pen, so he must have been a very last minute entry."

Hazel peered at the programme. "Ah, I've got it… he was number 105 and it says… '*P-H Cantin, Ecurie Automobiles Cantin, Bugatti T39'*. That makes no sense at all to me, I must admit."

"Well, Ecurie Automobiles just means Car Stables… a lot of teams called themselves that, so he's just calling his team Cantin Car Stables. And the car is a Type 39 Bugatti."

"Oh, I see." Hazel said doubtfully, wondering why they bothered with all that information. "It's all a bit… nerdy, like train-spotting."

"Maybe, but you must remember Hazel, the sport is called *motor* racing. It's all about the cars, not the drivers. In those days, if you built a car which won races, you would sell lots of those cars. That's how the sport began in the 1890s. The drivers became heroes later on." Toby Allen was clearly still very enthusiastic about motor racing, his eyes seeming to sparkle as he talked. "We were there to see how these cars, the British, French and Italian cars, would stack up against the mighty Germans. Well, we soon found out. Those German machines... the Auto Unions and the Mercedes, were so much more powerful than the rest, they basically made everyone else look primitive in one fell swoop. That was Hitler for you!"

"Hitler? What did he have to do with it?" Hazel passed the programme on to her mother, while Alex started sifting through the various newspaper cuttings, and copying each one.

"Hitler was a great motor racing fan. When he became Chancellor he wanted to show that German technology was the greatest in the world, including their cars, so he sponsored not one, but two different manufacturers, Mercedes-Benz, and Auto Union, so that they could race and beat every other car maker wherever they raced. They built very powerful, and very technically advanced cars, and usually entered three or four cars each per race, which ensured that usually one or other of those teams won the race. In that regard, he succeeded; they swept the board wherever they raced."

Hazel raised her eyebrows. "Oh, so Hitler wasn't all bad then?"

"He was evil! Pure evil!" The old man almost spat the words out, then paused before softening his tone slightly. "But... he did help to raise the bar when it came to racing car technology; I will allow that. It still doesn't excuse anything else he did."

While Hazel had a quick look down the list of

drivers, the old man pulled out an old magazine. "Here's the following month's Motor Sport, with a picture of Cantin and a short biography. At this stage, they know he's missing but no-one wants to admit he might be dead."

He flicked open the correct page, and handed it to Alex to look at. He read the short biography next to the picture, with Hazel peering across to look as well.

"*Pierre-Henri Cantin, the French racing ace missing after the Abbots Park accident, was born on the 13th of March 1908 in Lorraine… Cantin has raced with some success throughout Europe for various private entrant teams. Two wins in 1935 in a Delage entered by M. Montaleau, now driving a modified Bugatti entered by Reg Simmons.*" Alex read.

"That's him. That's my ghost, that's the face I see." said Toby.

"I need to copy this. Hold the magazine, Hazel…" Alex fumbled in his back pocket for this phone, and quickly took a copy of the page, and then a closer picture of the driver and his short biography.

Meredith had been watching and listening with interest. She waited until Alex had finished copying the page, and then asked to look at the picture.

"Hmmmm. He looks quite familiar, actually. Now, who does he remind me of…?"

"Don't tell me you've seen his ghost as well, Mum?" said Hazel, frowning.

"No, no. I'm trying to think… ah, yes, you know who he looks like? That tennis player from the eighties… Becker. Boris Becker."

"Never hear of him, Mum," Hazel said, "I wasn't around then, remember?"

"He's not that old! He still commentates on Wimbledon. Anyway, this chap looks a bit like him."

Meredith handed the magazine back to her uncle, who stared at the picture for a moment or two.

"Well… that's extraordinary. D'you know, I've never noticed that before. I've just always seen that face and thought 'Cantin'. But now you come to mention it, he does look quite Germanic and not at all Gallic. I'm just… well, I can't think why it never occurred to me before." The old man seemed genuinely puzzled.

"Well, it did say he was born in Lorraine, Uncle Toby. That's in France, isn't it?" Alex was aware of his totally inadequacy when it came to European geography.

"Yes it is. It's near the German border, though, so I suppose he may have had some German blood in his veins from way back. Or perhaps it's just the way he's styled his hair… I don't know. You've set me thinking all sorts of things now, young Meredith…" His voiced tailed off.

Alex continued to turn the pages. "Oh, there's some photos here of the race." He snapped some more copies, and then handed the magazine back to the old man.

"Ah, yes." Toby's eyes lit up. "I'd forgotten about these. There's the start, look… you can just about see the cars at the back. Difficult to spot Cantin, of course, but he was on the back row so he's one of those in there…" he pointed "and look, there's another of the leaders going over The Leap! Isn't that incredible?"

Hazel looked over his shoulder at the photo, which showed five cars in a snake coming over the pronounced hump in the track. The front car, which Uncle Toby told her was the leader, von Brauchitsch, had already landed and was just ahead of a similar car, which seemed to have its back wheels slightly airborne. Behind them were three other cars almost side by side, at various angles to each other and the ground.

"That's just insane, Uncle Toby! It looks so dangerous. No wonder they used to get killed a lot."

Toby Allen snorted. "Well, yes… it was pretty dangerous, but then, von Brauchitsch lived until he was 98, so it was also possible to survive it all. Good driver. I think he won it, actually. And… if you look at this picture, I can tell you, we were watching from on the right, just out of shot. That's where my father parked his car."

"Are there any pictures of the crash, Mr Allen?" asked Alex

"No. None at all. No-one took any photos there as it was a prohibited area. As far as I know, no-one took any at all, not even of the car afterwards. If they did, I've never seen them."

Alex went back to the programme which had the race details in it. Flicking it open, he noticed that there was a circuit map near the front. Handing it to the old man, he asked him where the accident happened.

"Right here." said Toby, pointing to a short straight section. "Can you see the gorge runs alongside, and the cars would come down this section, to a right-hand bend, turn onto The Ledge, as it was called because… well, it's like a ledge above the river really. Then they'd approach this fast right-hander here" he pointed again "and then over The

70

Leap. So, we started out here, and ended up here."
He pointed once again to the short straight known as
The Ledge. "That's where we watched from, and
that's right where the car came off the track."

"But… there's no photographs at all?" Alex
repeated. "That's a real pain. I'm just trying to
visualise it all. Did you say the track's not there
anymore?"

"Well, I'm sure it's there if you can find it. But
it's disused; part of it is in private hands, as it was
owned by the local landowner, and the other part is
in Leigh Woods, which is National Trust I think. The
Ledge is definitely in the woods, so you can probably
get in there, but you'd be hard pressed to find the
actual track, as its either been ploughed up, or it's so
overgrown you would need a shovel." Toby Allen
put the magazine down. "Still, that would be your
best bet… to go up there."

Hazel and Alex exchanged glances. "Did you
say it's not far from here?" asked Hazel.

"That's right. Bristol, this side of the Clifton
Bridge. It's really not that far."

Meredith raised her eyebrows, knowing what
was coming next.

"Mum…"

"Yes we can. But not today. I expect you'll
want to finish copying all of these cuttings for a start,
and frankly, I'd like to spend some more time with
my cousin and catch up on family stuff."

Toby Allen shuffled a few more papers from
the pile. "Here's something which I'd rather not read
again… it's from the Inquest. Copy it by all means,
but please don't read it out now; it still upsets me."

Alex took the cutting. It was a single column

71

and had been neatly cut out. He noticed that there was no headline, and that it was therefore only a part of the complete story. "Thank you... do you know which newspaper this was?"

"I don't, I'm afraid."

"Only, this is not the complete report. There's a bit missing at the start, and at the end."

"I know. This is the bit where I am mentioned, that's all. We didn't keep the rest of it, and I never want to read the rest of it either." The old man spoke quietly but his voice was wavering.

Meredith began to gather up her bag. "Well, I think you've been a great host, and very entertaining, Uncle Toby, but I think we've probably worn you out somewhat, so perhaps we should make a move."

The old man nodded silently.

"Hazel, can you and Alex finish copying those bits quickly, and start getting ready to go, please."

"Sure..." Hazel replied, and quickly passed various cuttings and pictures to Alex, who copied them without comment, while Meredith began to tidy the drinks and biscuit plates away.

Ten minutes later found the visitors ready to go, and making their goodbyes.

"If we find something really interesting, could we come and see you again?" asked Alex.

"Of course, young man. I don't do much these days, so I'd be glad to see you again; just telephone me first though." Toby got to his feet, and shook Alex's hand once more. "Perhaps you'll come back later this week and tell me how you got on at the old circuit."

"We will, Uncle, but we won't outstay our welcome next time, otherwise we'll wear you out!"

Meredith gave her great uncle a hug and a peck on the cheek.

As they drove off, Toby Allen stood in his doorway and waved to them all, before silently shutting the door, and sighing deeply as he went back into his living room. It had been an exhausting day but he felt quite invigorated by the enthusiasm of the two teenagers for hearing his story. He took another look at the magazines and cuttings he'd shown them, and then went over to an old antique writing desk in the far corner of the room. Unlocking it, he took out a small bundle of letters, still in their opened envelopes, held together by a large ribbon.

As he read them, one by one, tears began to well up in his tired old eyes. Once or twice he had to stop to compose himself, but still he read on. Eventually, overcome by deeper sobs, he had to stop, and he replaced each letter carefully in its original envelope before retying the ribbon around them.

He was used to being alone; usually he welcomed the silence after Julia left after her daily visit. He enjoyed the pleasure of his own company, but after today he realised that he craved another visit, and hoped that the two youngsters would find a reason to come back and ask him more questions, no matter how painful the memories were.

11

Geoff Burns slammed the back door of the Range Rover shut and slipped his backpack on over his waterproof jacket. He'd been caught out yesterday by the changeable weather and had ended up walking around Clifton in blazing sunshine with the heavy jacket slung over his shoulder. Today he could slip the jacket off into the backpack if it got too warm again. Looking at the cloudy sky he doubted that it would be anything but cold and overcast, but this was England in the winter and anything might happen with the weather.

His wife and the two teenagers were already making their way along one of the woodland paths, and he set off after them, walking at his usual brisk pace. There were only two other cars in the car park, and Geoff suspected they belonged to the dog-walkers he'd seen heading off in another direction.

As he began to catch the others up he could see that Meredith was holding an old Ordinance Survey map in her hands, while Alex was occasionally glancing down at his phone, presumably to check his copy of the circuit map. They'd spent a while looking at a map of the area online last night, but were still a little uncertain as to the exact route of the old circuit, so they'd decided to set off on the path which would lead them towards the manor house.

"I think we should bear right soon" said Alex "so that we come out along the path nearest the

74

gorge. Crikey, there are so many little trackways around here!"

"Those are for cyclists" said Geoff, having caught them up, "so we need to be a bit careful."

"Yeah, that would be pretty lame, wouldn't it?" replied Hazel, grabbing her father's arm. "To come all the way here to investigate a high-speed racing crash, and get run down by a low speed bike!"

"I think it's more likely we'll get sucked into a quagmire. Look at this lot!" Meredith leapt over a large muddy puddle in the path. "And these are the official walkways too."

The others followed her, their boots becoming more and more muddy as they trudged on. Soon they came to a large fork in the path. The route to the left was much wider than the pathway to the right. Alex looked at the track map again, and pointed to the wider route.

"I think that's part of the old track, or maybe… no, that's an access road. No, it's not… it's part of the track after The Leap."

"Make up your mind, Lexie!" Hazel teased.

"So… if it's where I think it is, The Leap is to our right, about a hundred metres or so." Alex pointed to the narrow path, which curved off to the right. "So, shall we head this way?"

"Well, if you're sure" Meredith said, "let's do it, because I can't make any sense of this map. It doesn't show any of these little tracks at all."

They followed Alex along the narrow path, which almost immediately dropped down a dip, then turned sharp right and disappeared up a steep slope. They trudged up the slope, with one or two stumbles along the way, but as he reached the top Alex called out "Yes! This is The Leap. It's right here!"

Hazel reached the top next, and suddenly she could see how the track had faded away into the woods as nature had been allowed to take its course. There, right in front of them, was a small ridge, and the bushy outline of the track edges. Due to the way the circuit had been abandoned, this short section of track was not accessible – there was not even a single pathway along the route. There was a broad clearing on the right, however, where only small bushes had grown, and Alex identified this as part of the spectator area.

"Maybe this is where Toby's parents parked their car." he speculated.

"Could be" said Geoff, looking at the track map on Alex's phone, "which means... we need to head off that way to reach the accident site." He pointed to the far corner of the clearing.

"You go. I'm going to stay and take some photos for Uncle Toby." Meredith put her bag down and rummaged for her camera, as the two teenagers set off. "Are you going with them, Geoff?"

"I think I will, actually. You've seen how steep that drop is; I don't want to have to scrape them up from the riverbank!" Geoff started to follow the youngsters towards the line of trees ahead.

"Well, just be careful, Darling. I don't want to have to scrape you up either!"

By the time he'd caught Hazel up, Alex had already disappeared through a small gap in the trees. As they reached the gap, they could see cars in the distance, and they realised they were looking at the road on the other side of the gorge. Looking down, Hazel saw Alex's head quite a bit lower down the slope.

"Wait for us!" she called out. Alex stopped and looked back up at them.

"It's an easy path from where you are, and it's quite wide and safe," he called up to them, "but a bit overgrown."

As they made their way down a short steep bit of path, Alex came back towards them. "I reckon this must be where the boys went, don't you? If we follow this path, it sort of goes back uphill towards the track. At least, I think it does, if we're in the right place."

The three of them trod gingerly along the path, which although not too narrow was very uneven and rocky in places. Hazel glanced to her right and nearly fainted when she realised how high up they were, and how steep the slope was at this point.

"Oh my God, look at that!" she gasped. "If we slip now, we'll go straight down and hit those rocks below."

"Well, just be careful then." her father cautioned.

"Actually, I don't think you'd fall far, Hazel." Alex piped up. "I had a quick look just now and there's actually plenty of bushes and trees to break your fall. You'd have to sort of push yourself out quite a way to drop straight down."

"Great." she replied. "Remind me not to do that then!"

"But you can see what your uncle meant about the driver 'springing out' of the car. He'd have had to, to go all the way down to the water."

"Hang on here for a moment." Geoff stopped and got his phone out. "Let's take a few photos, and see if we can work out where it all happened."

He turned and took some shots of the path they'd just trodden, and then turned back to take a few more of the gorge. Hazel had stopped, but Alex was out of sight.

"Smile!" said Geoff as he snapped Hazel standing awkwardly near the edge of the path, with the drop behind her.

"Dad, can we move on, I find this a bit scary."

"Of course. Mind you, I never had you down for being scared of heights."

"I'm not usually, Dad. It's just… knowing what happened here is freaking me out a bit." Hazel turned and started walking again. "Alex! Where did you go?"

Geoff followed his daughter to another sharp corner in the path. Suddenly he caught sight of Alex again, this time about ten feet above him.

"Gosh, he got up there fast, didn't he?"

"It's really steep here, Dad" said Hazel, then to Alex "Wait for us!"

Alex was already up another level. "It's so steep" he called down "it's no wonder they didn't let spectators come along here!"

He trudged along another short level section of pathway, and then suddenly found himself alongside what looked like a very wide lane. The tarmac was crumbling along the edge, which about at his chest level, and there were bushes and pockets of grass growing through the old road surface, but it was clearly a piece of the circuit.

"This must be it!" he called to the others, as they came up behind him. "Look! There's the track, and up there" he pointed to the right "must be where the cars came from."

"So this must be where it happened then" Hazel panted. "Assuming it's the same as it was back in 1937."

"Which we can't assume at all" cautioned her father "seeing as this should be a lot more overgrown than it is. After 81 years, surely this would be under two or three feet of forest floor by now?"

Alex clambered up onto the track, and then walked across to the inside. Ahead of him was another steep slope, which he realised was a large mound, with trees growing up the side all the way along both left and right. He turned and looked back. Hazel and Geoff were by now on the old circuit as well. Geoff turned left and walked along in the direction of The Leap. Hazel ambled across to where Alex was standing.

"We must take some more shots of this, and show them to Uncle Toby" she said. "You take them, I'll pose, then he'll have me and his old circuit in the shots, lucky uncle."

Alex grinned. "Actually, you should go and stand back where we came up, and I'll get a shot of you there. This is a bit like an accident reconstruction scene, isn't it?"

The two teenagers spent several minutes posing and taking pictures of the track from various angles. They wandered in the opposite direction to Geoff, and traced the track along to where it curved away from the edge of the gorge, turning every now and then to take a 'driver's eye view' of the old circuit route.

"It doesn't look as if anyone else has been here for ages, does it?" Hazel commented. "I mean, you'd think we'd see a track where folks walk or cycle, but it's as if no-one has been near the place."

"Yeah, it is a bit odd, isn't it?" Alex was still busy finding new angles for his pictures. He stopped and brought up the circuit map on his phone. "Look, this must be where the old marshal's post was. Just over there." He pointed. "So... our man was driving along here, and came around this bend, onto The Ledge..." Alex began to jog along the imagined route of the Bugatti. "He would have been blinded by the smoke from the engine, which was in the front of the car... and so he would have gone straight on from about here... to..." He pointed again. "Right there. Right where we were standing." They jogged back to the spot. "And then... he went... over here, and down there."

Alex pointed down the steep slope. "Crikey... that IS steep. I hadn't noticed it when I was coming up the pathway."

"Me neither." Hazel stood a short way from the edge. "This is still freaking me out, Alex. I just can't bring myself to come any closer to the edge."

"But... you won't fall down. Look..." and with that Alex flung himself off the edge of the track.

"Alex, no!" cried Hazel.

She gasped as he landed a little awkwardly and rolled over onto his back, but she saw that he had not left the path. "See? I'm still about a metre from the edge, and even then, there's another small ledge before the drop."

"Are you OK? That looked painful."

"I'm absolutely fine." He stood up and brushed himself down. "Where's your Dad got to, I wonder?"

"Good point. Dad!!" Hazel called out in the

direction of The Leap. There was no answer.

"Oh well, he's obviously exploring the rest of the track. Shall we do the same?" Alex clambered back up onto the old circuit. At the same moment, Geoff appeared on the path behind him.

"Hello Dad. Where have you been? How did you come back behind us again?"

Geoff Burns grinned at his daughter. "Well, I just walked around the track that way until I reached a fence, and then I turned left and clambered down the slope onto another path, and wandered back until it met this one."

"Oh, so this bit is fenced off then, from the public?" asked Alex.

"Quite. I assume we're probably either trespassing, or we've disobeyed some hidden sign or other, so strictly speaking we should be getting back to Mum."

Hazel ignored her father's suggestion. "Dad, we walked round the track in the other direction. We've found the marshal's post, and we reckon we know exactly where the accident happened."

The two youngsters led Geoff back up and around the old circuit, stopping to look back occasionally, and explaining how they thought the accident had occurred. Reaching the site of the marshal's post, they stopped once again and checked the circuit map on Alex's phone.

"I wish I'd printed this off," he said "then we wouldn't have to keep squinting to see it."

"Let's go even further, and see how far back round the old circuit we can get." Hazel suggested. "It shouldn't take us too long, should it? Mum's got her phone if she gets worried."

They set off back beyond the marshal's post, where the circuit did a sharp turn to the left and went uphill, in the reverse direction of the race. They were now on the side of the hill, and to their right was an open field. Stopping again, they worked out that the circuit skirted the field and then turned towards the spot where they were standing

"So, they would have come steaming over this hill, down there to the corner by the post, hard on the brakes, and taken the corner quite slowly, so... I suppose that was why they thought it was fairly safe along The Ledge, because they were basically pretty much going straight along it, from a relatively slow speed corner." Geoff Burns was thinking aloud as he traced the route with the tip of a pencil.

"Hoi!"

They heard a distant shout, from the other side of the open field. None of them could see anyone, but the shouting continued. There seemed to be two voices, then they realised there was a slight echo from a short vertical rocky slope on their left.

12

"You!! … Up there!! … Get out of here!! … What do you think you're doing!! … This is private land!!" They heard a pounding of hooves, and suddenly a horseman appeared from the other side of the hill, galloping hard, coming straight towards them on the old circuit. Instinctively Geoff raised his hand as a greeting.

"What the hell do you think you're doing?!" The red-faced rider was a middle-aged man, who waved his riding crop at them.

"I'm sorry, we…"

"This is private land, private property. You're trespassing. Now get off my land!" His eyes blazed at them, and his face was so red, Hazel tried to work out whether he was angry, or out of breath, or both.

"I'm genuinely sorry, Sir" said Geoff, calmly. "We came up the side of the gorge pathway. We had no idea this was private land; there was no sign…"

"Are you blind? There are signs everywhere!"

"I'm so sorry, we didn't see any, but if you tell us the shortest way off your land we'll go right now." Geoff's polite tones calmed the man down somewhat. The horse, meanwhile, leaned his head towards Hazel, who patted him gently on the nose.

"What are you doing here anyway? Are you travellers or something?" the man growled, jerking suddenly on the reins to try and pull the horse's head away from Hazel's hand.

"No, we're investigating a crash on the old race circuit. A car went off the side of the gorge…"

"This hasn't been a racing circuit since just after the war. 1949 was the last race here. 70 years ago, so there's nothing to see at all."

"Well, we did find out where it crashed; we were just tracing the old circuit back, but we genuinely didn't realise… anyway, look, so sorry we trespassed on your land, and I can assure you we didn't mean any harm."

"Right. Well… you can leave over there." He pointed a bit further back down the track. "There's a gate in the fence. It's locked but I'm sure you can climb over it, like you climbed over the other one."

"Ah, no, we didn't climb any gates at all. We walked down the pathway which goes down towards the gorge, and then came up and we were on the old circuit."

"Really? I didn't know… look, what did you say you were doing again?"

"We were looking into the crash… in the race… in 1937." Alex butted in. "And we found out where the car went off, but they never found the driver. I'm sure you must know about it?"

"I'm not that old, young man." By now the man had calmed down. "Here, you hold him for a moment." He passed the reins to Hazel, and slid out of the saddle to the ground, then turned and held his hand out to Geoff. "Charles Forster." He puffed, still somewhat out of breath. He was quite few inches shorter than Geoff, which made him seem much less threatening, Hazel thought.

"Geoff Burns. And this is my daughter Hazel and her boyfriend Alex."

"Pleased to meet you all. Look, I'm sorry I was so damned aggressive, but we've had travellers in here before and they absolutely wrecked the place."

"No, I quite understand, and if we really are trespassing…"

"Well, you sort of are, although there should be a public footpath through the woods and across this bit of land to the other side of that field. It's just it goes right along the edge of the gorge, and it's quite treacherous, so rather than spend a fortune fixing it, we've just blocked it off. Well, I thought we had. The National Trust own most of the woods and they've never complained, and no-one has seriously objected. I don't think it's even on the latest maps nowadays."

"So, do you own all of this land?" asked Geoff.

"Yes, indeed. It belongs to the Manor House, over there, just behind the trees across the field. We own the whole estate, and this part of the woods. My father and his father built the race circuit. It was very popular in the 30s, but then the war came. Of course, we couldn't possibly reopen it now, because half of it runs through the National Trust land and that's a nature reserve. And then you've got the safety, of course. When they started races after the war, people realised how dangerous it was to run alongside the gorge and they wouldn't come here unless father spent a bloody fortune on barriers and things. No-one seemed to mind before the war, but then that's progress for you!"

"Well, it does seem totally mad to race alongside the gorge."

"They didn't seem to mind!" Charles Forster took the reins back off Hazel. "So, what's all this about a crash?"

"Oh well… he knows more about it than I do." Geoff waved his hand over towards Alex, who told of the story of the accident.

"Now you come to mention it, I did hear about it but of course, that was all second hand. I'm sure they found the driver eventually, of course."

"Did they?" exclaimed Hazel and Alex, almost in unison.

"Pretty sure, but I stand to be corrected. I've got a room full of old stuff from the racing era; been meaning to archive it or send it to a museum or something. I'm sure it'll be in amongst that lot somewhere."

"Wow. That would be... I mean, is there any way of letting people see it?" Alex asked.

"Well, there's a lot of stuff. It'll need me to sort through it; probably take weeks... how did you say you got in here again? Along the path by the gorge?"

"That's right" said Geoff, "we cut down from the main pathway in the woods, and then went through a small gap in the bushes, and found the path. It was pretty close to the edge."

"It is. You don't want to be going down there really. One slip, and if you're not careful you're down a sheer drop. There's a railway line runs along there, which comes out just the other side of this field. I think it's in a tunnel where you were though."

"Yes, we saw that on the map - it is in the tunnel at that point. We're just trying to work out exactly where this car went over the edge. Alex thinks he's got it, but anyway, we've taken up enough of your time. Thank you for your understanding."

"I'll walk you to the gate." Charles replied, offering Hazel the reins again. "You can take him if you like. Anyway, I never did ask why you're so interested in this particular crash?"

They started walking further back along the old circuit, towards the field.

"Oh, that's down to me really" said Hazel. "My great great uncle was one of the little boys who was badly hurt when the car hit them, and he reckons he's seen a ghost of the driver several times since. And Alex and I… we solved the mystery of the Salmsham Railway Disaster and thought we'd try and get to the bottom of this mystery as well."

"What mystery, exactly?"

"The ghost… of the racing driver."

"Well I never. Your great… great uncle?" Charles Forster was incredulous. "What's his name, Methuselah?"

"Who?" The joke was lost on Hazel, whose biblical knowledge was non-existent. "No, Toby. Toby Allen. He's about 93 now."

"He'd have to be!" chuckled Charles. "1937… that's 82 years ago, girl! I'm surprised he can remember much about it."

"Oh, he's pretty switched on, I'd say." said Hazel, pulling slightly as the horse tried to lead her away from the others. "Whoa…!"

"He's okay" said Charles, "he just wants to off on his own. He's not been out for a couple of days, have you, boy?"

They reached the large padlocked gate, which Charles indicated was their way out. "You'll be alright climbing over it, I'm sure. I do have a key somewhere, but…"

"No problem, Charles" said Geoff, shaking his hand again. "and thank you so much for your understanding. We won't do that again, I promise."

"Look, er... Geoff, it was no problem. Good to meet you. I say, did you say you're from Salmsham?"

"No, actually, South Attwell, but we're staying the week with my wife's cousin in Henleaze. It was just the Salmsham Railway Disaster that they mentioned; we don't live there."

"I know all about that – my sister-in-law got involved. I think she's got something to do with the museum or something."

"Your sister-in-law?"

"Yes. You may have heard of her. Arabella Templeton-Stubbs. She's your M.P...."

"Bella! Yes, we know her. These two got to know her pretty well, actually."

Charles chuckled. "What a small world we live in. Look, did you say you were staying in Henleaze?"

"That's right, with my wife's cousin."

"Well look, that's not far at all, is it. Why don't you come over and have tea with us tomorrow, and then perhaps I can have a look for the details of the race. We could come out here on the quad bikes and explore the old circuit properly. I'd certainly like to hear more about your ghost."

"Well... that would be a great thing to do, if you're sure."

"Of course I'm sure; wouldn't have asked otherwise. I don't have a card on me, but I could give you my telephone number. Call me when you get home later, and I'll arrange it with my staff." Geoff got his phone ready and typed in two numbers; the Manor House, and Charles Forster's mobile. "Best if you ring the Manor House number tonight; we can arrange a time then."

"Thanks so much, Charles. We'd better go and

find my wife now."

They clambered over the gate, and Charles Forster got back up on his horse, trotting away with a quick wave.

"Phew! That was... interesting." Geoff smiled as the little group started off along the path away from the gate. "He could have been a lot nastier with us if he'd chosen to."

They had only walked about ten metres when Geoff's phone rang.

"Ah. It's your Mum." He turned away slightly as he answered took the call. "Hi Meri.... Yes... we're all okay. Are you still in the same place...? Oh, right. Well we're coming back a different way... yes, we found the old circuit... what do you mean...? Oh, goodness. Be careful... Look, that's meant to be out of bounds. We've... no, listen, it's private land. Yes. We've just met the landowner..." He cupped his hands over the speaker and said to the group "She's only gone and found the pathway by the gorge; only she's gone right down to near the bottom."

Hazel laughed. "Typical of my mother" she said to Alex, while Geoff continued chatting to his wife, "she gets into more trouble than I ever do. I just hope she doesn't end up on the estate otherwise *Chahhles*" she exaggerated his accent "will start to lose his patience with us."

Alex smiled. "Yeah, it might not go down so well with *Chahhles* next time."

"*Chahhles...*" Hazel giggled as they took turns to impersonate their new acquaintance. "On his *hawsse, dahhling!*"

"Oh *yahhs*, what a splendid fellow; *Chahhles!* And he's friends with *Arabellaaaah.*"

89

"Shush Alex. I quite liked Bella."

"You would – she's posh and sticks up for women!" Alex grinned and ducked as he said it, knowing it would elicit a reaction from his girlfriend.

"Someone has to stick up for us, to stop you silly little boys thinking you rule the world."

Geoff finished the call, and popped the phone back into his pocket.

"Right, folks. We've got to go back into the woods and then find that pathway again. Your mum's gone further down the slope than we ever did. I have warned her to be careful."

"Don't tell *Chahhles*, will you Dad."

"No, or he'll fetch his *hawsse* and hit us with his whippety-whip!" Alex sniggered and swung his arm about in a mock whipping fashion. Geoff chuckled quietly at them, as they carried on along the path for half a mile or so, and then took a left turn which took them along a short section of cycle track. Following Alex's circuit map, they turned onto another narrow path, and finally arrived back at their starting point in the clearing beside The Leap. As they found themselves passing through the same small gap in the bushes as before, Alex began to speculate.

"You know, I think I know what might have happened to this Cantin bloke."

"Go on." said Hazel, as they dropped down onto the lower path beside the gorge for the second time, and made their way in single file back towards The Ledge.

"Well, you saw how I jumped off the old circuit and down onto the path?"

"Yeah."

"Well, what if... what if he deliberately made

90

the car go off the track, and jumped off it as it crashed. Your Uncle Toby said it wasn't going fast at all. What if he staged the accident, and then ran off or something, and that spectator guy thought he saw Cantin being thrown out, but he actually saw the dead boy going down into the gorge?"

"Why on earth would he stage a crash like that?" Hazel asked, in a tone which suggested she thought it was a crazy idea.

"I don't know..." he began, but Geoff interrupted them.

"We should turn off to the right here, down to this track." He pointed down what looked like a ledge running below and parallel to them. "I think that's where your Mum said she's gone."

"That's insane, Dad!" Hazel was starting to feel uneasy about the gorge again. "Look, we're really close to the rock-face!"

Ignoring his daughter's protests. Geoff started down the steep track and found it was a lot less treacherous than it looked from above. "Come on, you two. It's perfectly safe."

Alex followed him, and Hazel reluctantly fell in behind him. When they reached the lower level, they found themselves on a wider path than before, and they were able to move easily down a slight slope. The path zig-zagged its way down the edge of the gorge, never seeming to trouble the sheer rock-face which always seemed to be just around the next corner. Looking up, Hazel realised they'd come about half-way down already.

"The only thing is, we've gotta get back up there soon." she observed. "Where's Mum anyway?"

The answer came as they rounded the next

91

corner. Meredith Burns sat with her back to them on a small protruding rock a few metres away, camera in front of her face, taking snapshots of the gorge.

"Found you!" Geoff called. "Didn't even see this earlier. How did you find it?"

Meri turned around, stretched her arms out, and yawned. "Oh, well, I guessed the route you'd taken, so just looked for any little offshoots, and here I am. I've found one thing which is very interesting though. I'm sure you'll want to take a look."

She pointed to an area about twenty metres away, and just above their level.

"You see that piece of rock sticking out? Well, I went around it and… there's a short tunnel there."

"A tunnel?" Hazel exclaimed.

"Yep. Man-made. I couldn't get far into it, as there was a metal grill over it, but there it is. I think it might have something to do with the railway."

"Where's the railway from here?" asked Alex. "I thought it was below us."

"It is, but maybe it was an access tunnel for the workmen when they were blasting the original tunnel. I don't know." Meredith settled back down on her rock again. "You could go and check it out, but please be careful!"

"We will" said Alex, starting off past her. "Come on Haze…"

Hazel sat down abruptly next to her Mum. "I'm staying here, if you don't mind. I'm tired, my legs are killing me, and we've got to go all the way back up. I need a drink." She pulled a water bottle from her small backpack. Instead, Geoff followed Alex the short distance along the path. As they reached the protruding rock, they clambered up onto the raised edge of the pathway and then pulled themselves up to a small rocky ledge. There, in front of them, was a nearly concealed tunnel entrance.

"Wow, you can't see that at all from the path, can you!" Alex exclaimed.

"No... and you can't see it from the river either... or from above... it's very cleverly hidden, isn't it?" said Geoff. "I wonder whether it was meant to be, or whether it just happened that way because of where it is on the rock-face."

They stepped inside, and Alex lit his phone torch. They could see the metal grill that Meredith had mentioned, which was only about five metres inside the tunnel mouth. There was a gate in the grill, which was padlocked. Walking up to the gate, Alex shone his torch through into the depths. The tunnel seemed to go on for quite a distance, but then either stopped, or curved away, he couldn't tell which. He shone it upwards, and they noticed the brick lining which struck Geoff as unusual.

"Now, why would they line it in brick if they were tunnelling through solid rock? Interesting...unless it's not all solid. What's the tunnel floor like?"

Alex shone his torch down.

"Concrete... some bricks. This is most unusual. I mean, I wonder what it was meant to be for?"

"I wonder where it leads to" Alex added. Slipping his phone into his pocket, he clapped his hands sharply together. The sound echoed back. "It seems to go quite a way in. I'd love to go and explore it further."

"Hmmm. It'd probably get you into even more trouble. Let's take a few pictures and go back."

13

Half an hour later, the group had retraced their steps back to the junction with the original path, which led up to the old circuit. Eager to show Meredith what they'd found, Alex once again led the way until they arrived at the trackside. Just as he was about to jump up onto the old circuit, they heard what sounded like a motor bike approaching.

"Quick. Duck, everyone!" said Hazel. "That'll be *Chahhles* on his quad bike!" The two youngsters leapt back down the path and hid behind a large bush, while Geoff and his wife ducked down below the level of the track. The engine sound got louder and then passed above them without slackening. Geoff raised his head in time to see a flash of blue disappearing to his left. Whoever it was stopped a few seconds later, and they could hear the engine ticking over. Geoff was about to move when the engine revved up again, and started back towards them. As it sped past, he looked up again and saw a blue quad bike rushing off into the distance, its helmetless rider's thick shock of blonde hair flaring out behind their head. Geoff couldn't tell whether it was a man or woman.

"I think it's time we left" he called out loudly "before anyone else comes down this way." The others got up from their various positions and the group set off back down the path, retracing their steps back up towards the remains of The Leap.

"It's amazing what we could see from that position, even behind the bushes." Hazel commented. "No wonder the boys watched from there, you could see so much of the track."

"We could see that quad bike from when it came around the far corner, right up to where he stopped by that fence back there." Alex added.

"Was it a he?" asked Geoff.

"Oh yes, definitely a man. But it wasn't Charles Forster. Some other guy, a bit younger I would say. And he wasn't wearing a helmet."

"Yeah, that's a point. Whereas *Chahhles* was wearing one on his *hawse*, wasn't he?" Hazel pointed out.

"You must stop calling him that, Hazel" Geoff smiled, "otherwise you might accidentally say it to his face when we visit him."

They made their way back towards the car, the teenagers doing '*Chahhles*' impressions all the way. By the time they were ready to set off, it was lunchtime. Meredith rang her cousin, as they'd agreed to meet somewhere for a light lunch. Martina suggested a nice pub in the next village, and twenty minutes later they were all settled around the lunch table, a drink apiece, the barman having taken their food orders.

"So, have you found out more about our family ghost then, you lot. Any theories yet, Alex?" Martina asked, sipping a lime and soda.

"Well, we've found the place where the crash happened, explored some of the old track…"

"Been caught trespassing…" Hazel added.

"And yes, I've got a theory that Cantin might actually have staged the crash…."

"And they found a tunnel…"

"And we met the owner of the Manor…."

"On his horse, and his name is *Chahhles…*"
Hazel sniggered as she did her impression again.

Martina looked surprised. "You mean you met Charles Forster?"

"Yep, that's right. The man himself" Geoff said. "We were trespassing, and he wasn't too pleased at first. Thought we were travellers. But anyway, once we explained ourselves he got quite chatty."

"Hmph. You were lucky then. Nasty piece of work, that man." said Martina. "One of my friends works up at the Manor House, says he's a real b… I mean, he's a right swine to work for. Treats his staff like slaves, talks down to them all."

"Well, we didn't see any of that, Tina. In fact, he's invited us to tea."

Martina nearly choked on her drink "To tea! What, today?" She put the glass down on the table with a firm clunk.

"No, tomorrow. We're going to get in touch with him later, and sort a time out. But it'll be this week, he said. Invited us all." Geoff couldn't resist smiling at his wife's cousin, testing her reaction.

"Well, count me out. I wouldn't be seen dead in that place. My friend'd never speak to me again."

"Really?" Geoff took a swig of his pint. "Oh well. We happen to know his sister-in-law, as a matter of fact. The M.P. who helped these two at Salmsham. Arabella Templeton-Stubbs. Anyway, Charles said he's got records of the races, and we could look at them if we liked. In fact, I was going to mention that to Uncle Toby as well. See if he wanted to join us."

Martina looked suddenly thoughtful. She stared at her drink, gently spinning the glass round on the table in front of her. "You know, after all these years of hearing that story it never occurred to me that it happened just along from where I lived. We could all have gone and explored the place, but I don't remember ever going there, do you Meri?"

"Nope, not once. I've never even been to Leigh Woods before."

"I'm sure my parents discouraged us going" Martina continued. "Isn't that where they found that woman's body in the '50s?"

Meredith frowned. "What woman?"

"Oh" said Martina, "I thought they'd found a woman's body, in the woods, but never found out who it was. My mother mentioned it a few times, which is probably another reason I never came up here. I've never really been along this side of the gorge at all. And I certainly hadn't realised that the Forsters had anything to do with the race either. You'd think…" Martina frowned.

"What's up Tina?" asked Meredith.

"Well, you'd think that… if the crash happened almost on our doorstep, that Uncle Toby might have taken us up there, or at least pointed it out to us when we were younger. I wonder why he didn't?"

"Perhaps it was too painful for him." Geoff said. "Don't forget he lost his best friend down there. And he did say he went back about 25 years ago didn't he?"

"Or maybe he didn't want to spoil a good story in case the real truth came out?" said Alex.

Martina Heath looked quizzically at him. "How do you mean, Alex?"

"Well…maybe it didn't quite happen as dramatically as he says. Maybe it was all a big cover

97

up, and the crash wasn't really a crash, and he saw what really happened and…" He stopped.

"If that was the case, what's with all the newspaper cuttings, and stuff."

"That's true" said Alex thoughtfully. "But… something's not right, is it?"

Hazel rolled her eyes. "Well, duh! I mean, of course it's not right. We've got a 93-year-old man who's convinced he's seeing a dead racing driver walking the streets. Of course something's not right!"

"I thought you believed in ghosts?"

"I do… no, I mean, I did. I thought I did but… you're right this is all a bit confusing."

Geoff Burns smiled. "You're both right. So, what I think we should all do is just collect lots of information. Isn't that what you did at Salmsham, you two?"

Alex looked into the distance. "Not exactly. I mean, we stumbled on a lot of it, and went up quite a few blind alleys. My dad did most of the detective work really. But in the end, yeah, we got loads of evidence together. Accident reports, newspaper articles, old photos…"

"Digging up bodies." Hazel added.

Martina looked surprised. "Bodies?"

"Just the one body, Tina, and that was in a graveyard" said Geoff. "But look, coming back to this story. We need to just establish facts. Work out what we know, and take it from there. I'll ring Charles Forster when we get back to yours, Tina, and arrange a time when he can see us."

At this point, the barman appeared with their meals, and after a few minutes the grown-ups had changed the subject completely, as they continued to update each other on their respective families. Alex stayed silent for a while, mulling over everything they'd found out so far. Hazel, who had briefly joined in until her mother had started discussing Max's school issues, nudged her boyfriend.

"'Sup then? You're in a world of your own."

Alex waited until he'd finished his mouthful. "Just thinking about… well, whether the accident really happened as Uncle Toby saw it, or what really. It's all a bit weird."

"Maybe we should do what you did for the Salmsham thing – do a timeline of everything that's supposed to have happened, and then check every single fact."

"Yeah, I was thinking that. The only thing is, there's so many things that don't make sense. I mean, we've seen the track, which is amazing, and if we were in the right place then… I just don't know what to think."

"Right. We know there was a crash, and we know Uncle Toby was there."

Alex nodded. "Okay, I get that. But then… Cantin was killed… except didn't Charles Forster say they found him? Was he dead or alive?"

"That's what I mean. Let's do a timeline of… what may have happened. Put everything in there, Uncle Toby's story, the newspaper stories; everything, and then we'll cross-check each fact. If *Chahhhhhhles…*" Hazel exaggerated his name even more "thinks the driver was found, we'll put that in as well."

"Good idea. We can do it later. Ah…" Alex grimaced. "You know I've gone and left my laptop at home. Did you bring yours?"

"No, because I've done all my homework."

"Me too. Oh well, we'll have to resort to paper and pencil. Old people's technology!" Alex said the last line louder, and grinned as Geoff looked across the table at him quizzically. Alex explained what he meant, and Geoff suggested using a large lined pad, and a ring binder.

"That way you can add stuff in, take stuff out, scribble odd bits on the sheets, and then you'll build up a picture."

"Great idea, Dad. Can we get some paper on the way home?" Hazel was eager to get started. "I don't know about you" she said to Alex "but this has really got me hooked. Even more than the Salmsham thing. Sorry, didn't mean that to sound mean!"

"No, I get it." Alex agreed. "Probably, because it's your family's ghost, you're sort of more into it, but you're right. I feel sort of energised. I just wish we didn't have school next week!"

"Oh Alex, did you have to swear like that?" Hazel grinned and hit him on the shoulder. "Dad... when can we get going?"

Two hours later Alex and Hazel were sitting at the desk in the attic bedroom, working on the timeline. They'd already got several different ideas about the fate of Pierre-Henri Cantin, so but they put them all on one sheet, headlined 'CRASH', with details of the track at that point, and theories about where Cantin's body ended up (if he had died), or where he ended up (if he had lived).

"I want to know where that tunnel leads to as well, Haze. I mean, what if he jumped off the car and escaped along the tunnel?"

Hazel sighed. "I thought we agreed to collect the facts and then work out what might have happened. Speculating won't get us far, will it?"

"No, but it makes it more interesting. And let's face it, it worked at Salmsham."

"Facts, Alexander. Facts!" Hazel pointed to the paper pad and Alex's pen. "Write!"

"Hellooo!" Geoff's voice called up the stairs. "How are you two getting on?" They heard him climbing the staircase.

"Mind the low beam, Dad!" shouted Hazel. "We're doing okay actually, but there's so much stuff we need to get straight in our heads."

Geoff stood up straight after bowing for the low beam, and came over to the desk. "I hope you've got some good questions for your friend and mine, Charles Forster then. He's invited us for afternoon tea tomorrow at 3.30, and he says he's managed to find an old envelope full of the details of the race."

"Wow! That would be amazing. Hopefully there'll be some pictures as well. Are we all going?"

"All except Martina… she doesn't want to set foot in the place, but that might be a good thing. Also, Mum's phoned Uncle Toby and asked if he was interested in coming and he refused, and then he got very… off with her, so she thinks she might have upset him somewhat." Geoff grimaced. "Oh, and dinner's nearly ready, so I think you should both come down now and help set up the table, don't you? Maybe pour the drinks, Hazel?"

Leaving the papers on the desk, the two youngsters followed Geoff down two flights of stairs and into the dining room.

"What did Uncle Toby say, Mum?" Hazel

asked, while she laid out the places on the dining table, taking adding an extra one for Martina's husband Andy, who was just flying in from a business trip to Sweden and was due home shortly.

Meredith frowned. "He was very off. I think he was quite upset that we'd just gone off and checked up on his story, as if we didn't believe him. And then, when I said we'd met Mr Forster, he went very quiet on me. I told him we were going to visit him tomorrow, and he just said 'Good luck to you' in a very offhand way. I said 'Would you like to come with us' and he just snapped back at me, something like 'Absolutely not!' and then he said he had to go, and put the phone down."

"Gosh. I wonder what all that was about. Maybe we should go and see him tomorrow morning, Mum, and see if we can cheer him up."

Meredith shook her head. "No, I've already told him we'll pop over on Thursday, and he agreed that. Mind you, that was before I told him about Charles Forster. It seems as if our Mr Forster has rattled a few local cages, what with Tina's friend, and now Uncle Toby."

14

Geoff Burn's Range Rover pulled up in front of the ornate wrought iron gates to the Manor House at just before half past three. He wound his window down and leaned out to press the intercom. As he spoke to announce their presence, his breath formed little puffs of condensation in the cold atmosphere, and he was glad to wind the window back up again as they pulled away through the gates and along the long gravel driveway.

A couple of minutes later, they pulled up in front of the Manor House. Before they'd had a chance to undo their seatbelts, a youngish-looking man with a thick shock of blonde hair, and dressed in a smart business suit, came down the steps from the main entrance and walked quickly over to them.

"That's the guy on the quad-bike" Hazel said. "I'd recognise that hairstyle anywhere."

"Okay, well let's not mention that. We weren't there, remember?" Geoff cautioned, as he opened his door and stepped out in front of the stranger.

"Good afternoon Sir!" said the man, who Geoff estimated to be in his late 20s. "When you're ready, please follow me. Mr Forster is waiting for you in the lounge."

"Thank you… erm…" Geoff fished for the man's name but he simply turned and walked back towards the house. Glancing at the others, and raising his eyebrows, he followed the man to the steps, turning to make sure everyone was following. Hazel had managed to get her jacket caught on the safety belt, and took two attempts to shut the door.

"You can lock the car now, Dad." Hazel said. "now I've managed to unhook myself from it."

Geoff zapped the remote key and the car flashed and bleeped as the doors double-locked.

"No need for that round here, Sir" said the young man humourlessly, looking out from the large doorway. "No-one's going to get near this place, and with all respect, we wouldn't be needing another car either."

"Sorry… force of habit." Geoff smiled at the man, but it made no difference. 'Perhaps' he thought, as the man closed the door behind them, 'he's been trained to remain expressionless at all times'.

"This way, Sir." The man led them down a long corridor, and indicated a room on the left, standing back to allow the family to enter.

"Geoff. Good of you to come over. Do come in, all of you." Charles Forster was sitting at one end of a large sofa in front of a long glass coffee table. He smiled and waved them to sit around the table.

"Good of you to invite us, Charles. This is my wife, Meredith…"

Charles stood up and took her hand, gripped it briefly and then promptly sat down again. "Lovely to meet you, Meredith." he said, but he didn't sound terribly convincing, she thought.

"Now then, everybody. We will be having tea and snacks shortly. Is there anyone here who would prefer not to drink tea? No? Five for tea then, Michael."

The man who had shown them into the room

nodded, and left, closing the door behind him.

"Is he your butler?" asked Hazel innocently.

"Not exactly... I have quite a large staff running this estate and my various businesses, and Michael is one of my aides, but he's not my Personal Assistant. Actually, that's his father's job. But Michael often looks after our guests and instructs the other domestic staff so that things run smoothly."

"Wow. I wish I had someone to assist me like that." Hazel looked at her parents demandingly.

"You do." Meredith said. "Me, and your father. Anyway, Charles, you have a lovely home, and what a great view of the estate." She looked past their host at the panoramic view beyond. The windows, although fashioned in a style roughly matching the age of the building, were very modern in construction, beginning just a foot or so above the floor level, and extending to the top of the highly decorated ceiling.

"Yes, it is a lovely home, Meredith. It's been in my family since the 1920s. My grandfather bought it soon after the first world war had ended. It had been used by the military and was quite run down. But he built it back up again, and although the army used it as a base during World War Two, they didn't take it over fully, so he and my father were able to stay here and keep the business running."

"So, forgive our ignorance" Geoff said, "but... what business are you in?"

Charles Forster smiled. "Ah, many things now, but originally farming and tyres."

"Tyres?!" Hazel exclaimed with a frown.

"Yes, tyres." Charles said matter-of-factly.

"Big black round things, one at each corner!"

Alex chuckled. "You dork, Hazel!"

"My grandfather was a keen amateur car racer in the '20s. Very amateur, actually. He was not really any good, but anyway, he was interested in all things automobile, and became an importer for Vendolet Tyres, which you won't have heard of, but they were a French company...."

"Didn't they sponsor the race in 1937?" Alex interrupted. "I saw their name on the programme."

"Oh, yes. That's right. Well, that was the height of their success really, but then they got into all sorts of difficulties in France with the authorities, and ended up selling out to the French government. By this time, the war had started and my grandfather had other business interests, all to do with engineering, of course...."

The door opened and Michael appeared with a large tea trolley, stacked with cups, saucers and a vast selection of cakes and biscuits. Charles ignored him and carried on explaining the business.

"Now, our group of companies runs various garage chains throughout the UK and America, some specialising in tyres and exhausts, others just general stores. We have another set of companies dealing in aviation parts, including a small private airline. We also run an import-export business. You won't see our name in lights because we have a very specific client base; but our current and future clients know who we are and where to find us."

"Quite exclusive then, the aviation side, for example?" said Geoff, accepting a cup of tea from the unsmiling Michael.

"Certainly. Our clients are the sort of people who don't go shouting about their wealth from the rooftops, and don't feel the need to be seen to be wealthy, but they do live busy lives and so we have several jets in the air at any one time, and one or two cargo planes."

"Wow!" said Alex. "So you can go from anywhere to anywhere else in the world, and not have to worry about queueing at security."

Charles Forster smiled thinly. "Well, we still have to clear customs and passport control, but yes, if I chose to I can just decide to travel anywhere. But I've no need to except on business, and today at least, my business is being done here. Please... help yourselves to cakes, biscuits, anything."

Michael had finished pouring out cups of tea, and was now silently placing plates and serviettes in front of each guest.

"We have toasted teacakes; Michael's speciality; highly recommended."

As the guests enthused about the choices on offer, Michael remained expressionless.

"Well, I love toasted teacakes" said Meredith, "so, Yes Please, Michael, and thank you!"

"I didn't actually make them, Madam, the cook did, but I don't mind taking the credit. They are certainly the best I've ever tasted."

'He has a voice, and perhaps a bit of a soul then' thought Meredith.

"So now, you told me of your interest in this racing accident. Remind me again of your connection to the whole thing?"

"Shall I?" Meredith asked the others. They all agreed, so she carried on, between mouthfuls.

"My great uncle was a young spectator, and he and his friend sneaked into the prohibited bit of the circuit, alongside the gorge, because they got a really good view of the cars at high speed. Well, then the crash happened, and the car hit my uncle's friend and he was killed, and my uncle… great uncle… was hurt. Well, he claims that many years later he saw the ghost of the driver walking down the street…"

"It wasn't the street, Mum. He saw him at one of the races where they service the cars."

"Oh yes, that's right. In the paddock, at one of the races, some years later. Anyway, he claims to have seen the driver who was killed. That's all really. We've seen a couple of cuttings from the papers at the time, and so we thought… well, these two youngsters thought…we'd look into it in a bit more detail and solve the mystery."

"Hmm. I see. I don't really see what the mystery is?" Charles Forster frowned. "This all happened a long time ago, and people believed in ghosts then, of course."

"Well, that's just it" said Alex. "Uncle Toby still believes it, and we're just trying to work out what he's really seen. I mean, he was 12 at the time."

"You know we mentioned" Geoff butted in, "that these two helped to solve the mystery of the Salmsham Railway Disaster. Well…"

"My ancestor was the signalman accused of causing the disaster" said Alex, "but it turns out he was framed and it was actually mass murder, and there was a conspiracy… anyway, Hazel and I managed to help get to the bottom of it all, and then when she mentioned her uncle's ghost story we thought we'd find out some more about it."

"What are you doing, then? Trying to find conspiracies where there are none? I mean, by all accounts this was a simple accident..."

"Except they didn't find the driver, and someone kept seeing his ghost." Geoff said.

"Well, actually they did find the driver, but that was some weeks later. He was washed up on the bank of the Severn, and buried in Langley, I think it was. I found the race file."

"Oh. That's ruined my theory then." Alex said. "I was convinced he'd escaped somehow, and carried on racing, maybe under a different name."

"Most unlikely." Forster snorted. "For a start, why would he want to do that?"

"Well… that's what I wanted to find out, but… I'm also fascinated by this accident anyway. It seems that we…" he glanced at his girlfriend "we always seem to end up at the scene of some historic disaster. We really didn't expect to find anything yesterday, but there it was, the old circuit, and the scene of the crash, just as Uncle Toby described it."

Charles Forster put down the cup and saucer he'd been holding, and sat forward on the sofa.

"Well… the reason I suggested you come over is, as I mentioned earlier, I've managed to find the papers relating to all of the races which took place here. There were about 22 race meetings in the 1930s. They were all organised by my grandfather. He was head of the local car club. Most of the papers are just general correspondence; there's very little about the races themselves, maybe some results sheets, and the accounts, of course."

"What, you mean, someone wrote about each race?" Hazel asked.

"He means money accounts, Hazel." Alex tutted, shaking his head.

"What!" she responded. "Just because I misunderstood what he meant; no need to keep having a go."

"Is there something we could see relating to this race then?" Geoff asked. "I mean, do you mind us having a glance at it."

"Not at all" replied Charles. "When you've all finished eating, we'll go along to the library; that's where we keep all the archived stuff relating to the circuit."

With that incentive, the four visitors finished their tea and cakes fairly rapidly, amidst some polite conversation between their host and Meredith, who told him a little bit more about her great uncle. Alex was the last to finish; as soon as he put his cup down, Michael appeared as if from nowhere and silently cleared the long table.

As they followed Charles along another long corridor towards the library, Hazel leaned across and whispered in Alex's ear "That Michael guy gives me the creeps."

Alex nodded and whispered "Me too!" in response. "I wonder if he's some sort of robot."

The comment made Hazel chuckle, as they entered a vast room at the end of the corridor.

15

For a moment, standing in the doorway, it was difficult to recognise the room's function, then they realised that what looked like grey and black walls were in fact tinted glass doors hiding vast, neatly arranged bookshelves. There was no impression of cluttered ancient collections here, and yet the room was deceptively voluminous. There was one long wooden table towards one side, and on the other side, another set of sofas and another long glass coffee table. There was also a discrete drinks cabinet just inside the door.

"Well, I must say Charles, this is not how I imagined your library to look!" said Geoff. "I had the image of an old wood-panelled room with thick wooden bookcases, and a creaking mezzanine balcony with piles of books on the floor because there was no more space for them. This looks very twenty-first century."

"Thank you, Geoff." Charles smiled thinly again. "I think these days we know a lot more about preservation of books, so we control the atmosphere and the temperature very carefully. Some of the older books over here belonged to the original owners, but actually modern books don't tend to last very long unless you really look after them. One of my people is responsible for this library, and manages to keep track of things most of the time."

"That must be a full-time job" said Meredith.

"Actually it's not, and we don't go collecting just any book, but anyway, Shelley looks in every day and checks everything is in its place. Over here is the motor racing bookcase." Charles showed them to a large area set against the outside wall, between two tall double-glazed windows. He flicked a small switch on the right, and the shelves lit up behind the tinted glass.

"Ah, when you say bookcase, you mean 'wall' surely?" said Geoff, pointing as he ran his eye along the various titles. "Gosh, you've got plenty of 'Limited Editions' up here, haven't you? Look at that… Bentley… Bugatti…"

"Cantin was driving a Bugatti, wasn't he?" said Alex innocently.

"Was he?" asked Charles. "Well, that's a limited edition book, about Bugatti the man and the marque. There might be a picture of your chap in there, but somehow I doubt it. We can always have a look later on but… this is what I was going to show you, just in here."

He pulled opened a drawer beneath the lower shelf. Nobody had even noticed the drawers; they were totally flush fitting and had no handles, and none of the visitors saw what Charles Forster did to open this one.

He pulled out a bulky buff coloured envelope, and, moving over to the long table, undid the clasp at the top and pulled out a neat stack of papers. Alex noticed that several small photos fell out from a smaller envelope which was in between some of the letters and various paper lists.

"Here you are. 9th of October 1937 - Trophy Race Meeting. We're talking about the Gold Trophy race meeting, aren't we?"

"That's right. The Abbots Park Gold Trophy

race, wasn't it?" said Alex.

"Yes, sponsored by Vendolet Tyres. In other words, my grandfather's import company put up the prize money, and all the starting money."

"Gosh, that must have been a lot."

"It was, especially for 1937. He was quite ambitious, but he was competing against another race in London, the Empire Trophy. The thing is though, the Crystal Palace track was too narrow for the big German cars, and he managed to persuade most of them to race here the week after Donington. He got a bigger crowd than he expected, so the whole meeting turned quite a profit, and he got massive coverage for Vendolet too."

"Mr Forster...would you mind if I took copies of this? I could use my phone."

"Well... actually... wait here a moment, I'll arrange to have everything copied and sent on to you. How's about that?"

"Well, it's no trouble to do it now."

"That may be, but these are our private papers, and there may be something sensitive which shouldn't be out there in the public domain." Charles stared straight at Alex, and his expression made it plain that there would be no copying now.

"But this stuff's over 80 years old!" said Hazel. "I mean, what could there possibly be..."

"Hazel!" said Geoff. "Please respect Mr Forster's wishes. Thank you, Charles, we are grateful to you for showing us this. Could we have a quick look through now?"

"Why don't you two children fetch those chairs from the corner, and we'll sit and go through these now. Oh... Michael, send Shelley in to see us."

Alex and Hazel, who were unamused at being called children by their host, started out for the neat stack of chairs. Michael's sudden appearance made them both jump, and as he turned to carry out Charles's instructions, they exchanged glances.

"I told you... he's really creepy." said Hazel, straining slightly as she picked up two chairs which were somewhat heavier than they looked.

Alex grunted, and promptly toppled forwards as he tried to carry three chairs from the stack.

"Crikey, these are made of lead or something."

"No, you're just weak" laughed Hazel. "Obviously the 'children' comment was aimed at you, not me."

The chairs having been delivered, they grouped themselves around the top of the table. Charles slowly peeled off the top sheet of paper.

The first item was a typed index, which Charles passed on to Meredith, who scanned her eyes over it quickly and passed it on to the others; Geoff to her right and beyond him, Hazel. Alex, who was at the end of the line, was tempted to get his phone out and start snapping away despite Charles's very clear instructions, but he felt it was far too risky. The next few sheets were general correspondence with the RAC, who were the officiating body for motorsports at the time. Charles then produced a bundle of letters which were tied together.

"Ah. This is all the correspondence to do with the starting money for each team. Probably make very interesting reading."

"How does that work then?" Alex asked.

"Well, I think he offered a very lucrative deal to Mercedes and Auto Union – they were the big

German firms – to race here. Then the lesser drivers would have all received something for starting money, even if it was only a few pounds."

"So, not prize money for winning then?" asked Alex, slightly bewildered.

"Oh, they would have received prize money of course. But the main attraction for spectators was to see a race, and so if you turned up and your car started the race, you would get your starting money. Of course, some people abused the privilege and would turn up with any of piece of junk and just get it to do a lap and then retire, but they didn't last long in the sport. Usually, you would enter your car, and the organisers would accept or deny your entry. If you were a well-known name you would be paid more, of course. Occasionally, you wouldn't receive anything, but they might still let you race."

"Oh, so what was the point of racing then?" said Hazel "apart from driving round and round in circles and getting thrown off the edge of cliffs."

"Well, ask any racing driver and they'll tell you it's the thrill of driving at high speed, and the danger, and the thrill of winning as well. Also, the motor manufacturers used their race cars as advertising. Certainly with touring car racing in those days, you could buy a car like the one you saw racing, and use it on the normal roads. So Vendolet might supply a team with free tyres, particularly a big team so if it won, they would get free publicity."

They sifted through several more sheets of paper until they came to another envelope, marked 'Accident reports'. Charles unfolded the end and pulled out a few more sheets of paper, a couple of newspaper cuttings, and two photographs.

"Here" he said, holding up the photos "are the pictures of the car after the accident."

He passed them along. "Young man, if you wish to, you may take a copy of these now." The photos were passed along to Alex. "I'm not sure if it'll help you but at least you have proof that this accident actually happened."

The first picture was off the car hanging awkwardly in the tree where it came to rest, pointing down the slope, its cockpit clearly visible. The steering wheel appeared to be intact, but the mangled front wheels were splayed out at almost ninety degrees each side of the severely dented bonnet; the one on the car's left was pushed back quite a way towards the driver's seat area. There was no apparent fire, but a dirty streak of liquid appeared to run from halfway along the left-side of the bonnet, up past the shattered windshield. The whole car appeared to be slightly bent around the middle, and there were clear signs of impact with a tree on its left.

"I wonder who the man is standing beside it?" Alex said. "Would he be a track marshal?"

"Most probably. Either that or the rescue truck driver. They must have had quite a job pulling that back up to the road level."

Hazel passed the second picture along, and as Alex lined his phone up to copy it, he noticed that it was of the car being craned onto the back of a flat-bed truck. They had used four large ropes around the car body, and the left front wheel hung drunkenly down towards the ground, attached by nothing more than a narrow strip of bent tubing. There was a liquid dripping from the smashed radiator.

"Ah… Shelley." Charles snapped. They looked

up to see a woman in her late thirties standing anxiously halfway across the room. "Shelley, I'd like you to copy this file for these people. Make sure you copy everything, but let me have both the file and the copies back before I hand them over, just in case there's anything confidential in there. There probably isn't but I'll decide that." then, to Alex "You'd better let me have those photos back, and I'll keep everything together."

He packaged everything back up again, and then handed the complete envelope to Shelley.

"Everything, Sir?" she asked.

"I just said that, didn't I?" he snapped at her.

"Yes, Sir." Shelley nodded and left, as Alex and Hazel exchanged glances.

"Right, well... why don't we grab the quads and ride down to the old circuit. Even though it's dark now, we'll be able to see something, and I'd like you to show me where you think this crash happened. Michael!"

Michael appeared again, as if from nowhere.

"Prepare three quads for us. We'll take a trek down to the old circuit in the woods."

"It'll be dark. Shall I put the park lights on?" asked Michael.

"What do you think? Of course I want the bloody park lights on!"

"Yes, Sir!" Michael turned and left, still totally expressionless.

"Ble-deep ble-deep!" muttered Hazel under her breath. "Robot alert!"

Alex grinned and shushed her.

16

A few minutes later found the four visitors and Charles Forster standing in front of three identical blue quad bikes in the brightly lit garage next to the stables. The visitors had gone back to Geoff's car and donned jackets and hats, as the temperature was dropping fast, and they were struck by the warmth of the garage, until Michael raised the overhead doors and the outdoor cold enveloped them again.

It had been decided that Geoff would drive the second quad, with Alex riding pillion, and Meredith the third, carrying Hazel. However, Meredith was not keen on taking the controls, and Hazel volunteered instead.

"I've ridden one of these before, Mum. Claire Dryden has one up at her stables. It's fine, I know what I'm doing."

After briefly showing Geoff and Hazel the main controls, Charles Forster led them slowly out and along the track which ran around the main field. He had explained that they would pick up the route of the old circuit and follow it round to the far gate, beyond where the accident had happened. Then they would turn and go back and stop by the accident site. The powerful lights on the front of each quad picked out the track ahead of them. They rounded the left-hand corner at the bottom of the field, and made their way up onto the rough tarmac remains of the old circuit, rarely travelling at more than twenty miles an hour, with Charles looking back frequently to make sure the others were safely following him.

As they crested the hill and made their way towards the sharp right bend before The Ledge, Alex looked to the right and saw that there were some lights lining the earth bank. When they turned the corner, he realised that there were lights all the way along the right-hand side of the old circuit, leading farther into the woods. They drove past the site of the accident, and around a mild right hand curve before Charles' brake lights came on, and they had reached the limit of his property.

"This is the gate which I thought you'd climbed over" he shouted back to Geoff, "before you told me you'd come up through the woods. Now you can take me to the scene of the accident."

"Okay!" Geoff nodded as he tried to be heard above the sound of the engines. "It's not too far back there..." and he gentle throttled up the quad and turned it around to head off back to the crash site.

"Here we are!" Geoff pulled up and pointed to the gap in the bushes on the right. Charles manoeuvred his quad so the headlights shone straight at the gap, and killed the engine. Hazel pulled up alongside him and did the same thing. Geoff took a little while longer to stop his.

"The batteries'll be fine for a few minutes." Charles said as he jumped off his quad. "Now then, show me what you think happened, young man."

Alex duly explained where Uncle Toby had supposedly been watching the race from, and jumped off the circuit onto the pathway to demonstrate one of his theories about how Cantin may have escaped from the car before it crashed down the gorge.

"I see what you mean, but I still think it's all a

bit far-fetched. I can't think why a man would want to go to all this trouble to stage his own disappearance. There are far simpler ways to do it, surely? And he would need a reason. Do you have any ideas why he would do that?"

"No, I must admit, it does seem a bit weird." Alex clambered back up onto the track again. "But then, we thought that about the Salmsham accident."

They talked for a few more minutes about the accident, and how the spectator had appeared and helped save Uncle Toby. Charles Forster walked back along the old track and then knelt down to try to get a driver's perspective of the accident site. Wandering back, he mentioned an idea of his grandfather's; to run a 24-hour race. The idea never came to fruition as the war intervened and then they closed the circuit.

"It would have been very spectacular, and utterly mad, I think" he mused. "Well anyway, you've seen enough here I'm sure. Thank you for showing me, and perhaps if we go back to the house now, your papers will be ready to take away."

They duly fired up the quads and followed Charles back along the old circuit, across the field to the garage. Hazel noticed that they were going a lot quicker on the way back, and her mother patted her shoulder and shouted "Take it easy, Dear!" in her ear as they bumped their way off the circuit onto the grass of the field.

When they got back to the garage, Charles was grinning widely – none of them had seen him smile like that since they'd met him.

"That was fun, I must say. I do love riding these quads, but it's been a while since I've had one out in the dark. I might do that more often."

"You weren't hanging about on the way back, were you?" Geoff commented, smiling just as much as their host.

"Well, I guessed that you all knew what you were doing, and where we were going, and young 'Valentina Rossi' there was trying to catch us up I think." He indicated to Hazel, who was trying to untangle her long blonde hair, which was now sticking out at all angles.

"Thank you for letting me ride this!" Hazel enthused. "I might just have to sneak it out of here and have another ride."

"They are great fun, aren't they?" said Charles as they made their way back to the house. "But anyway, I hope you've had an interesting and useful visit. I've got to fly out tonight on business, so I'm going to have to say good bye now, but before you go, do feel free to have a quick drink, and Michael will bring you the copies of those files." He led them back into the lounge where they'd first met, and then shook hands with each of them in turn.

"Do please email me if you want to know anything else, and I'd be interested to hear how your investigation progresses." With that, Charles Forster smiled his usual thin smile, turned around and left the room.

Before anyone had a chance to say anything, the door opened and Michael appeared with a tray of glasses and a selection of soft drinks. "Shelley is just bringing an envelope with your papers. She won't be more than another few minutes. Please help yourselves to the drinks." He disappeared silently.

"Well, that was a very interesting afternoon" said Meredith. "How lovely of Charles to have us

121

over, and show us the library..."

"... and let us ride the quads. That was awesome! Can we get one, Dad?" Hazel was still buzzing from the experience.

Geoff smiled as he poured himself a natural lemonade. "No we can't... hmmm, produce of Forster Foods. Natural ingredients only." He read from the label on the lemonade bottle. "That'll be another one of his businesses then."

They chuckled at that, and then chatted for several minutes about the trip on the quads. Meredith was the only one who hadn't enjoyed it.

"We should have been wearing helmets, you know. And I was quite scared, Hazel. You went far too fast at the end."

"Oh Mum, it was fine. But you're right, we probably should have had helmets on. I don't know why we didn't, actually."

"Well, it never occurred to me" said Geoff, "which is odd. I suppose, we'd seen Charles without one so we just followed his example."

There was a knock on the door, which then immediately opened.

"Excuse me," said Shelley "which of you is taking these papers?"

"Oh, they're for me." Alex leapt up from the sofa. "Thank you very much for copying them. Are they all there?"

"Everything's been copied." Shelley looked slightly nervous as she handed the envelope to Alex and left the room. The others stood to leave.

They noticed Michael standing in the corridor, and as Meredith led them out, he held his arm out to indicate that he would show them out of the building. Shutting the door behind them, he swiftly overtook them and guided them to the main door, which he opened for them, looking at the far wall as first Meredith, then the two teenagers, walked past. Geoff, who was bringing up the rear, felt he should acknowledge Michael's contribution to the afternoon's entertainment, and thanked him profusely for his hospitality, managing not to show any hint of sarcasm in his voice.

"You're welcome." Michael said insincerely, as he shut the door behind them. They waited until they were in the car, the engine fired up, before Geoff commented "I wonder if he's had a lobotomy or something. He seems totally devoid of any emotion."

"Gosh, yes" said Meredith. "I mean, there's being professional and there's being downright weird. Either he's got a personality disorder, or he's frightened to speak."

"He didn't look like the sort of chap to be frightened of anything or anyone, did he?" said Geoff, angling the car back towards the long driveway.

"He's just very creepy" said Hazel. "I hope he doesn't want us to invite *him* for tea. I'll be out…"

For most of the short journey back to Martina's house, they stayed silent. Alex was lost in his own thoughts, looking idly out of the window at the lights near the harbour as they crossed the suspension bridge. Hazel nudged him.

"You're being very quiet. 'Sup?"

"Nothing" he replied. "Just thinking about… well, what a strange afternoon it's been. I mean, it was very generous of *Chahhhhles* to invite us *to teeee*" he put on his 'posh' impression much to everyone's amusement, "but don't you think it was odd the way we were herded out to the quads, then let free for half an hour or so with no thought of safety or anything, and then we get back and *Chahhhhles* has to 'suddenly' fly off somewhere, and we get shown out as soon as we get those copies."

"Shown out? More like 'thrown out'!" said Hazel. "I thought Michael the Robot would have lifted us out if we'd dawdled."

"Well, I thought it was very good of Charles to show us around" said Meredith. "He didn't have to invite us at all, especially as he caught you trespassing originally."

"Yes, I agree, but… he didn't really show us anything, did he. If you think about it, *we* showed *him* where we think the accident happened." Alex had a number of conflicting theories in his head, each containing its own unique uncertainty, but he had a feeling they'd been led up a large garden path today and he couldn't work out why.

"He's given us all those copies of the papers though" said Hazel. "I mean, he didn't have to do that at all, did he?"

"Agreed" Alex replied "but only when I asked if I could copy them on my phone. And suddenly, he whipped them off us. I wonder what it was he was hiding from us?"

"Probably nothing" said Geoff, as they pulled off the road into Martina's driveway. "You've got quite a stack of papers there. I think Charles has been very generous, actually Alex. You're probably seeing conspiracies where there aren't any."

Later that evening, after a dinner which

Martina had insisted on preparing even though her guests had told her they were not hungry, Alex pulled the stack of copies from the envelope and placed it on the table in front of them all.

"Well, here goes… one by one, starting with the title page." He turned it over. "Oh that's good, she's double-sided the copies. There's an index to the documents on this side. Handy."

He passed it to Geoff, who scanned the list. "Correspondence with R A C and sponsors, Correspondence with entrants, Starting money, Prize Money, List of entries, List of officials, List of Marshals, Medical, Timekeeper's records, Observer's Reports, Incident reports…ah! Inquest Master H Levenson, Inquest P-H Cantin, Legal. It's all there – everything we need to get to the bottom of this."

"Crikey, that's so much to get through!" Hazel commented. "Where do we start?"

"How about the Inquest on Harry Levenson?" said Meredith. "Isn't that the thing that Uncle Toby said he went along to?"

17

"Right, young man. Sit down over there, and wait until you're called." The stern-faced reception clerk peered at Toby Allen over a set of thick-rimmed glasses, and then returned to his writing, occasionally flicking his eyes up to check that his instructions had been followed.

Toby limped across the room and sat nervously next to his mother, who was busy lighting up another cigarette. He glanced around the large waiting room at the Coroners Court. They had been instructed to attend the inquest into the death of Harry Levenson; Toby was terrified at the thought that he might be seen as being responsible for his best friend's death. He had cried almost every waking moment since the accident happened, and since he had hardly slept for the past two nights, that meant he had shed a lot of tears. Before leaving for the inquest that morning, his mother had put a fresh handkerchief in his trouser pocket, but it was already heavily stained with snot and tears, and so he had started on another, which was in the other pocket.

His mind was working overtime, a deep fear of the unknown creating all sorts of nightmarish scenarios in his imagination. He was sure that he would be punished for his and Harry's sins. Had they not disobeyed very clear rules? Did they not completely ignore the very important sign that told them to 'Keep Out' of the prohibited area? Did they not deliberately place themselves in a position of grave danger, beside a circuit teeming with the most highly powered cars ever seen on a race track? He could clearly picture the stern rebukes, to be delivered in public by a tall, unsmiling judge who bore a remarkable similarity to Mr Derrick, his unremittingly cheerless Headmaster.

'Master Allen, you have been found guilty of the most serious crime of trespassing beside a motor racing circuit, a crime punishable by public flogging followed by imprisonment with only bread and water for food, for the next twenty years...'

"Are you alright, Toby dear?" His mother interrupted his nightmarish daydream, and he became aware of the silent tear running down one cheek. He started to nod, but then sniffed and buried his head into his mother's shoulder.

"I'm... scared, Mum. What if they... I mean, Harry's mum and dad will be in there. I didn't mean it... we didn't mean to do anything wrong." He tried to speak quietly, but his voice had carried across the cavernous room.

"There, there, Dear" his mother said tenderly, her arm around his shoulder. "You just tell them what you told the policeman, nothing more and nothing less, and answer any questions they might have for you. It's not about whether you or Harry were doing the right or wrong thing. They just want to know what happened."

Toby looked up through tearstained eyes, and noticed the clerk was walking over towards him, his stern visage softening as he came closer.

"Don't worry, young man. It's not a court case and you're not on trial. Whenever there's a... an accident, or any sudden death, there's an inquest. All the Coroner is doing is trying to find out what really happened, just like your mother said, so they can try and prevent it happening again."

Toby nodded and sniffed again.

"He's a nice man too, the Coroner. He's called Mr Colcher, and he's got a young lad not much older than you, so I think he'll be very kind to you."

"Thank you, Sir." Toby sniffed and wiped his eyes on yet another fresh handkerchief, which his mother had just given him.

The door opened, and a youngish looking man walked in, stepping briskly over to the desk. The clerk turned and, equally briskly, returned to his place behind the desk.

"Good afternoon, Sir." he said to the visitor. "I take it you're here for the inquest, Mr...?"

"Watson. David Watson." Toby started to recognise the man. He had looked vaguely familiar, but now he heard the man's slightly clipped voice, it dawned on him who he was. He appeared much smarter than Toby had remembered, but of course he would not have dressed up in a business suit to spectate outdoors at a motor race.

"Mum. That's the man who helped to rescue me!" he whispered to his mother.

Watson chatted to the clerk for a couple more moments, and then he turned and headed towards Toby and his mother.

"Good afternoon" he smiled, politely. She thought he had a slight South African accent.

"Good afternoon" replied Toby's mother. "I understand you helped my son here?"

"Ah, yes. Tony, wasn't it?" Watson repeated

the error he'd made when he'd first helped the boy moments after he'd come round.

"We're so very grateful to you."

She offered him a cigarette, which he politely refused with a brief shake of his head.

"Thank you, but I have a pipe."

Toby's mother continued "Well, I'd like to thank you so much for all your help. I don't know what we would have done if you hadn't found him."

"Well, I'm sure someone would have found him, Mrs…erm…"

"Allen. Clarissa Allen."

"David Watson." He shook her hand and smiled disarmingly at her. Toby was aware of a slight hesitation in letting go of the man's hand. His mother appeared to be charmed by Watson, who he guessed was just a few years younger than her.

"This is such a ghastly business, isn't it?" She said "I'll be so glad when today is over, for his sake and… my friends', in there." She nodded towards a door behind the clerk's desk.

"Yes, it really is" Watson agreed. "Truly ghastly. You don't expect to be involved in something like this really, even though we know it's a dangerous sport."

"Quite. My friends… well, I don't know what I'd be like if it had been my son who died. It doesn't bear thinking about."

"Yes, I'm so sorry for them, losing their boy like that." He looked at Toby. "How old was your friend?"

"Th..thirteen, Sir."

"Thirteen… God, that's no age. No age at all." Watson shook his head.

"Where were you when the accident happened?" Toby's mother asked.

"Oh, I was just a short way along the track, on the outside of the next bend. I had my camera, you see. You can get the most amazing shots of the cars coming straight towards you. Very spectacular, and if you get the angle right, you can see the gorge in the background. I'm only amazed that I didn't see the two lads, but then again, I was trying to remain out of sight and so were they. It was certainly a big surprise to find them there. Gave me quite a start."

"So you saw the crash then?"

"Well, yes. It didn't look like a crash though, more like a little bit of heavy parking. The chap was going so slowly, you see, behind all that smoke, but then it was as if the car hit a spring; it suddenly bounced end over end and the driver...well, he came flying out high over the car. It was quite sickening. I'm certain the poor chap's ended up in the river."

The door opened again, and two men walked over to the clerk. Toby didn't hear them clearly enough to catch their names, but he recognised one of them as the man who had helped him to the ambulance and then stayed with him until they reached the medical tent.

The two men sat down, across the room from where Toby sat with his mother. One of them nodded and smiled but no words were spoken. Watson stood up and walked over to them, introducing himself as he approached them. As the three of them began to chatter, Toby pressed his head into his mother's arm again. Then, the door behind the clerk opened and a voice called his name...

130

18

Toby did not really know what to expect when he limped into the Coroner's courtroom. He and his mother were led to some chairs, where she was invited to sit down. He moved to follow her, but the clerk who had shown them in pointed to the witness stand, and motioned Toby to move there.

He noticed a low-level murmuring in the court room, and saw the Coroner sitting and making notes in the distance. He avoided looking at anyone else, but felt that many eyes were on him as he took the oath with his hand on a bible.

The Coroner watched him, and then, as the clerk took the bible away, he spoke.

"Thank you for coming here today, Toby. I know this is an extremely difficult time for you, so all I am asking you to do now is answer any questions put to you as honestly as you can. Hopefully you won't need to stay too long."

"Thank you, Sir." Toby replied, his voice quivering with fear.

"Now, you are obviously very nervous, so I would like to reassure you that you are not in any trouble. I'm here, and the jury are here, simply to find out how your friend died. We're not here to find out *why* he died, and no-one is looking to blame you for this. Do you understand that?"

"Yes, Sir. Thank you, Sir." Toby was sure everyone in the courtroom could hear his tongue trying to stick to the roof of his mouth as he spoke.

"Now, I have here a copy of the statement

which you gave to the police on Saturday evening, so I just want to ask you some questions so that the jury can form a picture of what happened to you and your friend."

Toby nodded and swallowed hard. "Y-yes Sir."

"You and Harry left your parents, with their permission, and walked around the spectator fence, in the opposite direction to the race. Is that right?"

"Yes… that's right, Sir."

"Thank you. And you came to a fence across the spectator area, with a sign which told you that you could not go any further."

"Yes." He could feel the guilt rising in him, and began to blush.

"So you turned right, and followed the fence into the woods where no-one could see you, and then climbed over it. Is that right?"

The tears began to well up, and Toby began to look down, pressing his lips together in a vain attempt to avoid crying. He nodded, and managed a barely audible "Mm."

"It's alright, Toby. We just want to know how you got to the point on the circuit where the car came off. You walked along a path which went alongside, but slightly below the level of the circuit, until you came to a spot where you could see the cars, and you stayed behind a small bush so you couldn't be seen from the circuit. Is that right?"

"Y-Yes, Sir."

At that moment an elderly juror raised his hand, and the Coroner invited to him to stand and ask a question.

"Toby, this path you were on. Was it near to the edge of the gorge?"

"Yes, very near, Sir. The gorge was to our right, but we felt quite safe as there were some bushes beside the path."

The juror thanked him, and sat down. The Coroner once again asked him a question from his statement.

"Now, you say that after you'd been in this spot for about ten minutes, you noticed the car, the Bugatti, smoking as it went past you."

"Yes, Sir. The driver was leaning over trying to see. I remember we thought it was quite funny, and Harry said we wouldn't be seeing him again."

"Is that because you thought the car engine would blow up?"

"Yes, Sir."

"But then on the very next lap the car came straight towards you?"

"Yes, Sir. It wasn't going very fast, but there was a lot of smoke, and I remember seeing the driver leaning out so he could see where he was going."

"And your friend called out to you."

"Yes, Sir. Something like 'Watch out! He's coming straight towards us'."

"And you say you saw the driver very clearly."

"He was looking… I think now, I remember he looked right at me. He looked really shocked, because I think he could see he was going to hit us if we didn't move."

"And then the car came off the circuit and went over you?"

"Yes. I jumped… to my left, Sir. Well, I threw myself to the left, and the car made so much noise, and I think I heard Harry shout something."

"I see. In your statement here you just say you

don't remember anything else."

"I know… it's sort of coming back a little now, Sir. I remember hearing Harry's voice shouting out."

"Did you hear what he said?"

"I think it was a swear word, Sir."

"You may tell us what you think he said."

"I think he said 'Damn!', Sir."

Toby became aware of a commotion in the gallery up on his right, and noticed Harry's mother and father for the first time. She had her head down and was shaking it; her husband had his arm over her shoulder and was leaning down to comfort her.

He carried on. "I thought… I thought my mother wouldn't like to hear him say that."

"Quite so. And then, you don't remember anything else about the accident?"

"No, Sir. I just remember waking up and the spectator, Mr Watson, helping me."

"You know Mr Watson?" The Coroner had put Toby's statement down.

"No, Sir. Not until today. But I know it was him; I recognised him. He was very good to me."

"You said to the police that he was leaning over you and calling you a 'little fool'. Is that right?

The guilty tears welled up again, and once again Toby's face puckered up as he nodded.

"And were you hurt in the accident, either by the car, or by jumping down to the ground?"

Toby looked up and nodded again. "I felt… as if I'd been strangled. I think a piece of the car… it may have caught me around my neck. It hurt a lot, but the doctor said later I was just bruised. It was probably a branch which caught me. I've also bruised my shin but that doesn't hurt as much."

"Thank you, Toby. I just have one final question for you, and it is a little sensitive but you must try and answer it. Did you see or hear of Harry after you had woken up?"

Toby shook his head, and opened his mouth to speak but no coherent sound came. He began to sob uncontrollably.

"Thank you, Toby. You've done everything we asked you to do, and I know this was a very hard thing for you do, but I have no further questions for you. I would just like to ask if any members of the jury have any questions... no? Then, Toby, you may stand down. Thank you."

Toby stepped back, still sobbing, and almost collapsed into his mother's arms. The clerk stepped forward and spoke to his mother. "You may leave if you wish, or if you would like to stay for the verdict, you may sit up in the gallery there."

Much to his surprise and horror, his mother elected to join Harry's parents in the gallery. "I haven't seen them since Sunday. Connie needs my support, she's one of my best friends" she said to the clerk. Toby followed his mother up the steps into the gallery, and along the front row, still crying. She bent down and gave Connie Levenson a friendly hug.

"Call David Watson!"

The call echoed around the courtroom, over the general chatter which had slowly become louder as the jury members and spectators chatted amongst themselves. Toby looked along the row behind, and saw two people urgently scribbling notes onto thick ring-bound pads. 'They must be from the newspapers' he thought to himself, and he wondered what they would write about him tomorrow.

His mind wandered, and he barely noticed anything that David Watson said at first. Most of it he'd already heard in the waiting room, but then the Coroner began to ask what he'd actually seen of the accident, and Toby started to listen intently again.

"Mr Watson, you say in your statement that you saw the car going straight towards the edge of the track 'in a cloud of smoke', to use your words."

"That is correct, yes."

"And was it going very fast?"

"It didn't look very fast, but then, I was looking at it almost head on."

"Of course. But you didn't feel that it was going very fast, compared, say, to the other racing cars around it."

"Not on that lap, no. I got the impression the driver was just trying to pull up."

"I see. And then you saw the car topple over the side of the circuit?"

"That's right."

"But at no point did you see either Master Allen, or Master Levenson, where the car went off."

"No, Sir. I didn't see them until after the accident. Well, actually, that's not correct. I never saw the boy who was killed at all, just Master Allen."

"I see. Now, as I mentioned earlier, we have not yet found the body of the driver and so this inquest is not strictly concerned with him, however, you say that you saw the car topple end over end, and the driver 'flung out as if on a spring'. Is there any way you might have mistaken him for Harry Levenson? That is, could it have been the boy you saw being flung out over the car?"

"I... I don't think it could have been, Sir? He

136

was wearing white overalls and I'm sure he was wearing a leather helmet too."

"So, to the best of your knowledge, you never saw Master Levenson either before, during, or after the accident."

"That's right."

"Now, you mention in your evidence that you were taking photographs during the race. Did you happen to take any at the time of the accident?"

"I did take a snap of the Bugatti when it first appeared, but I must have damaged my camera because none of my pictures has come out. The whole film is ruined."

"That must have been quite disappointing for you, Mr Watson."

"It was very distressing, Sir. I feel as if I wasted my day. I travelled up from London especially."

Toby heard a few chuckles from behind him, and turned around to see the two press men making fun of the unfortunate amateur photographer. He wondered what 'you can't syndicate a white snowstorm' meant; he assumed it related to the likely outcome of the photo negatives.

David Watson continued to give evidence about his actions in the aftermath of finding Toby, and then he was dismissed. After he had left, Clarissa Allen leaned over, gave Connie Levenson another big hug, then gathered her handbag and coat, and stood up. "Come on, Toby. Let's go and have some lunch."

19

Extract: Western Daily Press,
Thursday 14th October 1937

RACING DEATH 'MISADVENTURE'
The death of a schoolboy spectator during last weekend's Gold Trophy Race at Abbot's Park was the subject of the Bristol inquest last Monday on Harry Levenson (13) of School Lane, Yatton. A verdict of Misadventure was delivered after the jury heard evidence that the boy and a friend were spectating from a prohibited area when a Bugatti car left the track and plunged over the edge of the Avon gorge. The boy's body was found at the foot of the gorge. Death was almost instantaneous. The body of the driver of the Bugatti has not been found and is believed to have been washed out into the Severn.

20

"So that's that then." Alex Phipps turned over the sheet of paper with the copy of the inquest verdict cutting on it. "Misadventure. Not a lot of information at all – nothing we didn't know from Uncle Toby."

"Except it's proof that it really happened." Geoff Burns sat back in his chair. "Harry Levenson's death was fully investigated and his body was identified, and so it was definitely him they found at the foot of the gorge and not the driver."

"What's the next thing then, Dad?" Hazel asked.

"Inquest – P. H. Cantin."

Alex picked up another sheet. "Here it is. This should be interesting. I thought Toby said they hadn't found him."

"But Charles said they had, so I suppose we should look at this and see what it says."

Alex looked at the small writing on the sheet. "It's another newspaper cutting...dated Thursday, the 6th of January 1938. *'A body washed up on the shores of the River Severn this Boxing Day has been formally identified as that of the missing French racing motorist Pierre-Henri Canton'*... they've spelt it wrong... *'The body, which was much mutilated and decomposed, was identified by his widow, Madam Christine Canton, who recognised a large tattoo on his back. The cause of death could not be readily established as the body appeared to have been badly cut up whilst in the river, probably by a ship's propeller. The head and right leg have yet to be recovered. Following evidence given at*

139

an earlier hearing into the causes of an accident during the Abbots Park Gold Trophy race, the jury reached a verdict of Death by Misadventure.'

"So, Uncle Toby was lying when he said they never found the body." Hazel said earnestly. "How can we believe anything else he says, then? I mean, what is it about old people...?"

"Hang on, Dear, give him a break, poor man... or poor boy, which is what he was then, remember?" Meredith said in response. "I'm not sure his parents would have told him about finding the driver's body, would they? I mean, they probably wanted him to try and forget the whole thing. They certainly wouldn't have shown him that report. It's quite gruesome enough for us, isn't it?"

"I suppose so...maybe." said Hazel, sounding unconvinced.

Alex put the sheet of paper down and looked up, frowning. "This is actually becoming more of a mystery though, isn't it? I mean, I was so convinced that Cantin just slowed the car down, jumped off it and survived, and Uncle Toby was seeing the real Pierre in later years. Now... well, it seems, he really was killed."

He searched through the next few sheets, but found no more about the inquest into Cantin's death.

"There's some stuff here about the RAC investigation into the accident though." Alex flicked through a couple of the sheets, and pulled one out.

"Here. It's got... hey, this looks juicy! It's got the names of the witnesses and everything." He passed the sheet on to Hazel. "Look at that... it's a copy of the official report into the crash."

Abbots Park Motoring Club
Abbots Park Circuit
North Somerset

Fatal accident to Car 105 P-H Cantin

Initial report – 10th October 1937

On lap 15 the Startline Observer and others noted smoke from beneath the bonnet of Car 105, and after consulting with the team representative and mechanic, Mr Reginald Simmons, it was decided to black flag the car on the following lap.

Mr A.D. Prosser, the flag marshal and observer at Post 7, then reported Car 105 had left the track about a third of the way along The Ledge, where the track bears slightly right. The car went between two of the straw bales which were lining the track at that point. An immediate request was made for emergency assistance and an ambulance attended, along with Mr P.L. Clarke, the Chief Marshal. Mr Clarke reported that the car was stuck about 30 feet down the side of the gorge, hanging almost vertically in the trees, nose down, about 4 feet from the ground. The driver was missing. Two young boys who were in a prohibited area were struck by the car; I regret to say that one was thrown down the gorge and killed. The other was taken to the medical centre but his life is not in danger.

The accident was witnessed by Mr David Watson, who was also spectating from a prohibited area. He states that the car was going slowly, almost in a straight line towards the edge of the track with the driver apparently blinded by oil smoke. The car tumbled down the side of the gorge and the driver was ejected 'as if on a spring'. Mr Watson assisted with the rescue of the surviving boy.

The car was recovered after the race, and inspected by H.C. Selkirk of the R.A.C. He found that the oil line had become detached between the engine and oil gauge and that this most likely spilled oil onto the exhaust pipe, thus causing the smoke. The front of the car was extensively damaged through impact with the trees. There was no indication of any mechanical failure such as steering or suspension failure prior to the accident.

Comments from Mr Prosser and Mr Watson indicate that the driver may have been intending to pull over to the side of the circuit as his speed was not very high considering where he was on the track, and he must have misjudged his position.

Chief Inspector Willow of the North Somerset Constabulary informed me that after an extensive search of the gorge, no trace of the driver's body has been found and it is assumed to have been washed out into the River Severn.

It is our conclusion that the accident was caused by a detached oil line causing oil to leak onto the hot engine, causing an excessive amount of smoke, which prevented the driver from seeing clearly.

Kenneth Forbes-Hunter
Clerk of the Course

Appendices: Witness details

"So, the next sheet is just names and addresses of the people in the report." Alex scanned the list. "D. Watson is on the list... it says '*may provide photographs when film is developed*'. I wonder if he did?"

"He didn't produce any at the inquest, did he?" said Geoff, holding out his hand. "I'm sure if there were any, we'd have seen them."

Alex passed the papers to Geoff, who sifted through them. "There's a lot of stuff here about the car entries. Most of it is letters back and forth about starting money. I'm sure it is interesting to any motor racing folk, but nothing I think to help us."

"Well, I'm baffled" said Alex. "I mean, there was a crash, the driver was found... eventually. One poor boy was killed, the other one says he's seeing the driver's ghost."

Hazel looked at him. "I told you... Uncle Toby wasn't making it up."

"No, I know, but... there's something else here. There are no such things as ghosts, Hazel."

Hazel rolled her eyes. "Here we go again..."

"No, listen. They might exist in Uncle Toby's head, but they're not real. But something happened, so we've got to do some more digging."

"What do you suggest?"

"Well…" he hesitated. "If it's okay with everyone else, how about going along the bottom of the gorge tomorrow to see where they found the boy's body?"

Just then they were joined by Martina and her husband Andy, who had been working all day in his home office, having arrived safely the night before. He was familiar with the family story, but not with their investigation, and asked how it was going.

"Ah, so much to tell, Andy!" Geoff waved the papers in his hand. "This is just some of the evidence we're sifting through."

Andy Heath whistled through his teeth. "Rather you than me. I've got enough on my hands with international clients trying to get out of paying us."

He and Geoff carried on chatting about business, while Martina scooped up the empty drinks cups. Meredith stood to help her, and the two women retired to the kitchen.

Alex shrugged at his girlfriend. "What do you reckon? Walk along the bottom of the gorge tomorrow morning – see where they found Harry?"

"Yeah, I'm up for it. Just got to ask Daddykins here if he'll drop us off?" Hazel prodded her father's arm. "Dad, can we go along the gorge tomorrow?"

Just then the two women came back in from the kitchen, Meredith shaking her head. "Sorry, Hazel, not tomorrow. Martina is taking us to the Blaise Castle House Museum, and then Lucy's coming home. Martina's picking her up at 5.30. Then, on Friday we're visiting Uncle Toby again, remember?"

"Oh, Mum!" Hazel dropped her shoulders in protest. "What's so special about this museum? I thought we were here to solve this ghost story."

"Well, yes, we are, but this is my holiday too, and I haven't spent much time with Martina really. So, if you don't mind, we are all going to the museum tomorrow, then you can meet Lucy and have a good cousinly catch-up. You'll even get a lie in tomorrow morning. The museum's not open till 11."

"Well, how about me and Alex go before that then? Like, 8 o'clock? We could walk it."

"What, from here? How long will that take? I don't suppose you'll be back in time."

Alex shrugged. "It doesn't matter really. I mean, I think we've got everything we need anyway. I don't think we'll learn much from going along there." He exchanged glances with Hazel. "Anyway, I'm pretty tired. I might go to bed now, my head's spinning."

Half an hour later, after a quick shower to wash off the day's grime, Alex sat down at the little desk in his bedroom. Hazel had just texted to say she was coming to chat and talk about tomorrow. He opened the lined pad of paper they'd bought yesterday, tore off the top sheet which had their notes on the crash on it, and wrote the word 'Timeline' in capital letters on the next sheet, then underlined it carefully.

There was a discreet knock, and then he heard his girlfriend climbing the stairs. She bowed her head to avoid the low beam, grabbed a small stool and plonked herself down next to him. "What's you doing?" she asked, resting her chin on his shoulder.

"I've started a new timeline. Here, why don't you do it, and I'll list the people involved." He tore off the top sheet and handed it to her, along with his pen, then took a pencil from the pot on the desk, and

145

wrote '<u>People</u>' on the next page.

For the next hour or so, the two teenagers worked on a timeline of every event from the race in 1937 to the last known sighting of the ghost. Hazel wrote down every key event in the story, and every time a name came up, Alex would write it down on his list, and if it was a person of interest he would underline it. After they'd finished, Alex took a deep breath.

"I still really want to go along that towpath, just to see where Harry Levenson was found."

"How about we go walking really early tomorrow?" suggested Hazel. "It's only about two miles to Clifton bridge, and another two miles along the towpath. We could be there and back in two and a half hours if we walk fast, which you always do!"

They agreed to meet in the kitchen at half past seven. "We ought to leave a note though, saying we've gone for a short walk and won't be long" Alex said "otherwise it's a bit rude, isn't it?"

"No, because my mum will probably kill me. We should just go…"

"…and she'll kill you anyway." Alex paused. Maybe we'd better not go after all. It's not fair on your parents, and if anything happened to us, they'd have to face my folk, and anyway…"

"Wuss. I knew you'd wimp out of it. No wonder you're such a loser."

"Eh?" Alex flushed with anger. "I don't want to get into trouble, that's all. And I don't want you to get into trouble either."

"Hazel! Are you up there?" Meredith's voice carried up from the bottom of the attic stairs.

"Hi, Mum. We're just making some notes." Then, quietly to Alex. "Downstairs, tomorrow morning,

7.30, okay?"

Alex nodded, as Meredith started up the stairs.

"I thought you'd gone to bed, you two! Hazel, you shouldn't be in here." She reached the top of the stairs and beckoned angrily. "Come on… bed!"

"We've nearly finished, Mum. We've done a timeline. Look…" Hazel held up several sheets of handwritten notes as her mother came over and stood beside them. "And Alex is making a note of all the names we need to research. That's all."

Alex held up another couple of sheets. Meredith took them from Alex, and looked at the list.

"I've underlined anyone I think needs investigating. I'm very keen to know more about Mrs Christine Cantin… and also Reginald Simmons, the mechanic who was in the RAC report. If they staged the crash, maybe he was in on the plan."

"Right, well, you can continue this tomorrow. I'm sorry, Alex, but it's not really very appropriate for Hazel to be in here at this time of night."

"What are you on about, Mum? We're trying to sort through all this stuff and make sense of it?"

"Maybe, but it's late, and you're both in your PJs. Now go back to your room and go to sleep."

"I get it, Mum." Hazel got up and made for the stairs. "It's nice to know you don't trust me. Night, Alex, see you tomorrow."

As Hazel flounced off down the narrow stairs, Alex looked down at the desk. "Sorry, Meri. I'd never… I mean… it won't happen again."

"No, Alex. It won't." Meredith Burns said firmly as she plonked the papers back down on the desk, turned, and followed her daughter down the stairs.

21

"Here. This is the spot. This is right below The Ledge." Alex slipped his phone back in his pocket, and looked up the almost sheer slope.

The two teenagers had crept fairly discreetly downstairs at half past seven, only to find Andy and Martina sitting at the breakfast table. They quickly ate a bowl of cereal each and explained they were just going for a short walk, and would be back before ten, and Martina had innocently recommended several nice walks around the area. Thanking her for her advice, and pointing out how they were spoilt for choice now, Alex and Hazel pretended to be trying to decide which way to go when they left, but as soon as the door was shut behind them they turned right and headed purposefully towards Clifton.

"We're doing well today, aren't we?" Hazel commented. "First my Mum thinks we were up to something inappropriate in your room last night, and now we're 'going for a short walk' along the towpath, sort of against her wishes."

"Yup. What do you reckon? Bread and water for the rest of the week?"

"Rest of the year more likely. Oh well. Still, it's worth it... this. The view from the bridge. Look how high up we are. Glad I'm not scared of heights."

They stopped halfway across the suspension bridge, and looked down.

"Apparently" Alex observed presently, "Brunel

148

was the first person to cross here, hanging in a basket under an iron bar a thousand feet long... and it got stuck... so he had to shin up the ropes to free the pulley. Dangling up here, over the gorge. He must have been mad!"

"Crikey! I mean... we'd never do anything so daft now, would we?" Hazel grinned, and they set off again, hand in hand.

After crossing the bridge, they turned right into Leigh Woods and followed the signs to the towpath below, turning left at the bottom to head in the direction of Abbots Park, alongside the railway line.

"What was your Mum talking about the other day, about a body in the woods?"

"Oh, yeah... I dunno, I only heard what you did. It was in the 1950s though" Hazel said, "so nothing to do with our ghostie."

"True. Anyway, I'll get my Dad to look it up when we get home."

It took them just over an hour to reach the point which they'd identified as the most likely place for Harry's body to have been found. The railway had disappeared into a tunnel about fifty yards back, and the path was exceedingly narrow. Further on, about a quarter of a mile away, they saw the remnants of an old private harbour. Looking up, they saw the familiar outline of the trees at the top of the gorge.

"He must have been found about here, then." said Alex. "But there's a really big ledge up there... so the car must have really hit him hard to make him come flying out over the ledge."

"I wonder if we can climb up any of this." Hazel said, checking the almost sheer rock-face. "Maybe if we go along a bit."

They ventured a few yards further on. There was no sign of any possible path up the side of the gorge.

"Maybe, if we go back that way and climb up by the railway line..." Alex jogged back level with the tunnel entrance, and called out, "There's a sort of foot crossing here, but I think it's for the railway workers. It's all fenced in."

There was no reply from Hazel. He pursed his lips, shrugged, and scrambled up a short but steep rock-face, finding himself on a level with the railway line, right at the edge of the ballast. A fence bolted into the rock-face prevented him from walking onto the line, but he found a small path through the rocks to the right, which seemed to climb very steeply and then disappeared across the top of the tunnel. All he could see beyond that was a sheer rock-face.

He made his way to the foot of the steep climb. He couldn't work out whether it was man-made or not. It certainly didn't look very used. 'I expect it's just kids like me who clamber about up here' he thought to himself, as he carefully began to climb, checking each hand and foothold before pulling himself up higher. After a short while the climbing got easier, but he got a big shock when he turned around after a few minutes, for not only had he climbed up considerably further than he'd thought, but he could not see the foot of the gorge at all. He began to think he would not be able to retrace his steps; it looked very treacherous. He shivered slightly at the thought that he'd just climbed that way. Looking up, he saw he was not very far from the top. In fact, he thought he recognised the piece of slope which had the tunnel in it that Meredith had stumbled across a couple of days previously. He thought he should climb a bit more and find a safe resting place.

After a few more metres of climbing, he reached a small ledge which seemed to be on the top of the sheer rock-face where they'd stopped before.

His phone buzzed. 'Oh crikey – Hazel!' he thought. Sure enough, his girlfriend had texted *'Where r u?'* some five minutes ago. *'Nearly at top'* he typed, and was about to press send when a hand grabbed his shoulder.

"Beat cha to it!" Hazel's voice made him jump out of his skin.

"How the heck did you manage that?" he said.

"I found a path which went around this bit of rock-face. It's quite a climb. It'll be hard to go down."

"Same here. This side was almost a sheer climb, by the railway tunnel entrance." Alex realised he was quite exhausted from his exertions. "Looking at this bit, this must be about where the car ended up. I still reckon that Cantin should have landed around here. I mean, to go out over that sheer rock-face, he must have really been catapulted out from the car... it doesn't seem possible, does it?"

Hazel turned and went back along the path. "If you come back here, you'll see exactly where we are." She beckoned him, and pointed up to her right. There, as he'd suspected, was the old tunnel. They scrambled up another steep bit of pathway, and then reached more familiar ground.

"Come on... show me this tunnel" she said, and they clambered up onto the rocky ledge, and stood in front of the tunnel entrance.

"That's all there is to see, I'm afraid "said Alex, shining his phone torch past the grill into the dark.

"It obviously belongs to someone, because there's a padlock on the gate."

"So there is." Hazel grabbed the padlock, and pulled it a couple of times. "It's a combination padlock. Shouldn't be hard to crack."

"What?!" Alex watched as Hazel looked at the lock and started to slowly turn the numbers, one at a time. "You're not telling me you know how to pick padlocks, are you?"

"Shhh!" Hazel concentrated for a few seconds, then smiled as there was a very slight 'click'. "One down, three to go… Shine the torch this way."

Alex watched, impressed, as Hazel rotated the next number on the barrel. She fiddled about a bit, then went to the third number. Again, a little 'click'. Finally, after another minute or so she pressed the base of the padlock and it snapped open.

"How did you know how to do that?"

"Remember I used to do rowing, a few years back? We had lockers there and people were always forgetting their combination codes. Me and Bethany Walters worked out how to do it. Also, most people don't rotate the numbers very far… and once you've got the first three, the fourth one is a matter of trial and error."

By now, they had removed the padlock and swung the grill out just far enough to slip through into the dark. "What was the code anyway?" Alex asked, as they slipped the padlock back on to make it look unopened.

"One nine five four" said Hazel. "Or, 1954. Wonder who's birth year that was?"

They started to make their way into the tunnel. The ground was firm beneath their feet. Shining their phone torches down, they saw the floor was initially made of concrete, but then after a few metres, it was the same brickwork as the sides and roof of the tunnel. They made their way along to where the tunnel curved slightly to the right.

"Didn't your Dad say this was Victorian or something?" Alex asked "Probably to do with the railway workers."

"I don't know – I wasn't there, remember. But it seems to go on for ever." Hazel held her torch up. The beam did not project very far.

"Hang on, I'll take a flash photo."

Alex set his phone camera to flash, and took a photo. The double flash blinded the two teenagers for a few seconds, before Alex was able to look at the picture he'd just taken.

"Nothing!" he said, "apart from black blackness, with a bit of black…"

Hazel interrupted him. "What's that… down there, in the bottom of the picture?"

They peered again, and Alex zoomed in. "It looks like a wooden box or something. It's only about 20 metres away. Let's find it."

As they walked on slowly, Hazel grabbed his arm and shivered.

"Urgh. It's getting cold."

"You scared?"

"No!" She didn't sound very convincing. "Not really. Wait, there's the box."

By the light of their two phone torches, they could make out a long wooden crate, with metal hinges and the letters FG stencilled on the side. Alex lifted the lid, which opened stiffly but almost silently. The crate was empty. He let the lid go, and it slammed down with a loud thump, which echoed along the tunnel in both directions.

"Shhh!" said Hazel.

"Why? No one's going to hear us." Alex slipped his phone into his jacket pocket and cupped his hands to his mouth. "HALLOOOOOO!" he called. The sound echoed once again.

"You see, no-one. I really don't think this leads anywhere. We'll probably come to a brick wall soon, judging by the way that echo came back." Alex took his phone out again. "Come on, let's see how far it does go."

They trudged on silently for another few minutes, alternating their phone torches to save battery power.

"Have you noticed something?" said Hazel "We're going uphill now?"

"Oh yeah. If it was part of the railway, surely it would be going downhill, wouldn't it?"

"Yep. Anyway, shouldn't we be getting back? My 'rents will go spare if they find out where we are."

"Shhh!" Alex stopped suddenly. "Listen!" he whispered. "What the heck is that?"

They could hear a low throbbing sound, like a distant generator. Alex stepped back, and the noise stopped. "That's weird" he said, "you can't hear it until you stand right... here." He moved forward again, and the throbbing noise resumed.

"Look at that, those lights... on the wall" said Hazel, shining her torch upwards. "They start right here, and go on into the tunnel."

"Yes... and those are modern type bulbs. It's like they light the London Underground tunnels with."

"I thought the Underground tunnels were dark."

"They are, except at night. That's when they do all their track maintenance."

"Oh, right. Hey, we'd really better get back" said Hazel. "Look at the time. It's nearly 9.30! We'll be late for that museum thing."

"Ah, no way, Haze. We can't come all this way without seeing what's at the other end. Come on!" Alex grabbed his girlfriend's arm and walked firmly on towards the source of the sound.

The tunnel began to slope upwards even more, until the two teenagers could feel their calves straining as they walked on. After another few minutes, the slope began to ease, and then suddenly it was level, and a large concrete wall signalled the end of the tunnel. As they approached it, they noticed an opening to the left, which had a barred metal gate across it. This gate, too, was locked, but with a conventional padlock.

"I'm sort of glad it wasn't a combination like the other one" Alex said, on inspecting it. "Because, you know, I would have felt obliged to keep exploring."

"Yup. Hashtag Me Too!"

They peered through the bars of the gate.

"There's something up there... I can see a sort of dim glowing light." Alex took another flash photo. Suddenly, they heard the distant sound of an engine starting and being revved up, as if in response to the camera flash.

"That sounds like one of those quads!" said Hazel. "That means... we must be underneath the Manor garage or something."

As she spoke, lights began to reflect off the walls beyond the gate, and the engine sound grew louder.

"Oh crikey, you're right. We'd better get out of

here quickly!"

They ran as fast as they could back down the tunnel. The lights, and engine, got closer until they reached the barred gate. There was a screech of tyres, a revving of the engine again, and then the vehicle, sounded as if it was turning around and going away again. But the choking smell of exhaust gas confirmed their fears, and gave them an added incentive to reach fresh air as soon as possible.

It was only now that they realised just how far they'd walked along the tunnel. Running back, once again using their phone torches, seemed to take forever. The tunnel levelled off, but still seemed to go on and on. Alex was beginning to wonder if they'd accidentally turned into a different tunnel and were doomed to run forever.

"Wait, there's that old box" puffed Hazel. "We're nearly there. Oh no! Quick. They're coming back!"

The distant engine sound echoed along the tunnel. There was no doubt about it. They were being chased; whoever it was had obviously gone to get the gate keys, and then returned to chase them.

"Grab the end!" Alex shouted, and between them, they dragged the crate sideways so as to partly block the tunnel. "Haze - those letters – FG. Forster Group. Now, we'd better run for it!"

They could hear the engine rev up, and then start to accelerate down the tunnel towards them. Running for all they were worth, Alex and Hazel came to the bend near the tunnel entrance, and could finally see daylight again. Lights flashed off the tunnel walls behind them as they squeezed through the grill and slammed it shut again. They heard a screech of brakes, then the engine revved up again.

Whoever was on the quad had managed to avoid the crate across the tunnel, but at least they'd been held up for a few precious seconds.

"Quick, you run!" shouted Alex. "I'll sort the padlock out." He spun the barrel frantically and clicked the padlock shut, diving away from the gate just as the lights reached the bend in the tunnel. Dropping down to join Hazel on the path, he pointed along to the pathway they'd trodden on Tuesday, and they began to run up towards the top of the gorge. There was another screech of tyres as whoever was following them stopped at the locked gate, then, as the path took them across the top of the old tunnel, they heard the engine revving up, and then disappearing back down the tunnel.

Ten minutes later, they were resting in the woods, beside The Leap. Hazel phoned her mother to say they'd just forgotten the time and were now in Leigh Woods. Meredith gave her an earful, and told them to be at the car park in ten minutes.

"Wait, listen, there's another quad approaching!" said Alex. "Look, over there."

Through the trees they could see one of the quads approaching at high speed, on the old race circuit. It pulled up at the private gate, and Michael got off. He pointed at the two of them and shouted.

"You two! Come here!"

Alex looked at Hazel and called out "What, us?!"

"Yes! You two! Come over here, now!"

"Why?!" Alex called out.

"You know why! You were down in the tunnel!"

"What tunnel? We've just been up here, walking in the woods!" Alex called out, then quietly to Hazel "Come on. Let's get out of here."

"Come over here right now!"

Hazel called out "We're going home, sorry, we can't come over, my Mum's here!" and started walking away towards the narrower path. Alex followed her, and the pair of them walked purposefully away from their angry pursuer.

"Alex… look! He's following us!"

Looking back, they saw Michael climbing over the gate, his clumsy Wellington boots catching in the rungs. He stumbled slightly as he landed.

"Run! Come on…!"

The young friends ran as fast as they could along the path, taking the shortest route back to the carpark and passing several children and dogwalkers on their way. Suddenly, Hazel stopped beside a middle-aged couple walking two large labradors.

"Excuse me…" she said breathlessly, "there's a man chasing us… we're going back to my mum's car but if you see him following us, try and stop him."

"Why…?" the man asked.

"He's a weirdo!" shouted Hazel, starting off again, pulling Alex by the hand. When they reached the car park, it was Martina they saw.

"Quick, Tina! Sorry! We're being followed by a man!" Hazel dived into Tina's Volvo, and Alex followed suit, pulling the door shut behind them.

Martina was about to question them when she saw the look of terror on their flushed faces, and slammed the door shut.

"Right, let's go, children" she said pointedly. "And once we're out of here you can start thinking of what you're going to say to your parents, Hazel. Your Mum is absolutely livid…"

22

"I thought I told you not to go out!" Meredith Burns was standing in the hallway, shaking with anger, as they came through the front door.

"No, you didn't actually tell us not to go." Hazel screamed back. "You said it wasn't a good idea…"

"Because you would be late back! And guess what?! Look at the time!"

"Ah, that was my fault…" Alex piped up as they made their way into the living room, where Geoff Burns sat patiently on the sofa, coffee mug in hand.

"I don't doubt it, Alex Phipps! You're as bad as she is!" Meredith pointed a finger at him angrily. "Just remember, we invited you here as our guest. I expect you to treat us with the same respect you'd give your own parents, and not… lead my daughter into these stupid… escapades."

"I'm really sorry, Meri…" Alex began.

"Mum. Mum! Listen! We were chased by that Michael guy, from the Manor House, right? On his quad bike. We only just managed to escape. That's why we took so long…"

"What?! The Manor House?! I thought you were going to go along the towpath?"

"We DID go along the towpath. We found where the boy's body probably landed…"

"…then we climbed up to see how the driver could have possibly been thrown down into the river." Alex interrupted, determined to try and rescue Hazel from her mother's wrath. He carried on and explained about the tunnel, and their narrow escape from capture.

After he'd finished, Geoff Burns sat back in his chair and put his hands behind his head. "Hmmm. Secret tunnels all the way to underneath the Manor House eh? I must say, this is beginning to sound like one of Enid Blyton's Famous Five adventures."

"Except we're not five. We're the Terrible Two." said Alex lightly, immediately wishing he hadn't.

"That is not the slightest bit funny, Alex." Meredith snapped. "Thanks to you two, we're going to be late visiting the Blaise Castle Museum. But we ARE visiting it, and you two are staying with me all the way around, and when we get back tonight you are both grounded. Your cousin Lucy's coming home tonight, Hazel. You can spend some time with her, and if there's any more trouble from either of you, we'll simply go straight back home. Oh, and you will both stay in your own rooms tonight too."

"Hey, look at this" Alex called out, sitting in front of the remaining papers from the Manor. "I've found this cutting. It was out of order... in with the general correspondence. It's about Cantin's funeral..." He passed the paper across the dining room table to Geoff and Andy, who were chatting about the shipping firm which Andy worked for.

Martina and Meredith busied themselves clearing the table, pointedly working around the men, and ignoring Alex, who decided to carry on as if he hadn't received a massive telling-off earlier on.

Hazel and Lucy had gone to their room straight after tea. Alex had sent Hazel a couple of texts but she hadn't replied. He imagined the girly banter that was taking place, and was happy to be downstairs even if he was a little out of favour with Meredith.

Alex pointed to the cutting he'd handed to Geoff. "There's quite a few names on there we haven't seen before. Plenty to get our teeth into when I get home. I'll get my Nana to search for each one."

The two men scanned the cutting.

"Where's this?" Andy asked

"Langley. But I don't know where that is."

"I know" said Geoff. "It's in Berkshire, off the M4 near Slough, twenty miles outside of London. Interesting. I wonder why he's buried in Langley?"

Extract: Uxbridge & West Drayton Gazette,
Friday 25th March 1938

LANGLEY

The funeral of Pierre Cantin, the French racing motorist, took place at St. Mary's Church on Wednesday last. Mr Cantin was killed following an accident at a motor race at Abbots Park last October. His body was recovered almost three months later from the River Severn. The chief mourners were Mrs C. Cantin (wife), Mr André Cantin (brother), Mr & Mrs Reginald Simmons, Mr. M. Fepp (cousin), Mr P. Vendome, Mr & Mrs Andrew Forster, Mr. Etienne Boulet, Mr A.D. Prosser, Mr K. Forbes-Hunter, Mr H. Selkirk and many members of the automobile racing community. The Rev. E. S. Archer officiated. The wake was held at the Red Lion afterwards.

23

Arthur Prosser removed his coat, and sat in the fifth row, in the pew by the aisle, beside someone he recognised as one of the leading motoring journalists of the day. Normally, he'd have been happy to talk to this chap, but today he felt decidedly unsure of himself, and outside of his comfort zone.

Arthur had been a motor racing enthusiast ever since he'd been taken by his uncle to see a race at Brooklands in early 1921. As always, motor racing seemed to be the preserve of the rich or very rich, but Arthur had harboured a secret desire to get involved somehow or other, and when the Abbots Park circuit had asked for volunteers to marshal their races, he'd applied eagerly. The work was unpaid, of course, but the organiser's expenses paid for his return fare from Reading, and all the marshals were generally well looked after. A meal allowance was given, and generous amounts of drinks, of the non-alcoholic sort, were made available at each marshalling post. He'd been marshalling for the last three years, but this was the first time he'd seen a fatality first-hand, and he felt he ought to pay his respects to the driver and his family.

Arthur's boss at the yard had granted him a full day's leave, and Mr Carpenter, his boss's boss, a motor racing enthusiast himself, had sought him out especially and given him a free railway pass to Langley and back, for which he was extremely

162

grateful. His wife had seen him off early that morning, having arranged to have his best suit cleaned and prepared specially. He felt very smart, but at the same time, very uncomfortable. Having taken his hat and coat off in the church, he now felt quite cold, but was too afraid to make a fuss and put it back on again. The gentleman on his right, across the aisle, was still wearing his thick longcoat. Arthur shuffled about a bit, trying to cover his legs, and then his hat fell onto the stone floor between the pews.

"Excuse me… so sorry…" he gasped to the journalist, as he reached down awkwardly to retrieve his errant headgear.

"No bother, young man. I say, are you a relative or a friend?" The journalist spoke quietly, only just audible above the low murmuring chattering of the rest of the congregation.

"Neither, actually. My name's Prosser. Arthur Prosser. I was the flag marshal at the race track when he… erm… when he went off."

"Oh gosh, that must have been a bit of a rum do for you. Did you see it all happen then?"

"Well, I didn't see too much really, but I saw him go off the edge of the circuit, yes. Went down to help rescue the driver, but all we found was the young lad who survived."

"Quite. Ghastly accident. Poor lads; you can't blame them for wanting a good view, but… Paid the price and all that, poor little beggars. Ronald Preece, by the way. Motor Sport magazine."

"Yes… I know. Pleased to meet you, Mr Preece."

"Oops, we're starting. Let's have a chat when this is all finished, eh?"

"Erm… yes, right." Arthur stuttered, wondering

163

if he should really be talking to this man, who was, after all, a journalist. 'You never know how they might twist your words' he thought.

"Here goes. Heads bowed and all that..."

Forty-five minutes later, the congregation made their way slowly out of the church, onto the path that led around the around the side, to the freshly-dug grave on the far side of the churchyard. The wind, though fairly light, was bitingly cold. Arthur stood beside a large tree which kept the worst of the wind off him. He was little further back from the main crowd, but as he reasoned, he didn't really know anybody anyway. He could still hear enough of the vicar's recitations to say 'Amen' in the right place, and he was relieved that the final committal did not take as long as the church service had done.

After the coffin had been lowered into the grave, everyone began to make their way back towards the church entrance. He felt a tap on his shoulder, and turned to find Ronald Preece alongside him.

"Mind answering me one question, off the record, of course." Preece lit a cigarette, and then offered another to Arthur, who declined it.

"No, that's fine. Ask away."

"Between you and me, did you think that Cantin crashed the car deliberately?"

"No, I don't think so. I mean... it hadn't occurred to me. I remember he wasn't going very fast, but I just thought he was trying to pull over because he couldn't see, what with all that smoke. Maybe he just misjudged the edge of the track. Why do you ask?"

Preece took a long drag on his cigarette. "Well... it turns out he was on the run from the French police.

164

There was a warrant out for his arrest on charges of fraud and embezzlement, from Vendolet Tyres. His disappearance came at a very convenient time."

"Crikey… from Vendolet? But… didn't they put up the money for the race?"

"Yes. Which is what makes me think the fraud and embezzlement is a cover for something else. There's more to this than meets the eye. My contact in France says the French police weren't telling the British police the whole story. I wonder even if we've buried the right man today." Preece took another drag from his cigarette and looked straight at Arthur, watching for a reaction. Arthur frowned as the import of what Preece had just implied sunk in.

"Anyway, thanks for your time. Let's keep this to ourselves, eh? I didn't tell you any of that, and I promise nothing you told me will find its way into print." With that, Ronald Preece moved away. Arthur blew out his cheeks in astonishment as he watched Preece approach one of the drivers of the moment, Philip Westwood, and engage him in animated conversation.

Aware that he was now near the front of the train of mourners, he stood aside to let a few people past. Suddenly, he caught the eye of a man standing a few yards away, across the path. The man beckoned him over, and he recognised the Clerk of the Course, Forbes-Hunter, who he'd last seen when they were preparing the accident report. He was standing not far from the churchyard entrance, chatting animatedly to a man with a splendid military-style moustache. They evidently knew each other well.

"Hallo, young man. Arthur Prosser isn't it? Jolly good of you to come down. I say, did you come of your own volition or were you asked?"

"It was my own idea, actually, Sir. I felt I should pay my proper respects."

"Good man, good man. Oh, I say, allow me to introduce you two. This gentleman here is Harry Selkirk, the RAC scrutineer. He checked over the wreck after the crash."

Arthur shook hands with the scrutineer. He had heard of him as a man some mechanics feared, and most team managers treated with a hefty dose of distrust.

"Oh. That must have been a bit grim for you?" said Arthur. "How badly damaged was it?"

"Actually, not too much considering where it had been. The front was a bit done in, but I think they're repairing it for this season. Not that I think they'll put it in for any more big races."

"Oh, so… who owns it then?"

"The Forster family. They are the tyre importers who sponsored the Gold Trophy race. They own Abbots Park as well, hence the tie in. Well… it costs money to put these races on, so we need people like the Forsters to keep funding them."

They looked towards the church, where the close family were talking to the vicar.

"Yes, it's a sad day" Selkirk continued, "but at least they've got a body to bury." He nodded his head towards the family mourners. "I say, Ken, she looks far too young to be a widow. Still, I expect some other dashing young daredevil will swoop down and… erm…" He stopped, as the young widow made her way towards them. She kept her veil over her face as she spoke to them in halting, heavily-accented English.

166

"Sank you all so much for coming. Pierre would 'ave been pleased to 'ave zis many... erm... of peoples... you know... to come to him... now." She nodded as she spoke. It always amused Arthur that foreigners sometimes sounded as if they were putting on fake comedy accents when they were struggling to make themselves understood.

Kenneth Forbes-Hunter clasped her outstretched hand and nodded to her. "I'm so sorry, Madam. We felt we must be here to pay our respects. We were... the officials at the circuit."

"Ah, I see. Yes... sank you. Well, I must speak with ze others." She nodded briefly at each of them and moved away somewhat abruptly.

"You see, that's what officialdom does for us, Arthur" said Selkirk with a huge grin. "We frighten them off. It's only natural. They believe we think they're cheating all the time, and most of the time they probably *are* cheating, so we're to be viewed with deep suspicion. Even a flag marshal like you, Arthur. Them and us, old chap. Them and us. Right, let's go and have a jar across the road. Are you coming, young man?"

Arthur was unsure. "Well, I don't think I've been invited. My wife's expecting me back this afternoon."

"Yes you have" said the scrutineer cheerily. "We all have; you heard the vicar say so, on behalf of the family. And anyway, the first round is on the Cantins, and the second one is on me, so come in and partake, and don't worry about the little woman at home. I'm sure she'll understand."

The Red Lion was conveniently situated right across the road from the churchyard. Arthur followed the two senior officials into the bar and

167

ordered a pint for himself. Selkirk found a corner table with a good view of the bar, and the three of them sat down. Selkirk took out a pipe and lit it, puffing rather sweet-smelling smoke across the table. Forbes-Hunter watched him with amusement, then got out a cigar and lit it with some panache. Arthur was not a smoker himself, but was not in the slightest bit put out by others smoking around him.

He looked towards the bar, and recognised several well-known faces; some stars from the twenties, and a few from the contemporary top-line racing fraternity. He knew some of them were tee-total, but he was surprised that most of them seemed quite happy to sink more than a couple of pints in quick succession. He also thought that there was perhaps a little too much laughter for a funeral, but then, it was quite a while since the accident. Perhaps the shock had worn off somewhat.

"So, Arthur. Tell me. What do you think of his family, eh?" Kenneth Forbes-Hunter pointed to Mrs Cantin, sitting with a group of men in the opposite corner of the bar. "Anything strike you as a bit odd?"

"In what way?" Arthur was feeling very uneasy about someone he'd noticed, but was far too shy to mention it."

"That pretty wife of his... now she's got the veil off, you don't see much evidence of grief, do you? And I swear she's been making eyes at his brother ever since they came out of the church."

Selkirk nodded. "Ye-e-e-s, I saw that too" he drawled before taking another sip from his pint.

"Well..." Arthur hesitated. "If you ask me, that brother of hers actually looks like someone else I've met, but I can't quite place him."

"Oh well, it's obvious, young man. That's because he's the spitting image of his late older brother... but then, he would be, wouldn't he? That's André Cantin, by the way. He's a racer too, but in France. Never raced here, as far as I know."

"André Cantin?" said Arthur. "Hang on, I thought he was killed at the Nurburgring last year. Or maybe that was a different driver."

"Well, he's doing a damned good impression of being alive now, what?" chuckled Selkirk.

"I suppose so" said Arthur, "But I never saw Cantin except when he was racing past me. I mean, I've never seen his face but... there's another chap there who looks similar too. That one there, the one with slightly red hair. Did Cantin have more than one brother?"

"He might well have done, but no, that's a cousin of his, Matthias Fepp." Forbes-Hunter explained. "You see, they're all tied up with Vendolet Tyres. The cousin... Fepp... he's a Director of Vendolet France. Then there's Andrew Forster there... he's no relation, but he's their British importer, and he also owns Abbots Park. I think Cantin himself was a co-Director of the company as well. I'm not really sure. And that chappie there is Philippe Vendôme. He's the 'Vendo' in Vendolet. His father Marcel was the founder, and there's an old man around here somewhere, Charles Boulet, who was the co-founder. He's the 'Let' in the name. they're pretty much all here, in fact. We really should ask for a year's free tyres, what?"

Arthur was impressed. "How do you know so many of these people?"

"Because, my dear fellow, I deal with them day

in, day out, at these race meetings. Sometimes they're on my side, sometimes they're not. They're usually after some small favour or other on the day, but then, when you need them to cough up for another race meeting, they're only too pleased to throw their money around. And they like to be treated royally. I try to do my best."

"And I try to do my worst" grinned Selkirk. "Guaranteed way to puncture any pompous know-it-all team owner… frown and say 'What's this then', point to something innocuous under the bonnet, and watch 'em try and second guess what you've found."

"He's a wicked bugger, this one. Crossed him myself once or twice, when I used to race."

"I saved your life more than once, old boy. Some of those piles of junk you presented to me wouldn't have got round the first bend without collapsing."

The two older men carried on cheerfully teasing one another, and reminiscing about their past escapades. Arthur, meantime, found himself staring more and more at Pierre-Henri Cantin's brother. 'I know that I know him' thought Arthur. 'It isn't because he's related to Cantin, because I never knew Cantin'. It troubled him. Suddenly, he was aware that his stares were being reciprocated. He was about to look away when André Cantin gestured to him discreetly to go outside.

Arthur nodded. Cantin replied by holding up two fingers and mouthing what looked like "two minutes" to him. Arthur nodded again, and then gulped down the rest of his pint, grabbed his hat, and excused himself from the table. "Just off outside to get some fresh air."

24

Arthur waited furtively just outside the front door of the Red Lion, smiling weakly at various customers as they passed him for the door. He glanced over towards the graveyard. He thought, before he left today, that he should go back to the graveside for one last time. Presently, the pub door swung open, and André Cantin barged out, grabbing him roughly by the arm.

"Zis way, queeckly, before anyone notice us" he said with a strong French accent. He led Arthur across the road and back through the gates of the churchyard. "Okay, now walk normally. We go to the graveside. I must speak wiz you."

They walked hurriedly back around the side of the church, towards the freshly filled grave.

"You are working undercover?" asked Cantin.

"No? Are you?" Arthur's heart was thumping with excitement, but, oddly enough, not fear. Even as they walked towards the graveside, he thought to himself 'I have no idea what's happening here, but I'm excited and fascinated, and not a bit scared'.

"How did you guess?" came the reply, the accent suddenly much more English and less pronounced than before. "I don't know how I've got away with it so far, but no-one from Vendolet has realised that I'm not André Cantin. Not even his wife, not that she'd know. The real André never went to their wedding – bit of a family rift there, old chap. No, I'm actually working for… well, I can't tell you who. But let's just say it's a branch of the intelligence services and leave it at that, eh?"

"Oh, right." Arthur had vaguely heard of the intelligence services, but thought that they were all foreign spies working undercover in Europe.

"Now, old chap. I've seen you somewhere before, but I'm not sure where. Were you at the race?"

"Yes. I was the flag marshal. I saw the car go off the track."

"Ah, yes, good. Okay. So, how involved are you with the race organisers?"

"Well, I'm not. I mean, I'm a very low link in the chain of command at the circuit. I just turn up, watch the races and wave the flags whenever I'm needed."

"Quite, quite. So who are those two chaps you were drinking with, eh?"

"Oh, well, one of them was the Clerk of the Course. I only met him on the day of the crash. The other one I didn't know at all until today. He's the RAC man who scrut…"

"Quite, quite. Now, you see, let me tell you something you probably didn't realise. Your two drinking friends are in collusion with Philippe Vendôme to undermine the rest of the Board of Vendolet Tyres. Look… this is far too complicated to explain easily, but let's just say we are closing in on them. We didn't think they'd have the nerve to show up today of all days, but the fact that they did means that something is up."

"Oh, right." Arthur nodded, but his mind was somewhat confused by this sudden rush of information.

"I noticed them… cosying up to you. Now, your life might be in danger here…"

"Oh surely not!" Arthur chuckled and looked up

at André Cantin. Then he finally recognised him. "Oh, it's you! Of course! I knew I'd seen you before."

"Yes, it's me. So, now, listen… how did you get here today. Did they bring you?"

"No, I came down by train from Reading."

"Good, good. Now, are you planning to go back to Reading today?"

"Oh yes. I'm hoping to catch the 2.45 from Langley…"

"Good, good. Listen, do you have a railway timetable on you?"

Arthur nodded, and reached into his pocket.

"Right, now, see here…" the man calling himself Cantin unfolded the timetable and pointed, "what I need you to do is to let the other two know you're catching the 2.45, okay? Make sure they hear that and believe it. Have you got that?"

"Yes, okay. Then what?" Arthur wondered where this was heading.

"Then… do you have a wife at home?"

"Yes. She's expecting me back about 4.15."

"Right. Can you send her a message and tell her you're going to be about an hour late. Then, get on the 2.45 but get off at Maidenhead, and then wait an hour. See here, there's a train which leaves Maidenhead at 3.58. I need you to be on that train. Now, if you happen to see me on that train, don't react. Pretend you don't know me, alright? When the time's right I will come, and I will find you and tell you what to do next."

"Right. I'll be an hour later getting home then?"

"Yes, or maybe an hour and a half, if my plan works out. But remember what I said."

"I will" said Arthur. "Can we go back now? I'm

getting rather cold."

"Of course." Cantin took him by the arm again and led him back towards the churchyard gate. "Look, you go back in and tell your colleagues exactly what I told you to. Oh, and another thing. They might discreetly follow you onto the 2.45, but whatever you do, don't sit with them, okay? It's important. Ignore them, and if they call out to you, find a reason to move down the train. These really are life and death matters."

"Am I in a bit of danger then?" Arthur suddenly felt very uneasy.

"Yes, you probably are, just a little bit. But not if you do as I just asked. Then you'll be perfectly safe. My colleagues and I will be looking out for you on the train, right?"

"Your colleagues? So…what shall I tell my wife?"

"Just say you'll be leaving later as you're staying with a couple of guests and they've asked you for an extra drink, or something."

Arthur crossed the road and went straight back into the Red Lion. He was relieved to be back in the warm again. He went to the bar and asked if he could use the telephone. Putting some loose change on the counter, he rang home and gave his wife the message. Hanging up, he thanked the barman and looked towards the table where he'd been sitting, but there were two totally different people sitting there now; strangers who he had not seen at the funeral.

"Over here, young man. Hey, what can I get you?" Selkirk waved cheerily at him from further along the bar. "Pint of stout, wasn't it?"

"Erm… I wasn't going to have another actually"

"Too late, it's ordered…" he indicated another

pint to the barman. "What's the hurry. Train to catch, or did you drive here?"

"I have to catch the 2.45 back to Reading." said Arthur, pointedly.

"The 2.45, eh? Good for you. 2.45. Yes. Ah well. Plenty of time, look. It's only five past. Old Forbes-Hunter's had to shoot off back to London – important work he says. I reckon he's up to something, know what I mean?" He winked.

Arthur smiled weakly, noting how Selkirk's drawl seemed to be getting more pronounced. Either he was becoming drunk, or putting on a good act.

"Well, this has been an odd do, I must say." Selkirk continued. "The family have all disappeared. About five minutes after you went out, they all followed you. I thought they were off to get you or something."

"Oh, no… I didn't see them. I went back to the graveside. I just wanted to pay my last respects."

"Good man, good man. Yep, we're only here for a short time, so enjoy every day while you can. You never know if it'll be your last, what?"

A shiver went down Arthur's spine. His mind went into overdrive as he wondered what on earth the two race officials were really up to, and what their plans were for him.

"I say, you look very pale. Did you see a ghost in the churchyard or something? Old Pierre jump out of his coffin and say 'Hello?'" He took another large mouthful from his beer glass. "Mind, he'd be hard pushed to do that. They say one of his legs was missing. Gone walkabout I expect, ha ha!"

Arthur smiled thinly. "I think I'd better go, Mr Selkirk, but thank you very much for the drink."

175

"You've barely touched it, lad!" Harry Selkirk held out the glass and placed it in Arthur's hand. "Go on, down it in one. It'll keep the cold off you when you're waiting for that train. When did you say it was again?"

A voice in Arthur's head reminded him to 'make sure they think you'll be on the 2.45'. He told Selkirk the train time again.

"Better get going then, laddie. Listen, nice to chat with you; keep up the good work with that flag marshalling. We couldn't run these race meetings without you chaps. No-one really appreciates it, except we do. We really appreciate it. Go on, get on your train." Selkirk waved him away drunkenly.

Arthur arrived at the station with five minutes to spare. The brisk walk had sharpened his mind, and he was very alert to his surroundings. He was pleased to see several other people on the platform; complete strangers. When the 2.45 pulled in, a minute ahead of time, he found a carriage which had several people standing in the corridors, and got on at the busiest-looking door. 'Last on, first off' he thought, as the train pulled away.

They stopped at Slough, the next station along the line. Arthur peered nervously out of the window. One person got off, and several got on, but none of them looked suspicious to him. They rattled through Burham and Taplow stations, then slowed down for their scheduled stop at Maidenhead. Alighting as instructed, Arthur kept a watchful eye on the other passengers who left the train at the same time, but they all made their way out through the station building. Arthur picked up a Daily Mirror at the kiosk on the platform. Realising he was feeling a bit peckish, he made his way to the little tea shop. His wife had packed him a sandwich, which he ate whilst enjoying a refreshing cup of Great Western tea. Glancing at the front page, he saw the headline: "SOVIET SKY ARMY READY FOR HITLER." He smiled and thought 'if Hitler's aeroplanes are half as good as his racing cars, the Soviets will get a shock.'

"Mind if I sit here?" The voice came from a youngish man, who appeared to be not much older than Arthur himself.

"Not at all" Arthur replied, wondering if it was one of André Cantin's colleagues coming to keep an eye on him. The other man studied his paper without once glancing up. 'A true professional' thought Arthur, who became more and more engrossed in his own paper. He checked the time; 3.20. Still 38 minutes before his train left. He turned to the crossword page, and folded the paper so make it easier to write the answers.

'This looks easy' he thought. Arthur Prosser was very good at crosswords, especially the more cryptic ones, but still he was happy to pass the time lazily filling in these easier answers, without having to give it too much thought.

"Cad!" exclaimed the man sharing his table.

"Beg your pardon?" said Arthur, wondering who he was referring to.

"Oh, sorry, old man. Just doing this bally crossword. 36 down… Cad. It struck a chord with me, that's all. I've been dealing with one of those all day long. Oh, I see you're doing the same one. Great minds, eh?"

Arthur glanced back at his own crossword. He

had got as far as all of the across clues, but none of the down. He filled in CAD without thinking.

"What have you got for 37 across, old man? 'Strike out' is the clue. I haven't the faintest."

"Delete" said Arthur, slightly on his guard now.

"Ah yes, delete. Good idea. Actually, I'd rather like to delete the cad I've been dealing with today. I say, I wonder if this crossword's got any other advice for us, what?"

Arthur managed a weak smile. "I doubt it."

"Ah well. Maybe you haven't had such as bad a day as I have then." The man was clearly fishing for a conversation. "Mine's been pretty grim, I can tell you. Listen, if you ever decide to get married, don't do it, I say. Women. They're far too much trouble."

I am married, actually" said Arthur quietly. "And, I've just been to a funeral, so my day's not really been a bed of roses either."

"Oh, my dear fellow, I'm so sorry to hear that. How totally insensitive of me; I do this, you know. I don't think before I open my mouth. Was it… was it a close relative?"

"No, no. An acquaintance. I really only knew of them through my work. It was still a very sad occasion though."

"I expect it was. I'm so sorry. Jonathan Blake." He held out his hand.

"Arthur Prosser" said Arthur, shaking it weakly.

"You travelling far, Arthur?"

"Re… erm." He stopped and looked down. What if this was someone they'd planted to follow him? "I… can't really say, actually." Arthur stuttered. "It's a bit… private."

"Ah, Okay, I understand. Yes, quite. Well, I'm on

my way to Bristol on business, changing at Reading. Be glad to take my mind off other things, actually. I expect you're heading home eventually."

"Eventually, yes" said Arthur. "I have some personal matters to attend to first, in relation to today's funeral."

Jonathan Blake nodded, and picked up his paper again. "Look, sorry I interrupted you, Arthur. I'll get on with this crossword and leave you in peace."

"Thank you. It was alright, just the wrong day for a convivial chat, that's all."

The two men sat silently for the next 15 minutes, until the arrival of the 3.58 for Reading, when they stood up, said their goodbyes politely, and left the café. Arthur left a couple of shillings on the table as a tip, smiling and thanking the waitress as he left.

Two days later, Jonathan Blake remembered that he thought Arthur Prosser had seemed very distant and thoughtful, and clearly affected very deeply by the events of that day. He had tried to engage him in polite conversation, but noticed that Arthur had then got into a different carriage than he had, further down the platform. After another minor question from a juror, he was stood down by the Coroner, and thanked on behalf of Arthur Prosser's family.

25

Slumped in his favourite armchair, Meredith thought that Toby Allen looked much older than he had on Monday, when his eyes had sparkled as he related his ghost story. He had initially been pleased to see them again, and was keen to hear how they'd got on, but then something Alex had said about their visit to the old circuit and 'working out what really happened' had changed his mood and he began to withdraw from the lively chatter around him.

"Are you alright, Uncle?" asked Meredith. "Shall I get you another cuppa?"

"That would be nice, yes please, my dear."

"Hazel… you can do that, please." Meredith's request was clearly an order.

Hazel got up wordlessly, and took Toby's mug out to the kitchen.

"These two are not in my good books at the moment, Uncle. They got themselves into a bit of trouble yesterday, exploring on private property."

"Oh. Where was that then?"

Alex shuffled in his chair. "Oh, we found a tunnel in the side of the gorge, and went down it. It goes right under the old circuit, and ends up somewhere under the Manor House."

"Ah yes, well, of course, that's where old man Forster kept his collection of valuable cars. There's a huge underground space, a bit like a car park. He used to buy up anything of interest and then keep it hidden from view. Then, when the demand for

180

historic cars increased, he would put feelers out, create interest in a particular car, and then put it up for auction and make a killing."

"Oh, right. Well, we wondered what the point of the tunnel was. I mean, it's halfway up a cliff. There's no harbour…"

"That's where you're wrong, young man. There used to be a private harbour along there. Well, actually, several. The people who owned the Manor House before the Forsters used to import all sorts of goods from abroad. But the edge of the gorge has crumbled in places, so there's no longer anything left of the steps to the old harbour. In fact, I think the old harbour has washed away completely."

"Oh, right." Alex sat silently for a moment, recalling the ruined harbour they had noticed. "Oh, also, we got some papers copied from Charles Forster. He's got a library full of all the race details."

"Oh yes. I gather you've been to see him, Meredith. Rather you than me. Ghastly man."

"He was very nice to us actually. Took us out on his quad bikes, around the old circuit. Hazel drove one of them; I was too scared to drive it myself."

Alex took out the copy of a cutting, and passed it to the old man. "I think I owe you a big apology, Mr Allen. This is the details of Cantin's funeral…"

Toby Allen read the article slowly, nodding to himself, then pointing to the names.

"Well, well, well. Mr. and Mrs. Reginald Simmons. So he was involved as well." He paused, then muttered to himself. "Matthias Fepp…. They're all there, aren't they? These people…"

"And Cantin's brother André." Alex added, trying to work out where this was leading.

"So…Fepp knew the Cantin's did he?"

"Did you know Matthias Fepp then?"

"Oh yes. Well, I knew his younger sister very well. We were… it was some years on but we were… I was going to marry her. But she kept calling it off, then whenever I gave up, she came back to me."

He stared into the distance, apparently emotionless, both hands holding the cutting, his thumbs kneading the bottom of the sheet. Alex stared at him, wondering whether to speak. The silence was broken by Hazel's return.

"Here you are, Uncle Toby. One cup of tea." She placed it on the small table beside his armchair.

"Cantin's brother André…" he said, still staring straight ahead "was also a racing driver, but I'd heard he died the year before, at the Nurburgring. That's right…they were both quick drivers in their day, but Pierre was the faster and won more races. I must have got the dates wrong – he can't have been killed and then turned up at his brother's funeral." Toby came out of his apparent trance and turned towards Alex. "And Reginald Simmons ran a tyre dealership in Bristol after the war. Then I think he went to work for the Forsters."

"Perhaps they owned the dealership?"

"Yes. Yes, that's most likely. You will check all of this, won't you? All these names. I don't trust my memory these days. If I'm right, though, and André Cantin was killed in '36, someone must have been impersonating him at his brother's funeral."

"Another ghost, maybe?" said Hazel. "Your tea's there, Uncle Toby."

"Another ghost, or the same one?" said Alex. "This is getting more and more weird."

"Something's bothering me, young man." Toby continued. "Something doesn't fit. I need to have a think, and I need to read some old correspondence I have. Perhaps I can get back to you in a few days' time. I'm quite tired now."

"We're going back home soon, Uncle" said Meredith. "These two have to go back to school next week, but you've got my number anyway. In fact, we are going back to Henleaze now anyway. We're all off to see Annelise in the opera this afternoon."

"Ahhh, Annelise. What a beautiful voice that girl has. Please do send her my love, won't you?" Toby Allen sipped the tea Hazel had made for him, and pouted in disgust.

"How many sugars did you put in this, Hazel?"

"Three, wasn't it? Like my brother has."

"I don't take sugar…"

26

The walk from Martina and Andy's house to Bristol Harbour took less time than expected, and they had planned to arrive early in any case so that Geoff Burns could show the teenagers around the museum ship, while Meredith went off to find her sister. Alex was intrigued by the ship's history, Hazel less so, and Lucy had already seen it, so she and Hazel stuck close together. Whenever Isambard Kingdom Brunel was mentioned, Hazel rolled her eyes. She'd heard more than enough about the great engineer over the past year as Alex discovered more and more about him. Now they were aboard his former ship, and Alex was regaling Geoff with the story of the first Clifton gorge crossing. The two of them continued enthusing about Brunel's visionary engineering genius while the girls covered their ears.

An hour later they made their way to the Hayward Saloon, where the opera was due to take place. Meredith and Annelise were already there, and the singer greeted them all with hugs, and led them to the front row of seats. Alex was immediately taken with her striking looks; whereas Meredith Burns was quite tall, with dark hair, and dark brown eyes to match, her sister was a petite blonde with blue eyes, much the same height and build as her niece. 'She could actually be an older version of Hazel' he thought to himself.

"So, you're the gorgeous young man who's swept my niece off her feet then?" Annelise Dillon gushed as she gave Alex a hug. "I gather you're working on the family ghost" she continued, putting on a fully dramatic stage voice. "Any sightings yet? Any clues? Have you dug up any more bones? I heard all about your railway adventures last year!" Alex smiled and gave her the briefest résumé of what they'd discovered so far. Annelise seemed genuinely intrigued by it. "You will keep me informed, won't you both? I'm on Facebook – keep me in the loop, both of you" then she had swept away backstage.

"She's a bit over the top, but she's a cool aunt too. She's not got any kids of her own so me and Max are like her kids as well, if you see what I mean?" Hazel told Alex. "And you can stop blushing; you never swept me off my feet; she's just winding us all up a bit for a reaction."

"Deny it if you like, but I've got my birthday necklace…" Alex grinned and held up the gold bar with the romantic inscription. Hazel rolled her eyes.

Alex, Hazel and Lucy sat down and stared at the space in front of them. "Mum, is this it?" asked Hazel, looking at the plain floor, with just a small stool and a narrow backdrop, and a small area for the band in one corner. "Is this where they're actually going to do the opera?"

"Yes, Dear. That's why they're called Opera Anywhere. The gentleman selling the programmes told me they'd rather be doing the performance up on the top deck, if only it was summertime."

"I don't get it. I was expecting a huge stage, posh orchestra, lots of fancy costumes…"

"Just wait and see. Quality, not quantity…"

Alex and Hazel held hands through most of the

first act, although Alex was disappointed to notice that Hazel's other hand held her cousin's. He was not really expecting to enjoy the action on stage, but found himself drawn in very quickly by the powerful acting, and very well-projected singing, and the fact that it was all happening right there in front of them. When Annelise Dillon appeared, she was completely transformed from the bubbly person he'd met not twenty minutes ago. He was just about keeping up with the plot; something to do with the sailor not being allowed to marry the girl he wanted because of who she is, or who he is.

At the interval, as they joined the rather noisy queue for drinks, Alex commented to Meredith that he thought the man playing the Captain had been on stage as a sailor at the beginning, but he wasn't sure.

"Oh, more than likely" said Meredith. "They're only a very small troupe of players. They often have to double up roles on stage."

"It's not what I expected at all. It's really good, although the music's not really my sort of thing. It's a bit old fashioned."

"Well it *was* written 140 years ago, but the words… well, listen carefully. You'll find a lot of humour in them. W S Gilbert was very clever with words, and very perceptive about people."

"What did you think of Auntie Annelise then?" Hazel tapped him on the shoulder excitedly. "She's really good, isn't she?"

"She is *so* like you to look at, Hazel!" he said, struggling to be heard over the ever increasing crescendo of chit-chat. "I could just see you doing all that singing and acting and stuff, up on the stage, your name in lights…. if you could only do all that singing and acting anyway!"

He dodged her arm punch, nearly knocking the drinks from the table. "Seriously though, you are the spitting image of her."

"Are you saying I look forty whatever?" said Hazel indignantly.

"Is that what she is? Wow…!"

The second act opened with a solo aria from the Captain. Alex tried to listen to the words; they were old fashioned too, but Meredith was right, they were much funnier than the music implied. As the applause died down, Hazel appeared on stage and began to speak. Hang on? Hazel?!

Alex did a double-take, and then realised it was actually Annelise. She really did look so young. Alex watched with total fascination as she recited her lines, then as she began to sing, Alex tried to ignore her similarity to his girlfriend, and made himself focus on the words, just as Meredith had suggested.

> *Things are seldom what they seem*
> *Skim milk masquerades as cream…*

Alex found himself hearing the words again in his head: *Things are seldom what they seem*

Eh? What was that…? She was still singing. He had missed a line. What was she singing now?

> *Jackdaws strut in peacock's feathers*

Of course they do…

> *Black sheep dwell in every fold*
> *All that glitters is not gold*

Alex stopped listening. His mind was churning over so many confused thoughts in his head. *Things are seldom what they seem.* That was true. Nothing they'd seen or heard so far really added up. *Jackdaws strut in peacock's feathers.* Someone out there wasn't who they purported to be. But who was it? Someone was definitely up to something, all those years ago. *Black sheep dwell in every fold.* Who was the black sheep? Didn't Toby Allen raise his eyebrows when he saw the list of mourners at Pierre-Henri Cantin's funeral. *Things are seldom what they seem.*

He played everything they knew over and over in his mind, and then found himself clapping automatically with the rest of the audience; of course, the music had stopped. He tried to concentrate on the stage once more.

"Incomprehensible as her utterances are..." began the Captain. Alex zoned out on the word 'incomprehensible'. That just about summed it all up. Incomprehensible. Nothing made sense.

Things are seldom what they seem.

If he could just pinpoint the odd piece of the jigsaw... the piece which didn't really fit, he was sure he'd be able to work everything out.

Jackdaws strut in peacock's feathers...
Black sheep dwell in every fold...
Things are seldom what they seem...

"I loved that bit where they chucked the glasses over their shoulders, and the sailors caught them! So well done, wasn't it?" Hazel shouted to Alex through the applause, as the cast took a final bow, waved and then ran offstage.

"Yeah, really good." Alex realised he'd not

registered any of the last thirty-five minutes of the action, despite being in the front row, and having had one of the singers point at him during one verse.

"My favourite bit was when he hit Dick Deadeye's foot with the cat o' nine tails!" Lucy shouted "That was so funny! I don't know how they manage to keep going without laughing."

"Me neither" Alex responded, trying to remember ever seeing anyone with a cat o' nine tails on stage. As the lights went up, they stood and put their coats back on, then filed out of the Saloon and out onto the harbourside. Alex found himself deeply engrossed once again. 'Who was the black sheep'? he asked himself. 'Jackdaws in peacock's feathers'. Someone was clearly pretending to be someone else. But who? Who was pretending to be André Cantin? Surely, he couldn't possibly pass himself off as Pierre's brother in front of his widow? Who was that other guy that Uncle Toby mentioned? Simmons, that was it. He seemed surprised to find Simmons at the funeral. So, who were all those people at the funeral? What was their true relationship?

"Alex!!" Hazel dug him in the ribs. "Talk to me. You haven't said a word since we left the ship."

"Sorry… I got carried away. Listen, I think… I mean, I was thinking about everything we've found out this week…" Alex started to tell her, but she ignored him and leapt out of her seat.

"Annelise!! Over here!!"

Annelise Dillon pushed through the doors of the Watershed Café and made her way between the tables to join the family group, hugging and kissing them all 'in her artistic manner' thought Alex. Her family gushed forth compliments about her role, and exchanged anecdotes about how the performance went down with the audience in general. She sat herself down opposite Hazel and Alex and ordered a glass of white wine, which was swiftly delivered.

After a few sips, she smiled across the table at the two teenagers. "So, you two young peeps. What do you think of opera then?"

"It's not what I expected at all. You were amazing!" Hazel gushed. "How do you do it without microphones? And how do you get all those high notes and everything?"

"Oh, I'm a contralto. I don't go that high, you know. Not like a soprano like Sammy - she played Josephine – now she *did* have some really high notes. But anyway, it's just training, and lots of practice. I've been singing since I was five, so I've had... ooh, let's see now... at least 16 years of practice." She smiled at the joke. Hazel gazed adoringly at her; if she'd said she really *was* 21, Hazel might have believed her.

"How about you, Alex? What did you think?" Annelise gazed at Alex, smiling oh-so-sweetly.

Alex didn't reciprocate the smile, but came straight to the point. "That song you sang... to the Captain. About things not being what they seem?"

"Yes, '*Things Are Seldom What They Seem.*' What about it?" she asked, somewhat bemused.

"It set me thinking about this ghost story. I think it's really helped me start to make sense of it all. Black sheep... peacock's feathers... things masquerading... that sort of thing."

"Glad to be of assistance, Alex, Dear." She smiled sweetly again. "If you like I'll send you the

190

whole opera libretto. You never know, it might even give you the clue to the name of the ghost."

Alex blushed deeply as the rest of the group laughed. "Erm…actually, there was one other thing."

"Yes?" Annelise smiled even more sweetly, having recovered from her bemusement at his original question.

"Didn't the guy playing the Captain also play another sailor at the beginning?"

Annelise frowned. "Harvey? I don't know. I didn't see that bit. He probably did though. It's what we do when we have someone missing. You see, when the space is so tight, we can't have a full cast, so we cut down on one sailor and one girl cousin. That's why I doubled up as a cousin at one point."

"Of course! It's all making sense now…"

"At last!" Hazel glared at him. "Welcome back, Alexander Phipps. You've finally figured out the plot of the opera!"

Alex shook his head. "No, no. I mean, this whole ghost story thing is starting to make total sense. Listen, as soon as we get home tomorrow, I'm going to ask my Dad and my Nana…"

"And your sister, don't forget" Hazel butted in.

"No. Livvy's away at uni. But I'll get Dad and Nana to research all of those people on the list, and especially the ones at the funeral. I reckon I have a rough idea about what's been happening."

Annelise smiled at him again. "Ah… Monsieur Alex Poirot. Will you be letting us into your little secret any time soon?"

Her change of accent drew appreciative laughter from everyone, including Alex. 'She really is a fantastic actress' he thought.

"I would, but... I don't know any of the details. If I tried to explain what I'm thinking, it wouldn't make any sense. I mean, some of these people must have been genuine, but someone is a fake, but I just don't know who."

27

"Toast?"

"Please…thank you, Lucy." Alex shielded his eyes from the bright kitchen light. "Where's everyone else?"

"Mum's nipped to the shops, Dad's at work, Hazel's in the shower, and her 'rents are still in bed."

"Right. Am I up uber-early or something?"

"Not really. We're just all chilled. Oh, Hazel's told me all about your adventures, and all about that stuff from last year with the railway crash thing. Sounds really cool!"

Lucy put two slices of toast on a plate and put it down on the table next to Alex. He smiled appreciatively. She was taller than he'd expected; as tall as her cousin even though she was two years younger. She looked ever so thin and delicate, thought Alex, as if she might snap in half like a twig.

"So you went to Leigh Woods? Did my Mum tell you about the Mystery Woman they dug up?"

"Oh yeah, I think Meredith mentioned it, actually. It didn't really register with us though. I think it was the 1950s?"

"Yeah. They found this woman buried in a shallow grave. No-one knows who she was. They did a thing on it in the paper last year or the year before. You should look it up."

"Yeah, I'll google it sometime. It's nothing to do with our ghost though. He was from the 1930s."

"Next time you go tunnelling, count me in"

193

Lucy continued. "I'm up for lots of adventure!"

Alex frowned. "Nah, best stay safe, Lucy. You really don't want to get too involved with us, we do stupidly crazy things. Your cousin is a complete nutcase, by the way. She has a reputation at school… did she tell you about this?"

"Nope."

"Well, last year… they were playing netball, and one of the other girls committed a foul or something, and the teacher just picked on Hazel and sent her off. She'd been absolutely nowhere near the foul, but anyway, she got blamed. She was so annoyed that she totally lost it, lashed out and actually punched the teacher really hard."

"Crikey. I'm surprised she didn't get expelled."

"Well, *all* the other girls stuck up for her, and what's more, one of the TA's saw it all and reckoned the teacher had been picking on Hazel all the time, probably just for the hell of it. Probably because she's actually a really good netball player. So, anyway, she got off with a day's suspension, and the teacher left at the end of July. Now they call her Psycho Hazel, but she's not at all like that normally. She's just got a good sense of justice, and she knows how to stick up for herself… and other peeps too."

"But you said she was a nutcase, though."

"Yeah, but she's a cool nutcase and I happen to…" He stopped, thinking it better not to reveal his deeper feelings for Hazel just then.

"Oh, by the way" said Lucy, "Mum says her friend Katie who works at the Manor House is coming round in about an hour."

Katie Farleigh sat at the dining room table,

cradling a hot mug of coffee. She was a petite lady with a neat blond bob, but her slightly worn facial features made her look somewhat older than Martina; yet they'd been in the same class through both primary and secondary school. Martina had filled her in about the ghost story, and when Geoff had finally appeared, Martina introduced him.

"So you work at the Manor House?" Geoff asked. "We were there the other day as guests of Charles Forster. We were very well entertained."

"Oh, I'm sure you were" Katie replied. "He knows how to put on a show, he does. Let's you see what he wants you to see. Hides what he doesn't. I'm lucky, I work on the accounts side so I answer to Marianne Simmons. She's the finance manager, and she answers to Jeremy Forster, Charles's younger brother. He's the Group Financial Director."

"Ah yes, well Charles said it was a family business" said Geoff.

"Oh yes, it is. Very much so. They keep it all in the family. I must say, Jeremy Forster is a lovely man and I do enjoy working for him, whereas Charles is… well, probably the rudest man there is, to be honest. If he spoke to me the way he spoke to his assistants I'd slap him one, and then leave."

"We met one of his assistants" said Hazel. "We thought he was a robot, actually, didn't we, Alex?"

"Oh yes… Michael" Alex grinned, and the pair of them 'ble-deeped' in unison.

"Michael Simmons. Hmmm, a robot. Yeah, well, he is a really case study, that one."

"Wait a minute, did you say 'Simmons'?" Alex suddenly leaned forward.

"That's right. My boss's son. The Wild One we

call him, when she's not listening. He's got Charles Forster round his little finger. Yes, Sir. No, Sir. Anything you want, Sir. But I tell you, when Charles isn't there, the little sod does what he likes, and pushes all the other staff around too. His father's not much better either."

"His father?" Geoff said. "You mean, the whole family work there?"

"That's right. Michael's grandfather used to work for the firm apparently. He had a garage and tyre business which the Forsters bought out, and Michael's grandfather came with it. I don't know his name, he was dead long before I worked there."

"Who's his father?" asked Alex. "Only… well, there was a Simmons at the funeral of the racing driver. Reginald, I think his name was. That's right, he was Cantin's entrant and mechanic… so he must be Michael the robot's grandfather!"

"Oh, more than likely. Michael's father is James Simmons; he's Marianne's husband. Like I say, James' father had this garage which he sold to the family, and now the Simmons's work for the Forsters. All very cosy and very closed shop." Katie Farleigh finished her coffee, and stood up. "Well, I must be going, Tina. Nice to meet you all, and good luck with your ghost story, you two."

"Thanks" said Alex. "One quick question though. Do you know how old Michael is?"

"He'll be 35 in May. I only know this because the family are throwing a special party for him, and we're all expected to be there. I think I'll probably have to have a bone in my leg that week…"

28

Mark Phipps sat in his office and flipped open his laptop. He'd already briefed his mother-in-law and she'd been working on finding out more about Pierre-Henri Cantin long before Alex had gone away with the Burns family, but he was worried she may be overwhelmed by the list of names he had in front of him. He'd even offered to buy his own Ancestry membership and do the research himself, but Sheila Bagley was insistent that she should carry on being his 'research assistant'. In her last email she told him it gave her something to keep her mind occupied. Now he felt he was about to unleash a veritable brainstorm on her.

Alex had arrived home at tea time, looking fairly tired, but full of beans about the trip, with a stack of papers which he was now busy sorting out in his room. He'd briefly told the story to his family over tea, and then passed the report of Cantin's funeral to Mark.

"Dad, this would be a good starting place. Could you ask Nana to find out anything and everything about these people?"

Mark read the report of the funeral, and raised his eyebrows. He duly scanned the image of the newspaper report from Cantin's funeral, and typed a message to his mother-in-law:

From: mark@phippstribe.net
Sent: Saturday, February 23, 2019 8.52PM
To: sheilabagley@phonetalkinternet.com
Subject: Ghostly research!

Dear Sheila

Alex has just come back from a week in Bristol with
Hazel Burn's family, researching their family ghost!
Yes, honestly! Alex thinks it's all a sham.
Could you have a look at all of the names in the
attached clipping and see what you can find out. I'm
doing the same with the British Newspaper Archive.
Alex seems to think one of these people is an imposter
but he doesn't know which one, nor does he know who
they're trying impersonate. Oh what a tangled web, etc
etc!

Love

Mark

Sunday morning

From: sheilabagley@phonetalkinternet.com
Sent: Sunday, February 24, 2019 07.59 AM
To: mark@phippstribe.net
Subject: RE: Ghostly research

Dear Mark

What a can of worms! Hardly any of these people
make sense. I can't find who Mrs C Cantin is; the
only André Cantin I can find was buried in Metz,
France in 1936 aged 26. There are a few M. Fepps
but they were all from either Lorraine in France, or
Neckerau in Germany.

There are too many Reginald Simmons's for me to do any meaningful research on him, although there is one born in Langley in 1902

Arthur Daniel Prosser b 1912 Chippenham d 1938 Reading

Kenneth Forbes-Hunter b 1889 London d 1962 London

Harold Clifford Selkirk b 1892 Coventry d 1970 Chevening, Kent

There's an Andrew Forster who died in Bristol in 1959 aged 62

I've not got anywhere with Vendome or Boulet, there are too many of them – I need more information about them.

Let me know if you want me to dig deeper with any of these.

Love to all

Sheila

"He's not up yet, Darling." Freya Phipps poured a mug of tea for her husband. "I think this week's activities have worn him out. Apparently, he and Hazel got themselves into a bit of trouble and damn near got caught trespassing. Meredith Burns told me. She was a bit embarrassed because she really likes him, she thinks he's good for Hazel, but apparently, she really had a go at him. Oh, and she caught them in his room in their PJs, but she says they were just writing up notes or something."

Mark shrugged. "Well… I wouldn't worry about that. Knowing Alex, he probably was 'just writing up notes'. I expect the full story will come out in the next few days. Anyway, I'm off for a run in a bit. When he comes down, could you give him this from your mum."

Alex sat slumped at the breakfast table. Freya put a fresh mug of tea down in front of him, and a cereal bowl.

"Mum, could I have some bacon and eggs? I'm so wiped. I can't believe how tired I am after this week. We were up and out all the time; I don't feel as if I slept at all."

"Did you have a good time though?" Freya asked him, as she started cooking his breakfast. "You didn't really say whether you enjoyed it or not last night, you were just telling your ghost story."

"Yeah, it was okay, actually. Erm… I think we got into a bit of trouble with Hazel's mum but it's all okay, and I apologised."

"Trespassing, wasn't it?"

"No, sneaking out to explore the towpath when she reckoned she'd told us not to. No, the trespassing thing was before that, and we were with Mr Burns when that happened. What this?" He picked up the printout his father had left him.

"Oh, that's from Nana. Dad printed it out for you. It's all she could find so far. Not sure if it's much help. Anyway, what was all this about trespassing with Geoff Burns then?"

Alex ignored his mother and scanned the information from his grandmother's email.

"Wow! Where's Dad?"

"Out for a run. Back soon I expect. Why?"

"I need him to reply to this straight away. Also, I've got some other names for Nana."

"Can't you give the poor woman a break?"

"Oh, come on, Mum! You know she loves all this stuff."

From: mark@phippstribe.net
Sent: Sunday, February 24, 2019 10.37AM
To: sheilabagley@phonetalkinternet.com
Subject: RE: Ghostly research!

Sheila

Alex has asked if you can get the following from your list please:

Birth certificate for Reginald Simmons – the one born in 1902 in Langley, and if you can find his death any time that would be good.

Death certificate for Pierre-Henri Cantin (October 1937 but probably later as body found January 1938) and anything more on the Andre Cantin buried in 1936

There's also a name to check out. David Watson, date of birth unknown but he gives an address as C/O Christine Rocquefort, 18 Bonneville Garden Mansions, Kensington, W8 – do you have any way of checking directories or anything?

Mark

29

Mark sent the email to his mother-in-law, and immediately logged in to the newspaper archive, and typed 'Reginald Simmons Langley' into the advanced search page. He narrowed the dates down to 1937 and 1938. As always, the results threw up lots of spurious links; any reference to either Reginald, Simmons, or Langley, threw up a result but they were usually not linked. He tried again, this time putting Simmons in the 'Use exact phrase' box, leaving Langley as a general search.

"Well, well, well" he muttered to himself, as the first image came up. "Alex!"

His son came in from his room, where he'd also been busy online, trying to find any archived reports of the Trophy Race.

"Didn't you say they were into tyres?"

"Yep. Vendolet Tyres to be precise. Why?"

"Look at this advert from the Slough Advertiser and Gazette… '*Tyres, new or rebuilts.*' I like that. Not rebuilds, but *rebuilts*. '*Vendolet specialist. Free fitting. Simmons Garage Limited, George Green.*' He screenshotted and cropped the image, and printed it.

"Wow. Who the heck is George Green?"

"George Green is a place. Look, it's where Simmons had his garage. It's a little hamlet between Slough and Uxbridge, a couple of miles from Langley. So, Reginald Simmons had a tyre garage near Langley, selling Vendolet Tyres. Pierre-Henri Cantin was a Director of Vendolet... so there's a connection there. I wonder what else we can dig up... What's the next name on the list then?"

"P. Vendome."

Mark typed in the name, and just one result came up – the newspaper report of the funeral. Typing in Andrew Forster and Etienne Boulet returned the same result.

Alex went back to his room, and started exploring a Facebook group which dealt with old racing photos. It consisted of members posting any pictures they'd taken as youngsters. Whoever was the Group Admin had asked people to tag the date and place, but it was still hard to find all the pictures he was looking for. He searched 'Race of Champions 1968' and got all sorts of pictures, most of which were nothing to do with the race. He tried 'Brands Hatch March 1968' and got a completely different set of pictures. He went back to his notes, and tried to remember the name of the driver Uncle Toby had met... he had used a French swearword, so he must have been French. Mustn't he?

In the end, a google search for the race pulled up an entry list. He scanned the names. Didn't Uncle Toby say the guy hadn't started the race? He looked down the list. There were no French drivers. Then he looked again. At the bottom of the entry list was Jo Siffert, listed as DNS... Did Not Start. Siffert was Swiss. 'That explains why he swore in French' thought Alex. He went back to the Facebook page and typed in Jo Siffert 1968, and a whole host of photos came up. There were pictures of him on the back of a trailer, with a laurel wreath around his neck, waving to the crowd. There were several pictures of him in a dark blue car with a white ring around its nosecone, and strange wings on spindly stalks above the back wheels. Alex scrolled on.

"Alex!" He heard his father call from his office along the landing. He got up and ambled along to Mark's room.

"Bingo!" said Mark as Alex sat back down beside him. "Another mystery to add to your list of mysteries… look at this."

He handed him a copy of a newspaper cutting. "Before you read it, just look at the date."

"Monday the 21st of March, 1938" Alex read out aloud. "What about it?"

"Five days after your Cantin funeral. Read on."

"A verdict of Suicide whilst of unsound mind was delivered on the body of Arthur Daniel Prosser, a goods clerk, whose body was found beside the railway line about a mile from Twyford station…

Prosser, 25, was returning home to Reading from a funeral in Langley. His wife said he had left home in good cheer that morning. They had recently had their first child, a son. As far as she knew her husband had no financial worries and the funeral was of a racing driver whose fatal accident he had witnessed. Deceased had telephoned her to say he was staying on to have a drink with some fellow mourners. Witnesses gave conflicting reports as to his state of mind. According to Mr Kenneth Forbes-Hunter, a racing official and fellow mourner, deceased had seemed in a cheerful demeanour, and this was confirmed by two other witnesses. However, Mr Arthur Simmons, another mourner, said he saw deceased standing over at graveside after the wake, looking pensive. Mr Jonathan Blake, a travelling salesman who did not know the deceased, said he spoke with him on the railway platform at Maidenhead, and deceased seemed distant and vague about where he was going. He did not see him again after they got in separate carriages. Mrs Eileen Newson, a passenger on the train, said deceased walked up and down the carriage corridor several times but he did not see him sit down. After deceased had passed her three or four times she did not see him again. John Arthur Glennie, a guard with the Great Western Railway, said he was told by a passenger that one of the doors was open on the right-hand side in the last but one coach. He went along and closed it. He was certain it was not open when the train had left Maidenhead, as he had looked out of both sides of the train a few minutes beforehand. Deceased was found after the driver of an up train reported hitting something on the line. His body had been cut into several pieces by the wheels of the up train passing over it. A post mortem found death was due to multiple injuries.

"Why do I think that was not suicide, Dad?"

"Because you have a suspicious mind, oh son of mine. So, come on, tell me. Why is it not suicide?"

"Well, because… well, his wife says he's in good cheer. He's just had a kid, so presumably he's a happy family man. He's got a good job, so no worries about money, and he's cheerful right up until just after the wake, when he goes to the graveside. So, reading between the lines of this inquest, he must have seen someone, or something, at the graveside to make him want to take his own life."

"I love the way you assume that because he's got a job, he's got no financial worries. You have a lot to learn, son."

"Maybe, but… hang on. Who the heck is this Arthur Simmons guy who says he saw him at the graveside? I thought it was Reginald Simmons?"

"Another name for Nana then?"

"Yup." Alex's head was spinning even more. *Things are seldom what they seem*

"Talk of the devil" said Mark, "she's just sent another email. I asked her some more of your questions today. Let see what she's found out."

From: sheilabagley@phonetalkinternet.com
Sent: Sunday, February 24, 2019 3.20PM
To: mark@phippstribe.net
Subject: RE: Ghostly research!

Dear Mark

I've ordered those certificates you asked for. They can send PDFs now, so they don't cost as much - £6 now instead of £9.25

I've checked that address too. They weren't in a directory, but in 1939 there was a register taken in England and Wales, and 18 Bonneville Garden Mansions had a person named… guess who? Matthias Fepp, born 3rd June 1906, married, also Heidi Fepp, born 29th November 1906, married, and Natasha Fepp, born 6th August 1928. There is another child, but they must be still alive because the record is not available. Copy attached. There's no sign of Christine Rocquefort there.

Any more to follow up yet?

Sheila

"Crikey Dad! Please tell me I'm not imagining this… the address of the guy who witnessed the accident is the same address that the Fepps are living at two years later. What does it all mean?"

"I think it means you've opened up another family can of worms; except, of course, Hazel's family aren't directly involved in this, are they?"

"No, they're not. But… can I ask Hazel over now? If she wants to come?"

"I'm sure Mum won't mind. After all, the Burns's have put up with you all week."

Hazel arrived out of breath half an hour later, having cycled up from her village. She took a carrier bag from her backpack and handed it to Freya.

"It's from my mum. Alex left his dirty socks, pants and tee-shirt in the back of our car. Sorry! Mum has washed them, by the way."

Freya smiled. "Thanks, Hazel. The boys are up in Mark's office. You go on up, and I'll bring you a drink of squash in a minute."

Hazel bounded up the stairs. "So come on then, what's this exciting piece of news?" she said, giving Mark a quick hug, and then kissing her boyfriend on the cheek.

"Remember that song your aunt sang? The one about '*Jackdaws strut as peacock feathers*'?" said Alex, wiping his cheek.

"Yeah, what about it?"

"I knew, as soon as I heard it, that it was telling us something about your ghost story. Well, I think we've found ourselves a little jackdaw. A certain David Watson. Our witness, the spectator. The one who says he saw the accident happen; who no-one else saw before the accident, and who gave a 'care of' address in London rather than a real address."

"Why. What about him? How do you know?"

"Because, the address he gave in London... two years later, it's being lived in by a certain Mathias Fepp and his wife and daughter."

Hazel's jaw dropped. "You mean... this Fepp guy, who is the cousin of Pierre-Henri Cantin..."

"No, who we are *told* is the cousin of Fepp. But I tell you what, I don't believe any of this stuff in the paper. It's all a bit of a sham. That reporter's been led right up the church path, hasn't he. '*Things are seldom what they seem*' – that was the name of that song, and it totally applies to this ghost story, doesn't it?"

Hazel frowned and stared at the wall as Alex carried on with his theory.

"Listen...right, the car crashes. No sign of the driver. No *official* witnesses apart from that marshal... oh yeah, and he tops himself after the funeral too; I'll tell you what I think of that in a minute. Then this guy David Watson appears... but where from, and how quickly does he appear? Uncle Toby is half conscious so he doesn't have any sense of time. I reckon... I reckon that David Watson is a diversion. Cantin is trying to disappear, so he stages the accident, he jumps off the car as it rolls down the gorge, and he escapes into the tunnel and walks through to the Manor House.

"Meantime, this Watson guy, who is actually Matthias Fepp, appears as if from nowhere…maybe from the same tunnel, rescues Uncle Toby, makes a statement to the police and the coroner, and everyone believes him because everything he says adds up. Then… five months later, at Pierre-Henri Cantin's funeral, he sees Arthur Prosser, the marshal who was the first on the scene. Prosser recognises 'Watson' and confronts him, and then on the way home to Reading, he happens to fall out of his train, supposedly suicide."

"Can't be…" said Hazel, still staring thoughtfully at the wall ahead of her. "Cantin can't have escaped down the tunnel if he was being buried five months later, can he?"

There was a short silence, then Alex sighed.

"You see what I mean? Was he dead? Wasn't he dead? I mean, he was identified by his wife, wasn't he? By tattoos on his body, or something."

"Well, with respect, Alex, if there's something very odd going on here, I definitely wouldn't believe that identification." Mark Phipps could feel himself being drawn further into the mystery. "From what you're saying, you've only got David Watson's word about the accident; you've only got Cantin's wife's word that the body is his, and looking at that inquest, you've only got Arthur Simmons's word that Prosser was apparently suicidal."

"And the guy on the railway platform."

"Ah yes… so, who is Arthur Simmons, and who was this… Jonathan Blake. We need to check him out too. Maybe he was Simmons… or Cantin."

"Dad… how easy is it to get to Langley from here? I mean, could you take us next weekend?"

"I can't, no. I'm away in Berlin on Thursday for ten days. But… why? What is there to see in Langley, apart from the churchyard?"

"Well, that's just it. I'd like to visit Pierre-Henri's grave, and see if there are any other clues. Do you think your Dad will take us instead, Hazel?"

"Erm… I could ask him… or we could get the train and go ourselves… if we're allowed?" Hazel glanced at Mark Phipps to gauge his reaction.

"I don't think either of us would be happy with that. It's not that we don't trust you, but if anything happens you really need an adult…"

"Livvy!" Alex interrupted. "What if you got her to meet us? She's at Brunel University, isn't she? That's in Uxbridge. Didn't you say George Green was on the way to Uxbridge, from Slough?"

30

Saturday 2ⁿᵈ March 2019
St. Mary's Church, Langley

Alex reached into his backpack and retrieved his notepad. He'd made a note of the grave number from a PDF he'd downloaded on the church website. He led the others through the churchyard entrance, and headed around to the right of the church, following the footpath through the different sections detailed on the map.

"Ah look, we could have come in that way" said his sister. "You're leading us round the houses again, little bro."

Alex grinned. He didn't like to admit that he had missed having Olivia around at home. She'd helped out a lot with the Salmsham railway mystery, and although she wasn't particularly enamoured of Hazel, their mutual dislike had softened and she thought that any girl who could put up with her brother deserved some credit. When Alex had asked her if she'd come out and meet them in Langley, she'd jumped at the chance. They'd arranged to meet at the railway station, a decision made easier when Mark offered to transfer her bus and train fare money over to her bank, as well as money for a lunchtime meal. Freya had seen the two teenagers onto the train, and Olivia was waiting at the ticket barrier when they got off. She gave both of them a quick hug, and then introduced them to a young girl with quite dark skin and deep set eyes. "Ah, guys, this is Flavienne. She's doing the same course as me.

She's just coming along for something to do... and that guy over there having a smoke is Denis..." she pronounced it 'De-nee' "who is Flavienne's boyfriend. They're both French so you never know, they may come in useful."

"Are you all studying Modern History then?" asked Hazel.

"Non, Denis, he study ceeveel enzhineering" Flavienne said in a heavy accent. "We are at the right university, yes?" She smiled. "Brunel, yes?"

Hazel rolled her eyes. "Of course, Brunel University... Civil Engineering. How could I ever have guessed" she muttered under her breath.

On the way to the church, Hazel explained the ghost story to Flavienne and Denis. She wasn't sure whether they understood much, but there was a lot of polite nodding and 'ah yesses' from the young French students. She did establish, however, that Denis Fontaine was a fan of Formula 1 and particularly Charles Leclerc, the new Monegasque hotshot who was driving for Ferrari this year.

Alex stopped in the middle of the churchyard, and held out both his arms. "Folks. This... is Section S. We're looking for Pierre-Henri Cantin. Died 1937."

Most of the graves had headstones, so it was a case of walking up and down the lines of graves to find the one they wanted. There were a hundred and twelve graves to check, and they were just wondering if Alex had brought them to the right spot when Olivia called out.

"Over here. Here he is... the gravestone says 'Pierre-Henri Cantin... Racing Driver. Loving brother and uncle. 1908 to 1937. *Requiescat in pace*'."

"Oooh, get you and your fancy Latin!" said Alex, taking a picture of the inscription.

"Ah, yehhhs, Cantin!" said Denis, in sudden recognition. "Zis is a... how you say...erm... famoose man...driver. Yes, he race in a Delage and Bugatti and he, er... he win many races *en France*, long ago. I...erm... my fazher has books wiz Cantin and... he has a brozzer André who is... is died at the Nurburgring in Germany. Yes. Before ze war."

"Yes, and that's one of the mysteries we have. André Cantin was killed in 1936." Alex told him. "And yet... someone claiming to be André Cantin stood here a year later and buried his brother. Denis, does your father still have those books?"

"Why, yes. I sink he does. He is a journalist for local news journals, but he like to write about the history of the automobile, yes?"

Alex and Hazel exchanged glances.

"He'll know about Vendolet Tyres!" Hazel shouted. "There was all that stuff about fraud and everything. Denis, you are the greatest French genius in the world." She flung her arms around his neck and kissed him on both cheeks, much to everyone's amusement. "And so is your father, if he can help."

They walked slowly back through the graveyard towards the main entrance. Alex had pre-arranged that they would have lunch in the Red Lion, and he'd explained that the wake had taken place there straight after the funeral.

"What I want to know is, what happened to Arthur Prosser between the funeral and him going home, to make him go from being a happy young man to a suicide?"

213

"Oh look" said Hazel idly. "There's a Simmons family grave here. What was our guy called?"

"Reginald" said Alex. "He ran the local tyre garage at George Green."

"Here you go then." Hazel pointed at a large headstone. "Reginald Simmons, born 5th November 1902, died 17th August 1971 and his dear wife Ellen born 11th May 1904, died 24th January 1989."

"Nothing about any of his children" Alex said, "but there's some folk here who are probably his parents. Oh, and here's Arthur Simmons. Now, isn't he the one who was at this funeral?"

"Oh yeah. Oh, no actually. This one can't have been him; he died in 1916, aged ten. Oh, that's really sad." Hazel pouted her lower lip out. "Are you gonna snap these for the record?"

"Definitely." Alex carefully lined up his iPhone and took a few shots of the Simmons graves, before leading everyone back to the churchyard gates.

"So, come on then folks. You're Arthur Prosser. You've come to the funeral. You've seen the coffin lowered into the grave. You've come over here for a drink, and you're all... not happy, but you're feeling fine in yourself. Then you get up and go back to the graveside, then everyone who sees you after that says you're not happy or anything. Distant, I think one man said. So, what's happened to you to make you change your mood?"

Alex threw the question out to the others, while they waited for their food to be delivered.

"Either..." said Olivia cautiously, "Either someone's said something to you, or... you've seen something, or someone."

"André Cantin!" said Denis, suddenly. "You 'ave seen André Cantin, and you know is not possible because 'e is died in Germany the last year."

Alex nodded. "Maybe, except... how would Prosser know André Cantin?"

"Because... because 'e is also racing driver, so maybe Prosser saw 'eem."

"But Prosser is a flag marshal. They don't generally meet the drivers, so he wouldn't know him, would he? No, I reckon it must be someone else. Maybe Matthias Fepp?"

"Hold on" said Hazel. "remember Uncle Toby got all funny about your surname? He said he knew someone with a similar name. I wonder if he meant Matthias Fepp? It's a bit like Phipps isn't it? Especially with Toby's posh accent, what?"

"It wouldn't surprise me. I always reckoned the old devil's been keeping something from us."

"And then there's the perpetually mysterious David Watson..." Hazel started.

"Aaaaarrrrrgggggghhhhhh!" Alex's cry of frustration interrupted her, and caused some raised eyebrows from the other pub guests. "This is so confusing! All of my theories are being thrown out by this... these revelations. I feel as if we've been watching a horror movie, where all these things seem to be happening but nothing is quite right, and nothing is where it should be."

The walk back to Langley Station took them a leisurely twenty minutes, during which time the three girls discussed more up to date problems, such as choosing new clothes for the expected summer heatwave. Alex and Denis were content to amble along quietly behind them.

As they approached the railway, Alex tried to make conversation with Denis.

"Did you know that Brunel built this railway?"

"Yes, I 'ave made a study of eet. I go to Deedcot museum and I like ze Great Western Railway"

"Have you been to Bristol yet?"

"Not yet, but I like to go soon."

"Ah, you must. There's so much to see."

Alex smiled to himself. 'How lucky that this guy appears just when we need him, and he's a Brunel fan like me' he thought.

"You're a cool guy" said Alex admiringly.

"I know" replied Denis. "I am ze coolest!"

After seeing the three uni students onto their London-bound train, Alex and Hazel crossed to the westbound platform and sat down on the seat, speculating as to what was going through Arthur Prosser's mind after coming back from the funeral. Alex took out his ringbinder.

"We should have brought our laptops."

"What, and left them on the train. Sure Haze, that would have been clever."

"You're calling me Haze again, Lexy-baby…"

"Hang on! Look at Prosser's inquest report again. What does it say about Jonathan Blake?"

"'he spoke with him on the railway platform at Maidenhead, and deceased seemed distant and vague about where he was going.' Yeah, what about it?" asked Hazel, slightly puzzled.

"Don't you see it? He spoke with him where?"

"On the platform…"

"Yeah, on the platform at *Maidenhead*. And we're at Langley. What's he doing at Maidenhead?"

"Maybe… maybe he had to change trains?"

"Maybe… yeah, that's true. We need to get hold of an old railway timetable, don't we? And I'm waiting to hear back from my Nana about these people like Jonathan Blake and Arthur Simmons."

31

Hazel sat at her boyfriend's computer, looking through the pictures from the Facebook site. They'd finally found an album of thirty photos uploaded by 'Norman55' who had gone with a friend to the Race of Champions and had wheedled his way into the paddock. Hazel and Alex had been looking for any pictures of Jo Siffert; they'd looked at several other photos of him and knew they could recognise him. Most of these photos, though, were of mechanics bending over half-built racing cars. There were several shots of men wearing racing overalls, but neither of them knew who were. Hazel decided to flick through them again, this time looking at everyone else in the pictures, including the spectators crowding around the cars.

There was nothing to see. Sighing, she clicked on another album, called 'Simons Snaps'. Most of his pictures showed various different types of racing car on the track. There was one of a saloon car which had crashed; the driver was standing next to it looking a bit sorry for himself. The next picture was of the same car sitting forlornly in the paddock, its bonnet crumpled and the front of the roof crushed, and a member of its team inspecting the back of the car. Hazel scanned the faces of the onlookers, and then did a double take. She looked again, enlarging the screen image so as to zoom in.

"Oh. My. God! It's my Gran! Look... there." She pointed to a slim girl with long flowing hair, standing next to a tall man in his mid-forties.

Alex squinted at the screen. "If you say so. I've never met her. Is that your mum's mum?"

"Yep. Linda Allen, her name was then. Oh wow! This is amazing... hang on, isn't that Uncle Toby?" She pointed to the tall man.

"Crikey... you're right. There he is! This is incredible. I can't believe you've found them. Just as well you looked, I'd never have spotted either of them. When was this taken? Does it give a date?"

"Yep. Saturday 16th March 1968. He was there, Alex. He was really there!" She copied the photo into Alex's research folder, and scrolled on through, but most of 'Simons Snaps' were close-ups of car engines and gearboxes.

"I really don't see the fascination with this at all. Who wants to see another gearbox?" she grumbled. "I mean... they all look the same."

"Yeah" said Alex laconically. "It's a bit like clothes shopping for girls, isn't it? You know, who cares about it really?" He started to flinch as she slapped his leg hard, then suddenly spotted someone in the next photo. "There!!"

"Where?" Hazel looked back at the screen.

"That last picture. There's your uncle again; that's his jacket!"

"Oh yeah. From the back. I forgot he's got more hair, of course. He was only 42, and Gran was only 19. We need to get my mum up here."

Toby Allen had his back to the camera and seemed to be talking to another, shorter man who was partly hidden. Linda Allen stood on his right, holding his arm. Hazel copied the picture, and then flicked to the next one. It was obviously taken a few seconds later.

"That's Jo Siffert!" Alex exclaimed "So... if this is Toby talking with Siffert, like he said, where's the ghost? Ah, there's so many folk in the background." Alex ran his finger along slowly the screen.

"They all look pretty solid to me" Hazel joked. "No transparent people floating about..."

They had a copy of Cantin's biography with his picture on it, and compared the faces of everyone in the background. There were a fair number of spectators standing behind Siffert, but no-one in overalls, and no-one who looked anything like Pierre-Henri Cantin. Hazel clicked on the next photo.

This was of a mechanic wearing red overalls, bent over the front of a car, its workings exposed, the red and white nosecone placed to one side. In the background were two pairs of legs, which Hazel identified as belonging to Toby and her gran. "You can tell from the style of her jeans... you see, my knowledge of girls' clothing is useful stuff, not like engines and gearboxes!"

She clicked onto the next picture. Now, they could see that the photographer had moved in much closer. Siffert was looking at Linda Allen now and smiling. Toby was looking to the left of the Swiss ace, straight at a mechanic, who seemed to be staring straight back at him.

"Cantin!" they both said together, excitedly. There was no doubt about it, it was the same face as the one in the magazine.

"Quick, Haze, copy it, copy it. Mum!! Meri!!" Alex called to their mothers, who were downstairs chatting over a late supper which Freya had prepared for them. Meredith had picked the two teenagers up from the railway station earlier, a pre-arrangement which included supper at the Phipps's. Both their husbands were away on business, and Hazel's brother was at his best friend's birthday sleepover, so it was a chance for Freya and Meredith to get to know each other better.

A quick check of the remaining pictures drew a blank; no more shots of either Toby, Linda or the 'ghost'. They scrolled back through the other photos, as the two mothers appeared at the doorway.

"What's the excitement then?" asked Meredith. "Have you found something?" She and Freya sat down on the end of Alex's bed.

"Look." Hazel went into the folder and double-clicked on the picture of Cantin. "There. Look, Mum. There's Gran, there's Uncle Toby, and there…that's our ghost. Pierre-Henri Cantin."

There was a brief silence as they all stared at the image of the 'ghost', in plain green mechanics' overalls, staring fixedly at a younger Uncle Toby.

Meredith Burns broke the silence. "So, he's for real then. But who is he? This little mystery is becoming more convoluted."

"When was this taken?" asked Freya after a few more moments. "And where, come to that."

"Well, the place is the paddock at Brands Hatch Motor Racing Circuit in Kent. And the date…" Alex froze. "Oh… Hazel. March the 16th, 1968!"

"Yeah, we knew that. So?"

"That date is 30 years, to the day, after Cantin was supposed to have been buried in Langley churchyard… so, that's one heck of a clever ghost.

He'd be 60 in this picture, if he was still alive, if it was really him. Could this guy really be 60?"

"Well, he could possibly" said Freya. "He's a bit blurry, but he's got a full head of hair… difficult to say really. But why not? He could pass for 60."

"What about 30?" asked Hazel.

"I'd say… yes, he could pass for 30 as well."

"He was 30 when he was supposed to have been killed. I suppose we should make a copy of this and send it to Uncle Toby, and tell him we're sorry, and we believe him now."

"I think we should send it to Martina first" said Meredith. "She can show him, then you two won't be responsible if Uncle Toby keels over with the shock."

"Okay, but I want to go through these all again and see whether we've missed anything." Hazel said, scrolling back through the folder.

"We'll leave you to it, I think" said Freya.

The two mothers went back downstairs, leaving their offspring pouring over the screen. They must have spent another hour scouring for similar pictures, but to no avail. Alex did, however, post a comment online, under the original picture, asking if anyone could identify the mechanic standing behind Jo Siffert. Eventually, Hazel began to flag, struggling to keep her eyes open, and it was time for her mother to take her home.

After kissing goodbye to his girlfriend, Alex went back to the Facebook group and tried another date, bringing up a few pictures from the 1954 British Grand Prix, but only three from the paddock, and no-one in those pictures resembled looked familiar to Alex. Nonetheless, he still copied them, with the thought that Toby should see them, along with all the rest. His email 'pinged'.

'Ah, another missive from Nana' he thought:

From: sheilabagley@phonetalkinternet.com
Sent: Saturday, March 02, 2019 11.14 AM
To: mark@phippstribe.net
Cc: alex@phippstribe.net
Subject: RE: Ghostly research!

Mark

There are several Jonathan Blake's but the most likely one died in Maidenhead Sep 1973 aged 76

I've done some work on the Simmons family:
Michael Andrew Simmons, b23 May 1984 Bristol, mother's maiden name Da Costa. Looks like he is an only child.
His parents James Andrew Simmons, b 13 Oct 1954
Mother's maiden name Condon.
Married Marianne da Costa at Holy Trinity Church, Abbots Leigh, 30th July 1983
James's parents: Arthur Frederick Simmons b 17 Aug 1905 in Langley, died 4th November 1975 Bristol
Married Alice Condon at Holy Trinity Church, Abbots Leigh, 12 Sep 1953
I can't find Alice's death anywhere; there are lots of Alice Simmons in the Bristol area. James is their only child.

Also found Christine Simmons, aged 40 buried at Abbots Leigh in December 1951; I've ordered her death certificate, and also Matthias Fepp's – he died in Bristol in 1970.

Sheila

'Interesting' thought Alex. 'James's birth year 1954 – same as the code on the tunnel padlock...'

32

Heidi Fepp took a big breath, and blew out the five candles on the giant cake, suspended in front of her by her husband and son, each holding half of the large silver cake-tray.

"Happy Birthday, my darling!" Matthias Fepp said out loud, for everyone to hear. "May there be many, many more with you by my side."

A loud 'Ahhh!' went around the guests in the large ballroom, followed by much clapping.

"I'd just like to say…" Matthias raised his voice a little, until the chatter had died down, "that my wife has been a big part of my life… the most important part of my life, for as long as I can remember. I look at our children, my brilliant son Gerhard, and my wonderful daughter Natasha, who is as beautiful as her mother…" More 'aaahs' from the crowd "and… look, there she is. You wouldn't think she was 23, she looks about 15, and that's how my Heidi looked when I first met her, and I think she still looks as young!"

There was more applause, but Matthias waved it down. "But there is one thing I haven't done yet today and that's given my beautiful wife a present, and, well… if you listen carefully, Darling, you might hear it…"

The hall went silent, as guests looked at each other in puzzlement.

"Maybe we need to open the windows... just for a moment!"

Two servants flung open the French windows, and the guests could hear the sound of a high-performance engine in the distance. The engine note blipped, and then briefly died down before rising again and getting louder and louder. A large cloud of dust above the tree-lined road signalled the approach of whatever it was; suddenly there was a screech of brakes, more blipping and revving, and a small white sports car rushed into view, accelerating hard towards the house, finally executing a perfect half-spin to arrive backwards in a cloud of dust and tyre smoke, right beside the French windows. A neatly dressed figure with thick blond hair stood up on the driver's seat, hopped over the door, quickly took a bow, and then tossed the keys towards the astonished Mrs Fepp.

"Oh my goodness! It's that new Jaguar, isn't it? The one I've always wanted? Oh Matty!" Heidi jumped up and down excitedly, like a small child. Mathias slipped his arm around his wife's waist.

"Well, I think you've had enough of driving boring old saloon cars, Darling; time to spice up your life with this exciting little toy. Happy Birthday!" They went over to the car, followed by a large crowd of enthusiastic guests, all keen to have a closer look.

Meantime, the grinning driver ran up the steps and through the French windows, flung his gloves across the room towards one of the servants, and said "Right, this calls for champagne... and food! I am starving!"

As the guests milled around the car outside, Christine Rocquefort stood in the middle of the ballroom with a champagne glass in her hand, staring at the driver, who was talking to the butler.

"Whatever you've got, Sam, old chap. I'm starving... hello Darling?" He grinned at Christine as she slowly walked towards him, her face set.

"You bastard! You absolute total bastard. You've been with *her* again, haven't you?"

"Ahhh... if you mean, that small, beautiful, slender, high-revving pussy cat of a Jaguar out there, then yes, I have been with her. And very good fun she was too. I had her... in top pretty much all the way from Langley to here, and she let me do whatever I wanted with her...at the touch of my fingertips." He flinched and shut his eyes as the champagne hit him squarely in the face.

"You know perfectly well who I mean. That little tart from Chelsea..."

He wiped his face with his sleeve, flicked his hair back, and glared at her through steely blue eyes. "I don't know any little tarts from Chelsea. I don't know any little tarts from anywhere. They're all in your mind." He tapped his temple "You're a crazy woman. Now shut up and let me <u>eat</u>!"

He turned his back on her, picked up a sandwich from a platter in the middle of the table, and walked back towards the French windows.

"Good journey, Arthur old chap?" A figure appeared out of the small crowd on his right.

"Splendid, Andrew, really good. She's a real mover, that one. Floored her all the way. She's most definitely run in now, I can tell you."

"I bet, I bet. How was Reg?"

"Reg was… being Reg. But he's doing alright, and he's happy we're putting so much quality business his way."

"Good, good. Erm, there's someone over here I'd like you to meet. Give him the bold, full frontal Arthur Simmons treatment, but probably best not to mention too much about your… erm, rapid journey. It's the new Chief Constable; lovely chap, important to keep him onside, if you know what I mean?"

Andrew Forster gently guided Arthur towards two tall gentlemen admiring a large painting. They both turned as Andrew spoke. Martin Geldman, the Forster's lawyer, stood back and nodded to Arthur, as Andrew spoke to the other gentleman.

"Chief Constable, I'd like you to meet Arthur Simmons, my right-hand man, as it were. Arthur, this is Chief Constable Willow."

"Call me Tom, old boy!" He gripped Arthur's hand firmly, and looked him squarely in the face. "I say, have we met before? You look quite familiar."

"Only if you've been a traffic copper, Tom?" said Arthur, grinning boldly. "I used to be known to most of them, once upon a time. Not any more, of course. I'm too grown up and sensible for all that."

"Apart from just now, eh? I saw that. Beautiful bit of parking, what? I bet that little cat belts along, doesn't she? I hope you gave her some stick… erm, down the lane, of course."

"Oh, you mean around the old race track. Yes, I did do a little detour, just for show. Got to be fairly gentle with her, of course; she's not really run in yet."

"Quite, quite. Tell me, I was thinking of getting one of those myself… What do you think? I'm not too old for one am I? I'm quite an enthusiast, you know. Often thought of giving it a go on the track, once I've retired from this lark."

Arthur grinned. "Why not? I'm sure you could handle the Jag. And there's plenty of motoring clubs you could join too. You don't need very much to go racing, just a decent car and a bit of skill, and I'm sure you've got that from all your police training."

Tom Willow nodded. "Oh, yes. That's true. Used to do a bit of high speed chasing back in my day. Love to try one of those beasts, though." He pointed to the painting of Manfred von Brauchitsch, driving a pre-war Mercedes to victory at the Abbots Park track.

"Ah yes, the old Merc" Arthur sighed.

"Old Merc indeed. What a machine! I was here for that, you know. The Trophy Race. '37, wasn't it? Saw him win it. Amazing driver… amazing car. There were three of them that day, I think. Bloody krauts really had us whipped, didn't they? Showed us how it was done then. Do you know, that beast was so powerful, if you put your foot down in any gear… any gear mind, it'd still spin its wheels."

"Is that so? Gosh, well I never knew that."

"Bet you did, you know. You were here too that day, weren't you? I'm sure I recognise you."

Arthur felt suddenly unnerved. His stomach knotted and he felt his heart thumping. He looked squarely at the policeman with a quizzical look on his face, but said nothing.

"Yes, of course" Tom Willow continued, still staring at Arthur. "I know who you were. You were one of the officials, weren't you? We had that damn stupid accident, when that bloody Frog drove off the edge of the gorge, killed himself and took a young boy with him. That's right, weren't you the marshal fellow? First on the scene and all that."

Arthur smiled in genuine relief. "Nothing gets past you, does it, Chief Constable."

"No, old boy. Once a copper, always a copper. I notice little things no-one else does, you know, and I always remember important details. Part of the job. That's how I can recognise you 14 years on. Yes… sad business that. I remember when we fished that Cantin chap out of the Severn a few months later, what was left of him. Fair chopped up, he was. Ship's propeller most likely. Not sure how his wife recognised him; any of him, to be honest. Only his bloody tattoo; been in the army or something. Had a number on his shoulder, and some fancy picture down his back. Pretty much all there was to see."

"Quite… well I must circulate, Chief Constable. I haven't actually spoken to the Birthday Girl yet."

Arthur said a quick goodbye to both men, and backed away, leaving the policeman pointing out some detail on the painting. Making his way out through the French windows, Arthur thought he saw Heidi Fepp, and was about to pinch her playfully when she turned round, and he saw that it was her daughter Natasha.

"Dammit, girl. You and your mother are so alike. Just as well you turned then. or I would have probably done something…"

"And I would have slapped you one. Go away, Arthur, I'm not one of your little tarts."

"That's enough of your cheek, young lady. Just remember who you are, and where you are."

"Oh I know who I am, and I know who you are. I remember everything, Mister Arthur Simmons, so just you keep that in mind, and keep your filthy hands to yourself. Ah, Mother…"

Arthur shrugged and turned back to go into the house. As he made his way back up the steps, Christine appeared from the inside.

"You never stop, do you. She's only 23, for God's sake. Like that little tart…"

"Oh shut up! Just stop!" Arthur hissed at her.

"I'll stop when I like" she said venomously, while maintaining a wide smile for public view. "I'm not falling for any more of your family's lies and tricks. Just remember, all I have to do is to go over there and tell dear old Chief Constable Tom Willow everything I know."

He smiled back. "But you won't, Christine, my dear, because you'll be in just as much trouble as the rest of us." They smiled at each other, and she clinked her half-empty champagne glass against his.

"I might though. Cheers."

"Oh no… you won't. You really won't."

It was at about 3.30 in the morning, after the last of the guests had left, the family had retired to their beds, and the staff were in the middle of clearing the ballroom, that the call went out when Alison Whiteley, one of the young housemaids, came rushing downstairs.

"Someone, please phone for a doctor. Quick. It's Mrs Simmons. She's been taken ill. Mr Simmons has just found her and she's… not moving."

"Not moving. What is it?" the butler asked her.

"She's taken some pills…"

33

"I expect you both know why I've called you in" Sharon Lightwater said, sitting down behind her desk. "I don't need to tell you we are very concerned about your whole attitude this term, and your test results. Now, I don't know what is going on between you two, but I thought we made it clear that these two years are vital for your future careers. So, would you like to tell me what exactly is going on? Hazel?"

Hazel shrugged and looked at the floor. She had sat through several of these chats in the last year or so, and in her opinion they were complete waste of time, as no-one ever listened to her explanations.

"Alex? Would you like to explain why there has been a sudden dip in your results?"

Alex looked across at Hazel for a moment. "Miss, that 'sudden dip' was one small maths test, which I rushed; I just wasn't focussed, that's all."

Sharon took a deep breath. "Look, I know you two are more than just friends, but you mustn't to allow personal relationships to get in the way of your futures. Now, is there anything you want to tell me?"

"No, Miss" said Alex. "There's nothing to tell."

"Really? I'm sorry, but I just don't believe that, Alex. Look, are you... in some sort of trouble, perhaps? At home?"

"Trouble at home?!" laughed Alex. "No!"

"Hazel? You haven't said anything. Do you want to talk to me... in private?"

Hazel frowned in astonishment. "Why would I want to talk to you in private? I'm fine. We're fine. Everything's fine. I'm just a little behind in my homework, that's all. Something's come up, and…"

"We're investigating… another mystery. From the past… like last year." Alex said, awkwardly.

Sharon rolled her eyes. "Another mystery? I see. What is it this time, the sinking of the Titanic? The Bermuda triangle? Or another train crash?"

"It's a ghost story, if you must know" said Hazel, "in my family… my mum's great uncle keeps seeing a ghost, only… we've already uncovered two suspicious deaths, and there's a lot more to this than everyone thought."

"A ghost story!" said the teacher, shaking her head disbelievingly. "What are you two like?"

"We're like… private investigators, actually Miss." Alex shifted uncomfortably in his chair. "And we've found out stuff that lots of adults have missed. Important stuff… life and death stuff." As he spoke, he realised how very dramatic it all sounded.

"We actually found a secret tunnel under a Manor House" said Hazel, determined to inject some real-life drama into the conversation. "And then we got chased… by a man on a quad bike."

"Right. This has gone on long enough. I think I'm going to have to chat with your parents…"

"Oh, they know about it. My Dad was with us when we got caught trespassing on the old race track where the crash happened…"

"Race track? What race track, Hazel? And why was your Dad with you?" Sharon was beginning to lose her cool. "Look, I've known your Dad a while.

He doesn't strike me as the sort of man to lead two young people into 'life and death' situations."

"You don't really know my dad then" muttered Hazel, under her breath.

"I beg your pardon, Hazel Burns? What did you say just then?" Sharon stared at her fiercely.

Hazel shook her head.

Alex took a deep breath. "Look, Miss, can I just explain about our investigation, so you know we're not making all this up as an excuse to miss out on doing our schoolwork."

"Go on then, Alex. This had better be good."

Alex briefly outlined the details of the story, beginning with the accident, and the death of Harry Levenson, and only mentioned the ghost once, concentrating instead on the anomalies in the factual evidence that they'd gathered so far. With some input from Hazel, he thought he'd summarised the mystery very clearly.

Their teacher was unimpressed. "From what you're telling me, Alex, I would say this is a police matter. You should hand it all over to them and they can investigate it. I'm going to write an email to your parents, both of you, spelling out why we've had this conversation, and why this has all got to stop."

"But Miss…"

"Hazel! You listen to me. You've got a track record of trouble-making at this school. You're an intelligent young lady, with a bright future, but you can't let yourself be sidetracked by these… childish adventures. This isn't an Enid Blyton story, you know, this is real life."

Alex threw his head back and laughed loudly. "That's what her dad said… 'it's like an Enid Blyton

233

story'. Only we're not the Famous Five, we're the Terrible Two. That was just after we'd been chased by the guy on the quad."

"Exactly my point. This is all too fantastic…"

"So what you're saying, Miss" said Hazel, "is that even though we've found out that someone who was supposed to have jumped from a train was probably pushed, and someone else who supposedly witnessed two deaths is not actually who they said they were… none of that's important, but because my homework might be a bit late the world's going to come crashing down around us."

"Yes, Hazel Burns, I am saying that. And believe me, your world *will* come crashing down if you don't pull your finger out. And yours, Alex Phipps. You, of all people surprise me. Up until now, you've had an exemplary record at this school, and your results have been excellent. Don't let yourself be dragged down by… associating with…"

Suddenly Alex saw red. "Associating with who? Hazel's dad? Or just Hazel? We're best friends, okay! No, actually, we're not. We're much more than best friends. She happens to be my girlfriend, okay? And she really helped us to solve the Salmsham mystery last year, and you might remember that we actually rewrote a bit of history…"

"Enough! Don't you dare speak to me like that again! Either of you!" Sharon stood up. "Wait here! Don't leave the room! I'm going to call Mr Bolton over, and you can think about what you're going to say to him to explain I shouldn't sanction you both."

She stormed out of the room, slamming the door behind her. Her brisk footsteps echoed down the corridor, and they saw her stride out of the doors of the B Block, and along the path towards the main school offices.

"Hmph. That's another fine mess you've got me into, Hazel Burns" Alex chuckled. "I mean, I could be the world's greatest at anything and everything, but you're just dragging me down, and down, and down..."

"Yep. It's my job in life. I wreck futures, you know" she grinned. "Actually, Alex dearest, I do think we are quite a bit in the muck, aren't we?"

"Yup."

"Parents will have to get involved."

"Yup."

"Yours will probably ban you from seeing me."

"That I *very* much doubt" said Alex. "My dad has a real soft spot for you, and he likes your dad too. And our mums are firm friends now."

"My dad... well, he can't say much, can he? He got us into the muck too. And my mum... I mean, it's her ghost story. If they try to poo-poo it to her, she'll probably throw it back at them."

Alex laughed again, then frowned. "I tell you what though, Haze. When the Head gets here, we need to at least pretend that we'll do as were told, and that we take it all seriously, and so on."

"Oh right. You mean... take this all on the chin? And make out we're sorry, and it won't happen again?"

"I won't sanction you this time, but rest assured, if we have any more issues with late homework, or poor attitude..."

"You won't, Mr Bolton" said Hazel "We're really sorry. We've had a chance to chat while Mrs

Lightwater was gone, and we've both agreed to work really hard and not to let our… investigations get in the way of school anymore."

"Alex?"

"Hazel's right, Sir. We'll prioritise our school and homework over any investigations we might be involved with."

"Ah yes. These investigations. If what you say is true, you should simply talk to the police…"

"But Sir, they won't…"

"Please, Alex. Don't interrupt me. We have agencies, such as the police, in our society who deal with problems and investigations, and criminal activity, and everything else that you shouldn't be concerning yourself with. Leave it to the adults, and focus on your school work."

"Leave it to the adults?!" Alex snorted angrily. "Would they be the ones who send the wrong people to prison, and think every murder is a suicide…"

"Alex! Remember what we agreed" said Hazel sharply, with mock seriousness. "Now, come on. Don't give them a chance to think I've been leading you astray. We agreed we'd focus on doing our school work, and focus we will, okay? Now, please apologise to Mr Bolton."

Alex apologised, managing to suppress an urge to giggle at his girlfriend's mock anger. "Thank you, Alex, and you Hazel" the Head acknowledged as the two students stood up to leave. "Now, there is one last thing I'd like to say to you both, so please sit down again."

They both sighed, and sat down.

"I'm not stupid, you know, and I know that you're probably going to ignore my advice, but let me just say this. Reputations are often built on perceptions, and very often those perceptions may only have a tenuous link with the facts."

Hazel and Alex exchanged glances.

"Hazel. Your school career has been defined, to some extent, by what happened last year in the netball incident. Whatever the rights and wrongs of it, and I don't want to go into all of that again... the perception of you amongst your peers, and some of your teachers, as some kind of teacher-beating 'psycho' will be with you, I'm afraid, throughout the rest of your school life, unless it gets the chance to be... how shall I say it... overwritten by some other occurrence. As for you, Alex, you have the reputation for being a very sensible boy, and yes, a bit of a sleuth in the eyes of your fellow students, but don't spoil it. I've heard you both described with great wonder, as 'private investigators' by other pupils, but just remember, you weren't the only ones involved with the Salmsham mystery, were you. And one successful investigation doesn't make you ace detectives." He paused. There was no reaction from the teenagers. "So, let's hear no more about this ghost story. Save it for the holidays, and let's get you through the year and prepare you for your GCSEs."

"Thank you, Sir" Alex said. "Erm... will you be still be contacting our parents at all?"

"Yes, Alex. I will be sending them an email just mentioning that we've had a chat. Nothing sinister, just for the record, really. But, if anything else happens, we'll be talking directly with them, yes."

34

"Great, so what you're saying is, I'm grounded till Easter? Really? Okay, thanks a bunch, Mum!" Alex threw his school bag down hard and kicked his shoes off, hard enough that one of them bounced off the wall and flew halfway across the hallway.

Freya Phipps stood in the hallway, arms folded, trying to remain calm. "Throwing your bag down like that isn't very clever, is it? Your laptop's in there. And no, you're not grounded. I just said, I don't want you seeing Hazel until your school work is up to date."

"Mum, it is up to date. I don't know what the school have said…"

"It's not the school, it's Meredith. She's… concerned… that Hazel is getting behind."

"But… we were going to do her homework tonight, Mum, and then work on the Cantin thing."

"Well… you're not now, so you can calm down, and put your things away neatly, and do whatever schoolwork you've got tonight, and I'll have tea ready in about an hour."

Alex slammed his bedroom door shut, fell onto his bed and grabbed his iPhone. He typed "'*Sup*" and pressed Send. Hazel replied straight away.

'rents have got da email. I'm grounded'
'me too'
'your mum says I'm a bad influence'
'she told me your 'rents say it bout me'
'We're both bad peeps then'

'Yh'
'Shall we keep being bad'
'Yh l8r gonna check emails I love you xxx'

He logged in and checked for any new messages. There were none. Then he opened the Facebook group page. There was a reply to his comment on the Brands Hatch picture. Someone called jerry62 had posted *"According to my Dad that was Arthur Simmons, sometime saloon racer and mechanic. Aka 'Minute' as in 'back in Arfur minute lol. Hope that helps?"*

"Thanks very much, yes it does" he typed in reply. 'Arthur Simmons' he thought. 'Where was he in all of this?' He reopened the email from his Nana. He realised he hadn't done anything about the information in it. There was his name, birthdate, marriage date, death date. Ah, of course. His death. Alex noted that he died in Bristol, yet he was buried in Langley, next to his brother Reginald. Back home with his family. Alex picked up his phone again and flicked through the pictures he took in the churchyard. There it was, Arthur Frederick Simmons. He sent the pictures to his email so he could see them better; the writing on the headstones was quite faded even in real life.

He opened up his email and saved the attachments to the research folder, then opened one of them. It was Cantin's grave. He clicked on the next few pictures, until Arthur's grave appeared.

Alex frowned, and checked the information his Nana had sent. He quickly rang Hazel.

"Can you talk? Great… look, you're not going to believe this but…"

"Alex Phipps! Did you not get the message not to contact Hazel?" Meredith Burns' voice barked severely down the phone. Alex could hear Hazel objecting in the background.

"Yes, but Meri…"

"No buts, Alex. You're not to ring her."

"Fine, but actually, this is for you and Uncle Toby. We've got the wrong Arthur Simmons, or there's two of them born on the same day."

"What are you on about. Who's Arthur Simmons?" Meredith's voice was severe now.

"Your ghost. Someone on Facebook has identified your ghost in that picture at Brands Hatch. The ghost of Cantin that your Mum and Uncle Toby saw was a racing driver called Arthur Simmons."

"Okay, so Uncle Toby made a mistake then. That's still no reason to be calling Hazel…"

"No, sorry, listen, Meri. This Arthur Simmons died in Bristol in 1974, and they gave his birth date as the 17th of August 1905."

"Yes, but…"

"We found his grave, in Langley last weekend. I've got a picture of it here. It says Arthur Frederick Simmons, born the 17th of August 1905, died 9th February 1916."

"What are you trying to tell me, Alex?"

"That our ghost, who was masquerading as Arthur Frederick Simmons, brother of Reginald Simmons, of Langley, is a fake. Whoever he was, he's stolen the identity of Reginald's real brother who died when he was 10. And I wouldn't mind betting that Reginald helped him do it."

"I don't understand it." Meredith said softly. "If it wasn't Arthur Simmons, who was it?"

240

"That's my point. We don't know. What we *do* know that whoever was prancing around the racing circuits of England in the 1950s and 60s calling himself Arthur Simmons was a fraud. There was no such a person. Oh, and he just happens to be Michael the robot's grandfather."

"So, Katie's boss isn't really a Simmons then."

"Oh yes, he will be. If he was called James Simmons at birth, and registered as that, then it's his real name. It's just, his father used an alias, that's all."

"Okay. Thank you, Alex. Look, you'd better get back to your homework, and we'll speak soon."

"Okay. Thanks Meri, and sorry for phoning Hazel. I'll back off, I promise."

"Mum, when's Dad back?"

"Tomorrow afternoon. Why?"

"Oh, I think I might need his help on something. To do with the motor racing stuff."

"Well… now, I've just had a long chat with Meredith on the phone, after she spoke to you. We've decided that you and Hazel…"

"Look, Mum, we're fine, we're good for each other. She's my best mate and I love her…"

Freya put her hand on his arm. "Will you please stop, and listen to me. We've decided that once Hazel has finished this weekend's homework, she can come over, okay?"

"Mum, you're the best!"

"I know. But let's have a bit less of this 'I love her' stuff, until you know what it really means."

From: livvyphipps@brunel.ac.uk
Sent: Saturday, March 08, 2019 8.25 PM
To: alex@phippstribe.net
Subject: Denis's dad

Hi Li'l Bro

Remember the mad Denis? He's only gone and asked his
Dad for some help. Do you mind if he emails you directly
from France?
Give my love to the rents
Vive la France
Lxvvy

From: alex@phippstribe.net
Sent: Saturday, March 08, 2019 9.04 PM
To: livvyphipps@brunel.ac.uk
Subject: RE: Denis's dad

Hi Sis

That would be awesome. I'll brush up on my
French… un peu (ooh, get me!)

That Arthur Simmons boy who's grave we saw,
died aged 10. He's our ghost! Someone using his
identity was the ghost Hazel's uncle kept seeing.

Lightwater threw a wobbly and me and Hazel this
week. She got the Head in to lecture us about our
attitudes and all that jazz. We've managed to
ignore most of it so far. They got all the olds
involved but so far we're still allowed to go out
during daylight hours…

Alxx

35

Sunday 10th March, 2019 – South Attwell
Chess game

"Fabulous buffet, thank you Meri. I'll give you a hand tidying it all up…"

"Later, Freya, later. I'm keen to see what the Terrible Twosome have come up with today."

Geoff Burns had set up a large white mat on the dining room table. The two families had come together, at Meredith's invitation, to try to piece together what was becoming a more complicated problem. Meredith's mother Linda had arrived early to help her daughter with the buffet, and both Burns children had apparently finished all of their school work assignments by early Saturday evening.

Alex had suggested, and Hazel and her parents agreed, that they should set up a series of 'events' on the table, using sheets of A4 paper, and some chess pieces, starting with white figures.

"What we'll do" said Alex, "is talk through each event on our timeline, and every time a person is mentioned, they become visible to us, so we'll use a white figure for that person. Once they've gone, they're invisible and we can reuse the figure. If we can use the same figure for the same people that would help. For anyone not directly relevant, we'll use one of the pawns, and Max is going to make a note of who is who. If there's someone who we think isn't who they are claimed to be, we'll call them 'unreal' and use a black figure, okay? Right… here goes. 9th October, 1937, the Abbots Park Gold Trophy race."

Armed with copies of the race and accident reports, and witness statements from the inquest, they started placing chess pieces onto the sheet marked RACE. Max carefully noted the names of Pierre-Henri Cantin (knight), Arthur Prosser (rook), Harry Levenson (knight), Toby Allen (king) and David Watson (bishop), and then Alex started to place them in the appropriate places.

"Right. The crash happens... now. Cantin... disappears. Harry... was hidden, but appears, and dies – we'll leave him out for now. Toby was hidden, but now appears. Prosser is there all the time. David Watson was hidden and now appears. So far, so good. Except, where is Cantin?"

"In the river" said Hazel.

"But we can't see him... so he's not there."

"But he is there...they fished him out three months later."

"Nah, listen everyone. They fished *someone* out three months later but we don't yet know who. Let's work on what we have as evidence which cross checks. Cantin is nowhere to be seen. Everyone thinks he's in the river. But... who saw him go into the river?"

"David Watson." Geoff said. "Yes, I see what you mean. If your theory is right, and Cantin has really jumped from the car, and gone down the slope and into the tunnel, Watson was lying..."

"Exactly" said Alex, with a finger on the Watson figure. "And... no-one saw Watson before the crash. I mean, he could have been hiding there, but surely Toby Allen would have seen him. Now, he said he never saw the boys, and Toby said they never saw him. I say, if he'd been hiding in the same place as them, he would have seen them. I think he's come out of the tunnel as Cantin went in…"

The next 'event' was the investigation by the RAC, followed by Harry Levenson's inquest. "And then… here's the odd thing. We never see or hear about David Watson again. But we know that he gave an address in London 'care of' Christine Rocquefort. So, I reckon we should list him as an 'unreal' person, and let's swap his white bishop for a black bishop."

"Agreed" said Hazel' "but also, Cantin the driver."

"How do you mean?"

"Well… we don't know anything about him. No-one at the race seems to have known him, there's not much written about him, and he was due to race in Crystal Palace, wasn't he? I mean, he could have been absolutely anyone."

"Ah. Good point, Hazel." Mark Phipps leaned forward and pointed at the Cantin white knight. "What if the real Cantin was ambushed on the way to Crystal Palace, and a substitute…" Mark swapped the knight for a black one as he spoke, "…appeared at the very last minute at Abbots Park. The substitute 'disappears' or is 'killed', and then the French police have no-one to chase. Meantime, Cantin lives on…"

"Until he's washed up on the shore three months later, in pieces" said Geoff.

"If it's his body. Let's see, who identifies him?" Alex was starting to warm up. "Why don't we do the inquest on Cantin next?"

Some more pieces were produced, representing the people at the inquest.

"So… the only people named at the inquest are the coroner, and Mrs Christine Cantin. Let's have a Christine figurine, shall we?" He smiled at his little rhyme, and placed the black queen on the table. "I think we should make her one of the 'unreal' people too, don't you?"

"You forgot someone" said Hazel. "Here, at the inquest. You forgot Pierre-Henri. He's here, isn't he, in the adjoining mortuary."

"Good point, good point. But let's use another piece for the dead Pierre, because the only thing linking the live Pierre with the dead Pierre is the evidence from the 'unreal' Christine."

The funeral in Langley was the next item. A collection of pieces built up on the paper, including new ones for Reginald Simmons's wife, Matthias Fepp, and André Cantin, and once again the 'dead Pierre' was used. André was also logged as 'unreal', (black bishop) as he was alleged to have been killed the year before in a German race.

"Right, I'd like to stretch the funeral day out to include the train journey to Reading" Alex added.

"Because" added Hazel, "Arthur Prosser gets on the train, and is seen by Jonathan Blake…"

"Rewind, rewind. What about the scene by the graveside? Arthur Prosser is fine, happy, cheerful, full of beans, then he goes to the graveside and is seen by Arthur Simmons – ah! We need an Arthur Simmons. Let's make him 'unreal' too…"

By the end of the afternoon, the group had covered every known incident from the fatal race, to the paddock at Brands Hatch, with Toby Allen and his niece, the former Miss Linda Allen, now Mrs Dillon, Meredith's mother, who insisted on being a white rook, for reasons only she understood.

"Okay, so now you think we know what happened at these various times" said Geoff Burns, "what we are missing is the big 'Why?'"

"I know, I know" said Alex. "I'm waiting on some more details from my Nana, and also an email from this French journalist guy who Livvy put us onto. Then, I think, we've got the mystery solved."

"Wait a minute" Meredith piped up. "Didn't Uncle Toby mention that Matthias Fepp had a younger sister. He dated her or something."

Alex looked up from his notes. "Oh yes. Did we get her name at all?"

"I'll have to ask Tina to go around and have a chat. He said he'd read some old correspondence and get back to us, didn't he?"

Alex put his pen down, puffed his cheeks out, and stretched his arms. Hazel grabbed the list he'd compiled and ran her finger down the page, nodding as she went.

UNREAL
Pierre-Henri Cantin (black knight)
David Watson (black bishop)
Christine Rocquefort (black pawn)
Christine Cantin (black queen)
Pierre's body (black rook)
André Cantin (black bishop)

Arthur Simmons (black knight)

<u>NEED MORE INFO</u>
Cantin brothers
Vendolet tyres
Matthias Fepp
Fepp's sister (Toby's g/f)

"You know, there's another occurrence we haven't done" she said, to the accompaniment of a collective groan from everyone else. "Our little meeting with *Chahhhhles Fawwwster* and his robotic minion, the wonderful Michael Simmons."

Alex shook his head. "No, let's not. Not now, I'm wiped, and besides, we've sort of confirmed their information. I mean, they're not really part of the ghost story, are they?"

36

From: marcel.fontaine@editionfontaine.com.fr
Sent: Sunday, March 10, 2019 4.37 PM
To: alex@phippstribe.net
Subject: Cantin racing pilots

Dear Alex Phipps

My son is telling me how you are interested in hearing about Pierre-Henri Cantin. Please forgive my not perfect English. I am a French writer for many years about the history of French Grand Prix pilots, and I can tell you some things about Cantin and his brothers.

Here is everything I know from books in my house.

There were two brothers Cantin, Pierre-Henri and André. Pierre-Henri is born the 3 Mars 1908, André the 18 Octobre 1909 They were born in Metz, Lorraine.
They both liked to race cars. Pierre-Henri win some races in 1930 and André start to race in 1933 but Pierre was often faster and win more.
Pierre-Henri was paid by Vendolet Tyres and promote the tyres wherever he goes. He makes André use the tyres, so they enter him both for the Eifelrennen at Nurburgring. He tested at the circuit the week before the 14 Juin 1936 he died when the tyre blow up, and the car roll a lot down the mountainside and André was thrown out and instantly died. It was badly damaged and cut up for spare parts, but they keep the engine which was still good. André's body is come home to be buried in Metz.

Now it is Décembre 1936 and finds Pierre-Henri is having a liaison with a young girl, but he is a married man, his wife found out about them. His wife then died suddenly and people think it was him who killed her but the police cannot proof it. This girl is also the girlfriend of one of the Directors of Vendolet Europe so they tell him no more money for racing, but then some money was missing from Vendolet and the police suspect several people and one of them is Cantin. They then think he might have killed his wife and they find more evidence so they try to arrest him but he leave France and go to Germany. All this is in 1937 and now he is wanted by Police in Europe. Then his team enter him for the Empire trophy at Crystal Palace and so the British police try to arrest him, but he is racing instead in Abbots Park and that's where your accident happens.

Vendolet is losing money and there is some fraud with some Directors but I am not knowing who is the bad ones. Philippe Vendome is good man I think but he go into prison but then let out later. He was a victim like the rest. His partner Boulet, he died in 1938. Then French government take over Vendolet for war tyres then sell it all later to bigger company.

I think one of your writers at Motorsport investigate Cantin's death in Britain but he die before he can write it down. His name was R Preece.

I hope this helps. Ask me some more but I am not sure I can help more.

I would like it if you tell me what happens at British end of this mystery?

Yours most sincerely

Marcel Fontaine

From: alex@phippstribe.net
Sent: Sunday, March 10, 2019 11.41 PM
To: marcel.fontaine@editionfontaine.com.fr
Subject: RE: Cantin racing pilots

Dear Marcel

Thank you so much for writing to me. I met Denis when we went to find Pierre-Henri Cantin's grave and we both like Isambard Brunel!

I read your email and it is very interesting. I have some questions which you might know the answer to:

Who was Pierre-Henri Cantin's wife? We have her down as Mrs Christine Cantin, and she was alive at his funeral.

Can you find out about her death? Was there an inquest?

Who was the girlfriend?
Who was the Director at Vendolet?

I think this mystery is becoming more difficult.

I should tell you that I don't believe Pierre-Henri Cantin died in the crash at Abbots Park, I think he escaped. The crash looks as if it was staged.

I don't know who the body is in Cantin's grave in Langley, but I don't think it is Pierre-Henri Cantin.

I must stop now as I have to go to school tomorrow and I am already in trouble there!

Alex Phipps

From: alex@phippstribe.net
Sent: Sunday, March 10, 2019 11.58 PM
To: sheilabagley@phonetalkinternet.com
Subject: Most ghost stuff

Hi Nana

Sorry this is so late, please don't let on to Mum but I've just had loads of information from a contact in France and I can't sleep anyway.

The André Cantin buried in Metz is Pierre-Henri's brother.
We're looking for Pierre-Henri Cantin born 3rd March 1908 in Metz
André Cantin born 18th October 1909 (the one who was killed) in Metz
Pierre-Henri married someone who died around 1936/7 can you find out anything about who?

Anything at all you can find out about Matthias Fepp and his wife Heidi would be great.

The person calling himself Arthur Frederick Simmons has been identified as our ghost in 1968, but he actually died 9th February 1916. Please could you get his 1916 death certificate for me? And the 1974 one? Dad will pay, I'm sure!

Love Alexxx

37

"So you see, I think we're looking at murder again" said Alex dramatically, as he and Hazel followed the rest of their form across the car park area between the science block and their form room. "Marcel Fontaine reckons that Pierre-Henri Cantin probably bumped off his wife…"

"But he can't have done – she was at the funeral, wasn't she?" Hazel suddenly slowed down. "Watch out, Lightwater's about. Just walk slower."

"If you mean Christine Cantin, she's one of our 'unreals' though, Haze. So, she might not have been his wife at all. And anyway, if he wasn't Pierre-Henri… oh this is doing my head in." They turned into their form room and put their bags down together on a desk at the back of the room, just as Sharon Lightwater came in.

"I hope you two are concentrating on your history coursework, and not discussing personal issues from outside of the school."

"Personal issues? No, Miss. We were actually discussing a bit of French pre-war history." Alex managed to keep a straight face.

"Really." Sharon stared at him disbelievingly. "Well, just make sure you two sit apart from each other, please."

"Happily" said Hazel. "I don't even like him anymore, anyway. His sister smells and hangs out with French people."

The rest of the class laughed as Alex grinned and sat down at the back of the room, next to Jason Roebuck, who responded by jabbing his pencil into Alex's arm. Hazel picked up her schoolbag, went to the front of the room and plonked herself down between two other girls in the front row.

"So, in 1929, the French, fearing a German invasion, started building the Maginot Line, which was a vast undertaking, as you can see from the map. It wasn't just a line; in some places it was many miles deep as well. As you can see here…the section along the Franco-German border was over 280 miles long, and was the strongest section of the whole line…"

"Miss!"

"Yes, Alex?"

"I presume that was the strongest section because it covered Alsace-Lorraine?"

"Well yes, it did indeed cover the border between Alsace-Lorraine and Germany."

"Is that because Alsace-Lorraine was part of the territory that Germany had ceded to France after the first World War." Alex's question brought murmurs and a few jeers from the rest of the class.

"Well, they didn't exactly cede it, Alex; it was disputed territory which the French annexed until it was recognised in the Treaty of Versailles. Now…"

"What about Metz, Miss?"

"What about Metz, Alex?"

"Well, as I understand it, the Germans had made Metz into a sort of stronghold during World War One and changed all the street names into German, and so now the French saw it as one of the industrial cities most under threat from the Germans, leading up to World War Two."

"Erm.. you could well be right, yes Alex. Why this sudden interest?"

"Well, I've been wondering just how much the people of the region considered themselves to be French, and how much they considered themselves to be German? I mean, there are a number of families there with Germanic surnames, especially in Metz."

There were several murmurings in the class, ranging from derogatory calls of 'swot' to 'you show her, Alex'.

"That may be the case, but that's not entirely relevant to the coursework I've set you, is it?"

"No Miss, but you have to admit, it's a very interesting question, and of course it could have had an influence on the future outcome of the war, if some people in France, especially in Alsace-Lorraine, felt strongly affiliated to Germany."

The class fell silent.

Sharon Lightwater could sense that she might be heading into a trap, but decided to play Alex at his own game. "I'm not sure that the majority of the population felt very strong ties to Germany, Alex."

"But some must have done, Miss. With your permission, may I do a little bit of extra study on this subject. I find it really intriguing." Alex managed to keep a straight face. Most of the rest of the class looked at their teacher in mock seriousness. Hazel and the two girls she was sitting with were desperately trying to suppress their giggles. Even Alex's enemies in the classroom were impressed to see how his line of questioning had slightly befuddled their teacher.

"Okay, Alex, if you are genuinely interested in this, you may of course do some extra work on it, but only after you've completed all the other history homework I've set you."

"Thanks, Miss!"

"So, coming back to the Maginot Line as a military structure…"

"Erm, Miss!" Alex's hand went up again.

"Yes, Alex?"

"So, may I make my area of research relate to the ethnicity of the families in Metz, please, as well as the political scene?"

Sharon Lightwater suddenly felt her face flushing with anger, and she slammed her hand down onto the desk in front of her, causing the front row of students to jump in surprise.

"Right, that's it! Alex Phipps! You can go to Mr Bolton's office right now, and explain to him why you are disrupting my class, and I shall be along after this lesson is over to find out what your game is."

Alex stood in front of the headmaster's desk, and put on his most earnestly serious face.

"I really am genuinely interested, Sir. I mean, imagine if, say, East Anglia had only recently been returned to Britain after Germany had ruled the area for fifty or so years? There would be people there with strong British and German family ties…" He stopped, as Stephen Bolton held up his hand.

"Alex. Is this directly relevant to the lesson that Mrs Lightwater was delivering?"

"Well, I thought it was, Sir, as we were talking about the Maginot Line, and I wondered about the impact it had on the border between Germany and

Alsace-Lorraine, but then she just sort of exploded at me. I think she thought I was doing it to annoy her, Sir. But I really, really want to know."

"I see. What's brought on this sudden interest in the people of this part of France, hmm?"

"Well, as you know, Sir, I've been quite interested in family history for a while now."

"Really? In France? Now, that is a surprise. I had no idea you had family in France."

"I don't, Sir. At least, I don't think I do. This is just general social interest. I just thought it was a very valid question. By the way, if you ever want me to trace any of your family history… that is, if you haven't already done it…"

"My family history… such as it is… is absolutely none of your business, Alex Phipps, okay? Nothing to do with you!"

Alex raised his eyebrows. He had clearly hit a raw nerve. He decided he'd probably pushed his luck a little too far this time.

"Sorry Sir, I didn't mean to offend you. But, anyway, I still think the question of the political affiliations of certain families is a very interesting subject."

"Well, in that case, I think you should definitely do some more detailed research on this subject that you are so passionate about."

"Yes, Sir?"

"However, I want you to keep it separate from all your other homework, okay?"

"Yes, Sir. Thank you, Sir."

"…and I'd like to see a thousand words on it by the end of next week."

38

As he walked somewhat smugly towards the bus stop, ahead of his usual group of friends, Alex found his way suddenly blocked by Jason Roebuck and another troublemaker from his class, Ben 'Beefy' Hall, who put his hand onto Alex's shoulder and stopped him.

"So come on Phipps, what was all that stuff about, sucking up to Lightwater back there?" Jason faced up to Alex, while Ben tried to pull his schoolbag from his shoulder.

A couple of years ago, Alex had been terrified of these two and a third boy, Dale Grafton, who had since moved schools following a serious incident. Nowadays, being taller than the others, Alex felt a lot more confident and, emboldened by the afternoon's events, he decided to stand up to the two bullies.

"Hardly call it sucking up, Jay. Being sent to the Head and all that. Oh, get off, Beefy, it's only got schoolwork in it and you wouldn't know what to do with it anyway." He wrenched his bag away from the other boy.

"Yeah, well. She reckons you were winding 'er up. I'm not so sure, all that poncy stuff about that town and all that."

"Well that's why she sent me to the Head, isn't it, Jay. She thought I was winding her up. And yeah, I suppose I was a little bit. So what."

"What did Bolton say?"

"Gave me a thousand-word essay to write, by next Friday. Like I said, I was hardly sucking up."

"Showing off to that bimbo girlfriend of yours, I suppose. I dunno what she sees in you, Phipps."

"More than she'll ever see in you, that's for sure…oof!" Alex wasn't quite ready for the stomach punch, and bent up double, completely winded. He saw a shoe coming towards his face, and tried to move out of the way but found he just couldn't move quickly enough.

The kick never reached him. Instead he heard a squeal of brakes and a couple of shouts, and became aware that Beefy Hall was lying awkwardly on his back, half in the road, and groaning. He heard a car door slam and managed to get his breath back a little.

"Come on, lads, what's up here?" Alex heard a familiar voice. "Up you get, come on. You were lucky I didn't run you down; that's what happens when you mess about beside a busy road. Oh, hello Alex. Are you alright?" Chloë Smith stood in front of her dark grey BMW and faced the three boys.

"Fine, thanks, Miss. Nothing serious." Alex felt a bit wobbly but wasn't going to let Jason Roebuck know that. Ben Hall was just picking himself up from the road, where he fallen after losing his balance from trying to kick Alex. He rubbed the back of his head and checked for blood, but there wasn't any.

"Alright, boys. I'm Detective Chief Inspector Smith, Hallowfield CID and I can't begin to tell you how much paperwork I'd have to fill out if I'd have run you over just then. What's your name?"

"Ben Hall, Miss" said Ben, somewhat forlornly.

"Okay, Ben. Next time, save your kicking for the football, okay? And what's your name?"

"Jason."

"Jason who?"

259

"Jason Roebuck, Miss."

"Look me in the face when you talk to me, Jason, okay? Now, I saw you punching Alex just then. Why was that? Has he provoked you?"

"No, Miss. We were having a game, that's all."

"Really? A game? Is this true Alex?"

Alex shrugged. Just then, another group of schoolchildren arrived, Hazel in their midst.

"Ah, so you've finally been found out, Jason Roebuck" one boy said.

"Go on, Miss, arrest him! He's a bully" said another.

Hazel pushed to the front of the group, who had now stopped on the pavement behind the boys.

"Hello, Chloë" she beamed confidently. "Nice to see you here, hope everything's okay…?"

"Hazel, hi. So, this is where you guys go to school then? Yes, everything's fine, isn't it Alex?"

Alex nodded shakily.

"Good. Right, everyone, you've all got a bus to catch, so why not just move on, and let's have no more playing around beside a busy road. And you three…" addressing Alex, Jason and Ben "no more fighting, alright? I know who you are, so if there's any more trouble you won't get off so lightly."

The group started to move away. Alex picked up his bag, which had come off his shoulder when he dropped to the pavement. Hazel brushed down the back and arms of his jacket.

"Are you guys going back to Milnefield?" asked the detective.

"I am, she's going to South Attwell" said Alex.

"Right. Hop in both of you… front seat, Alex."

As they drove off, under the watchful stares of their fellow schoolchildren, Hazel couldn't resist chuckling "This will totally reinforce our street cred with the others."

"Yeah, and hack off Lightwater even more when she finds out!" grinned Alex.

"So, guys, you mind telling me what all that was about?" Chloë swung the BMW round the roundabout and floored the throttle.

"Woah! This has got some power!" Alex said. "Yeah, anyway, I got sent out of class today for asking the wrong questions, and they thought I was being a swot, so they jumped on me for that. I don't care too much."

"If you're getting bullied, you should speak with your teacher."

Both teenagers laughed.

"She's the problem actually" Alex grinned. "You see, we're working on another historic crime. And they told us to hand it over to the police, but we don't have enough evidence."

Chloë Smith rolled her eyes briefly, then sounded her horn as an elderly driver meandered across her lane without signalling.

"Old people in cars…" she sighed "What, you mean you're finding more bodies for me to dig up?"

"No, but we've found a suicide which we think wasn't a suicide, and a fatal motor racing accident which we think was all staged. Apart from that, nothing which would be of interest." Alex was still smiling as he said it. He'd always got on well with the DCI; while they were in the depths of investigating the Salmsham disaster, she'd always treated the youngsters as adults. He felt he could tell her anything, and he also knew she wouldn't be interested in this case as it was outside her area.

"When was all this?"

"1937" Hazel piped up from the back seat. "And we've identified a man in 1968 who wasn't who he claimed to be. My great uncle thought he was a ghost, but it was this guy called Arthur Simmons. But the real Arthur Simmons died in 1916."

Chloë laughed. "You guys are serious, aren't you? Where do you find these stories?"

"My family. This ghost story's been with them for years, but we're just exposing it as a big fraud. Not so much the story, but the story behind it."

"Do tell…"

For the rest of the journey home, Hazel and Alex gave an outline of the story to the DCI, who listened with interest, asking a few questions here and there.

"Well, of course, this really would not be of any interest to the modern-day police, but do let me know if you dig up any more skeletons. Oh, and both of you… I know you're not stupid, but please do be very careful not to go trespassing, or breaking any other laws. I mean it. I don't want you wrecking your futures 'cos you think this is all just a big adventure."

"We won't" said Hazel, as they swung into her road. "Just along there on the left. Thank you very much for the lift. See you soon, bye…"

They eased back out of Hazel's road onto the main road to Milnefield.

"So, now you say you're in trouble at school? That's not like you really, Alex."

Alex smiled again. "I know, right. Me and Hazel were told not to have anything to do with each other. We've ignored them, of course. And today, I was asking about Alsace-Lorraine because that's where the Cantin family were meant to have come from. I got told I was being disruptive, yet all I did was ask a genuine question about the city of Metz. Anyway, I got sent to the Head, and now I've got an essay to write for him. I don't mind, though. He's going to get a detailed run down of the case. It'll help me get my thoughts straight on all that stuff."

"You're incorrigible, Alex Phipps!" grinned the detective, as they pulled up outside his house. Chloë checked her watch. "Well, it seems I've got time for a cuppa, so you'd better make sure it's a good one."

Alex fumbled for his front door key, but the door opened before he found it. Sheila Bagley stood in the doorway.

"Nana! What brings you here?"

"You'll never believe what I've found out! Oh, Chloë, hello my dear, how are you?" She embraced the detective. "I'll put the kettle on in a moment, but look, you must see this, Alex!"

They went through into the kitchen, and Sheila picked up a sheet from the table, handing it straight to Alex, who started to read the list of names.

"I've underlined the significant information, Dear" said his Nana, flicking the switch on the kettle. "I think you'll be in for a bit of a surprise… I take it you'd like some tea, Chloë dear?"

"Yes, please, Mrs Bagley. That's very kind of you. I've just brought this supersleuth home, as I bumped into him outside his school and was heading past here anyway."

Alex blew his cheeks out as he read the sheet. "Wow, Nana. This is dynamite!"

Metz, Moselle, Lorraine, France
BIRTHS

Name	Matthias Fepp
Mother	Marie Thérèse Cantin
Father	Heinrich Fepp
Birth	3 Juin 1906, Metz

Name	Heinz-Peer Fepp
Mother	Marie Thérèse Cantin
Father	Heinrich Fepp
Birth	3 Mars 1908, Metz

Name	Jürgen Fepp
Mother	Marie Thérèse Cantin
Father	Heinrich Fepp
Birth	18 Octobre 1909, Metz

Name	Andreas Fepp
Mother	Marie Thérèse Cantin
Father	Heinrich Fepp
Birth	18 Octobre 1909, Metz

No records of Pierre-Henri Cantin or Andre Cantin births in Metz in that era.

Name	Christine Rocquefort
Mother	Hélène Louise Bernard
Father	Robert Rocquefort
Birth	4 Decembre 1913, Belfort, France

Name	Heidi Neugebauer
Mother	Suzanne Schroll
Father	Wilhelm Neugebauer
Birth	29 Novembre 1906

MARRIAGES

Name	Matthias Fepp, fils de Heinrich Fepp, Ingénieur
Spouse	Heidi Neugebauer, fille de Wilhelm Neugebauer, Illustrateur
Married	12 Juin 1927, Metz, France

Name	Pierre-Henri Cantin, fils de Henri Cantin, Ingénieur
Spouse	Yvonne Alice Lévy, fille de Jean-Pierre Lévy, Sculpteur
Married	13 Août 1932, Metz, France

BURIALS

Name	Yvonne A Cantin
Age	26
Buried	15 Janvier 1937, Metz, France

No record found of Yvonne Alice Lévy's birth around 1910

264

"So, Pierre-Henri Cantin was born Heinz-Peer Fepp? Is that what this is saying?"

Sheila poured the kettle into a large teapot. "It seems so, doesn't it? That also makes Matthias Fepp his brother."

"Didn't you say in an earlier email that Matthias died in Bristol in late 1970?"

"That's right, Dear. He was only 64. He got cancer, poor chap. But his date of birth ties up with the information from Metz, you see, so I know it's him we've got."

"I must tell Hazel and her Mum straight away. It's all starting to make sense now."

Chloë Smith looked on with amusement.

"It seems like you should all start up your own detective agency!" she laughed. "I'm kidding, of course, Mrs Bagley, but it appears you've all uncovered another mystery."

After the DCI had left, Alex and his Nana chatted again about the list she'd brought over.

"Oh, Nana, can you do me a favour please?"

"What now, dear?"

"Can you find out a bit about my head teacher's family? His name's Stephen G Bolton, he's about 55 or 56, and he was *very* offended when I offered to look up his ancestry for him."

39

Ronald Preece swung the blue Morris 25 Coupé out of the main gates at Brooklands, and made his way rapidly through the streets of Weybridge, until he turned onto route A3, accelerating quickly up to sixty miles an hour. The Morris, which was on loan from the factory as he was meant to be doing a write-up for them, was surprisingly nimble for its size, and he was pleasantly surprised at the quality of the handling.

As he reached the outskirts of the town, he decided to see just what the car would do, and floored the throttle. At first the car seemed reluctant to go any faster, but then gradually he felt the slight push in his seatback, and noticed the dial winding itself up to beyond seventy. He grinned to himself. 'This is what real motoring should be about' he thought, 'forget all those killjoys who'd have us drive everywhere at twenty.' He was so busy enjoying the open road that at first he didn't spot the powerful Mercedes coming up from behind, but he couldn't fail to notice the headlights as they flashed into his rearview mirror.

"So… you want a race, eh?" he said to himself as they approached a gentle bend in the road. "Come on, then…"

The Mercedes suddenly pulled out and drew alongside. Ronald turned his head briefly but could barely see the driver, who seemed to be staring

266

straight ahead. As the bend got nearer, Ronald eased off slightly, sensing potential danger if someone were to come the other way around what was a blind bend. As his car slowed slightly, so did the Mercedes. He accelerated, and the Mercedes matched him, still alongside.

"What the hell are you playing at, you bloody fool!" he shouted out to no-one in particular.

By now, the bend was upon them, and Ronald had already decided to let the Mercedes go. Much to his relief, it pulled ahead, and began to pull in. Suddenly, the brake lights came on, and Ronald realised he was going to hit him. He aimed his car between the Mercedes and the verge – there was just enough room, but as he got alongside, the Mercedes pulled right over again and for the first time, Ronald realised this was all very deliberate.

"I don't believe… what the hell…!" He looked aghast at the other driver, and suddenly everything fell into place. By now, neither of them were travelling very fast, and suddenly the Mercedes stopped and let Ronald back onto the road. The driver gave a cheery wave as Ronald Preece drove off into the distance, flicking a 'V' sign as he did so.

Half an hour later, he sat in his living room, his hands shaking as he drew on his third cigarette. He picked up the telephone.

"Operator, which number do you require?"

"Get me Slough one-zero-four-seven please."

There were a few clicks, and then he heard the phone ring at the other end.

"Hallo?" a man's voice answered. "Who's this please?"

"I want Mr Fepp, please."

"Who shall I say?"

"Tell him… it's Lindsey Foulkes about a set of tyres for my new Jag. I met up with him yesterday at Brooklands."

"Yesterday, you say? I think you must be mistaken, Sir. Mr Fepp wasn't at Brooklands yesterday."

"Oh right" said Ronald. He was ready to play his joker now. "Well, I don't know who it was, then, but he said he was your representative, and gave me Mr Fepp's name and number…" This was a lie, but he wanted to see how the garage assistant would get out of it.

"Oh, that'll be Arthur Simmons, Sir. He's our representative. I don't know why he would have given you Mr Fepp's name though. I mean, we look after all the sales in England, you see." The young man at the other end was clearly trying to be helpful.

"Oh, I see. Perhaps he ran out of his own cards. It had this number written on it, you see. Perhaps I could speak to Mr Fepp anyway?"

"Who did you say you were?"

"Foulkes. Lindsey Foulkes."

"Oh, well, I'm really sorry Mr Foulkes, but Mr Fepp is actually down there at the moment… at Brooklands. He'll be back later on tonight, but I'm happy to take your order."

"No need, I'll call him later."

Ronald hung up. So, he wasn't wrong; the mysterious Mr Fepp and Arthur Simmons must be the same person. Whoever he was had been driving the Mercedes, and had tried to drive him off the road earlier. Perhaps he was showing off, but more likely it was a warning.

268

Had Ronald Preece realised just how ruthless his adversary was, he would have taken steps to protect himself immediately. As it was, he decided that if the worst thing Fepp/Simmons would do was try to push him off the road, he was more than capable of handling himself.

He sat down in his armchair and began to relight his pipe. It still had a small amount of tobacco left in it from earlier on. He took a few puffs until it caught, and then sat back and contemplated the events of the past day.

He was certain he was getting closer to the mystery of the disappearance and death of Pierre-Henri Cantin, but there were parts of the puzzle that didn't quite add up. He took a few more gentle puffs and let the smoke build up in the room. Suddenly, he leapt up from the armchair and made his way purposefully to the large bureau in the corner of the room. He turned the key in the lock, and heard it click, then it seemed to click again.

'That's odd' was his first thought, but then his brain seemed to be processing several ideas at once. He felt a cold chill go up his back, and turned around. There was nobody there apart from Selwyn, his old black cat, who yawned at him from the cushioned sofa, stretched a paw out briefly, and then promptly curled up and went back to sleep.

He pulled the bureau lid down and opened the file of papers at the back, sifting through, taking note of the odd name here and there.

"Aha" he said out loud. "This is the one."

He picked up a sheet of thin typing paper, which had a list of names typed on it in purple coloured ink. He began to read the names on the list.

Since the last time he'd read it, two names which had previously been unknown to him were now familiar; he could even put faces to the names. Taking a pencil from his jacket pocket, he ticked the two names. There were just three remaining, and one had a question mark beside it.

He heard another click, and once again, turned around. There was another, slightly different sound. It seemed to be coming from outside the room.

Ronald got up silently, and tiptoed across the room to the door. There was that sound again, but what on earth was it?

"Hello?" he called out. There was no reply.

He turned the door knob and suddenly pulled the door open. Silence. He moved into the hallway and looked towards the front door. It was shut. He turned and looked up the staircase. The sun shone through the landing window, exaggerating the brightness of the hallway. He looked past the staircase towards his kitchen door, which was closed.

"That's odd" he said to himself. He remembered leaving the door open for the cat. He walked stealthily along the hallway, past the ever-open dining room door, and put his hand on the kitchen door handle. It was the last conscious action Ronald Preece ever made. At the same moment, a hand appeared from behind him and pressed a damp cloth over his nose and mouth. He tried to take in a breath, but almost immediately felt his world spinning as he inhaled through the cloth. His last lucid thought was regret that he had not sent everything to his editor before heading off to Brooklands that morning.

40

Extract: Motor Sport, May 1938

RONALD GRAHAM PREECE 1889 – 1938

We are sad to announce the death of our popular motor racing correspondent Ronald Preece, who died in a house fire at his home in Shamley Green on the 7th April. A full appreciation will appear in next month's issue, however I believe it is sufficient to say that all of our lives are much the poorer for the loss of this fine gentleman. We have received many messages from readers who never met RGP yet feel that they knew him well through his writings. Their loss is keenly felt; those of us who knew him personally are grieving at the passing of a great friend and honourable man, and feel that the least we can do in his memory is to follow his example by continuing to aspire to absolute integrity in all our journalistic researches and reporting.

41

Meredith Burns chewed over the information Alex had sent her by email. There were so many unanswered questions, but she didn't want to get Hazel or Alex too excited as they were in enough trouble at school as it was. Hazel had told her about the previous afternoon's scuffle with the boys in her class, and how that DCI had got involved. But the mystery was getting deeper and deeper and she knew she wasn't going to be able to ignore it.

Today was her half-day at the Post Office, and like most Tuesdays, business was quite slow. She'd just helped one of the local pensioners pay a couple of utility bills. She'd known Jimmy North for years, from when he used to tend the church gardens. Now he was a frail, lonely widower, always up for a chat, and still quite flirtatious, with a twinkle in his eye. She remembered one conversation she'd had with him a year or so back, when he told her she reminded him of a young lady he used to date. He'd winked at her again today, and it brought that memory back again. That reminded her; she needed to ask Uncle Toby about the Fepp girl he'd dated, but she didn't want to upset him too much. On the other hand, armed with the knowledge about the Fepps and Cantins being the same family, she thought she could gently tease more information out of him.

Perhaps she should go and visit him, but not take Hazel. He would probably open up to her if she was alone, or maybe if she just went with Martina. She was trying to remember how long it took to drive to Yatton from her home.

She sent a text to Martina, and another to Geoff. Martina texted her back in ten minutes to say she'd rung Uncle Toby and he'd be delighted to see them both this afternoon.

At 1 o'clock sharp, she closed the counter. She'd already started the cashing up (as it was still called) long before closing time, and it only took another twenty minutes to complete. Handing it all over to Sanjay, the proprietor of The Stores, she grabbed a chicken sandwich and bottle of water from the cold display shelf and paid Anita, Sanjay's wife.

"Off in a rush, Meri?" Anita smiled

"Last minute change of plans, Neets. Off to see my elderly Uncle up Bristol way."

"Okay. Have a great time. See you tomorrow!"

It was 4 o'clock before the two ladies arrived at their uncle's house in Yatton. Meredith had driven via Henleaze to pick up her cousin, and she filled her in on the new developments on the way.

"I haven't told Hazel where I am today; I just sent her a message saying I wouldn't be home till late, and she's got an after-school revision session anyway, so Geoff'll pick her up on his way home."

Martina smiled. "I'm lucky. Andy's working from home today so I haven't had to tell Lucy where I've gone either. You know, she'll message Hazel if I did tell her. No secrets in this family, eh?"

"Not nowadays. But I think" said Meredith, as she swung the car into her uncle's driveway, "we'll have to prise a few out of dear old Uncle Toby."

"You want to know her name?" asked Toby. "Well, I can't think that it'll do any harm. It was Tasha. Or Natasha. I called her Tasha. I met her at that race meeting I told you about. The one where I saw the ghost. 1954 British Grand Prix. That was it. Beautiful girl she was... we met in the paddock, and... well I don't know what made us talk, but anyway, I ended up with her telephone number and address, and I wrote to her and... well, I don't remember all the details, but it wasn't long before we met up. Either I'd get the train to London, or she'd get the train to Coventry."

"So, let me get this clear" said Meredith. "Natasha was a Fepp, yes?"

"Yes, I'm sure her brother was either Gerhard or Matthias..."

"Gerhard. Matthias was her father." Meredith interrupted.

"Her father? No... she kept talking about her uncle living in Bristol. And she also kept talking about Gerhard and Matthias... she never called him Dad, just Matthias. Oh, and another thing, she changed her surname from Fepp to Phipps. She wanted to Anglicise it; she got fed up with people calling her insulting names, like 'kraut'."

"Ah... now I understand why you questioned Alex. He's a Phipps, but there's definitely no German in his recent ancestry."

"That's right. I thought they'd sent him to find me." Toby frowned and looked down at his feet.

"To find you?" Martina exclaimed. "Who'd sent him? And what do you mean, to find you? You're here, in plain view, aren't you?"

"Yes, I am." Toby Allen looked thoughtful. "But I feel they've always... always been watching me. I don't know why. In fact, I don't know a lot of things any more. None of it makes much sense."

Meredith exchanged glances with her cousin.

"Erm... Uncle Toby, there's something else we've discovered which is going to throw things up in the air a bit more."

"Go on."

Meredith took a deep breath. "Pierre-Henri Cantin and André Cantin were Matthias Fepp's brothers. They were born Fepp, but took on their mother's maiden name. And there was another brother, Jürgen Fepp. He was André's twin."

There was a long silence while Toby Allen processed all of this information. Meredith looked straight at her uncle. He was looking at the far wall, clenching and unclenching his jaw. She was about to say something when he took a deep breath.

"So" he said slowly, "I've been really taken for a fool. All these years... All my life, since that crash."

The two women remained silent.

"Tasha often mentioned her uncle, the racing driver. You're right, it wasn't Matthias. It was always Jürgen. He was the wild one. But I never put two and two together. Of course!" He sat up and looked straight at Meredith. "That's how we met. She was there because her uncle was racing that day, but he was... wait a minute. Wait right there. I need to go and get the race programme."

Martina offered to make tea while he was searching. It was ten minutes before he reappeared with the box of papers Meredith had seen when they first visited him. He rummaged through the box and finally pulled out the race programme for the 1954 British Grand Prix. He flicked through to the supporting races.

"He drove in the big sports car race. I remember it well, because it was actually dry for that race. It had rained for most of the Grand Prix. That's odd." He ran his finger down the entry list.

"What's the matter, Uncle?"

"Well, there's no Jürgen Fepp here."

"Uncle... there's something else." Meredith said tentatively.

"Wait a minute. He was racing in a C-type Jaguar. Here they are, all the C-type Jags. Titterington, Sanderson, Rolt, Head, Simmons, Hamilton, Dunham, Davids, Connell, Baxter.... Those are all the names in the list."

"Uncle. I meant to tell you. We've identified your ghost. Or rather, Alex has."

Toby Allen looked up. "Go on."

"He found a picture from the Brands Hatch paddock, in 1968. There's you with my Mum, and Jo Siffert. The person standing behind Siffert... your ghost... is someone called Arthur Simmons. Apparently, he was a well-known saloon car racer. He died in '74."

"Simmons. Oh my..." The old man looked down at the entry list. "Here he is, look. Arthur Simmons, Jaguar C-type. But he can't have been... unless I saw him and thought it was Cantin."

"Well, is there a Cantin, or a Fepp listed anywhere on the entry list?"

"No, there isn't. But..."

"There's something else, Uncle. This ghost of ours, Arthur Simmons, is an alias, an impostor. You

276

see, the Arthur Simmons he claimed to be actually died in 1916 aged 10. Oh, Uncle… what is it?"

The old man suddenly dropped his head into his hands and began to sob. Martina jumped up from the sofa and sat on the arm of his chair, putting an arm around his shoulder. Meredith fished a packet of tissues from her handbag and passed them over to her cousin. They remained in the same place for a minute or so – at one point Martina thought Toby had stopped breathing, but suddenly he lifted his head again, his eyes moist with tears.

"I'm afraid I've been a stupid… credulous fool. For all my life… well… since the accident. So stupid, so bloody stupid. And because of that, my whole life has been a complete waste."

"Oh no, you can't say that, Uncle" said Martina, holding him tightly. "You've lived a very full life, surely? You were always regaling us with stories of your exploits."

"Yes, I was. All based on this… lie. This ghost… this… Look at me. Look at me. You're looking at a fool!"

"No…" Meredith began.

"Oh yes. Remember when your daughter asked me, was I ever married? Did I have children?" His voice rose "She really hit a raw nerve there, bless her. I… wanted to marry, I wanted children… so much…"

Tears streaming down his face, he looked up at his great niece Martina, who was still sitting on the arm of his chair, hugging his shoulders, gently squeezing him.

"But I only ever really wanted one woman."

The two cousins looked at each other in silence.

"Natasha?" asked Meredith, tentatively.

42

"Natasha" nodded Toby quietly, looking over towards Meredith. "She… I asked her to marry me. Twice I asked her. Both times, she said 'yes'. The first time… she broke it off after a few weeks. Told me… wrote to me, that it wouldn't work out. Well, that hurt me, but I got over it. She even sent the ring back. Then, we met again by accident, at a function in Coventry. That's right. It was 1956, in January. Her father was there; he was something to do with aviation engineering or something, and my firm was supplying his firm with expertise and parts. And she was there. I tried to ignore her, but she came over and found me, and told me she'd made a terrible mistake, and she wanted to get back together with me, only this time it was 'for real' – I remember then wondering what she meant, as if the first time was a sham. Well, we started to see each other and then… well, I'd had another girlfriend who I'd… let go, when Tasha came back into my life. Then… well, we'd only been together another two months when we got engaged again. I gave her the same ring; I'd always kept it. Well, we couldn't do anything straight away. She wrote to me a week or so later and said she was going abroad for a while. Wouldn't say why, or where, but told me to wait as she'd be in touch. Well, then I got a very strange letter from someone claiming to be her friend in Germany, saying that Tasha was marrying a German man, and had asked me to forget her, and move on. She said she'd send the ring back, but she never did."

There was another silence.

Finally, Martina, who had been gently stroking her uncle's shoulder while he told his story, kissed the top his head, and sat up on the arm of his chair.

"So, did you ever see or hear from her again?"

"Never."

"Did you ever try to contact her?"

"No. But I had my suspicions... oh... I can't even begin to... I think. Please, please girls, please know that I would never harm a hair on her head. I wouldn't hurt anyone... ever."

Meredith took a deep breath. "Of course you wouldn't. What are you saying, Uncle?

"I'm saying that... well, someone in her family killed her. I had my suspicions at the time."

"But why?" asked Martina softly. "Why would they do that?"

"I didn't know at the time. But I can see it all now. Look... please, don't involve the police because they'll think it was me."

"What do you mean?" said Meredith. "How could you have killed her if she never came back?"

"They found her body."

"But you just said you never heard of her again. How do you know they found her body?"

"The girl in the woods... Leigh Woods."

"What... the Mystery Woman?"

Toby Allen nodded.

"Uncle Toby, that was years and years ago Aren't you getting a bit confused?" Meredith looked at her uncle quizzically.

"I'm not confused, Meredith, my dear. I may be an old man, but I've still got all my marbles, and I've still got my memory. When they found the body, I knew who it was."

"But… hadn't she been dead for several years? When they found her?"

"Yes… up to three years, they said. But she was wearing a ring. Our engagement ring – the only clue to her identity, and the police held out hope that someone would recognise it. Well, I did. I knew."

Meredith took a deep breath. "So what would have been the harm in telling the police? Did you think they would accuse you of the killing?"

He shook his head. "No" he said simply, "I don't even think the police would have been stupid enough to accuse the person who identified her. No, I just… knew not to say anything. I don't know why… I couldn't ever put my finger on it, but I felt in great danger. But now, I think I know why. It's starting to make sense."

Martina looked puzzled, and glanced at her cousin, but Meredith began to nod at their uncle.

"The ghost" she said softly. "Did you know all along, that he wasn't really a ghost?"

"I suppose I did, deep down. But I couldn't explain… who it really was, and why I kept seeing them, so I convinced myself… and… of course. Of course! Natasha… she… I told her about the ghost when we first met. She told me I was seeing things. But the next time we met up, she kept telling me she had some powers. She claimed to be a medium. In those days folk were very much more superstitious than they are now. I believed her when she told me… please, don't laugh, but she told me I had an aura about me, and I was probably seeing the dead racing driver because I was the last person he'd seen alive."

"Well..." began Martina.

"Don't you see, though? She was fooling me. Now we know why, don't we?"

"I don't. I don't understand it at all" Martina said. "It sounds as if she was as gullible as..." she stopped before belittling her uncle.

"You're right, I was gullible. Not about the ghost, but about her. I thought she was seeing me because she loved me, but I'd told her about the accident. She knew all along that it was her uncle. I realise now, what that young man said before..."

"Alex, you mean?" said Meredith

"Yes, Alex. Alex Phipps. You see, even when I was 12 I found it difficult to believe the driver had been killed. You know what? I think I knew I'd seen him after the accident."

"You mean... he was David Watson?"

"Exactly. He... when the accident happened, I swear I saw the driver come out of the car before it hit us. I had so many images in my head, but I sort of remembered the ones which had been suggested to me at the time, and went with them because... well, I was 12. Who would believe a 12-year-old who says he saw the driver jump out of the car, and then strangle his best friend and throw his body over the edge of the gorge, and then try to strangle me too?"

"Hang on, did you say he strangled Harry?"

"Yes. I'm sure he did. I'm sure I saw him. With my own eyes." Toby Allen's voice was very quiet now. "Except... yes, he did do it. And somehow he sort of seemed to change his clothes. It's like... when he came out of the car, he was wearing a white cotton top, but then he was wearing something different. So maybe it was a different man... I can't think clearly.

Anyway, I was stuck under the front of the car. If it hadn't stuck in the trees I'm sure it would have killed me. I thought I was dreaming, but I saw him choke Harry, and just throw him over the edge. I didn't dare speak, so I just crawled out from under the car and tried to crawl away, but I'd hurt my leg... bruised it badly. I thought it might be broken. Anyway, then someone else appeared and he... Watson, had to pretend to search for us. Anyway, I tried to crawl towards the other rescuers but he saw me, and came over and put his hands around my throat and started to squeeze. I thought... well I knew then that he was going to do to me what he did to Harry. Then someone approached and suddenly he let go of my throat and called out to this other person. Then... and I'll never forget this. He looked right into my eyes and said in a low voice 'if you ever breathe a word of this, I'll come and find you and you'll be next', and then he started to be really friendly and try to help me."

"So, David Watson was really Pierre-Henri Cantin then?" said Meredith. "That's what Alex and Hazel were thinking anyway."

The old man looked straight at his great niece. "Maybe. But...who was Pierre-Henri Cantin? I mean, who was really the driver? I'm as baffled as you are, Meredith. But... I'm so sorry. I've led you all round the houses. I've lied to you all my life, but please believe me when I tell you, I really did believe I was seeing a ghost... most of the time. But it wasn't Cantin, it was David Watson... but... that's the other odd thing, you know. Cantin in that picture, and the ghost of Cantin; they had a moustache. Splendid French thing. I swear that Watson didn't..."

43

From: marcel.fontaine@editionfontaine.com.fr
Sent: Tuesday, March 12, 2019 6.02 PM
To: alex@phippstribe.net
Subject: Re: Cantin racing pilots

Dear Alex

I have some more of the information you ask for.

Pierre-Henri Cantin marries to Madeleine Barrilot on 6
Avril 1931 but she die in 17 Juin giving birth a child.
Then he marries to Yvonne Alice Lévy 13 Août 1932
I told you last email that he have a liaison with a girl and
his wife find out, but now I think was not what happened.
That story was made up by Jürgen Fepp, another racing
pilot. We now have the story that Yvonne before she
marry Pierre-Henri was also with Jürgen, and when
Pierre-Henri marry her Jürgen was now with another
woman but he did not like the wedding and he get into
argument with Cantin and then he killed Yvonne, she die
Décembre 1936.
Well also Pierre-Henri Cantin was a Director with
Vendolet Tyres and he was taking money from Vendolet
for his racing. The other Directors find out and told the
police who start to investigate.
Jürgen Fepp was also a Director of Vendolet, and the
boyfriend of Christine Rocquefort and she bought his
racing car a Maserati, she get money from the Rocquefort
family. She also payed for him to race. He raced a lot in
France and Germany but not in England. Reading reports
at the time most people think Jürgen tried to frame Cantin
for the murder of his wife. In 1937 Jürgen disappears and

is never heard from again, so police start to go after Cantin, then he go to England and the race happen.

Best Wishes

Marcel

From: alex@phippstribe.net
Sent: Tuesday, March 12, 2019 9.20 PM
To: marcel.fontaine@editionfontaine.com.fr
Subject: RE: Cantin racing pilots

Dear Marcel

Wow! This is amazing. Did you know that the Cantins were brothers with the Fepps? Pierre-Henri was born Heinz-Peer Fepp and André was born Andreas Fepp. Jürgen Fepp is Andreas' twin brother!!! Cantin is their mother's maiden name.

Every time I think I know what has happened, something new crops up, but I now think that the racing driver who was buried is either Jürgen Fepp or Pierre-Henri Cantin…

Alex

From: marcel.fontaine@editionfontaine.com.fr
Sent: Tuesday, March 12, 2019 6.02 PM
To: alex@phippstribe.net
Subject: Re: Cantin racing pilots

Dear Alex

What you say explains a lot. What a familly eh? I want to hear what you find, and maybe we write a book together? It could make a crazy story, no?

Marcel

44

Mark Phipps sat and stared in disbelief at the newspaper report on his computer screen, one hand around a mug of his usual mid-morning coffee. He had been granted a two-day break from his office, having been recently abroad on business working non-stop for ten consecutive days. The previous evening, Meredith Burns had phoned excitedly to tell him about her meeting with Uncle Toby, and asked Mark to search the newspapers for reports of the Mystery Woman of Leigh Woods.

It had been the work of a few moments to find the reports from late 1959, and the subsequent description of the headless woman's remains. Even without the sensationalistic descriptions which were commonplace in the media of the time, Mark felt a shiver up his spine when he read about the discovery. She had been buried in a shallow grave quite a way away from the main pathways in the woods, and there were no fragments of clothing found with her, only a ring – the ring which Toby Allen claimed was the engagement ring he had bought for Natasha Fepp (or Phipps, as she called herself). Her body was extremely decomposed, but even so, the pathologist had concluded that she may have been in the early stages of pregnancy.

Mark had copied all the reports he could find into the 'Ghost' folder he had set up, but then he had gone back to the screen to see what else the search had thrown up. Something with his name on it had caught his eye, and he right-clicked on the initial headline to open up the full newspaper report:

Extract: Bristol Evening Post,
Wednesday 15th February 1961

MYSTERY MURDER OF CHELVEY MAN

Police admit they currently have no leads in their investigation into the murder of Anthony Allen, a 33 year-old single man, of Chelvey, who was found in a pool of blood in his back garden last Friday. There was no sign of forced entry into Mr Allen's home, and no sign of burglary or any damage to the property, which was owned by his mother, to whom he paid rent at full commercial rates.

Mr Allen, an engineer with Bristol Siddeley Engines Ltd, was described as a quiet man who had no known enemies. He had been engaged to be married two years ago, but he broke off the engagement following family pressure. His then fiancée has since married and claims to have had no contact with him since her wedding day, when she received a message of 'sincere goodwill' from him. His neighbours say he was a quite quiet but cheerful man who generally kept himself to himself. He occasionally entertained small groups of friends at home, and was recently seen in the company of a young woman who has not yet been identified.

His body was discovered by Mr Gerald Phipps, a delivery driver, who was attempting to deliver some gardening equipment which Mr Allen had ordered the previous day. When Mr Allen failed to answer his doorbell, Mr Phipps called on a neighbour in case they had a key. By chance the neighbour did have a spare key and was able to let Mr Phipps into the back garden where he was intending to leave the equipment. It was then that the gruesome discovery was made and the police were called. Mr Phipps later told our reporter that he'd been very shocked to find the man's body. "I'd seen him just a few days earlier to discuss his order. He was about my age and seemed so pleasant and cheerful. We talked a great deal about aeroplanes over a cup of tea. I never expected this at all. This is a very big shock and I feel so sorry for his friends and family."

"Freya! Freya, come and look at this!"

His wife rushed up the stairs, and came and sat beside him at the desk.

"Look. Read that" said Mark.

Freya scanned the newspaper report.

"Oh gosh!" she said. "He's not a relative of yours, is he? I mean, do we know a Gerald Phipps?"

"No, we don't. I'll get your mum to find out more about him. It's one heck of a co-incidence, though. Here we are, searching for a mystery murder victim in Bristol, and it throws up someone with a connection to our surname, even if it is a tenuous connection."

"Hmmm, I wonder what our home-grown Sherlock Holmes will make if it. He'll probably see a conspiracy where there isn't one!"

Mark chuckled. "I don't think we should be too harsh on him, he's been on the nail so far with this ghost story, hasn't he?"

From: sheilabagley@phonetalkinternet.com
Sent: Wednesday, March 13, 2019 12.17 PM
To: mark@phippstribe.net
Subject: RE: Gerald Phipps

Dear Mark

I can't find anything about this man at all. There are several Gerald Phipps' but they are all accounted for in your family tree, and none of them fit the time and place. I wish we knew how old he was then I could narrow it down. Perhaps you could find the inquest records?

Sheila xx

"Hi Mum, Hi Dad. We're home!" Alex kicked off his school shoes and put his bag down in the hallway. "I've got Hazel with me, Meri's going to pick her up later."

"Hi, you two" Freya said, coming out of the living room. "Dad's made in interesting discovery so I'll bring a drink up for you both in a moment, okay? Hazel, would you like tea, coffee or a cold drink?"

"Tea please, Freya. Has my Mum been in touch about yesterday's meeting with Uncle Toby?"

"Oh yes. Mark's done little else today... but as I say, he's got something to show you guys. We're not sure what to make of it."

Alex scanned the newspaper report. "Dad, this is too much of a co-incidence. Gerald Phipps is the anglicised name for Gerhard Fepp. He was Matthias Fepp's son! You know, he's probably the one who was blanked out on that register from nineteen thirty-nine. That means he's still alive. We should be able to find out where he lives from the Electoral Register online."

Mark puffed his cheeks out. "That's a bit of a wild guess, surely? How do you know he's our Gerhard Fepp."

"Because, Dad… who was the victim?"

"Anthony Allen. He's no relation of Hazel's family, is he?"

"No, but he'd have been known as Tony Allen. Didn't David Watson keep calling him Tony and not Toby? I wouldn't believe any of that rubbish about 'having a nice chat over a cup of tea' or whatever. I bet they thought this was their man. He's the right age, he's been recently engaged and he's not any more. Gerald-slash-Gerhard chats with him to make sure he's got the right guy. I reckon they thought they'd silenced Uncle Toby for good after this."

"Hang on" said Hazel. "Are you saying that Gerhard Fepp was the murderer?"

"I don't know, but if he's family… he's Jürgen Fepp-slash-Arthur Simmons's nephew. Jürgen could have sent him along to do the digging, to make sure he was the right 'Tony' Allen, and then had him talk to the press openly as a distraction. I bet the police checked him out thoroughly and he was clean, so probably Jürgen did the murder."

"This is *so* confusing!" Hazel sighed.

"Well, dearest Hazel of mine, sorry to say this, but it's your family mess, not mine!" Alex grinned as Hazel rolled her eyes at him. "Look" he continued, "let's get my Nana to do a quick Fepp-stroke-Cantin family tree, with all the aliases in it, because this is getting really ridiculous, trying to keep track of it all.

Dad, can you ask her to do another big chart, like she did for the Salmsham thing.?"

"When I've finished this search, yes." Mark was tapping away on the screen. "There you go. There are twelve Gerald Phipps's listed in the U K … here they are. All over the country… Liverpool, Kent, Midlands… and ah! There's one in Abbots Leigh! On the Electoral roll from 2002, to the present day. Let's get the address…"

Three minutes later, and Mark picked up the phone to directory enquiries.

Half an hour later, the scene was set, as a slightly nervous Hazel Burns dialled the number.

"It's ringing… oh, hello. Is that Mr Gerald Phipps…? I'm so sorry to ring you, and this is very random, but my name's Hazel Burns and I'm… no, I'm not selling anything. It's about the murder of Anthony Allen in… yes, that's right. I'm a schoolgirl from Atwell Academy and I'm doing a project on unsolved murders, and I need to get really good marks for it, so I wondered if I could come along and interview you? Yes, of course… yes… well, can I put my parents on? Oh, okay… well, this isn't my parent's number, I'm actually ringing from my friend's house… I'll put his Dad on… bye for now, thank you so much." She handed the phone to Mark.

"Hi… Mr Phipps? Yes, I'm Mark Phipps, from Milnefield. Yes, well, that's what made Hazel want to call you. I doubt we're related… no, my family are from Salmsham and Hallowfield… yes, that's right… well, yes, the school are doing a massive historical project and Hazel is determined to make hers the best ever, so what better way than to do her own interview. Quite, quite... Well, that would be really great. Listen, I'll get her mother to call you later… or could we email you? Oh… okay, fair enough. Oh, right, I'm sorry. Yes, my parents are the same. Okay, well you'll be hearing from Meredith Burns later on, okay? Meredith… Burns. That's right. Thank you so much, Mr Phipps. Speak soon."

He put the phone down, and they all let out a collective chuckle or relief.

"I was so nervous, thank you, Mark" Hazel said. "He thought I was about to sell him some double glazing or something."

"Well, he said he's 85 years old, which is why he doesn't have the internet" said Mark, "so that's something for Nana to get her teeth into. She couldn't find anything about him – birth, marriage or anything else."

Alex piped up "That's because she needs to search for Gerhard Fepp, remember?"

"Of course. Right… another massive missive for your Nana." Mark grinned as he started typing.

45

A Metz Family History (Work In Progress)
Alexander Phipps – 10SEL

This essay is about my research into a mixed-ethnicity family from the town of Metz, in Alsace-Lorraine. In the early 1900s, Heinrich Fepp, a German-born Engineer and resident of Metz, married Marie Thérèse Cantin, whose family had lived in Strasbourg for over a century before. Alsace-Lorraine was an Imperial Territory created by the German Empire in 1871 after its victory in the Franco-Prussian War. The area remained bi-lingual, although Metz suffered greatly during WW1 when the Germans changed all the street names into German and then suppressed the use of French speaking in public. There is evidence to suggest that the Fepp household was politically benign, however, as will be shown by the various children they had.

After WW1 Alsace-Lorraine was annexed to the French Republic.

Heinrich and Marie Thérèse Fepp had four sons, Matthias in 1906, Heinz-Peer in 1908, and twins Jürgen and Andreas in 1909. Matthias seems to have retained his German name even when living in England in 1939, but in the 1920s and '30s Heinz-Peer used the name Pierre-Henri Cantin when he started his career as a racing driver. It appears that his brothers also tried their hand at racing; Jürgen using his real name, while his twin also changed his to André Cantin.

At some stage their father became involved in a tyre manufacturing business with Marcel Vendôme and Charles Boulet, the founders of the Vendolet tyre company, which was big in Europe after WW1. The Fepp/Cantin children also became involved in various ways with Vendolet, who certainly sponsored Pierre-Henri and André Cantin so they could go racing. Sadly, André was killed in 1936 in a race in Germany, and was buried in Metz.

Meantime, Pierre-Henri got married, and the details are a bit murky but it seems that his wife found out he was having an affair and he may have killed her, although it has also been suggested that Jürgen Fepp killed her and tried to implicate Pierre-Henri. There was also some evidence that money was being taken from Vendolet, and evidence seemed to point to Pierre-Henri as the thief, although I personally think again, it was not him. Whatever happened, the police became involved and were actively searching for him when he appeared on the entry list for a race in London in 1937.

The police went to Crystal Palace to arrest him, but he did not show up at that race meeting. Instead, he appeared at another race the same day, in Bristol. During that race his car left the road in an apparent accident and he was allegedly flung out of the car, over the edge of the Avon Gorge and into the river. Three months later his headless torso was washed up in the River Severn, and identified to the satisfaction of the coroner by someone claiming to be his wife.

I personally believe, based on other evidence, that Pierre-Henri Cantin had been murdered before the race by his brother Jürgen Fepp, who seems to have taken over his brother's identity, staged the accident, jumped from the crashing car and then reappeared as a spectator and witness, thus giving a false impression to the police that Pierre-Henri was dead. The wife who identified the body seems to have been Jürgen's girlfriend Christine Rocquefort, a scion of another wealthy family from Alsace-Lorraine. Jürgen wanted to continue his racing career in England but decided to use an English name. For reasons which I believe to be entirely criminal, he stole the identity of the brother of his business partner, one Reginald Simmons. Reginald's younger brother had died in 1916 aged ten. Jürgen Fepp thus took over the identity of Arthur Simmons, and raced extensively under that name, in sports cars, throughout the 1940s and right up until the early 1970s. As Arthur Simmons, he continued in a relationship with Christine Rocquefort who used his surname. She died in suspicious circumstances in 1951, and then 'Arthur Simmons' married Alice Condon, and they had a son James Simmons, who is still living in Bristol, and who has a son Michael.

Meantime, Matthias Fepp had married a German-born girl, Heidi Neugebauer, in 1927. They had a daughter Natasha in Metz in 1928, and a son Gerhard who was born in England in 1936. Both Natasha and Gerhard anglicised their names during WW2, so she became Natasha Phipps and he became Gerald Phipps. It appears that Matthias retained his German name for business purposes, although he may informally have used the name Matthew Phipps in English social circles.

In the mid-1950s, Natasha became involved with a young man, Toby Allen, who had been witness to the racing car accident in 1937. My firm belief is she had been sent in by her uncle Jürgen to find out how much Toby knew. She then broke off the engagement, but a few months later she met Toby again and they became engaged again. A mysterious letter was sent to him soon afterwards claiming that Natasha had gone to Germany and was now marrying a German man. Two year later, however, a headless body was found in Leigh Woods, wearing the engagement ring that Toby had given to Natasha. At the present time this information has not been passed to the police and the body's identity is officially unknown. However, in 1961 a man named Tony Allen was murdered by an unknown killer, and conveniently discovered by Gerald Phipps. It is my firm conviction that all of these events are linked, and the common cause is Jürgen Fepp alias Arthur Simmons, who appears to have suffered psychopathic tendencies from an early age, which his family endeavoured to put up with. I have yet to discover how much Gerald Phipps was involved, and whether he was an innocent victim of his uncle Jürgen's sick behaviour, or a willing and complicit assistant.

In summary:

Matthias Fepp – came to England with his wife Heidi and their two children, Natasha and Gerhard, who became Natasha and Gerald Phipps (no relation to me!). Died of cancer in August 1970 aged 64.

Heinz-Peer Fepp – became Pierre-Henri Cantin, and was murdered sometime around late 1937, probably by his brother Jürgen.

Andreas Fepp (twin) – became André Cantin, killed at the Nurburgring in 1936

Jürgen Fepp (twin) – became Arthur Simmons, probably murdered at least five people, possibly more. Died in 1975 (I have not yet found out how he died – that research is ongoing).

I firmly believe that the complicated geo-political situation in Alsace-Lorraine may have been a trigger which caused an individual within this family to become psychopathic in his behaviour, in such a way that the family themselves defended rather than treated this behaviour. It may also have triggered the family's propensity to display a dysfunctional public identity.

Alex Phipps (aged 15)
15th March 2019

46

Mark turned into Sandy Lane, and drove along slowly, passing the address they'd been given by Gerald Phipps. The large detached houses, which had been built in the 1930s, all had individual characters, but Gerald's house looked a little more weather-worn than the others.

"Some of these houses are worth well over a million pounds" Mark commented as they drove on for another quarter of a mile or so. "I think one further along has been valued at over two million. I'm not sure Gerald's will fetch so much unless he scrubs it up nicely."

Mark turned the car around, and drove back to pull up outside Gerald's house. Meredith, Hazel and Alex jumped out and said their goodbyes, agreeing to keep in touch, and give them ten minutes warning when they needed picking up. Mark and Freya had been given a mission by Alex to try and find the spot in Leigh Woods where the body of the Mystery Woman had been found.

Meredith and the two teenagers walked up the driveway towards the large house. To the left was a garage-cum-carport, half open to the elements. They could see a royal-blue Rolls Royce parked inside, slightly obscured by a large wheelbarrow – someone had been clearing the winter spoil from the garden. The right-hand side of the house was some distance from the fence, but a large wooden gate indicated the way through to the back garden.

"Hmmm. Nice car" said Meredith. "A Rolls. I wonder if he'd miss it!"

"You drive, I'll be the look out" joked Alex. He glanced at Hazel, but she didn't smile.

"I'm starting to feel really nervous now" she said. "Are we getting in too deep here, or what?"

"You'll be fine, Haze. Just act the part of the enthusiastic teenager. I'll makes notes and watch his reaction. Just make sure you don't mention Uncle Toby, or the race crash, or the Mystery Woman in the woods. If I think it needs that, I'll play Bad Cop to your Good Cop. Oh, and if I ask for the loo and take some time, just keep him distracted, okay?"

Meredith rang the doorbell, and then stepped back away from the door.

There was a long pause, and Meredith stepped forward to ring the bell again, but then they heard a bolt being drawn back, and the door eased open. A middle-aged woman's face appeared, peering through a shock of unkempt blonde hair, and stared at them wordlessly.

"Hello" said Meredith brightly. "We're here to see Mr Phipps. We contacted him earlier in the week. My daughter here is doing some…"

"You better come in then" said the woman with a strong Bristol accent. "Our guests are 'ere!!" she shouted, then "'E's in there."

She pointed towards a large side room, and Meredith led the two teenagers through the door. Her first impression was that she had travelled back in time to the 1960s. There didn't seem to be a modern implement in the room at all; there was an old TV cabinet with what looked like a small black and white set in it. The furniture seemed well worn although its original quality was still evident, and Meredith was surprised to see an old dial telephone sitting on a sill in front of the bookshelves. Even the fireplace looked as if it was still used for the occasional coal fire, but the room was also very warm, the source of which was not evident.

Meredith looked for Gerald, but there was no sign of anyone. She turned and was about to call out to the woman who'd let them in, when a man's voice called out "Are you Hazel?"

Startled, Meredith turned back and realised that what she'd identified as a large bundle of drab grey and brown cushions on the settee contained a small figure. Gerald Phipps looked very ancient and frail, and began to stand up to greet his visitors.

"Meredith Burns. I'm Hazel's mother. I'm so pleased to meet you, Mr Phipps." She held out her hand and he grasped it to steady himself, and then pumped it gratefully.

"Pleased to meet you too, Meredith. Hhhh." He made very wheezing, breathy noises as he spoke. "You must be Hazel then. Hhhh... Please, do sit down all of you. Hhhh... Susie will bring some tea."

Meredith and Hazel sank deeply into two very comfortable old armchairs, as the old man dropped back into his original place on the settee opposite, and stared at them intently, slightly unnerving them. Meredith stared at him, and behind the sunken grey face, recognised the Germanic features she'd noticed in the photograph of his uncle, Pierre-Henri Cantin, taken all those years ago. 'Definitely an old version of Boris Becker' she thought.

"Erm... this is my boyfriend Alex" said Hazel, "and he's working on the same project as me, although he's not studying this case, but… we're going out later which is why he's here."

Alex smiled and nodded to the old man, and sat at the other end of the settee, pretending to make himself comfortable whilst finding his phone and switching on 'record'.

No-one spoke at first, until Meredith nudged her daughter and mouthed "go-on" to her.

"So…" began Hazel nervously, "we've been asked to find out about unsolved murder cases, and I did a search and found this man called Anthony Allen and I read an old newspaper report which mentioned you, and I thought… well, my case is more recent than anyone else's so I thought it'd be cool…erm, good, to actually interview someone who was there. My school said it was alright as long as my Mum came with me."

"I see" said Gerald Phipps, nodding. "Well… Hhhh… what you read in the papers is probably all there is to it. You know how I found him, of course?"

"Well, sort of" replied Hazel, pretending not to remember what she'd been cramming in the car. "Something about delivering a lawnmower?"

"Yes, that's right. Hhhh. Except it wasn't a normal lawnmower. It was… Hhhh… a tractor with a mower, but it had other fittings as well, like… Hhhh… well, like a snowplough, and a rake mechanism for collecting up autumn leaves. Hhhh. Hhhh. Oh yes, it was our top of the range model."

"So… what did you do for a living then?" Hazel. "Were you a salesman or something?"

"Well, I worked for the… a family firm, Simmons Garages." Hazel and Meredith both raised their eyebrows, but Gerald was well into his stride now, and the breathiness was becoming less obvious as he spoke. "Simmons had all sorts of garages, car dealerships, tyre depots, and they also had a branch which imported these tractors, so they began to specialise in garden equipment, mainly aimed at the big commercial landscape companies, but we'd sell to anyone who'd buy, of course. I was the sort of general gopher for them. My... I had a relative who worked for them as manager, and I usually did all the running around. It was good fun while it lasted.

"Well... one day this chappie called and said he wanted a motorised lawnmower, and my boss took all his details and then said something like 'how much are you looking to spend' and the chap had no idea, so I was sent out to find out all about him and try and sell him the top of the range equipment. Well, I drove out to Chelvey to meet this chap..."

"Anthony Allen?" interrupted Hazel.

"Well, we had him down as Tony, yes. So, I called in and... well, as you can imagine, this was a long time ago but that meeting is very... vivid. Well, he let me in and before I'd had a chance to ask him anything, he'd made me a cup of coffee and got some biscuits out. I noticed a picture of an aeroplane on his kitchen wall, and we got talking.

"Well, it turned out, he worked for the Bristol Siddeley Engine company, which made aero engines. He was an engineer, you see, and so was I. Well, I was very interested in all of that so we must have talked for a good half an hour before I realised I hadn't discussed his garden equipment at all. Anyway, he showed me into his garden, which was... I could see why he wanted a tractor for the lawn, and we talked about... I remember asking him whether he lived alone, and he said he did. He told me he'd been engaged but that was a couple of years back, and he said... erm... what was it... oh, that's right. His mother wanted him to focus on his career, and I remember thinking it was odd until he told me he rented the house from his mother and she told him he'd have to find another place if he got married, or something like that. So anyway, he'd broken off the engagement and she'd married another man, and I think that was it. The thing is, I may have got some of that from the inquest, but I do remember him talking about his ex-fiancée with a great deal of affection and... well he seemed very sad about it.

"But anyway, then he ordered the top of the range tractor and mower, and all the extra trimmings; I mean, he... money was no object, it seemed. I remember writing all this down, and then I went back to base and gave my boss all the details, and thought no more of it.

"Well, anyway, about a week later my boss asked me if I wouldn't mind delivering the gear to this Tony chap, so I agreed and that was it really. I went round there and... well, there he was."

Hazel looked at Alex, who made 'go-on' gestures with his left hand.

"Erm... this is going to sound a bit crass but... what was it like to find him? How did you feel?"

"What was it like? You mean, to find his body? It was awful. I remember almost being sick."

"Weren't you with someone at the time?"

The old man nodded. "Yes... his neighbour. You see, I'd rung the front doorbell and got no answer, and I had instructions on the delivery sheet to take the gear round the back and leave it in the back garden if there was no-one in. Well, I couldn't get into the garden, but I'd had lots of experience of delivering other things, like cars, and so-on, and I knew that lots of people trusted their neighbours with keys and things, so I knocked on the nextdoor's house, and this older chap came out, and saw what I was doing, and… he didn't have a key to the house, but he showed me how to get into the back garden. He helped me with the gear, and we both went round the back. Well, we both saw the body, but I think I ran over to it and then I… touched him to check for a pulse. He was still warm-ish… I got the neighbour to check as well, so I couldn't be mistaken. Then he went off and called the police and I just waited there, quite stunned, beside the body.

"I think I was quite upset because… well, because he was such a nice chap, you see? I couldn't understand how it was that someone so nice and pleasant and harmless could be just chopped down. In broad daylight."

"And to this day, no-one knows who did it?" asked Hazel, innocently.

"No idea at all. You see…" and then he stopped talking.

Meredith was just about to say something to restart the narrative when the door opened and Susie appeared with a tray of tea, which she placed silently on the low table in front of the settee.

"There's sugar, milk an' flapjacks. 'Elp yerselves, we don't wan' any left now" she muttered, and without a glance at Gerald, she turned and shuffled out of the room, not quite shutting the door behind her.

"Oh, flapjacks!" said Meredith enthusiastically. "I love flapjacks, Gerald!"

"Oh... Hhhh... yes, I do too. Better than biscuits, eh? Hhhh" Alex noticed the wheeze had come back, and wondered at which point he should step in and challenge Gerald about his real identity.

As Meredith poured tea for everyone, and passed it around the table, Alex stood up and asked if he could use the toilet. Their plan had been to extract as much information about the murder as they could, and then reveal their true interest in the investigation. As Gerald gave him directions to the downstairs toilet he nodded discreetly to Hazel, and as soon as he was out of the room he ignored his host's instructions and made his way upstairs, knowing that the housekeeper was still downstairs and probably listening to their discussion.

47

Hazel sat up and started to talk. "You know you mentioned Simmons Garages? I had a relative around here years ago who knew them, I think. Either worked for them, or did business with them. Didn't they have a really big tyre business or something. I can't remember all about it, but my relative mentioned some French firm."

At this the old man sat up and stared intently at her.

"What did you say? What French firm? I don't recall any French firm" he snapped. There was no huffing or wheezing; Gerald Phipps was on the alert.

"Oh, I can't remember the name…"

"Who was this relative anyway? What was his name? And why are you really here, eh?"

"Oh, he was my Great Great Uncle. It was a long time ago." Hazel was careful to use the past tense to describe him.

"What's your surname? Burns, isn't it? I don't remember anyone of that name working for us."

"So who ran the Simmons Garage again? Was it a Mr Simmons? I think my uncle knew him."

"My dear girl, what exactly has this got to do with the murder of Anthony Allen?"

"I think" began Meredith, "she's just trying to get some background…"

"Well, Simmons Garage has got nothing to do with it. Nothing whatever. Nothing!"

Alex reappeared at the doorway, and took a deep breath. "I disagree there, Sir" he said in his most serious voice. "Surely, when Tony Allen put in his order, someone at Simmons's recognised his name as someone they wanted to... bump off, for whatever reason, and they sent you out to ask lots of searching questions, then, when they'd established they'd got the right man, they went round to his house and killed him, just before you arrived with the delivery. They probably thought the police would thoroughly investigate *you* as the person who found him, then eliminate you, and therefore Simmons, from their enquiries, and then... job done."

"Who the... what is this? How dare you? You're not the police, are you? What's the game, eh? You... you invite yourselves into my house on some pretext..." the old man stood up shakily. Meredith reached out to hold his arm.

"Get off me!" he growled. "You can all get out of my house."

"So you *do* know who murdered Tony Allen then. It's as we thought folks. Arthur Simmons..."

"I told you..." Gerald started, but Alex shouted over him.

"Arthur Simmons, your uncle, murdered Tony Allen because he thought Tony had seen him crash the Bugatti at the Abbots Park race in 1937, and fake his brother's death."

"My uncle... was not Arthur Simmons... and what crash? What race?"

"Either you know everything, or you have had so much wool pulled over your eyes..."

"Get out! Susie!! Get them out!"

"You're right though, your uncle was not Arthur Simmons, his real name was Jürgen Fepp and he murdered your sister Natasha and dumped her

306

body in Leigh Woods!" Alex shouted, as Susie came into the room.

"Susie. Show these people out…" Gerald called out desperately.

"Look, Mister Gerhard Fepp, we know pretty much everything there is to know about the whole affair. We're actually preparing a case file for the police…"

"Impossible!" snapped Gerald. "Everything you've said is pure fantasy. My sister was certainly not killed and dumped in the woods. You can't prove anything."

"Oh, but we can" said Meredith, calmly. "You see, Hazel's great great uncle is still alive, and his name is Tobias. Tobias, otherwise known as Toby Allen. The little boy who saw the accident. The young man who was engaged to be married to Natasha Fepp…"

Hazel picked up where her mother had left off. "… or Natasha Phipps, as she called herself. Your sister. So your uncle, having murdered your sister, also thought he'd murdered her fiancé, having arranged for him to receive a weird letter telling him Natasha had married another man in Germany…"

"Except your lovely Uncle Jürgen got it wrong" Alex said, "and murdered an innocent man named *Tony* Allen, leaving Toby Allen to relate the story to us all these years later."

Gerald Phipps sank back down onto the settee. The three visitors also sat down again. Susie, the housekeeper, just stood by the door.

"That's not all, is it, Dad?" she said.

"Dad?" Hazel gasped. "You're his daughter?"

"Stepdaughter… kind of. 'e never married my Mum, but they lived 'ere together for many years. Now she's dead I stayed on to look after 'im…. For a retainer, I 'asten to add. But 'e's not telling you all, is 'e, the old devil. Look at you, Dad, sitt'n' down there pretendin' to be all frail an' wheezy. 'E's eigh'y-five, grant you, but 'e can jolly well move 'imself around when he wants to. I tell you something else… when he 'eard you was coming round, young lady, 'e thought his luck was in until your mother said she was bringing you. Yes, that 'e did."

"What do you mean?" asked Hazel.

"Tell 'em, Dad. Go on, tell 'em about them schoolgirls?"

Hazel gasped. The old man just stared straight ahead silently, looking out of the front window.

"Right, well, I'll tell 'em then. He used to like his young ladies, did my old Dad over there. Only one time, he started following this nice, decent young schoolgirl up near Blaise Castle Park, and she ran away, but while she was runnin' away, someone else got 'er and done 'er in. That scared 'im, that did. So anyway, then he starts seeing another one, and then 'e gets 'er in the family way. Luckily for 'er, the parents took over and brought up the child, and threatened 'im never to go near 'im. Young lad grew up decent, at least."

"I paid them off, you know" said Gerald, fixing his gaze on Hazel. "I loved that girl, I really did. I… my family paid them a lot of money, over quite a few years, so the lad got a decent education. I gather he's a schoolteacher now. I have no idea where."

Hazel shivered slightly, as Susie continued.

"Then there was Alice Simmons…"

308

Gerald stirred. "What? How did you know…"

"I'm ain't stupid, Dad. I listen, I learn, an' I snoop. Let's face it, I've 'ad a few lessons from you, ain' I. I 'eard about what you got up to with Alice. This is 'is Auntie by marriage, if you like!"

Hazel shivered again, and wished she was in another room, away from the leering old gentleman.

Alex nodded. "Wasn't she Arthur Simmons's second wife?"

"After 'e bumped off his first one, yeah. Well, she's had this son, James. 'E works up at the Abbots Manor House now, for them Forsters, but anyway, Alice gets tired of Arthur knocking 'er about and having affairs and treating 'er like a piece of dirt. So, she casts around and finds this" she pointed to Gerald. "Well, 'e was a young man back then, quite 'andsome, so I were told, and she seduces 'im, and then… well, then *she* disappears, doesn't she, eh? Eh, Dad? Everyone was told she'd run off with another man. But you always reckoned Uncle Arthur done it, Dad, but you don't know where he hid the body."

"Natasha wasn't killed by Uncle Arthur, you know" said Gerald suddenly. "That can't have been her body in the woods. And even if it was, no-one could ever prove it."

Alex leaned forward. "But the body was found with Natasha's engagement ring on it. Toby Allen knew it was her."

"Oh, yes… that ring. It was a plant." Gerald laughed knowingly. "Uncle Arthur put it on the body to draw Toby Allen out into the open, because he knew the truth about the crash."

"See, that's what I said" said Alex. "And I knew you knew all about that."

"No, you said it was Natasha. But I'm telling you, my sister was very much alive when they found that body in the woods."

"So… who *was* she then?"

Gerald Phipps smiled eerily at them. "You'll never know. You'll never ever know."

There was a short silence, then Hazel asked "So, what happened to Natasha? Is she still alive? I think my uncle would like to know."

"Your uncle… is probably better off thinking she was the body in the woods" he said finally.

Suddenly, Meredith stood up. "Well, I think we should leave now. It seems to me we've opened up a lot of old wounds, and I'm really sorry it had to be like this, but still… thank you for your hospitality, and you, Susie. Alex, would you text your Dad and ask him to come and collect us please?"

"Already done. He's outside right now."

Gerald Phipps remained on the settee. "Susie will see you out. And see that you don't come back, any of you…"

As they stood on the doorstep, Susie pulled the door closed behind her and herded them along to the right of the doorway, on the other side of the house to the room they'd left the old man in.

"Listen… you've hit a raw nerve now… 'e'll be after you. 'E's not as 'armless as you think. See if you can't get them police round 'ere, and tell 'em they might want to do a spot of gardening out back."

Meredith gasped. "Are you saying there's someone buried out there?"

"I'm sayin', and this is only speculation, mind, but there's folk gone missin' round 'ere over the years, 'specially young girls." She stared straight at Hazel, who glared back at her incredulously.

"How can you possibly live with him if you think that?" she asked.

"Oh, I don't live 'ere, I come in durin' the day. Won't catch me in there with 'im in the dark."

"Why haven't you told anyone before? I mean, if you knew about them all."

"I never had the courage… 'e'd know it was me and then… well, I'd go the same way. I'm dead serious. Until you folk came today I jus' put them things to the back o' me mind."

"Susie!!" Gerald's voice called out from the house. "Susie!! Have they gone yet?"

"Right, we'll get moving. Bye, Susie, and you take care, won't you" said Meredith discreetly, as they set off down the driveway.

48

"Quick Dad, we have to go and rescue Uncle Toby!" Alex slammed the car door while Hazel and Meredith belted up.

"What are you on about?" asked Hazel. "Rescue him from what?"

"Gerald. We let slip that Toby is still alive. I bet you anything he'll try and get to him."

"Don't be daft, he doesn't know where he lives. Mum never mentioned Yatton."

"He's not daft, Haze, he can find him in an instant. Just like we found Gerald!"

Mark Phipps pulled away gently from the kerbside, and began a sharp U-turn which ended up being a five-point turn in the middle of Sandy Lane, pointing the car towards the main road.

"Would you mind explaining just what is going on, please Alex?" he asked. "And where is Uncle Toby's house, and where are we taking him?"

"Right, Dad. Gerald Phipps is a nutter. He's a liar, a psycho, like his Uncle Jürgen. He was complicit in the murder of Tony Allen, and his stepdaughter told us to get the police to dig up the garden back there."

"Are you being serious?"

"Oh God!" exclaimed Meredith. "Alex is right. I'll ring Martina and see if she can take Toby in. Mark, you'll have to turn back around again and head off in the other direction. Yatton is about eleven miles from here. I'll get the postcode off Martina."

"If all this is true" said Freya from the front

seat, as her husband turned the car around again in the entrance to a side road, "we need to involve Chloë Smith pretty quickly. Shall I give her a call?"

"Yes please, Mum. She'll probably listen to you. But before you ring… just tell her… tell her we think we can definitely solve two historic murders… no make that three, 'cos we know Harry Levenson was murdered, and we think there may be some more. And we may be able to name someone who is suspected of molesting girls."

Hazel looked at him oddly, and was about to comment when Meredith piped up "I think that's going a bit far, Alex. He didn't actually molest girls, did he? I thought Susie just said he had affairs with them when he was younger."

"Nah, say it anyway, Mum" said Alex. "Oh, and you might mention that his housekeeper says the police need to do a spot of gardening there."

The in-car conversation stopped while the two women were on their phones. Alex was fascinated to find that he could to absorb the gist of both simultaneous conversations if he concentrated hard enough. When both calls were finished, Hazel turned to her mother.

"You're really going to have to stick up for me next week, Mum. School are going to go ape when they find out about this."

"Don't worry about the school. I think we can handle them" Meredith replied, "as long as you do your best to do *all* your coursework and revision."

"Coursework is totally up to date, Mum. Revision is what I'll do on the way to lessons…"

Toby Allen was completely taken aback. "What do you mean, I have to go with you? And who are these people, Meredith?"

"This is Mark and Freya Phipps, Uncle. They are Alex's parents, and they are nothing to do with Gerald Phipps, who I think you might know about."

"Good grief! Gerald Phipps…"

"Gerald Phipps, or Gerhard Fepp, knows you are still alive. He was the person who discovered the body of Tony Allen in Chelvey. Tony Allen was murdered by Arthur Simmons in 1961 because he thought it was you. Gerald also thought it was you, but he knows now that you are still alive. We think you're in quite a lot of danger, Uncle. You really have to come with us."

"No. Let him come here. I'll sort him out."

"No, Uncle, I simply won't allow that. You're not a young man any more…"

"Nor is Gerald."

"No, but he is ruthless, and probably armed."

"Armed? Hmph! Where are you taking me?"

"We're not… Martina has just arrived. She's taking you home with her, just for a few days, just until the police can ensure your safety."

Martina and Meredith helped the old man pack a few belongings, while Alex offered to take the papers relating to the ghost.

"I think I'll keep them, if you don't mind, young Alex. But I do have something you may borrow until you've read them. I wouldn't normally let anyone see these but… well, now you pretty much know everything anyway, you will find these may have a few more clues." As he spoke, he had unlocked the bureau and took out the bundle of letters, handing them to Alex. "I'm not naïve enough to think you won't copy them, or show them to the others, but please remember, this is my personal and private correspondence. I don't know how much you two are really in love, or if you even know what it really means yet, but… well… please forgive what I wrote all those years ago."

"Thank you, Uncle Toby" said Alex humbly. "I promise you I will look after these as if I'd written them myself."

"Oh, that reminds me, Uncle" said Meredith. "According to Gerald, the body in the woods was not Natasha, but they planted the ring on her to make you think it was, and to draw you out. They fully expected you to go public, and then they would have found you and… well, what they did to Tony Allen."

The old man nodded. "Thank you for that. It still doesn't explain who the body was."

"Oh" said Alex, "I reckon I know. It was Arthur's second wife, Alice Condon. She had an affair with Gerald, and Arthur bumped her off and made Gerald help him dispose of her body. At least, that's my hunch. DCI Chloë Smith will, of course, demand my evidence…"

They helped Toby Allen into Martina's car, and said their goodbyes, while Julia, who Toby had called while he was packing, went around the house with Meredith to make sure the place was secure. After about twenty minutes Julia locked the house and got back into her red Astra and drove off, while the others got back into Mark's car.

"Well, well, well. That's very interesting" Mark said, looking into his rearview mirror as he drove off.

"What is, Dear?" asked his wife.

"We have a Rolls-Royce following us."

"Really? Who's got a Rolls-Royce?"

"Well, unless I'm very much mistaken, your friend Gerald had one tucked alongside his house, didn't he? So, that either makes two identical Rollers, or our friend and namesake Mister Gerald Phipps has already found Uncle Toby's house."

Hazel felt a chill go up her spine.

"Wow. If we hadn't come straight here…"

"Don't say it, Hazel. I feel quite sick thinking about it." Meredith opened her window slightly as they pulled off.

"Must say" said Mark, "I've never been tailed by a Rolls-Royce before. I wonder if he thinks we've got Toby with us?"

Mark drove well within the speed limit, and made sure he acted as if he had no idea that they were being followed.

"Alex, old chap" he said in a mock upper-class accent. "Do the decent thing and open up the map on your phone."

"Certainly, chauffeur" grinned Alex. "Where would one like to go?"

"How about a jolly old police station, eh?"

"Spiffing idea, Father! How about, I take some footage and try and film his reg number as well."

"Jolly good plan, old chap."

While Alex discreetly filmed their pursuer, Hazel turned on her voice recorder app and gave a running commentary. After crossing the Clifton Suspension Bridge, they drove into the city centre and straight to Bridewell Police station. As they pulled up outside, a police officer came over and tapped on the passenger side window, which Mark opened for him.

"I'm sorry Sir, you really can't stop here."

"I know that, Officer, but we are being followed... correction, we were being followed by that Roller which has just driven past."

"Why's that, Sir. Did you cut him up?"

"If I explained right now, you'd never believe me, so I'll leave you in peace. Thanks anyway."

Mark wound the window up and drove away slowly. Suddenly, he wrenched the wheel left into a narrow one-way street and floored the throttle pedal, much to the consternation of his passengers.

"Crikey Dad!" cried Alex. "Is he behind us again? I can't see him."

"No, he's not, but he's probably circling around to go past the police station again, so I want to get as far away from it as I can. Let's drive up some more of these back streets, then turn on the SatNav for home once we're away over the other side of town."

"Mum. What did Chloë say?" Alex asked, once they were safely on the main road back to Milnefield, and not being followed.

"Well..." Freya began. "She wants to see you two nutters tomorrow, and she's said under no circumstances should you do any more prying into people's private lives without talking to her first."

"So, she doesn't believe us then?"

"Actually, do you know, I think she does believe you, just like she did before, but remember she has to act on factual evidence, not on guesswork and hunches."

49

DCI Chloë Smith sat thoughtfully at the dining room table at the Burns's house, surrounded by odd sheets of paper, which included copies of photographs, newspaper cuttings and screenshots of various online reports. Both the Burns and Phipps families were there, excepting Olivia Phipps who was still at university. Max Burns, Hazel's 10-year-old brother, had sat disbelievingly through the afternoon's conversations, having only had a vague idea about the family ghost story.

Chloë smiled and chuckled to herself, then took a deep breath. "Well…" she began, "this is getting to be a habit of mine, spending my Sunday afternoons picking up the pieces of your investigations."

"If it's any consolation, we're not going to build a scale model of the race-track" Mark grinned.

"Why not, Dad?" Alex said with mock enthusiasm. "I'm sure Chloë would love to come and play racing cars in our back garden."

"No Chloë would not" said the DCI. "I'm not actually sure I can do much with all this information. My boss will probably have a stroke if I tell him."

"You'll be able to take the credit for solving two historical cases" said Hazel, innocently.

"Listen, do you two realise… no, all of you, just how dangerous this whole thing could have been for you?" The DCI was being serious now. "Seriously, Meredith… Geoff… everyone. Really, what were you thinking, letting these two walk into dangerous situations, like inviting yourselves into the home of someone you suspect might have been something to do with a murder. I mean… I mean, I wouldn't send one of my constables in to a situation like that without back-up. Ever! Do you understand, all of you, how flippin' … crazy this is?"

No one spoke.

"So now, I've got to take what evidence there is here, and probably reopen… well, I'll get whichever force dealt with it to reopen the two murder cases. I'm not sure how we'll find out who the mystery woman was though. She was reburied in a known grave, so we could exhume her, but who would we compare the DNA with?"

"James Simmons" said Alex straight away. "If I'm right, and it's Alice Condon, she was James's mother, and Michael's grandmother."

"Ble-deep" said Hazel under her breath, making Alex chuckle out loud.

"Okay. I have to say… oh, you two!! I want to give you the world's biggest telling off, but at the same time… yeah, you've done a good bit of sleuthing but… for goodness sake, back off now. It's done – you've solved your mystery. You know who the ghost was." Chloë collected up her papers and began stuffing them into her large pilot case. "Look, my case is full, and it's all your blasted papers!"

"What are you doing about the search?" asked Alex. "You know, the one at Gerald Phipps's house?"

"And his garden" added Hazel.

"Nothing, Alex. Firstly, it's not on my patch, and secondly we have no evidence of a crime…"

"Oh, what?!" exclaimed Alex. "I've got a

recording of him confessing!"

"Well, then, let me have the recording, please."

"Can I copy it onto my PC and send it to you."

"You can, but of course I still can't act on it."

"But…"

"Alex! Listen to me. There's a thing in this wonderful country of ours called the law. Everyone has to abide by it, you, me, the police… everyone."

"Apart from the people in charge…"

"Everyone, Alex Phipps. The people in charge, politicians, judges, lawyers, members of the Royal Family… you know, if you watch the news, even the Duke of Edinburgh has to wear a seat belt, right? So, I can't just go and dig up someone's garden unless I have a very very good reason to suspect there's anyone buried there. I mean, do you have a name? Is there a missing person you know is buried there?"

"You dug up Jack Dove last year…"

"Because you gave me good evidence that he was buried where we found him. You know, name, dates, documentary evidence. Here, you just say you think this guy might have had something to do with missing persons. That's not good evidence at all; it's hearsay, tittle-tattle, gossip. I need names, dates, evidence that he was able to be involved, okay? Right… I've said my piece, and I'll be off. But just remember, all of you and especially you too youngsters, you've done enough. No more, okay?"

After the DCI had left, the Phipps family prepared to go, but Geoff and Meredith insisted they stay for dinner. While the adults chatted and mucked in with the preparations, Hazel and Alex went up to Hazel's room, with Max in tow.

"Can I stay with you two, please? The grown-ups will make me help with the table otherwise."

Hazel was about to kick her brother out, but Alex persuaded her to let him stay. As they sat in silence, Alex sent his girlfriend a text: *'I have an idea'*.

'Wot'

'Talk about school stuff, but use text to plan'

'Yh'

"So, what sort of mark d'you think I'll get for that essay about the Metz families, Haze?" he asked.

"No idea, Lexy-baby… I s'pose it depends if Bolton thinks you're taking the mick."

"I bet he'll have learnt something he didn't know though." *'So wot's the next plan?'*

"Yeah, like, he has a major nerd in Year Ten who loves writing about obscure foreign history topics." *'Dunno. Need to get my Nana to do more stuff on Gerald – like any children? Marriage?'*

'Didn't she say she found no info on him?'

'Oh yh. Daymmm'

"Hazel, can I play a game on your laptop?"

"Okay, li'l bro, if it keeps you quiet." She flipped the lid up and typed in her password, as Max slid onto her chair and typed in his favourite games website. "There you go… until dinner, right?"

Max nodded and became instantly absorbed. Hazel watched him for a few moments, then went back to texting Alex. *'I have an idea'*

'?'

'gotta delete txts before we do it'

'??'

'don't tell rents'

'k'

'don't tell anyone'

321

50

"Has anyone seen Hazel Burns today?"

Sharon Lightwater scanned the form room. One or two heads shook, some turned towards Alex, who pretended to be revising an English text.

"Alex? Have you any idea where Hazel is?"

"No, Miss. I'm sure she'll be here soon. I hope so, we're going out to the coffee shop at lunchtime."

"Oh, is that right. I thought you two weren't meant to be seeing each other?"

"That's right, Miss, we're not allowed to at home or school, so that's why we have to meet at the coffee shop to have a catch up."

Sharon grimaced disbelievingly and shrugged as she marked the 'Absent' column in the register. The school office would follow up any absentees, after listening to all the answerphone messages.

'Shall I text her, Miss?"

"No, Alex, you shall not text her. Your phone shouldn't even be out while you're in class. You know the rules…"

"I do, but…"

"…and you know better than to break them."

"Yes, Miss, but…"

Sharon walked over to Alex's desk, her hand held out.

"What, Miss?"

"Phone. Come on, Alex, you can have it back when the lesson bell goes, but right now, you can

322

hand it over."

"Okay, if you insist." He slapped the phone down hard in her hand. As she walked back to her desk and placed the phone on the shelf behind her, there were a few pointed comments.

"Careful, Miss, he'll have the police onto you."

"Yeah, he's got friends in high places."

"He'll have you arrested…"

"Or murdered…"

She thumped her palm down on the desk. "That's enough, Year Ten! You're meant to be nearly approaching adulthood, so please try and act your age. If you want me to treat you like children then just carry on like primary school kids. Your choice."

Just then the phone buzzed, and instinctively she glanced at it. The message on the display made her blood run cold.

'Hi, don't tell ne1, I've arranged to meet Gerald at his house. Am on train to…'

"Alex, come here please?"

Alex sighed. "Oh, what now, Miss? I wasn't doing anything."

"I know, Alex. But you really need to come here right now." Sharon held up his phone. "There's a message on here… we need to go outside. Everyone, please… this is really genuinely urgent. Please all stay quiet. Erm…Fiona, would you go and ask Mr Bolton to come here urgently. Miss Kendall will look after you all for a minute."

She bundled Alex out of the door, and handed his phone back.

"Who is Gerald?" she asked, as Fiona Martin slipped past them on her errand to fetch the Head.

"Eh?"

323

"Who is Gerald? Please… read the message."

Alex unlocked his phone and read the message from his girlfriend, his mouth opening wider and wider in shock. "Oh… my… God! Oh my God!" He put his hand up to his forehead. "No! Miss, you've got to… she's… she's in so much danger. This guy, calls himself Gerald Phipps… lives near Bristol. He's really Gerhard Fepp. He's been implicated in at least one murder, and helped to dispose of a body after another. He's also… my God…" Alex started to shake, dropped his phone and held his hands up in front of his face, the tears starting to form. He rubbed his eyes to try to hide the flood but felt his cheeks flush and the tears rolling down them.

"Right, Alex… please, tell me where this is."

"It's in… it's Abbots Leigh… Bristol way. I can't remember exactly where. My Dad drove us there on Saturday… this guy is a complete nutter. I mean, he's… he'll kill her. You've got to help her, you've got to help! I'll send her a message, shall I?"

"Erm, yes, do that."

'Don't go anywhere, Hazel. ur in danger. Please tell us where u r and I'll get my Mum to pick u up'

'I'll be ok'

'No!!! You won't!!! Please!!! I l u xx'

'Too late im at Bristol im gettin taxi from da station. l u 2 xx'

Alex sank to the floor, dropping the phone as he went. Stephen Bolton appeared in front of him.

"What's going on, Sharon?" asked the Head, looking down at the sobbing Alex, who was slumped against the wall of the corridor.

"It's Hazel Burns again. I'm afraid she's… she's taken it upon herself to carry on this crazy investigation, and she's arranged to meet a man… on her own, at his house, near Bristol. Alex says he's a murderer. She's on her way there now. Alex is trying to persuade her not to do it."

Alex looked up tearfully through his glasses, and handed his phone to the Head. Stephen scrolled up the message screen, and then back down, and handed it back to Alex.

"Keep her talking, Alex, the way you have already. Do your best… and come with us to the office now. Sharon, we need to get the police in, now! And call Hazel's parents straight away too!"

'Hazel. School no & dey calling ur rents. YOU HAVE TO STOP!!!'

'In taxi now. L be ok. Lu x'

'No. This guy is rally dangerous. He wants to kill Uncle Toby'

…

'Hazel. Pls reply xx'

Meredith Burns put her phone down, her face white as a sheet. Her boss looked at her.

"What's up, Meri? You seen a ghost?" Sanjay smiled inside at his little quip, having heard the ghost story from her a few days before.

"It's Hazel… she's missing from… she never went to school… oh God!"

"Okay" said Sanjay, his face instantly becoming serious, "you need to go. Go now. Don't worry about anything here, just go. We'll look after the counter."

"Yes… erm… yes. Wait, I'll call Geoff."

She rang her husband's number, but there was no reply. With the feeling of ever increasing panic, she tried the house phone.

"I just can't get hold of Geoff. He's not at work today as he had to work Saturday, but he's not answering either phone."

"Just go. Go home, and think what to do once your there. Good luck – I'm sure she'll be fine, she's a very bright girl, Meri."

Meredith grabbed her bag, put her coat on and dashed out of the door of the stores.

"Listen, if you need us, call…" Sanjay called after her.

Two minutes later she swung the Astra rapidly into her driveway, narrowly missing her husband's Range Rover. If his car was there, why hadn't he answered the phone? She rushed to the front door, barely able to put her key into the lock, her hands were shaking so much.

"Geoff! Geoff!"

There was no answer. She dashed upstairs, checked the en suite, and continued to call his name.

"Geoff! Where ARE you?! I need you, now!"

She stumbled back down the stairs, and heard the back door click shut.

"Geoff? Geoff?"

She heard a movement from the kitchen, and ran along the corridor to push open the door.

"Well," said a familiar voice. "You're in a right state, aren't you? What's going on?"

"Where's Geoff? What's happened to him?"

51

"POLICE!!! OPEN UP!!"

Four police officers stood on the front doorstep of Gerald Phipps's house, one of them holding an enforcer, a sort of one-man battering ram. Another two officers ran down the side of the house, kicking the gate open as they did so.

Two more officers waited by the front gate.

"POLICE!!! IF YOU DON'T OPEN UP NOW WE WILL FORCE ENTRY!!!"

A few seconds later, the officer holding the heavy enforcer swung it towards the front door. It took just two attempts to force the lock, and they burst in, with shouts of "POLICE!! STAY DOWN!!", and spread themselves out swiftly throughout the house, checking every room.

Moments later, the radio on Chief Inspector Terry Barnard's lapel crackled into life.

"We've found her...Sir. Upstairs on a bed, she's bound and gagged. We'll need an ambulance."

"Get an ambulance, now!" Barnard barked at one of his assistants.

"There's one already on the way, Sir."

A couple more minutes elapsed as the officers continued to sweep through the rest of the house, before the 'All Clear' was shouted, and immediately two paramedics, who had arrived a few moments earlier in the ambulance, rushed into the house.

"Upstairs!" They were guided by an officer

standing in the hallway, and at the top of the stairs another officer showed them into a room at the back of the house.

She had been lying face down on the bed, her long blonde hair spread untidily across the pillow. Her hands and legs had been tied, and the young officer who found her thought he'd detected a weak pulse, so he and another officer had gently rolled her onto her back. The first officer had pulled the gag away from her face, while the second cut through the ties on her wrists and ankles and quickly massaged her hands and feet.

"Hang on, there's another gag stuffed in her mouth… what sick bastard did this, eh?" The first officer pulled a small handkerchief from her mouth, and she began to cough and gasp for breath.

"Thank God, we found her in the nick of time!"

"What's her name please?" the first paramedic asked, shaking her gently on the shoulders.

The officer radioed his Chief Inspector. "The girl's alive, Sir. What's her first name?"

"Hazel." The reply came back loud and clear.

"Hazel… Hazel… can you hear me?"

More coughing. Her head rolled to one side.

"We need to get her oxygenated fast…"

"Pulse is weakening…"

"Cardiac arrest!"

The first paramedic began to perform CPR while the second unpacked a portable defibrillator. The police officer stood back as the second paramedic placed the two defibrillator pads on her body and called "Stand back" as she delivered the first shock.

"Restart CPR! Back on the chest."

While the first paramedic continued the CPR in the upstairs room, the officers who had gone into the back garden were busily searching inside and behind a large greenhouse, two other outbuildings and the overgrown shrubbery for signs of life.

"Can we get the dogs round here?" one of them radioed to the Chief Inspector. "We've got two outbuildings full of old garden tools and rubble. Anything could be in there."

"Over here!" The call went up from behind the greenhouse. Police Constable John McArthur waved his colleagues over, and showed them a freshly-dug trench, about six feet long and three feet deep. The excess spoil had been placed on a compost heap further long the plot. "I wonder how many more of these he's dug over the years?"

The Chief Inspector went up the stairs into the room where the two paramedics were packing away their equipment. The young officer stood up and turned away from the inert figure lying on the bed. "It's no use, Sir. We couldn't save her. We thought we'd got here in time but she went into cardiac arrest. The paramedics have tried everything."

"BBC News at Eleven o'Clock. Police searching for a missing Somerset schoolgirl have found a body. The 14-year-old girl, who failed to turn up at her school today, was thought to have arranged to meet a man in Abbots Leigh, near Bristol. The girl's name has not been released until a formal identification can be made. No arrests have been made, and police are urgently searching for the driver of a blue Rolls-Royce, index number 36 FEP, last seen in the Bristol city centre area this morning."

52

"Geoff! Geoff! Where have you been? Didn't you get the calls and texts?"

"I left my phone in the living room, sorry! Look, we need to call the police…"

"Hazel's gone missing… they say she's gone to meet Gerald Phipps."

"What!? Is this the old guy who followed you in the blue Roller? 36 FEP?"

"Yes, that's the one. Why?"

"I just saw his car as I pulled into our road. He's heading towards Milnefield."

Linda Dillon interrupted them. "Meredith, your phone's ringing…"

"Hello? Yes… yes… oh. Yes, I'll do that, yes."

She slumped down onto the chair.

"What is it, Dear?" asked Linda

"Yes, come on, what in heaven's name is going on?" said Geoff.

"The police have told me to stay right here, they're sending an officer round straight away."

"Oh no…"

He looked at his wife, and saw the same fear in her eyes that he was feeling. He was about to speak when Meredith's phone rang again. "Oh, it's from Freya Phipps… Hi, Freya?" she said tearfully.

"Meri, listen, I just had a message from Alex to say I must ring you and tell you; Hazel is okay! She's here with me, she turned up a minute or so ago. I don't know what the hell is going on, but Alex said it was really vital I tell you straight away. Hazel is fine, she's just nipped to the loo."

"Freya... oh, thank goodness...." She cupped her hand over the phone. "Hazel is fine. She's with Freya. She didn't go to Bristol."

Geoff suddenly reached out and grabbed the phone from his wife's grip.

"Freya, it's Geoff! Listen, I've just seen Gerald Phipps's car heading towards Milnefield. The blue Rolls, yes. Lock your doors and call the police. Tell them you think your life and Hazel's is in danger. Tell them she's with you, okay? Tell them whatever you need to, but whatever you do, don't answer your door until either I or the police arrive, okay? I'm coming straight over." He handed the phone back to his wife. "Linda, can I use your car again please? Gerald won't recognise it."

His mother-in-law nodded, and he grabbed his jacket and rushed out of the front door, slamming it hard behind him.

"Darling, what on earth is going on?"

"If I told you... actually, I'm not sure myself, but anyway, you haven't explained why Geoff was out in your car."

"Oh, well, there's something not quite right about it, so I popped over to see you, and totally forgot you worked now. Anyway, Geoff was here and offered to take it for a drive as long as I sorted out the garden waste for the binmen, so that why I was outside when you got home."

A few minutes later, the doorbell rang. Meredith could see the outline of two figures dressed

331

in blue. As she answered the door, she just hoped and prayed that the message from Alex was true.

"Mrs Burns... may I come in?"

"Yes, listen, I know you think my daughter is missing but she's not..."

"Mrs Burns, may we come through and sit down somewhere? My name's Janet, and this is Simone... we're from Attwell Police..."

"Hazel is alive. We've just had a message from her boyfriend's mother. She's in Milnefield."

"Mrs Burns, I'm afraid we've found a body."

Meredith took a deep breath. For a moment she was wracked with doubt, but the call from Freya had been so definite that she felt confident enough to ask them to check their facts.

"Use the house phone if you like." She handed them the receiver, but before Janet could press dial the phone rang, and she handed it back.

"It's my husband. Hang on... Hi Darling, the police are here... she's safe, and with you? Okay, I'll tell them."

Meredith put the phone down. "Look, you only know part of the story, but this is a complex situation and... well anyway, my husband has Hazel with him right now. They're at a friend's house in Milnefield."

"Well, that's a real relief, but would you mind explaining what is going on, Mrs Burns?"

"I wouldn't mind usually, but listen... the man who she was supposedly meeting is chasing her and us and... well, his Rolls-Royce has just been seen in Milnefield, and I think you should go over there right now. Here's the address..."

53

"Thank heavens you're safe, Darling".

Geoff Burns hugged his daughter tightly as he entered the Phipps hallway. "I've rung the police, and I've rung the school as well, and they've told me Alex is alright, but he's assisting the police at the moment… in a nice way, apparently." Freya Phipps put the kettle on, as Geoff sat down at the kitchen table and checked his phone for messages.

Hazel stood in the kitchen doorway. "Oh, Dad, I'm so glad he's okay. Look, Freya. I'm really sorry, I'm afraid I've gone and done a pretty awful thing, but Alex truly wasn't anything to do with it, so if he gets into trouble…"

Hazel was interrupted by the doorbell. She glanced at the door and recognised the outline figure on the doorstep.

"Dad" she said, quietly but urgently. "Please. Can you answer that? I think it's Gerald Phipps. He doesn't know you. Erm… you can pretend he's got the wrong house, or something."

Geoff Burns stood up from the table, raised himself to his full height and strode purposefully to the front door, casually opening it as if expecting a parcel delivery.

"Hello" he said, smiling brightly to the elderly gentleman standing on the doorstep in front of him.

"Mr Phipps" said the old man in a rasping voice. "You know why I'm here, of course?"

"Mr Phipps?" Geoff sounded puzzled, and frowned at the old man. "I think you've got the wrong house, sir. I'm not Mr Phipps, I'm afraid. Wrong name altogether, sorry." He slammed the door shut and walked casually back to the kitchen, well aware that his profile was visible through the door glass.

Gerald Phipps stood frowning for a moment, staring at the front door. This wasn't in the plan. He checked the house number again against the piece of paper he had in his pocket. No, this definitely seemed to be the right house, although he didn't recognise the car on the drive. Still, the writing on the paper was a bit small and blurry. He searched for his reading glasses, and had to let go of the knife he'd been gripping in his pocket. While he was patting his jacket trying to remember which pocket his glasses case was in, he saw a reflection in the door glass in front of him. In his younger days he would have reacted instantly, but he had been so completely thrown by the strange man who had answered the door that he was not quite as alert as usual.

Before he had time to think, both his arms were grabbed firmly and he heard a woman's voice.

"Mr Phipps? Mr Gerald Phipps?"

"Who wants to know?" he wheezed.

"My name is Constable Janet Culshaw, and I'm arresting you on suspicion of the murder of a person at your home in Abbots Leigh..."

"Piffle!"

"You do not have to say anything, but it may harm your defence…"

"Yes, yes, yes. Blah blah blah…"

"… if you do not mention when questioned…"

"Ha! Arrested by a woman…"

…something which you later rely on in court."

"If you knew anything about me…"

"Anything you do say may be given in evidence."

"…you probably wouldn't want to stand so close to me, my dear."

"No matter, Sir. That's why we use handcuffs. And look, you're actually being arrested by *two* women officers. I'm sure that must make it even more interesting for you."

"I'm an old man… Hhhh… I'm very frail… you're being… Hhhh… unnecessarily brutal."

"Of course we are, Sir. And to prove it, we're filming it too so the court and the jury can check just how brutal we really are…. Oh look at this!" Janet Culshaw pulled the knife from Gerald's inside jacket pocket. "Evidence, lovely evidence."

54

Detective Chief Inspector Julius Grant glared at Alex across the Head's table. Stephen Bolton had given up his seat to the DCI, but remained in the room as an adult representative.

"Right, young man. Do you mind telling me exactly what's been going on, and why you didn't come to us before?"

"Well, actually we did, Sir. Yesterday we had a nice long conversation with DCI Smith from Hallowfield, and she told us we didn't have enough evidence for the police to act on."

"Why Chloë Smith? She's from Hallowfield, we're Bristol. Why were you talking to her?"

"Because we know her well. And she knows us. You see, we worked with her last year on solving the Salmsham Railway Disaster, and… murders."

"Ah, that was you, was it? You had her digging up a graveyard, I seem to recall."

"Yes, Sir, that was us. I think if you ring Chloë now she'll confirm we spoke about this current case."

"I'm sure she will, but I'd like to hear it all from you, young man. Everything. All you know."

Alex puffed his cheeks out. "Where to start? Erm… 1937…Vendolet Gold Trophy Race…"

"Hang on, stop right there. I want to know what's been leading up to today, not what happened eighty-whatever years ago."

"Well, like I said, it started in 1937 with a faked

death and a murder…"

"Wait a minute, wait a minute. Okay, I think I need to talk to DCI Smith before you spin me this yarn. Will you both leave the room please…"

Less than five minutes later, Alex and his Head Teacher were back in the Head's office. DCI Grant was not in a good mood.

"You…" he pointed at Alex, "are in seriously hot water, young man. And your friend Hazel Burns is likely to end up in court for pulling that stunt today, wasting police time on searching for her. Have you any idea how many people put resources into rescuing her from that nutter's house… and she was on her way to your house all the time!"

Alex, who would probably have shrunk in terror at such a torrent of anger a year ago, simply shrugged. "I think, Sir, when you've finished searching that house and garden, you'll be thanking us both for solving a couple of unsolved murders… maybe a few missing persons, and most certainly saving the life of others in the future."

"Alex!" Stephen Bolton interrupted. "That is no way to talk to the Chief Inspector. Your behaviour is intolerable, and the way things are, you are heading for serious sanctions…"

"Sir, I think I may have done you a favour too, although I doubt you'll see it that way."

"What?! Done me a favour? Causing havoc in my school? Encouraging your… girlfriend to commit an offence. How is that a favour?"

"You… your mother brought you up single-handedly, didn't she? After your family made her leave your father, but made his family pay

337

generously for your education."

"What do you mean? My mother? What has my private life got to do with this… with you? What are you on about anyway?!"

"Your mother? Jennifer Bolton? She was only seventeen when she fell pregnant with you, and her parents supported her, and you, on condition she gave up any contact with your father."

"How do you know all… I'm sorry, DCI Grant, this is all a bit… Alex, what's my family background got to do with this… this crazy scenario?"

"Sir, didn't your mother ever tell you who your father was?"

"No, and she won't tell me even now, but anyway, that's got nothing to do with you whether she told me or not."

"I think she probably didn't. But that's okay, because I can tell you. His real name is Gerhard Fepp, but he's known as Gerald Phipps, and he's the man the police have just arrested for trying to murder my parents, and Hazel, and Hazel's Dad, and Hazel's Uncle Toby…"

"Enough!" said Julius Grant. "You…" (to Alex) "are coming with me to explain everything down at the station. And you…" (to the Head) "are coming with him until his parents arrive. And, Mr Bolton, I'd like to know just how much you knew about your estranged father's activities too."

"I can assure you" said Stephen Bolton, his voice shaking, "that I have no idea who my father was, and I still don't know whether this is a load of rubbish invented by this young man, or not."

Alex stood up. "Sir, I honestly didn't mean to shock you, but I think, if you ask your mother, you'll find this is all true. My family, especially my Nana, and Hazel's family… between us all we have a great way of finding out information from the past. It's how we solved this ghost story."

"Come on!" said the DCI. "Let's get going."

"Erm… Mr Bolton?"

"What is it, Alex?"

"Did you ever read that essay you asked me to write, about the families of Metz?"

"Oh, yes, I did. It was very well researched, Alex, and well written. I meant to talk to you about it earlier, before all this blew up."

"Well, just so that you know, they're your ancestors I was writing about. That's your paternal ancestry, right there in that essay."

"My God, Alexander Phipps, you have got some nerve, you and that girlfriend of yours." Chloë Smith said, grimacing as she sat down across the interview table from Alex. Freya Phipps sat next to her son, and the young duty solicitor sat on another chair just beyond the end of the table. Alex grinned.

"I really don't know why you're grinning, Alex. If Hazel had actually gone round there… listen, I'm telling you this, the Chief Inspector here at Bristol actually thought they'd found Hazel's body. Think about that for a minute. If she'd gone there…"

"But she didn't, Chloë…"

"You can call me DCI Smith, okay."

Alex raised his eyebrows. It was obviously going to be one of those confrontations.

"If this is a formal interview, you need to turn on the recorder" said the duty solicitor.

"It's not a formal interview, Mr Sharma. It's not even an interview. It's a friendly chat. Alex has done nothing wrong in the eyes of the law, but he's caused a lot of ructions…"

"Like solving murders which the police had been sitting on for nearly sixty years, and preventing several more murders taking place. By the sounds of it, you should be employing him to help with a few more of your cold cases."

"Thank you, Mr Sharma. I'm not a fool, and I know the true value that this young man has brought to these cases, but he has to be aware of the tremendous risks he and his girlfriend have taken." She stared icily at Alex as she spoke.

"Look, Chl… I mean, DCI Smith" said Alex, "I know what we did was not altogether correct, but you know that we were really worried about Gerhard Fepp and what he was going to do with Uncle Toby. That's why we asked to see you yesterday, and that's why Hazel pulled that stunt today. By the way… who was that person that they thought was Hazel?"

"I'm not in a position to say."

"Ah. It must have been Susie Phipps then."

Chloë Smith glared at him in silence for a few moments. "Susie… Phipps? Not Phipps. Hang on, how did you…? How much more do you know?"

"I didn't know. I was just speculating… with no real evidence… a hunch, which you always advise us against. But seeing as she was the only other female in the story who would have been hanging around his house…"

"Very good." Chloë sighed and dropped her shoulders. "Okay, Alex, yes, I'm afraid it was Susie Hale – she was never a Phipps."

"Of course. I forgot, she's only his step-daughter. She wasn't his flesh and blood."

"Sort of stepdaughter, yes. Her mother never married Gerald. But yes, it was her. We're not sure of the motive though."

"Well, she told us on Saturday that we should get the police to dig up the garden. She also said she was scared to stay there, but too scared to leave him, if you get what I mean. I think probably Gerald thought she'd been something to do with us finding him in the first place?"

"I don't know… I really don't know. Anyway, listen. I'm not really working this case. I'm only here at the request of my boss, to help Bristol CID with a bit of background. I'm away now, so you'll have to deal with DCI Grant from now on. But hey… he's calmed down a bit now, he no longer wishes to string you and Hazel up; in fact he's beginning to realise that you are a good team. I've given you the lecture about not going into these things without telling the adults; I know you'll completely ignore me but anyway, if you need any assistance or support with the school situation or anything, let me know."

"Thanks, DCI Smith." Alex smiled sweetly.

"Stop that! It's Chloë, okay, you cheeky little… Bye Alex, bye Freya. Mr Sharma…" and with that, DCI Chloë Smith left the interview room.

55

Hazel sat, shoulders slumped, head down, the tears splashing onto the desk in front of her. She had known from the start that she would be in a lot of trouble, but she had been prepared to take that risk just to get the police to search Gerald's house. She remembered feeling very empowered, and confident in the calculating way she had planned the stunt for maximum effect. She knew, from reading about other cases, that the school and the police would act very quickly if they suspected abduction, or if they knew that she was in any sort of potential danger.

Everything had gone to plan.

What she hadn't considered was just how 'life and death' the whole scenario would turn out to be. The Chief Inspector, no less, had been in to see her and described to her in no uncertain terms his feelings when he was dealing with the dead woman at the house that day. She could sense the restrained anger in his tone, as he explained that he'd genuinely believed that the body was her, Hazel Burns. She had seen the fear in his eyes. At that very moment, too, Meredith Burns began to sob, and Hazel realised just how close she had been to getting herself killed.

She sobbed uncontrollably as she recalled how she was originally going to take the train to Bristol to confront Gerald Phipps on his doorstep – on her own! A petite 14-year-old girl, confronting a strong, not-as-frail-as-he-looked man whom they suspected of murder. What on earth was she thinking? Thank goodness Alex had talked her out of that scenario. He had suggested calling the police to say there was a disturbance, but they'd surmised that the police would just knock and ask if everything was alright, and see a frail old gentleman who wouldn't hurt a fly. That's when she decided to bunk off school without telling anyone. She told Alex the outline of her idea without too much detail, and promised faithfully to not go anywhere near Gerald's house. They had cleared the chat from their phones, so the only conversation saved on their devices was the one they had started that morning.

As she sat sobbing, her head down, the door opened and Julius Grant came in. She didn't look up.

"Hazel" he said, gently. "Hazel, I'm DCI Julius Grant, and I'm the detective in charge of this case. Hazel, would you look at me please?"

She looked up through tearstained eyes, still sobbing fitfully.

"Hazel… I know you might think you're in a lot of trouble, but I just want to thank you actually. You probably didn't realise just what sort of a man Gerald Phipps is, but then, neither did we, nor did anyone else. We couldn't save his step-daughter today, but as you know we stopped him trying to get into your boyfriend's house, and he would have tried to kill you, and Freya Phipps, and your Uncle Toby."

He held out a box of tissues. Hazel took one, and passed the box to Meredith, who was sitting beside her daughter, staring up at the wall behind the detective, tears rolling silently down her cheeks.

"As far as I'm concerned" the DCI continued, "unless I find some evidence to the contrary, you've been nothing but a great assistance in this case. You

343

and your family, and your boyfriend."

Hazel nodded, and swallowed hard.

"Is he okay?" she sniffed.

"Alex? He's fine. He's a very fine actor too. They tell me he was shedding genuine tears when you were texting him that you were in that taxi, even though he knew you weren't anywhere near Bristol. I'm not sure what's going to happen about your school though. It's pretty serious, bunking off like that, but I have a feeling your Head teacher might be slightly more lenient than you'd expect, bearing in mind he's just had a pretty big shock too."

"Oh? What sort of shock?"

"Well, I can't tell you as it's a little sensitive, but I'm sure Alex will let you know all about it."

"Do you mind me asking" Meredith piped up "about Gerald Phipps? I mean, has he confessed to anything, like killing his step-daughter, or the mystery woman in Leigh Woods?"

"No, not yet, but he's gone from denying everything, to boasting. I like it when these people boast, because they just can't help telling us everything... much more detail than we actually know. He's convinced that you folks know about all his dirty deeds, so we'll just keep asking him questions, and listening to him sing his heart out."

Just then, there was a knock, and a constable put her head around the door. "Excuse me, Sir. Mr Burns is here. Is it okay for him to join you?"

"Yes, of course. Come in, Mr Burns."

"Thank you. Meri, we have a serious problem... The school have decided to exclude Hazel for the rest of the week, and they've also reported us to Social Services..."

56

"I'm sure you'd like to hear the good news first hand… that we've decided that there will be no further sanctions against either of these students." Stephen Bolton smiled as his eyes swept from left to right, from Geoff and Meredith Burns, to Hazel and Alex, to Freya and Mark Phipps.

Hazel and Alex looked at each other and smiled, and Alex started to say "Thank you…" when the Head held the palm of his hand up to stop him.

"However, their exclusion from school until next Monday will still apply, and I would like it very much if the two of them could just focus on their schoolwork from now on. I know I can't stop them being friends, and nor would I want to, but…"

Mark Phipps interrupted him brusquely. "We get the message. And we appreciate the decision of the Governors and yourself not to sanction them further, although I would like to add that you would have been on difficult ground, especially in the case of Alex, who I believe has not once - *not once* - failed to produce the work expected of him."

"Mr Phipps, I don't want to get into an argument, or discuss the details, or play one student off against another…"

"Of course you don't. But, as we know, and the police have acknowledged, Alex has done nothing wrong at all, and I'd like you to backtrack on your decision to exclude him from school this week."

"Look…"

"Good. Glad that's settled then." Mark Phipps smiled and looked straight at the Head. "We'll send him back in tomorrow morning."

"Erm… very well, Mr Phipps. Yes, alright, Alex. You can start back tomorrow morning."

"And while we're on the subject of exclusion" said Geoff Burns, "I think you've been particularly harsh on Hazel, considering that, thanks to her initiative and persistence, several lives have been saved this week, ours included, and a suspected serial killer is now in custody."

"Hazel's case is… a little different from Alex's, I'm afraid. She has deliberately and knowingly flouted school rules and…"

"We're not particularly wealthy, Mr Bolton, nor did we have wealthy parents" Meredith Burns said. "so we haven't all had the benefits of a well-funded private education, unlike your good self, however we do have a very well-defined sense of natural justice, which we have instilled in both our children…"

"Yes, I don't doubt it…"

"So you see, we find it hard to credit the school's… or rather, your decision to damage her school record irreparably when her net contribution to society as a whole has been immense."

"Yes, Mrs Burns, I'm afraid the decision of the Governors…"

"…was wrong, Stephen. Just plain wrong." Freya Phipps interrupted. "Whatever the rights and wrongs of these two compromising their own safety, they did the right things for the right reasons, and for you to punish either of them for that is simply unfair. And I'm not going to sit here while you let Alex off but punish Hazel…"

"I'm sorry, Mrs Phipps, but Hazel is not your child and so…"

"Oh no, you see, we're all involved together in this, all of us. This whole saga is so much bigger than a couple of kids apparently breaking your school rules. You must be well aware of the national interest in this case. I'm absolute certain that there are elements of it which are not yet known, which might cause unnecessary embarrassment to both you and the school, should the press ever find out."

Stephen Bolton blushed, much to his annoyance. He had half-expected this to become an issue, but this sounded like blackmail to him, and he decided to confront it. "If you are talking about my… my family background… that sounds suspiciously like blackmail to me!"

"Who said anything about your family background?" said Meredith innocently. "None of us did. That's your business; your cross to bear, if you like. We're talking about the school's decision-making process."

"What…?" Stephen began.

"Last year, as you well remember, my daughter was unfairly targeted by one of your teachers, partly because she was very good at netball – almost too good, and that teacher apparently couldn't handle having someone with that much ability in her netball group, and so she picked on her and humiliated her in front of her peers, and pushed her to react as any fair-minded young person might react. You might recall that one of the sports TAs stuck up for Hazel, so she was exonerated of any wrongdoing. But now, she's once again being picked on, perhaps to make an example to the rest of the school – who knows?"

"Look, Mrs Burns... all of you. May I please get a word in? Look at it from the school's point of view. If your daughter is allowed to just bunk off school as she did, and no punishment is given, what message does that send out to other students and parents?"

"Well, of course, put like that, it makes complete sense." Meredith glared at him. "But she didn't 'bunk off school' did she? She tried to prevent a crime, which, I should add, the authorities failed to prevent despite both our families reporting it to them in detail less than twenty-four hours beforehand. Now we understand that there was a lack of hard evidence, but we've had Social Services round twice this week and even they've concluded that what Hazel did was brave and heroic and she should be commended for it and not punished."

"I see..." Stephen Bolton knew he was beaten. "I'll see what I can do." He picked up the stack of letters and papers on his desk, shuffled them and straightened them out before placing them back down neatly, in a gesture of finality. "Thank you, all of you, for coming in anyway."

"Oh, it's alright. We're not going anywhere yet" Geoff said brightly. "Not until you make that decision..."

"...and promise to treat Hazel the same way you've treated our son" Freya added.

58

"So you see, Mr Allen, you were right all along to believe you were seeing the 'dead' racing driver – because you were indeed seeing the man who drove the Bugatti at you and your friend. We've managed to piece together, as best we can, what actually happened that day. Gerhard Fepp cannot stop boasting about his uncle's… exploits, nor his own."

Toby Allen sat impassively in his armchair and looked straight at Detective Chief Inspector Julius Grant, who sat on the sofa opposite him, armed with a large folder of notes which he kept referring to.

Martina Heath had driven Toby home that morning, after his very relaxing and enjoyable stay at the Heath's house, where she had pampered him so much so that he was a little reluctant to leave. As well as Martina and her husband, he'd enjoyed the company of his young great great nephew and niece after school each day. Martina had not known quite how he would react after she had taken him in on Monday evening, but it hadn't taken her long to realise that, whilst he may be slightly frail in body, in mind Toby Allen was as tough as they come.

"I'm fascinated to know how that… man was able to do all the things he did, and have the wit to get away with it, and yet he failed to notice that I was still living not twelve miles from him."

"Quite so, Sir" said DCI Julius Grant. "I'm no expert, but I think a lot of people like him, with psychopathic tendencies, tend to be a little too confident in their own invincibility. They think that because they've got away with certain things, they have total control over everyone and everything else. I suppose he must have thought, along with his Uncle Jürgen, that Tony Allen really was the person they were looking for, so they stopped looking for you because they thought they'd got you.

"What I can tell you is, young Alex Phipps had it pretty much worked out correctly, in terms of what you actually saw. The driver of the car, Jürgen Fepp, posing as his despised brother Pierre-Henri Cantin, colluded with his mechanic, Reg Simmons, to rig the oil line to the oil gauge on the fascia. When he chose to, he could yank the thing away from the engine block, and oil would pour onto the exhaust pipe and create a fair amount of smoke…"

"Hang on though" interrupted the old man, "I know a bit about those old Bugattis. They didn't have high pressure oil lines. That wouldn't have been very effective."

"I know, but we've run it past a couple of experts and they found that enough oil splashing onto the exhaust would create more than enough smoke for their purpose. We think they probably rigged up some additional oil capacity but whether they did or not, we have no idea. The car was repaired and sold on many years ago, and then destroyed in a fire in America in the late '50s. Anyway, when the time was right, once the field was spread out a bit, the driver yanked a piece of wire which loosened the oil line, and made the car smoke.

"The driver pretended he couldn't see because of the smoke, which in reality wasn't that thick, but anyway, he had pre-selected a section of track where there were supposed to be no spectators, and there was a drop to the river. He drove slowly enough off the edge of the track so he could easily jump off the car, unseen, rip off his fake moustache, turn his jacket inside out quickly and become David Watson, who then gave false statements about seeing the driver ejected as if from a spring, and all that rubbish. The thing he didn't expect was two find two small boys, both witnesses to what he did, and both still alive. He strangled Harry Levenson, your friend, and threw him down the gorge. He tried to strangle you too, but you were saved by the ambulanceman being nearby. Instead he pretended to be your saviour. By the way, we looked again at Harry's post mortem results. He had died from asphyxiation, but it was thought at the time he'd choked on his own blood as he'd lain on his back at the bottom of the gorge. Now, of course, we believe he was strangled by Watson, and already dead when he hit the ground.

"Watson then had the brass neck to turn up and lie his way through Harry's inquest. His evidence was never seriously questioned. For example, when he appeared at Race Control after the race, to make his statement, no-one asked where his camera bag was, yet he made a big thing about his photography at the time. He'd never been near a camera at all.

"Meantime he… Watson, or rather, Jürgen Fepp, took over Reg's late brother's identity and became Arthur Simmons. When Arthur saw you in the paddock the first time, a few years later, he had no idea who you were, except he knew you'd recognised him. But when you saw him again at the 1954 British Grand Prix, he realised who you were and so he got his niece to try and capture your attention. Apparently, although she didn't like her uncle very much, she did as he asked because he wielded a lot of power in the family, and she also thought it would be harmless fun… according to her brother Gerhard at any rate. As soon as you became engaged, she was made to break it off, which she did. However, she met you again and this time she really did want to marry you. When Jürgen Fepp found out about the second engagement he sent her straight out of the country, to Germany. But she didn't marry there, despite what you've been told. She seems to have disappeared. We have the German and French police working on finding out what happened to her. Gerhard claims to know nothing about her whereabouts, but says he didn't care much because they didn't get on at all, and he was glad to have her out of the way. Lovely chap, this Gerhard.

"He's also admitted that he worshipped Uncle Jürgen, and helped him with the mystery body in the woods. It was another German girl who Gerhard had met and befriended. She started to ask awkward questions about their business, and then found she was pregnant so Jürgen strangled her and planted Natasha's ring on her finger. He and Gerhard then buried the body, thinking it wouldn't be found for a few months. It was actually nearly three years."

"So what you're telling me" said Toby, "is that Natasha Fepp has disappeared off the face of the earth, and no-one knows where she went? Not even her brother. I find that hard to stomach."

"So do I, Mr Allen, but I'm keeping an open mind. We're starting to dig the garden up now at the Fepp house…"

59

"BBC News at One O'Clock on Thursday the 21st of March. Good afternoon, I'm Tom Forsyth. Police investigating the murder of a woman at Abbots Leigh, near Bristol, have uncovered the remains of at least three people in the garden of a large detached property in Sandy Lane. An 85-year-old man arrested earlier this week on suspicion of murder has been named as retired engineer Gerald Phipps, of Abbots Leigh. A spokesman for Avon and Somerset Police said that they are re-opening investigations into the disappearance of several people in the Bristol area over the past sixty years. Our correspondent Lisa Andrews is at Abbots Leigh. Lisa…"

"Thank you Tom. I'm standing here, outside this large detached house in an exclusive area of North Somerset, where police searching for a missing schoolgirl earlier this week found a woman in an upstairs room in the house. She had beaten bound and gagged and paramedics fought to save her but sadly she died at the scene. Today it was confirmed that they have since found the remains of two people following extensive excavations in the rear garden of the property, and have also uncovered the skull of a third person."

"Lisa, do the police yet know who these people are?"

"Well, Tom, I asked the question just about 20 minutes ago and was told there are a number of leads they are following but until the remains can be taken away for examination they will be unable to confirm anyone's identity. I can also confirm that police are investigating the alleged disappearance many years ago of Natasha Fepp and Alice Simmons, both of whom may be related to the man Gerald Phipps who is in custody now."

"And what about the dead woman who was found

on Monday? Do we know any more about her?"

"Well initially, the police thought they had found the body of the missing schoolgirl, but she was found safe and well near her home, shortly after the discovery of the body, however police have since named the dead woman as 45-year-old Susannah Hale, who they believe was employed at the house as housekeeper. An elderly man, who is believed to live at this address, was subsequently arrested some miles away in Milnefield. That man, who the police have named as Gerald Phipps, a retired engineer, is now being questioned about a number of disappearances over a long period of time, perhaps even the last 60 years."

"60 years! That's a long time, Lisa. Do you have any more information about who some of these people may be, and their connection with Gerald Phipps?"

"Well, Tom, the police are not giving away any more information at the moment. They say that the investigation is in its early stages and they are reluctant to name some of those people whose disappearance they are looking into as it could cause unnecessary anguish for their families, but I understand that the whole case was brought to their attention by the actions of the teenage schoolgirl who went missing. She cannot be named as she is only 14 years old, but she is believed to be known to the authorities as one of the people who helped with last year's historic investigation into the Salmsham Railway Disaster, which you may recall was found to have been caused by sabotage, and which turned out to be a major murder investigation in its own right."

"Gosh, so are you saying that this girl may have been conducting her own private investigation into these disappearances?"

"Well, Tom, I tried to speak to her family earlier on today, but they were unavailable for comment, but speaking to some of their friends and acquaintances I can tell you that they live in a small village in Somerset which I've been asked not to name at this time. It appears that this schoolgirl and her 16 year-old boyfriend have been conducting a private investigation with the aid of their families, into an old family mystery, and they discovered some evidence of a possible historical identity crime, and as part of their own research they found a pattern of untimely deaths and at least one suicide, which at the time did not appear to be linked, but which they subsequently concluded may have been suspicious deaths, linked in some way to one particular family."

"By which, Lisa, do you mean these deaths could possibly have been murders?"

"I think, Tom, that's the conclusion these families have come to. Now, I'm hearing that the police were notified of the families' suspicions last Sunday but could not proceed without more evidence, which may have been why the schoolgirl went missing, so as to trigger the police search, in which case she may have to answer to the authorities for misleading the police."

"I was going to say, Lisa, surely her family will be under investigation themselves for lying to the police about her disappearance?"

"Well, Tom, this is what I thought but I have been informed that she acted entirely alone and did not collude with anyone inside or outside of her family. The police have told me they will be taking no action against her or her boyfriend or their families over this incident."

"Thank you, Lisa."

"Actually Tom, I've just been joined by Detective Chief Inspector Julius Grant of Avon and Somerset Police. Julius, thank you for coming and talking to us in the middle of what must be a busy time for you."

"Thank you. Good Afternoon, Lisa."

"Now Julius, what can you tell us so far about what

355

you've excavated, erm… uncovered here in the grounds of this property."

"Well, we've uncovered two bodies which appear to have been buried in quite deep graves for some considerable time, and a human skull which was buried under the foundations of a large garden shed."

"What condition were the bodies in?"

"They are actually just skeletal remains, and there is no evidence of any clothing buried with them, which is making dating and identifying them quite difficult."

"And you say the skull was buried on its own?"

"Yes, that's correct. There were no other remains nearby and, without going into detail, it was evident that the skull was deliberately placed there in isolation."

"I see. Do you have any idea who any of these people are yet?"

"Well, our investigations are at a very early stage, but we do have a number of serious leads which we are following up. We have not yet finished excavating the garden but at the moment, from the information we've been able to obtain so far, we are not expecting to find any more remains. I'm afraid I can't say any more than that at this moment."

"I understand that, but people will be asking why it's taken years, maybe up to 60 years, for the bodies of these missing people to be discovered. Surely when they first went missing their disappearances were fully investigated at the time?"

"Well, what is actually one of the biggest problems with this case is that these people have never been reported missing; in other words, they were believed by people who knew them to have gone elsewhere and so no-one has ever made any formal report to the authorities, so none of them were ever investigated as missing persons."

"I see. And can you tell us any more about the

young schoolgirl who triggered this investigation in the first place?"

"I'm afraid I can't comment any further other than to say she is no longer part of this investigation."

"Is it true, though, that she and her family reported their suspicions about this case to the police last Sunday?"

"I'm not making any more comment about this, sorry. As I say, she is not part of our investigation, and nor is her family or her friend's family."

"One final point, though, about this girl. She is not being prosecuted for any offences?"

"I can confirm that she is no longer part of our investigations, and that's correct, she is not being prosecuted for any offence."

"Thank you very much, Detective Chief Inspector Julius Grant. And now back to Tom in the studio."

"Thank you Lisa. That's Lisa Andrews, reporting from Abbots Leigh. There's clearly a lot more to this story, and we will be reporting any further developments as we hear them..."

60

The black Daimler limousine pulled up outside the front steps of Abbots Manor, and the elderly chauffeur, who introduced himself as Jack, slid out of his seat and opened the door behind him. At the same time, Michael Simmons appeared on the other side of the limousine and opened the other door.

Mark and Freya Phipps emerged first, followed by the two teenagers, and finally Geoff Burns. Just behind them, Martina and Andy Heath pulled up in their Volvo Estate, and Meredith Burns got herself out of the driver's side back door, while Martina leapt out and opened the other rear door, and helped Toby Allen to his feet.

As Michael Simmons led the party up the front steps, Charles Forster stood smiling just outside the door, and shook their hands one by one as they went in. He took a little more time shaking Toby Allen's hand than he had with the others.

"Lovely to meet you, Mr Allen" he said' "after all this time. We owe you a lot, I think."

"We've got a lot to talk about" said Toby.

"There's plenty of time for that. Now, please do come this way." He led Toby along the corridor behind the rest of the group, and into the large lounge where he had entertained the Burns family and Alex just a few weeks ago.

"Please, everyone, have a seat and make yourselves comfortable. There's someone I'd like you to meet... well, he'd very much like to meet you."

Charles indicated a well-dressed man in his mid-60s, carrying a little excess weight, and with a large mane of hair, greying but still with plenty of dark colour, making him look younger than his true years. The man sat down beside Charles.

"This is my right-hand man, James Simmons. James, I'd like you to meet Geoff and Meredith Burns, Mark and Freya Phipps, and Hazel and Alex, who did all the crazy digging into the murky past. And, of course, Toby Allen, who sparked this all off."

"Hello everyone" James Simmons began, "I'm not usually lost for words, but this is a strange occasion for me. You see, my relationship with my father Arthur Simmons… Jürgen Fepp…was a very difficult one; to be honest I was closer to Charles's father than my own. Nothing that you've found out about him has come as a surprise to me… and neither has the discovery of my mother's body at my cousin's house. I was told she had gone away with another man, but I didn't ever really believe that."

Alex shuffled uneasily. "Are you saying, Mr Simmons, that they've found your mother?"

"The police have taken DNA samples from me, and confirmed that one of the bodies was my mother. Also, the skull was of a close relative, either an uncle or a cousin…."

"Pierre-Henri Cantin" interrupted Alex, "otherwise known as Heinz-Peer Fepp."

"I believe that will be proved, yes. But the other body… they have no idea who it is, and nor do I."

"Could it be your cousin Natasha?" asked Hazel. "She went missing in the late 1950s."

Charles Forster took a deep breath. "No, it's definitely not Natasha." He looked straight at Toby

Allen. "Toby… this might come as a bit of a shock."

The old man stared back at their host.

"Mr Forster" he began slowly, "this whole affair has pretty much consumed my life. Nothing would shock or surprise me now. Nothing."

Charles Forster turned and spoke softly to Michael. Recalling the moment later, Hazel realised it was the first time they'd heard Charles ask, rather than demand. Michael nodded, and left the room.

"James?" said Charles, looking at his right-hand man. "Over to you."

"My family owes you a great deal in so many ways, Mr Allen. I… I don't know exactly how we can make it up to you, but please… please let me say, I had no knowledge of the extent of my father's psychopathic tendencies until this whole affair came to light. The least we can do is…"

His voice tailed away as the door swung open, and Michael pushed a wheelchair in. Everyone sat up and looked at the frail figure whose head bounced slightly as she was wheeled in towards them. There was a hushed silence as the old lady in the wheelchair raised her head and gazed at each of them, one by one. As she stared at Hazel she smiled slightly. Hazel blushed, smiled back and then lowered her gaze. Alex looked at the others, and noticed their general bemusement.

It was Toby Allen who spoke first, in a hushed voice. "Tasha? Is that you?"

The old lady nodded. "Yes, my dearest Toby… it's me. We have a lot of talking to do. And I have a lot of explaining to do, but please… may I join you all and have a drink, please?"

"Michael…" Charles indicated with his finger,

and Michael moved the wheelchair so that Natasha was sitting alongside Toby. Still no-one spoke.

The old lady reached her left arm out, and grasped Toby's right hand. She looked at him, such a loving look, thought Alex, and the old man returned the look, and smiled, and said very simply "You're still beautiful. You're still the most beautiful girl in the world..." and at that moment Alex saw past the wrinkled visage, saw the piercing blue eyes and homely smile, and knew why Toby Allen had fallen so hopelessly in love all those years ago.

He turned to Hazel to speak, but she was weeping silently, as was her mother, and Martina. Even Geoff was looking close to tears. Alex looked down to avoid making eye contact with anyone else.

"He sent me away, you know" said Natasha. "My charming Uncle Arthur had me bundled out of the country. I went to Canada and worked there in an outpost, teaching in one of the group's company schools. I never... saw, or married anyone else. I was happy doing what I was doing. I never thought I'd see you again. I've had a good life, you know. The satisfaction of teaching generations of children is the best substitute for parenthood I can imagine. I came back here occasionally, but never for very long, and after 1975 I stayed away until I retired in 1998; then I came back and lived here."

"I've been in Yatton all this time..." said Toby tearfully. "If I'd only known..."

"I thought they'd killed you in 1961. I've been grieving too. But... here we are." She smiled again.

Charles Forster stirred and coughed slightly. "Well, I think... I think this calls for a toast, and then I think we should all have something to eat."

361

61

"Our business links with the Fepp family were once very strong" said Charles Forster, after the dinner plates had been cleared away, "but my grandfather and father were careful to keep their core business separate from the main Fepp-stroke-Cantin tyre business, so although my family owned shares in Vendolet, the Fepp's didn't own any shares in what became the Forster Group. Grandfather could see then how... erm... volatile the Fepps were, and especially Jürgen, who you all know of as Arthur Simmons. He was a wild young man, and claimed at one point to have served in the French Foreign Legion, which we can well believe. He seemed to have a ruthlessness about him which is common in all successful FFL recruits. But he also had a certain sparkle to him too... he could really liven up a party, cheer you up if you were in the most miserable of moods. Actually, that's how I remember him from my youth. But he clearly had a dark side, and although Matthias was the bigger brother, and was able to contain Jürgen's excesses most of the time, he was also quite frightened of him.

"By the way, you probably didn't realise but the brothers were all educated privately in France and in England, which is how they were able to speak fluent English, when it suited them.

"I have to say, until you people turned up on my property, I really had no idea what had been going on back in 1937, and neither did James. We knew nothing about the faked racing accident. When you first told me, I thought it was a piece of fantasy. I presume my grandfather knew something; that whole Vendolet business was pretty murky, but my father Andrew never once mentioned anything. It's been quite a shock for us all, but especially for James. The police have been swarming over us since you made them search Gerald's place, which, by the way, officially belongs to this estate. Once they've finished digging up the garden, we're going to sell it off."

"Do you mind if I ask a couple of questions?" asked Alex, tentatively.

"Go ahead, Alex" said Charles.

"I mean, to Mr Simmons here?"

"That's fine" said James, who was sitting between Charles and Toby.

"Well, we're sure that your father, Jürgen… Arthur… staged the accident, and turned himself into David Watson… but who really was the body washed up in the river three months later?"

James Simmons puffed his cheeks out. "We've been told by the police that all the evidence they have points to it being the real Pierre-Henri Cantin. He and my father never got on, and… I'm sorry, this is difficult for me…" His voice faltered and he looked down at the table, trying to suppress his emotions.

Charles Forster patted him gently on the shoulder. "What James is saying is that his father, Jürgen was, in the beginning, driven to do what he did by Pierre-Henri's actions. You see, Jürgen was dating a young lady called Yvonne Lévy in Metz, Pierre-Henri was so jealous, he started an affair with Yvonne, and then somehow convinced her that he was the better prospect, and married her. But she was still in love with Jürgen and they carried on

363

behind Pierre-Henri's back until one day, she told him she was just using him and she didn't love either of them. Well, Jürgen couldn't handle that so he killed Yvonne, but in such a way as to frame Pierre-Henri. The French police could not find enough evidence to convict him though, so at first they put it down as 'unsolved'. Meantime, Jürgen was now seeing Christine Rocquefort. Pierre-Henri also tried to seduce her but she was wise to all his tricks and didn't fall for it. Her family were very wealthy, and they sponsored Jürgen and his twin brother Andreas, or André Cantin, as he was known, the one who was killed at the Nurburgring. At the same time, money began to go missing from Vendolet and everything pointed to Pierre-Henri, as they had cut his sponsorship moneys. He escaped to Germany for a while until things cooled down in Metz, but he thought he was invincible and the temptation to race against the top drivers in his class at the Empire Trophy in Crystal Palace was too much, so he organised to have Reg Simmons run his car in the race. Now Reg Simmons was one of Vendelot's best garage owners in England, so he was known to my family, who were the main importers. Reg had a garage and tyre business in George Green, near Langley, which they used as a base for the Bugatti.

"Meantime, the French police were now beginning to suspect Jürgen of the murder of Yvonne Cantin, so they were now after both of them. Jürgen decided to get rid of his brother Pierre-Henri by staging a public accident, but Crystal Palace was not the place to do it. That year's Empire Trophy was the first British race to be televised live – and there were too many cameras about for his liking. So they contacted my grandfather, who as Vendolet Tyres GB was sponsoring the Abbots Park Trophy, and persuaded him to allow the last-minute entry. Pierre-Henri thought he was going to Crystal Palace but Jürgen killed him and brought his body here.

"In those days the subterranean tunnel, which I believe you two youngsters discovered a few weeks back, led down to a derelict harbour, so Jürgen hid the body in the tunnel until early in the morning of the day of the race, then decapitated him and dropped his body into the river…"

"Why did he decapitate him? Surely, if he wanted him found in the river, he wanted him identified correctly?" asked Geoff.

"Because if he was found before the race, he wouldn't be identified, but anyway the tide was strong and by the time the race started, the real Pierre-Henri Cantin was already floating towards the Severn. Jürgen and Reg Simmons, who was in on the plot, expected him to be found sooner, but it was really convenient in a way that it took three months.

"So, during the race, Jürgen posed as Pierre-Henri – they were brothers, the main difference from a distance being Pierre-Henri's moustache, but that was easy to fake. Then he staged the accident, and became David Watson… witness to his own 'death', as it were…"

"And killed my friend." Toby interposed unexpectedly, causing a collective gasp.

"I'm… truly sorry, Mr Allen" said James, sincerely. "I want you to know that I had no idea what my father was like until very recently."

"He tried to kill me later on too, except he got the wrong person" Toby continued. "He kept thinking my name was Tony, not Toby." Toby Allen stared straight at the son of the man who'd tried to kill him all those years ago. "But listen, James. I'm grateful to be alive, and to have had 93 years on this planet, when so many others have the misfortune to die younger than me. You don't need to apologise to me for your father's actions."

"Thank you. Thank you very much…"

Charles patted James on the arm and then, as Michael and a waitress served dessert, he carried on relating the story. "We now know that when Pierre-Henri's body was found, Christine Rocquefort posed as Mrs Cantin to identify him. Amazingly the British authorities took her at face value… I think she had a forged marriage certificate or something. Anyway, when they went to bury him, they realised the press would be there, and Jürgen Fepp was on the run from the police so he must not be seen. Jürgen called himself André Cantin at the funeral, but he was recognised as 'David Watson' by a marshal from the crash, and there was a journalist from Motor Sport Magazine who also knew that André was dead. Well… I only know this because he, Jürgen, wrote it down in his secret journal… he posed as a secret agent working undercover and persuaded the marshal to catch a particular train home, and killed him on the train and then threw his body onto the line in front of another train. Pretty ruthless… but he didn't stop there. He also caught up with the journalist, Preece. The coroner ruled that this poor chap died in a house fire, probably caused by his pipe tobacco setting fire to his settee, but it was Jürgen who did it using chloroform to knock him out. By the time he came round he was surrounded by flames. The post mortem found that he'd died of asphyxiation from smoke inhalation. No trace of any chloroform by then, of course."

James Simmons butted in at this point. "My father… Jürgen, also wanted to keep racing as he had in Germany, so he persuaded Reg Simmons to let him use his dead brother's identity, and became Arthur Simmons. He could pose as Reg's half-brother, and it suited him because no-one working for the business questioned anything he did. Arthur Simmons is the man who married my mother Alice, and that's who I really thought he was, not Jürgen Fepp." He grimaced as he finished the last sentence.

"But before that" said Charles, picking up the story once more' "and while he was already dating Alice Condon, he had married Christine Rocquefort, in Austria, as himself, Jürgen Fepp, but in fact, she was to all appearances Mrs Arthur Simmons. Anyway, Christine found out about Alice and threatened to tell all, so he gave her an overdose after a family party in this very house, and she died in her sleep. The police were suspicious, but somehow he had enough witnesses, including the Chief Constable, who was here at the party, to say they'd had a row and she'd just drunk too much, and the coroner returned a verdict of suicide. So then Arthur, as he was now known, was able to marry Alice Condon, the girl he'd been seeing before."

Charles took a mouthful of dessert before continuing. "Well, then Toby here bumped into Arthur at a race meeting and recognised him – saw Cantin's ghost, if you like. The first time, Arthur couldn't work out who it was, but he soon remembered and so he persuaded his niece, Natasha, to befriend Toby and find out all he knew."

Natasha raised her hand to stop him, and spoke in a frail but spirited voice. "I didn't need too much persuasion. I thought it would be a bit of fun and… well he's a very handsome man." She smiled at Toby. "But after he asked me to marry him, Arthur made me break it off. He was very… threatening. It was hard for me, but I valued my health. I regretted it as soon as I did it. My father, Matthias, wanted me to marry another man, a German friend of his, but…"

Charles picked up the story as she faltered.

"Natasha and Toby met again by chance a few months later, and renewed their engagement, but this time Arthur had her sent to Germany to marry this other man…"

"…but" Natasha butted in "I managed to make my way to Canada, and Andrew Forster, Charles's very dear father, kept in touch and found me a position in the company's school in a mining town, and that's where I've been since, until now."

"What about your brother, Gerald?" asked Alex, who was trying to work out how he fitted into the story.

"My brother and I… never got on. He had a very low view of women, even our mother. He treated her like dirt, and I barely existed in his eyes. He idolised his Uncle Arthur."

Charles carried on the story: "Gerhard Fepp, or Gerald Phipps, was… is as psychopathic as Arthur. He was very controlling, and had a string of young girlfriends; each one thought they were the only one, so life often got complicated for him. To be honest his preferences bordered on the lower end of the legal age range – he had been out with at least three schoolgirls that we knew about. Well, he had persuaded some young girl to come over from East Germany – smuggled her out on the pretext she'd have a better life. Well, she was a bit of a live wire by all accounts, and started to ask awkward questions. Then, when she got pregnant, Arthur and Gerald killed her, leaving her in the woods with Toby's engagement ring on. She was never reported missing from Germany, of course, so there were no clues as to her origins. She became known as the Mystery Woman of Leigh Woods.

"Arthur wanted Toby to come forward and identify her from the ring so he could trace him and then kill him, but Toby remained silent, so he had to try other means. Well, imagine his good fortune when someone called Tony Allen ordered some equipment from the family firm. He sent Gerald to recce the place and talk to Tony, and then on the day of the appointment, Arthur went round a bit before Gerald got there, killed Tony, and then left. Gerald was able to put on a good act for the police, and as his story was essentially true, it all checked out fine. I imagine Arthur was pretty upset when he realised many years later that he'd killed the wrong man."

"So when Uncle Toby saw him at Brands Hatch in 1968, Arthur was as surprised as Uncle Toby then. Is that what you're saying?" asked Alex.

"That's right. But by now, Arthur was quite relaxed about Toby. If he was going to make a fuss about seeing Cantin's ghost, he would have done so years ago, so he really didn't care about seeing him again. By then he and Gerald were running the garage together. They also ran a car in the British Touring Car Championship which Arthur was still driving, despite his age. Gerald's father Matthias died in 1970 of cancer, and his mother Heidi died in 1977 – she had been in poor health for some time, and had a series of strokes before the last one which killed her.

"Well, then we come to 1975. Arthur was racing at Thruxton, and had a really big shunt at Allards which put him in a coma. He was on life support for a while, but then there was a power failure in his ward and the machine simply stopped working, and he died in his sleep. We were all fairly suspicious as Gerald had visited that morning, but he had a genuine alibi for the time the machinery went off; he was with other family members so they knew they couldn't pin it on him."

Natasha squeezed Toby's hand, and said quietly. "It doesn't matter now, does it? Arthur was already dying. He wasn't going to recover properly…even if he'd come round from the coma, he would not have been the same person. I don't get on with my brother, but I'm sure he had nothing to do with Arthur's death. I'm absolutely certain of it."

62

From: marcel.fontaine@editionfontaine.com.fr
Sent: Tuesday, March 26, 2019 2.35 PM
To: alex@phippstribe.net
Subject: Re: Mystery solved

Dear Alex

Thank you for telling me the outcome of the Cantin ghost mystery. I will now have to rewrite all my history that I was writing, but this is a good thing, no? Gerhard Fepp sounds even worse than his uncle Jurgen. You say he killed other people not in his familly as well?

It seems like this familly was trying to self-destruct! Maybe they were a model for what was happening in Europe at this time. I don't think we will ever know what Jurgen Fepp did in the army but I will try to find out more.

Perhaps when I finish all my writing I can give you a copy of my book – I have spoken with my publisher and he wants me to write the book in two months!

When I am next visiting Denis in London I will let you know, I would like to meet you and your family.

Thank you for telling me what happened and I send warmest wishes to you, your family and your girlfriend Hazel, and also to her family.

Marcel

63

Tuesday 6ᵗʰ August 2019 – South Atwell

"Mum! Listen to this! *'Bristol man guilty of multiple killings. Bristol serial killer Gerald Phipps has been found guilty of the murder of five people over a period of nearly sixty years. The jury took just two hours to reach unanimous verdicts on all five counts, and a majority verdict on the manslaughter of a sixth person. A seventh charge of the murder of his uncle, Arthur Simmons, was dismissed early in the case due to lack of evidence. Phipps will be sentenced in early September.'"*

"Well, that's a relief. I'm sure Uncle Toby will be very pleased about that. I must give him a ring." Meredith replied. "Are you seeing Alex today?"

"Yep. He's walking over now. Oh, and he's got those love letters to return to Uncle Toby – I said we'd take them back next time we visit him… whenever we can, Mum."

"Yes, I think he'd like that, poor man. He hasn't got over the shock of Natasha's death yet. He told Martina they were going to marry in September. Cancer is such a cruel disease."

"I know, it's so sad. He never did get his girl, did he? I just want to give him a massive hug."

"Me too, Dear. Oh, there's something I forgot to tell you. Alex will be interested in this too."

"What's that then?"

"Well, Martina told me that just before she died, Natasha confessed to Uncle Toby that she was the person who turned off her uncle's life support, not Gerald. She didn't regret it for one moment, after all he'd put her through all those years back."

"Crikey! What a family! And I thought she was a genuinely sweet old lady." Hazel shook her head in disbelief. "It makes you wonder what people are really capable of... and what secrets they carry with them. Urgh. This is all a bit unsettling, isn't it?"

"It is, isn't it? Still... it's all over now. Poor Uncle Toby, as you said. I think we should visit him sooner rather than later... and make it a regular thing too. In fact, I'm going to make it my duty to see him once a month at least."

"I'll come with you too, whenever I can" said Hazel. "I feel a real connection with him."

Meredith Burns got up from the kitchen table and flicked the kettle on. "I expect your young man will want a cup of coffee when he gets here."

Hazel grinned and nodded. "Yup – he will."

"What are you and Alex doing today?"

"We're actually going to go to the cinema – we haven't been for ages. It'll be nice not to worry about investigating anything this time... Oh yes, we've decided, Mum. No more mysteries."

"Until?"

"No. Never. No more." Hazel paused and looked at her mother thoughtfully. "Ever..."

"Until?" grinned Meredith.

"Well... until after GCSEs at least."

The doorbell rang, and Hazel sprang up from her stool and rushed into the hallway.

"Well, you two just keep your heads down then" Meredith called after her. "There's still four weeks of school holidays for something else to rear its ugly head..."

AUTHOR'S NOTE

Whilst the main characters in this book are fictional, there are many references to real life people, events and places. The motor race in October 1937 is a fictional event which contains real-life drivers from that period, and whilst the race on the same day at Crystal palace was a real event, the real-life René Dreyfus was not a participant. Likewise, the circumstances surrounding Jo Siffert's non-appearance at the 1968 Race of Champions was a real event which provided the backdrop for a part of the story – I know because one of the enthusiastic onlookers in the Brands Hatch paddock that weekend was a very young me!

I have also used a fair amount of artistic licence by inserting an extra half-mile of land by Leigh Woods, alongside the Avon gorge, and adding a fictional Manor House and disused race circuit. I apologise unreservedly to the residents of Abbots Leigh for distorting the geography of their area, and for placing a dubious character in their neighbourhood.

The real Arthur Frederick Simmons was my wife's great uncle, but sadly she never knew him. He died early last century aged just 9 years, allegedly following some 'corporal punishment' delivered by one of his schoolmasters. Tragically his death certificate simply says "Natural causes" – a travesty of justice if ever there was one.

ACKNOWLEDGEMENTS

Ewen Getley of Kingsbury Racing, and Derek Hinchman for their expert technical advice on all things pre-war Bugatti. Anna Harcourt and Emma Barnes for their intimate knowledge of the Bristol area. Jay Wilkinson for information about Brunel University. Richard Peake, Luke Marshall, and my daughter Katie for advice on police procedures, past and present. Wendy Stonehouse for her help with emergency paramedic procedures. My brother Jon for the loan of various historical motor racing books from his vast library. Emily Fisher, Emily Jackman, Hazel GoldenSmith and many more of my younger friends for a youthful perspective. My daughter Jen for her suggestions for the cover design, and Libby Holcroft for realising it.

374

Manufactured by Amazon.ca
Bolton, ON